WILTED ORCHID

A DARK MAFIA ROMANCE

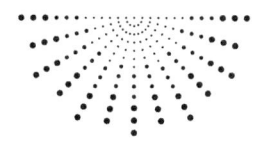

LOXLEY SAVAGE

The unauthorized reproduction or distribution of a copyrighted work is illegal. Criminal copyright infringement, including infringement without monetary gain, is investigated by the FBI and is punishable by fines and federal imprisonment.

Please purchase only authorized electronic editions and do not participate in, or encourage, the electronic piracy of copyrighted materials. Your support of the author's rights is appreciated.

This book is a work of fiction. Names, characters, places, brands, and incidents are the products of the author's imagination or used fictitiously. Any resemblance to actual events, locales or persons, living or dead, is entirely coincidental.

This is a Reverse Harem Contemporary Mafia Romance and is not suited for those under the age of 18.

❦ Created with Vellum

Copyright @ 2022 Loxley Savage

Wilted Orchid (Mafia Wars)

First publication: February 18, 2022

Cover by Maria Spada

Editing by Jessica Rousseau with Elemental Editing Services

Formatting by Vellum

All rights reserved. Except for use in any review, the reproduction or utilization of this work, in whole or in part, in any form by any electronic, mechanical or other means now known or hereafter invented, is forbidden without the written permission of the publisher.

Published by Loxley Savage

LoxleySavageAuthor@gmail.com

❦ Created with Vellum

SPECIAL THANKS

To my alpha team, Kala, Kelly, Christine, and Kendall. Thank you for all your open and honest feedback, my book is better because you've been a part of it.

To my beta team, Desiree, Lauren, Sabrina, Holly, and Katie. Thank you for your hard work on this one, and from your emotional comments that always make me smile.

To my husband, for always supporting me.

To my editor and friend, Jess. You're amazing and I'm so lucky to have your expert eyes on my work!

To my dear friends Alyssa, Sara, and Jane for your constant love and support.

To my PA, Allison Woerner. I seriously don't know how I ever survived before you came along. Thank you for all you do for me.

To Brandi Slater for busting your ass to read the ARC copy for me when I was in a pickle.

And finally, to the authors who joined me in this crazy idea almost 2 years in the making. **Katie Knight, C.R. Jane, Susanne Valenti, Caroline Peckham, Ivy Fox, and Rebecca Royce.**
Not only has this been one hell of a ride, but it's almost been an amazing experience. I love how close we've all grown, how supportive you all are, and how you made my dreams of this shared world come true.
Thank you.

DEDICATION

To my niece, Payton.
We've had such an amazing ride together. Our relationship has grown so much over the past two decades, but we've always stayed close, and I'm so blessed for that.
You are a constant support for me and my girls, you're giving, sweet, and loving. You help me every single chance you get without a second thought. I love our inside jokes, how we laugh together at the most random things, how we finish each other's sentences and seem to have our own language when we're together.
You are selfless, silly, smart, and beautiful. My life is better because you're in it. So, minime, this book is for you.
I love you. Always. - 72 & 90

WARNING

This is a dark, contemporary, reverse harem mafia romance intended for readers above the age of 18.
Within these pages are scenes of graphic violence, explicit sex, group scenes, kidnapping, kink exploration, discipline, foul language, and more which may be difficult to read. If such material triggers or offends you, please do not read this book.

If you're brave, enter the dark and fucked up world of the Mafia Wars.

YOU HAVE BEEN WARNED

MAFIA WARS AND TERRITORIES

Chicago - Italian Mafia - The Outfit
Moretti Family

New York - Italian Mafia - La Cosa Nostra
Rossi Family

Mexico City - Mexican Cartel
Hernandez Family

Boston - Irish Mafia
Kelly Family

Vegas - Russian Mafia - The Bratva
Volkov Family

London - English Mafia - The Firm
Butcher Family

PREFACE

MAFIA WARS

Since the dawn of time, waging war on those who have wronged us has been ingrained in the very fiber of mankind's true nature. The thirst for vengeance and retribution has always prevailed over turning the other cheek to one's enemies, and creating chaos and bloodshed is preferable to being subjected to vapid dialogues of peaceful negotiations.

None hold this way of life more sacred than *made men*.

Honor.

Loyalty.

Courage.

These are the codes of conduct of every mafia family.

However, the same cannot be said when they are dealing with their enemies.

Through the decades, in the midst of civil evolution, an ancient war was being fought. On both sides of the globe, blood was spilled in the name of honor, while the brutal carnage each family bestowed upon the other was anything but noble. Soldiers, kin, and innocent lives were lost on all sides, and the inevitable extinction of the mafioso way of life was fast approaching.

In the most unlikely scenario, six families came together in an

PREFACE

undisclosed location to negotiate a peace treaty. As the leaders of the most influential crime families in the world, they recognized that a cease-fire was the only way to guarantee their endurance. Should this attempt fail, then their annihilation was all but inevitable.

The treaty was effectively simple.

Each family would offer up one of their daughters as a sacrifice to their enemies. Marriage was the only way to ensure that the families wouldn't retaliate against one another. It would also guarantee that the following successor's bloodline would be forever changed, creating an alliance that would continue through generations to come.

Not all in attendance were happy with the arrangement.

The deep scars gained from years of plight and hatred couldn't be so easily healed or erased. However, even the cynical and leery knew that this pact was their best chance of survival. Although the uncertainty of the treaty's success was felt by every mob boss present, they swore an oath that would bind them to it forever.

As the words spilled from their lips and the scent of blood hung in the air, they made sure innocent lives would yet again be deemed collateral damage to their mafia wars one last time.

Their daughters would have to pay the price for peace, whether they wanted to or not.

PROLOGUE

TEN YEARS AGO...

Giovanni Moretti

Don of the Outfit, Chicago based Italian Mafia

TORRENTIAL RAINS and powerful winds pound the sides of the hotel, threatening to bring the whole fucking thing to the ground. On a small island, like Bermuda, there's nowhere to hide from a storm, you simply must endure it.

As the tempest rages outside, my excitement heightens. For me, it only amplifies the tension in this room as this monumental event unfolds before my very eyes. I never thought I'd see the day where the bosses from London's Firm, Boston's Irish Mafia, Russia's Bratva, New York's Cosa Nostra, Mexico's Cartel, and of course me, Giovanni Moretti, Don of Chicago's Outfit, would commit to being in the same room without the allure of an easy kill. Of course my sidearm is tucked safely away. I wouldn't go near these fucks without some protection. I'd be a fool if I did. Even under the pretense of peace, there's too much history here, too much blood spilled throughout decades of the mafia wars for any of us to truly feel safe.

The Butcher brothers, the cock suckers from the Firm, aren't fucking here yet. As I think of the countless ways I could murder them with my bare hands, the door opens and they walk in. "You're late," I growl, fingering the handle of my coffee mug.

Benny Butcher waves me off as he pulls up a chair, sitting in front of his brother Danny. Both men are covered in dried blood. "We're here, aren't we? Count your blessings, Giovanni, that we came at all."

Count my blessings?

Fucking *bastardo*. It takes all my willpower not to stand up and backhand Benny for speaking to me without an ounce of respect. However, that would ruin the entire reason we're here today—a peace treaty.

We've been pitted against each other for our entire lives, trying to outdo one another. Kill counts and stacks of cash don't mean anything if you're dead, though, so here we are, several of the most powerful men in the world, sitting around a table as if we've gathered here for a fucking brunch after Sunday mass. Looking around the room, I lock eyes with Irishman Niall Kelly, who appears as annoyed as I am at the Butchers' tardiness.

He mutters something in his native tongue to his son, and I'd bet all the cash in my wallet that it has something to do with the Butchers. The brothers are new to leading, as their father died only a week ago, so I'll cut them some slack today, but just this once.

Their nonchalance irritates me, and I pray when this is all said and done that my sweet daughter, Lily, won't end up in their blood-covered hands.

Carlo Rossi, don of our rival Italian Mafia from New York, clears his throat, gathering our attention. "We all know why we have come together today. Every head of family sitting here has realized that to preserve our way of life, sacrifices need to be made by all. We must put past grudges aside in order to guarantee our future."

I bite my tongue, wanting to blast Carlo into the future with the Ruger tucked in my waistband. The fucker talks about sacrifice and grudges as if he's above it all when we all know he probably murdered Travor Butcher only last week.

Carlo continues, "This peace treaty comes at the expense of our pride, but it's a sacrifice we all must make to ensure our survival."

The big Russian, Vadim Volkov, and Tiernan Kelly lock eyes. Vadim bares his teeth at Tiernan. "What are you looking at, Kelly?"

The two men begin to argue, but before it can escalate, Carlo slams his fists onto the table and shouts, "Basta!" then demands the men get a hold of themselves and remember why we're here.

I don't engage in futile arguments, instead I sit back and watch it, taking it all in and confirming my previous opinions are still true—I don't want Lily going with the Englishmen, Russians, or the Irish for that matter. That only leaves me with the Hernandez family, and God forbid, Carlo Rossi's boy.

"We came here to ensure peace so we can continue our livelihood," Carlo adds in a low tone. "That will not happen if pride cannot be set aside and sacrifices aren't made."

Benny snarks at Carlo, and I've had just about enough. Rising from my chair, I interrupt their bickering. "Are we going to sit here and do this whole song and dance of who has the biggest cock, or are we going to come to an agreement on how to stop killing each other?"

Silence engulfs the men, and for once, the Butchers look slightly ashamed of themselves, as they should be. Even Volkov shuts his mouth. Tiernan whispers something to Niall, and although Niall Kelly looks bored, I have his attention.

I fiddle with the crucifix around my neck, asking God to give me strength not to slaughter this entire room of men. "We all know why we are here and what needs to be done. Now, are we men who want to ensure that our way of life continues, business as usual, or should we just kill each other and save us all these childish tantrums?"

"As much as the idea of gutting your bellies open like a fish amuses me, Giovanni is right. Business should come before pleasure," Miguel Hernandez, Don of the Mexican Cartel, agrees.

I flick my gaze from Miguel to his son, Alejandro. The young man has maintained his composure and acted respectfully throughout this whole meeting, even as tensions have soared. I pray my Lily ends up as his bride.

Carlo speaks again, his words cold and deliberate, reiterating what we already know with just the hint of a threat. "It has been a year since we started our deliberations, and the time has come to put them into action. I admit, it will take some time to get used to this new reality, but resistance is futile."

A year…

It's hard to believe the negotiations that started as a mere whisper, a false hope of peace, are now finally coming to fruition. I just hope that when my sons and daughter learn of what I've done, that I've sealed their fate without their knowledge, that they will understand why I had to do it.

And so begins the discussion of using our daughters as sacrificial lambs. Each name is thrown into a hat, their futures scrawled across a piece of torn paper. Each family will choose a paper at random, and the girl's name written upon it will then forever belong to their son.

Niall Kelly tosses an empty fruit bowl in the center of the table, then drops a torn segment of yellow paper inside it. One by one, we all do the same, writing our family name on a scrap of paper and placing it inside the bowl.

After each family has added their name, I stand and pick up the pen resting on the pad of paper, then slice it across my palm. For a moment, I'm lost in the way my blood so easily comes to the surface, marveling at the deep color before holding my hand over the bowl. "On my blood, I swear to protect and care for the woman who will ensure the life of the Outfit. Let her sacrifice bring union to the *famiglias*."

Truer words I've never spoken, because as much as this treaty is necessary, it's also unnerving. Lily's life is on the line here, and if I can say or do anything to ensure she is safe and cared for, then I will.

Taking a deep breath, I reach into the bowl, pull out a bloodstained piece of paper, and unfold it. "Rossi." My gut twists as I flip the paper around for all to see. The Rossi girl, of all the women, is whom I wanted least. It is no secret that the Outfit and the Cosa Nostra hate each other more than any other two families in this room. Though I suppose it could be worse. At least, for now, Lily is safe from the calloused hands of one of Carlo Rossi's sons.

Sitting back down, I fix my attention on each man. The bowl makes its way around the table, each don adding his own blood to the mix and swearing his own oath before pulling a name. I think about my son, Salvatore, and his twin brothers, Fausto and Armani, who were brought into the world only eleven months after Sal was born, wondering which of them will marry the Rossi girl. I pray I haven't doomed one of my sons to a life of misery.

"Moretti."

Hearing my family name, I glance up from the table and see Miguel Hernandez holding the piece of paper with our name on it. I nod before looking to Alejandro who continues to stare forward, his lips pulled into a thin line. I have to wonder what he's thinking right now, knowing his future father-in-law is in this room and he is now forever linked with my family.

I can't help but feel relieved that Lily didn't end up with the Butchers or the Rossi boys, but on the same note, there's also a sense of foreboding. Now, my family's fate is tied with the Rossi's. Now, my true enemy will forever be bound to me by blood.

I've never made a harder sacrifice, and I'm not even the person who will suffer for it.

Ten years remain until the youngest girl, my future daughter-in-law, comes of age and the trading of our daughters will begin. Ten years until, in a sense, their freedom is snatched right from under them. Ten years until life as they know it will change forever.

CHAPTER ONE

6 Months ago...

Salvatore Moretti

Don of The Outfit for the past five years, eldest son of Giovanni Moretti who is now deceased.

WITH ONE HAND gripping the wheel, I silence the unknown caller for the third time. Fucking telemarketers wanting to sell me new insurance or some bullshit like that. I don't have time for this shit or the patience. Checking the clock, I see I only have ten minutes to get there to make sure the deal goes through. Sure, Armani and Fausto are there, overseeing things, but this is a big transaction, and I have to see it with my own eyes.

My phone rings again, and I almost crush my finger through the fucking dashboard as I accept the call. "Who the fuck is this?"

Static crackles, and a moment later, terrified cries and pained whimpers fill my ears, sounds that often make my cock stiffen.

Not this time, however, because I'm not the cause of her pain. A sinister voice orders, "Check your messages," and then the call disconnects. Checking traffic, I pull my car over and grab my phone, frantically entering my passcode. I know that probably seems old school to some, but I'll be damned if a deal went wrong and some asshole was able to knock me out then unlock my phone by holding it up to my sleeping face.

I open my messages as my phone pings that a new one has arrived, also from an unknown number. Tapping the screen, a picture fills my phone, one that makes my blood run cold. An address soon follows, and I enter it into my GPS before swerving back onto the road.

It's nighttime in Chicago. The cool, fall air foretells of a cold and snowy winter, but in spite of the chill, I roll down my windows, the chill keeping me focused and aware.

I should be calling for backup and telling *me familia* where to meet me, but I need my brothers to run this deal if I can't do it myself. That's rule number one as a don—trust no one.

Running through red lights and taking turns hard, I drive my car like it's stolen, praying a cop won't see me. Soon, the busy streets give way to a long, gravel driveway leading to an abandoned steel factory.

A single light illuminates a parking lot riddled with potholes the size of those pointless Fiats. I maneuver around them, screeching to a stop not far from a work van that's rusted and windowless.

The factory looms in the star-filled sky, maybe six stories tall. Unworking towers and huge containers that held God knows what scratch at the dark night. Empty piping connects it all, like once slithering snakes that suddenly turned to stone.

Unwilling to take a risk, I pull my nine from its holster and disengage the safety before jogging toward the factory. A single door is propped open on the side of the building, and I slowly open it wider, peeking inside. A darkened hallway greets me, followed by an agonized scream.

The scream seems to surround me, echoing on all sides, and I glance around, trying to discern its origin. Sobbing follows, and I run toward it, turning a corner before emerging into a vast, open space.

Old machinery sits dusty and unused, the scent of oil and metal still thick in the abandoned air.

High windows allow the moonlight to shine through, giving the place an eerie feeling. The loud smacking sound of flesh colliding with flesh grabs my attention, so I jerk my head in that direction and find a set of metal stairs.

"No, please," she cries, begs, as I hurtle myself up them, taking two or three steps at a time. The scent of blood and sweat and gunpowder fills my nose as I ascend, making my heart hammer and my stomach clench.

I already know what's happening. It's a scene I've often envisioned in my head and sent many a prayer up to the Lord begging him to prevent this from happening.

Yet here it is, just as I'd imagined.

I try to keep my cool, rounding the stairs, my hand now gripping a cold, metal door handle. I listen hard, trying to determine who might be inside, racking my brain to figure out who would do this to me, Salvatore Moretti, Don of the Outfit. Who would do this knowing I could fuck their world up with a single phone call?

I let out a shaky breath and pull the door open. This room might have been an office at one time. The whole space is surrounded by windows, a place where the boss might sit and watch his employees work below, but my eyes are straight ahead, because hanging against the cinderblock wall, with her wrists secured in rusted, iron shackles, is the love of my life.

Gianna is everything I'd ever hoped to find in a woman. She's sweet and kind, but also very aware of the inner workings of the Mafia. She's not scared of violence or death, and she doesn't shy away when I come home covered in blood that isn't my own. She doesn't ask questions or shoot cautious, unforgiving looks in my direction. Instead, she welcomes me and my darkness, understanding what I must do for my family.

As the first-born son of Giovanni and Lucianna Moretti, I was groomed to take over as don when my father could no longer hold the position. No one could have anticipated, however, that five years ago, my parents would both perish in a very suspicious boating accident, thrusting me into the role at the age of twenty-eight, decades before I intended to take over.

Dad told me about the pact during our yearly family vacation to Bermuda that would, unknowingly, be our last. He told Mom and our baby sister Lily that he wanted to have a night out with his sons. Little did we know then that he would drop a bomb on us. Well… just me really. My twin brothers, Fausto and Armani aren't affected by this, though if I chose to do so, I could pawn her off on one of them.

I can still see him leaning forward with his dark eyes fixed on me. Soft music played in the background, our outdoor table allowing the salty ocean breeze to cool my sweat slicked skin.

"I sealed the pact with my own blood, the blood of a Moretti. You have no choice but to marry the girl from Cosa Nostra. If you don't, our name will be tainted, our reputation tarnished, and you'll have the other five families as life-long enemies. You have no choice."

I remember Fausto stiffening next to me. "This is bullshit. The Cosa Nostra? Anyone but them."

Armani rubbed his temples, the vein in his forehead popping like it always did when he was angry. "Why not give Sal the woman from the Firm? He deserves better than those bitches from New York."

My father leveled my brothers with a glare so cold it made me shiver, even in the hot Bermuda heat. "It has been decided, son. Salvatore will wed the girl from Cosa Nostra when she comes of age. My decision is final. There is no need for a discussion, not when our family's blood is involved. I've made a pact. There's no turning back now."

I don't know what I thought would happen when I met Gianna. I didn't even try to hide our relationship. With our parents long dead, I had hoped the pact would die with them, but that was foolish of me, because five more mafia families are involved. Five more bosses to ensure everything goes as planned. More than just my brothers and I knew about it, and selfishly, all I could think about was how it would affect me, never really caring how Lily would feel about it. Soon,

Alejandro Hernandez will marry my baby sister, and just like me, there's nothing she can do about it.

So, as my eyes adjust to the meager light, I'm not shocked to see Carlo Rossi, boss of the Cosa Nostra, standing next to my sweet Gianna, his hands covered in her blood.

"Let her go," I warn, trying to keep my voice steady while I walk closer. Gianna stiffens at the sound of my voice, and though her eyes are hidden behind a black blindfold, I can see hope bloom in her features.

"Sal?" she calls, turning toward my voice, her voice quivering. "Help me, please!"

"Who? Her?" Carlo gestures toward Gianna casually, ignoring her cries for help. "No, my dear boy, she is my prisoner, and you have ensured her death. You were a fool to think you could renege on a deal sealed with your father's blood, the very blood that runs through your veins." Carlo drags the back of his hand over Gianna's chest, a yellowed grin playing on his face. It takes everything in me not to shoot him then, but I have to play it cool, because I can guarantee he's not alone even though it appears that way.

Carlo slides his hand lower and fingers the snap of Gianna's low-rise jeans then flicks it open. She thrashes in her shackles, and I see now that her ankles are bound too, restraints cinched above her strappy black heels. She's completely trapped.

Carlo bares his teeth, the display sinister and foreboding. "And now, because of your indiscretion, this woman will die. It is *my* daughter you will marry. How dare you tarnish *my* daughter by sticking your dick in this filthy slut." In a quick movement, he swings his arm back and backhands Gianna on the cheek so hard I grasp my own. Blood flies from her mouth, misting my face.

No one hurts what's mine.

Red blurs my vision, my pulse thumping in my ears. All sound fades, all emotion, until anger consumes me and the need to spill his blood becomes overpowering. I raise my gun, only for it to be knocked from my hand. It skids across the floor, and that's when I notice Carlo's men hidden in black outfits with masks pulled over their faces.

"Talk about her like that again, and—"

"And what?" Carlo interrupts, turning to face me. He snaps his fingers, and two of his goons seize my arms and force me to my knees. "Threaten me one more time and I won't just kill your little slut, I'll order my men to fuck her raw and force you to watch."

Fuck.

Gianna sobs, blood dribbling over her chin as Carlo tugs down her zipper, revealing the top of her red lace panties. Tears trail down her face from behind the blindfold, and her chest heaves, the once baby blue tank now stained red.

Cursing myself for the pain my woman is going through, I stare down Carlo, but the fucking bastard doesn't even blink.

I should have brought my brothers with me, but I wasn't thinking straight, not when I got the text message with a picture of my woman chained up and blindfolded. There was no time for rational thought, I just reacted, and now here I am, alone and unarmed, being forced to watch whatever plans Carlo has for me unfurl.

Carlo Rossi rolls up the sleeves of his burgundy dress shirt as if to intimidate me. "You thought you could fool the Cosa Nostra, did you? Fool us into thinking you were a man of your word, like your father?"

"Do not question my honor, *bastardo*," I sneer. "I never agreed to any of this." I spit at his feet, and one of the masked men punches my cheek before taking a fistful of my hair and yanking my head back.

Carlo steps in front of Gianna, grips her tank top in his blood-stained fists, and tears it down the middle, exposing her perfect breasts clad in a red lace bra.

"Neither did she," Carlo growls. "But now I must learn for myself what is so unique, so perfect about this girl that you'd put the treaty at risk." Carlo drags his hands down her sides, slipping his filthy fingers under the top of her jeans before tugging them down her hips.

Gianna cries, and my anger rages. My entire body shakes as I contemplate all the ways I could tear his head from his neck.

"Oh, very nice," Carlo comments, tugging on the thin straps of her panties sitting high over her hips and slowly dragging them down her shaking thighs.

"You wouldn't dare!" I fume, knowing I have no clout. My threats are as worthless as the warning label on a pack of cigarettes.

"Then you don't know me very well, boy," Carlo rasps, tearing her panties from her tan thighs.

Gianna's cries echo off the old cement walls as I shift my gaze from her half-naked body to Carlo. The small man sneers then kneels in front of me, leaning in so close that I can smell cigars and brandy on his breath. "You dishonor the Rossi family with what you've done, and for that, you will have to pay the ultimate price—or, at least, she will."

Before I can blink, Carlo has a firearm pointed at Gianna and he shoots.

The sound is deafening, and a scream launches from my lungs.

Gianna! No!

As I thrash between the men holding me captive, agony seizes my heart and sorrow pulls the air from my chest. Before I can even contemplate such a loss, I'm hit hard on the back of my head, and all the lights go out.

CHAPTER TWO

Valentina Rossi

Present day

Finally, the bell rings.

The last few minutes of class always seem to drag on, yet I can't tear my eyes away as the second hand slowly crawls around the dial. After shoving my books, folders, and spirals into my backpack, I toss the heavy thing over my shoulder and walk out the door.

Everyone is getting antsy. Spring fever hangs in the air as it always does when May approaches. As it's my senior year at Oakwood Prep, this might be the last time I experience such a thing. I'm sure the more mature, college-aged kids can keep their shit together, unlike the mindless high school boys I go to school with.

Hiking up my backpack, I head to my locker and trade my calculus book for government, knowing I have a paper to write this weekend on the most recent tax break for the rich. My family benefits from these tax cuts, but something about them doesn't sit right with me.

Maybe it's the faces of the poor kids bussed in from the inner city, their academics paid for with grants and government funding, that have jaded me. Comparing my life to theirs, I find it impossible not to think differently and think that things should change

Sighing, I slam the locker shut, double-check my lock, and head down the brightly lit hallway to the students' parking lot. Once through the double glass doors, I inhale deeply, enjoying the smell of spring in the air. As I walk over to my car, I notice the flowers blooming, the floral scent of lilac wafting across the school grounds from the freshly blossomed trees. Overhead, the sky is bright blue, the sunshine uninhibited by a single cloud. It's hard not to smile on days like this.

Stepping up to my car, I grip the handle before I hear someone shout, "See you Monday, Val!" I recognize Payton's voice immediately and turn toward her, waving goodbye before clutching the handle of my white BMW. The car unlocks itself, and I toss my backpack into the passenger's seat before plopping down and shutting the door.

I press the brake pedal and push the start button, and my car revs to life. I back out of my spot, pulling into the long line of cars trying to exit the parking lot. It's Friday night, and I know most people are excited to get home, change, and head out for the evening, but not me, even though I wish that were the case.

No, my brothers keep me locked up tightly in the suburbs of Hanover, a beautiful town in New Hampshire, even though they are miles away in New York City. Subterfuge is one of Father's best attributes. He uses it often, attempting to trick me into thinking he isn't as bad of a man as the rumors I've heard imply.

I nod at his lies and smile, but I know the truth. Even as a young child, I knew he wasn't a good man. That much was obvious by the condition of my mom. She was a disaster, a woman whose self-confidence was destroyed by a husband who would blatantly cheat. Prescription drugs couldn't console her, and neither could the copious amounts of wine she'd guzzle every night.

I hope she's happy now in heaven, and I hope, for her sake, that when it's his turn, Dad has to atone for his sins before joining her. It's been three years since Mom died, three years of me living mostly alone in our suburban hideaway house, tucked away from the dark world that consumes my dad and devours my brothers.

Even though I don't know them well, I miss them—my brothers, that is, not my parents. Dad's never really been here for me, and he sure as shit isn't a good father to them. I can only imagine what it's been like for them, growing up in the thick of it. I've always suspected that he is violent with them, abusive, though I try not to allow myself to think about it, because what could I possibly do? Mom found her solution and it killed her. During nights when she drank too much, she'd cry about them, about how she failed them. She'd call my dad and scream at him to "fix her boys."

But of course nothing changed.

Nothing has ever changed. Even after losing my mom, there was no difference. She's been dead to me for a long time, my dad too. He attempts to make up for his lack of a relationship by purchasing expensive gifts for me. Every year it's a new computer, the latest iPhone, a better car, or a shiny pair of diamond earrings. While I appreciate having nice things, it doesn't make up for not having a father in my life.

So I'm on my own, and sometimes I think it's better this way. I keep my head down, pretending to be someone I'm not—a casualty of being a mafia princess—and no one here knows any better. Here, at Oakwood Prep, I'm Valeska Anthony, but in real life my name is Valentina Rossi, daughter of the infamous mafia boss, Carlo Rossi of New York's Cosa Nostra.

I sometimes wonder what will happen to my brothers once Dad's dead. Who would take his place as boss? Tradition would put Lucian on Dad's throne, but something tells me Raphael will be his successor. Like my dad, my brothers insist that I keep a low profile. I can't allow anyone to get close to me, and I'm not allowed any social media profiles either, but I've worked my way around that, creating them with my fake name then blocking my brothers accounts. So far, it's worked for me.

Pulling into my driveway, I open the garage door and quickly shut it behind me, not daring to exit the car until it's fully closed. That's one thing my brothers, especially Raph, impressed upon me. "Watch your fucking back, sis, or you might find a knife in it," he'd say.

And so I do, living my life more cautiously than others but also more alone.

As I get out of my car, I wonder how things will go next year. They can't keep me locked up like this once I'm away at college. I've applied to several schools, all out of state. I'm done with New York and hiding. I want to live my life, have friends, and go to dinner whenever I want.

I'm so sick and tired of being treated like a porcelain doll who will break should I make one little decision for myself. They think I'm incapable, yet they do nothing to help me be more independent. It's kind of stupid if you ask me, considering how long I've lived alone and done everything on my own without my brothers' or my parents' help.

Before entering the house, I open the security app on my phone and scroll through all of the cameras. Only one person is inside, the same person who comes by every night to make me dinner and prepare other foods for the week—Theresa.

Some might call her a maid or even a servant, but to me, she's my only friend, even if I'm forbidden to talk to her. I know I'm monitored at all times, aside from when I'm in my bedroom and bathroom. Other than the normal courtesies of "please" and "thank you," or answering a few questions about what I'd like to eat this week, all communication with her is prohibited.

Closing the app, I pull my backpack from the car and head to the garage door. I press in the code, and after a beep, the lock disengages and I step inside. I can immediately tell Theresa has been hard at work, the distinct smell of her famous pizzicati cookies hanging in the air. She even makes homemade jam to fill them with.

"Good afternoon, Theresa," I greet, entering the quaint kitchen. She smiles and dips her head, greeting me in return without uttering a single word. She knows as much as I do what's on the line if we break the rules, and she has much more to lose than I do.

My mouth waters as she opens the oven and pulls out a baking sheet filled with cookies. I want to reach for one and stuff the sweet treat into my mouth while totally risking being burned, but I don't. She'd swat my hand away before I could even touch one.

I know after watching her make these dozens of times that they have to cool. And, as a final, delicious touch, she adds powdered sugar to the top. I don't think that's how they are traditionally made, but she knows that's how I like them.

Theresa wipes her hands on her apron then pulls open the fridge, removing a small, wooden tray and offering it to me. It's filled with cheese, crackers, and cuts of cured meat. "Thanks," I say happily, taking the treat to my bedroom. I've just put the tray down on my desk when my phone goes off, and my heartbeat quickens when I see who the text is from.

CHAPTER THREE

Valentina

Marco Capelli is everything I've ever dreamed to have in a boyfriend. Granted, he's not my boyfriend yet, but I hope that my single status might change soon. We met several months ago at a family wedding, and I haven't been able to stop thinking about him since.

He has perfectly styled dark blond hair that's longer on top and piercing blue eyes that make my heart jump and my belly get all fluttery. But it's his smile that gets me. He has straight white teeth behind a set of plump lips, lips I want to kiss.

He is perfection.

During the wedding, to my surprise, Dad allowed him to dance with me. My brothers looked shocked by this, and Lucian in particular was almost outraged, but not Dad. He barely glanced at the two of us as we strode off, Dad in a deep conversation with Marco's father, Alfonzo.

My hand shook in his as he led me to the dance floor. It felt as if all eyes were on us as he softly pressed his palm against my lower back and tugged me close to his body. I remember looking up into his eyes, fascinated that someone like him would ever want someone like me.

"You look beautiful," he purred, guiding me in a slow dance. I was so grateful for the dark lighting, sure that my cheeks were aflame. He made me all giddy, and I forgot how to speak when I was near him. He spun me, and I laughed the first real laugh I had in a long time. It was a moment where I felt carefree, a place where I didn't have to pretend to be Valeska.

At the wedding, I was Valentina Rossi, and I couldn't be more proud of it.

Marco pulled me in for a hug after the song ended, my face pressed hard against his chest. I still remember how good he smelled—the scent of a man, not the dumb boys I went to high school with. Marco even looked older than them, and he acted older too. Where the boys at my school were constantly making stupid jokes about dumb shit, Marco was poised and proper.

A gentleman.

Back at the table, Marco pulled my chair out for me and thanked me for the dance before going to sit next to his father again. When the bride, my cousin, threw her bouquet into the gaggle of single women, it was me who caught it.

Me!

I couldn't believe my luck. Everything felt right in that moment, from the smell of the flowers to how he made me feel.

Seen.

Wanted.

I sat down with a grin on my face, while Marco smiled at me from across the table. Alfonzo, red-faced from too much wine, clapped his aged hands and gripped my dad's shoulder. "Looks like we might have another wedding in the future, eh? Your Valentina and my Marco would make a handsome couple."

Dad didn't look up from his drink, and I felt some of my happiness drain. "Come, Alfonzo, let us discuss the future over whiskey and cigars."

Smiling, Alfonzo followed my father to the smoking lounge, making the dinner table awkward with only Marco, my brothers, and me remaining.

Raph shot Marco the evilest of looks, and Lucian, my eldest brother, pulled out his gun, placing it on the table in front of him.

"Tell me your intentions for my sister," Raph demanded.

I wanted to die.

Right there.

But Marco didn't even flinch. "A smart man like you has surely figured that out by now." Marco flicked his gaze to me and licked his lips, hands folded on the table in front of him. "I wish to court her."

My heart hammered, and I felt my lips part in shock at his blatant admittance that he did want to pursue me. I glanced at my brothers, terrified of their reactions.

Gabe smacked his lips, his gaze focused on his glass, while Raph shifted uncomfortably in his chair, his eyes locking with mine with what seemed like an apologetic gleam.

Lucian, however, made a show of pulling back the slide on his 9mm Ruger, checking to make sure a bullet was loaded in the chamber. "Sounds like you two will have the perfect family, doesn't it, Gabe?"

Gabe's eyes widened, and he whispered something to Lucian that made his lips curl into a sneer.

Lucian brushed Gabe off with the flick of his hands. "Oh, you worry too much, little brother. Let the two love birds have a little fun."

Marco's smile widened. "What do you say, Valentina? May I formally court you?"

Heat bloomed on my cheeks as I nodded my head a little too fast. "Yes."

This was followed by another awkward moment during a night where there were plenty of them. Marco took a breath to speak again when his dad, Alfonzo, came barreling out of the smoking lounge. Looking disgruntled, Alfonzo pulled Marco up from his seat. "We're leaving," he growled, not taking a second look at my brothers or me.

Marco didn't argue. Instead, he stood up and walked over to me, grasping my hand. "I'll be in touch soon," he whispered, kissing my knuckles. The moment his lips touched my skin, my breath caught in my lungs, but as he released me, I felt a piece of paper press against my palm.

And then he left.

I haven't seen him since.

I quickly hid the paper in my purse, pretending to look for my lip gloss. When Dad came back to the table, I asked him if something had happened, but true to his form, Dad would neither look at me nor answer my question. Instead, he tossed five hundred dollars on the table and told me to go buy something nice for myself.

That's how Dad solves all his problems, with money. Except money doesn't solve everything. Sometimes, it only makes things worse. Look at my life, for example. Because of the copious amounts of money exchanged in the many hands of the Cosa Nostra, I've had to live in hiding, I've had to live in a separate state from Dad and my brothers, and I had to watch my mom slowly kill herself over the course of several years.

Money didn't fix her and it sure as hell hasn't made my brothers' lives any better. Lucian is almost as cold as Dad these days, Raph is sweet to me when no one is looking, but I know he craves violence, and my youngest brother, Gabriel, is a man whore. Everyone knows it. He sleeps with anything that has two legs. Starved for affection because of an absent mother and a father who showed them no mercy, he finds attention in the arms of women. Any woman.

So excuse me if I'd like a little normalcy for myself. I want no part of the ever shrinking walls of the Mafia. Not the money, not the drugs, not the constant worry.

For once, I'd just like to go to Target and not have to double back to ensure I haven't been followed. I'd like to go for a walk outside and not on a treadmill. I'd like to go see a movie with my friends, have one of them sleepover, and get a fucking fancy coffee from Starbucks…

But I can't have any of that.

Soon, I hope, that will all change, because next year I'm off to college. I have my eyes on Dartmouth. It's close to where I live now, and many of my friends are hoping to go there too. I've already applied, requesting to live on campus as well. I'd take the crappiest, smallest dorm room they have over this whole house if it meant I no longer lived alone.

I'm tired of being isolated, so when I see Marco's name pop up on my phone from an incoming text, I decide right then that I'm all in.

I'll give all I have to see this through with Marco. I'll give him my heart if he wants it.

Marco: Hey, Valentina. This is Marco Capelli.

You might wonder how I have his phone number. Well, the piece of paper he slipped to me that night at the wedding had his information scrawled across it. I still have it tucked into the back of my desk drawer.

Me: Hey, Marco. How are you?

Marco: I got your text a few weeks ago. I apologize that this is the first chance I've had to respond. You know how crazy family life can be.

Me: Has it been that long? Seems like that wedding was only yesterday.

Of course I'm lying, I just don't want to seem too eager. He doesn't need to know that I check my phone a dozen times a day to see if he's responded.

My phone is silent for a moment, and I fill the void by shoving a cracker topped with a piece of cheese into my mouth.

Marco: How do you feel about us? About me courting you?

Wow. He's so bold. I like it.

Me: I feel good about it.

Of course I feel much stronger emotions. I'm excited, scared, and elated, but he doesn't need to know that.

Marco: Good. Me too. I'd like to formally request for you to join me on a date.

A date? With Marco? Hands shaking, I respond, maybe a little too quickly.

Me: That sounds awesome. Let me work on getting my dad's approval.

Then he does something I did not expect, he sends me a selfie. A fucking selfie. I can see that he's lying on powder blue pillows, his black-rimmed glasses only enhancing his eyes and boyish good looks. He's not wearing a shirt either, and I can see the smooth skin of his chest.

Good Lord, he's gorgeous.

Marco: How about you send me one back? I want to see your pretty face.

I almost choke on the fucking cracker. He wants a picture of me, and here I am, still in my school uniform, with my hair thrown up in a messy bun, totally disheveled with cracker crumbs on my shirt.

I rush to my bathroom, pull out my hair tie, and spray my hair with some dry shampoo before desperately trying to fix my face. I add some fresh mascara to my lashes, smack my cheeks for some color, and add light pink gloss to my lips.

After rubbing in the dry shampoo, I fix my long, dark brown hair as best as I can then open Snapchat to find a good but not obvious filter. I don't actually have any friends on Snap, but I do play with the filters when I'm bored at home.

I find one that almost makes it look like I'm not using a filter and take at least fifty shots of myself, moving my lips in various ways, hoping that I don't look like a fish but look hot at the same time.

I shuffle through the pics and decide on one. My chest squeezes as I send it off. I close my eyes, cringing to see what he'll say in response. After what seems like an eternity, my phone vibrates with an incoming message, and I preview it on my home screen.

Marco: Wow. Those are… interesting.

Interesting?

Sliding open my phone, I see what he's talking about. To my horror, I sent the entire series of fifty pictures.

Every.

Fucking.

One.

The fish pics, the ones where I checked my teeth for a rogue cracker seasoning, the cheesy winking pic.

Oh God.

I want to fucking die.

Just take me, Lord. Let me find a cliff to jump off, let me find a hole and bury myself in it.

Me: Oh my God! I didn't mean to send all of those!

My embarrassment increases by the second, and I wonder if he'll still want to court me after this.

Marco: Let me know what your dad says. Talk soon.

I don't even respond.

I can't respond.

What could I possibly say that won't make me look like more of an idiot? I close his messages and open Raphael's. It's been a while since we talked, I mean really talked. It used to be all the time, but over the past year, he's grown more and more distant.

Me: Hey, Raph. I need some advice.

His reply is almost instant.

Raphael: What's up, sis?

Me: It's about Marco Capelli. He wants to take me on a date. How do I approach Dad about it?

Instead of texting me back, Raph calls, and I answer on the first ring.

"I think you should wait until you're eighteen."

That's not what I wanted to hear. "Is that how you say hello these days, big bro? Not even a hey or how are you?"

Raph keeps his voice low, almost like he's whispering. "I just think it's better if you wait."

To my horror, I hear Lucian speak in the background. "Wait for what? Is that Val on the phone?"

"Hang on," Raph says, and then the phone goes silent. I wonder if he's trying to slip away where Lucian can't find him, but when the phone is unmuted, my oldest brother is on the line.

"So you want to go on a date with Marco Capelli, hmm?" Lucian asks.

"She should wait until she's eighteen," Raph repeats from the background.

Lucian scoffs at Raph. "Why should she wait? Don't you think it's best if she's not too wet behind the ears when the time comes?"

Wait. I'm so confused. "Time for what?"

"Don't worry your pretty little face, dear sister. I've heard it causes wrinkles. I'll make sure Dad approves. You'll have your chaperoned date. I promise."

Then the phone goes dead, and I look down to see the call has been disconnected. Why did Lucian sound so suspicious? Something is up, my spidey senses are tingling.

The question is…

What?

CHAPTER FOUR

Armani Moretti

I can't believe the time has finally come. Today, Lily is getting married and I'm not fucking ready for it. My baby sister looks gorgeous in her dress, her red hair so out of place down here in Mexico City.

The cathedral is large and old, the walls lined with arched, stained glass windows depicting the ten commandments. Old, exposed beams tower overhead, and an ancient organ gleams in the corner, its tune still beautiful yet haunting.

The priest, my sister, and Alejandro Hernandez, the oldest son of Miguel Hernandez, the previous leader of the Mexican Cartel, stand at the altar in front of a small gathering of people.

Tugging at the collar of my suit, I can't stop myself from glancing around. Sitting in a room filled with men who were once your enemies is anything but comfortable.

My twin, Fausto, who is probably annoyed by my constant shifting, elbows me in the side. "Chill the fuck out, bro. We have the treaty protecting us. Remember?"

"Will you two shut the fuck up and pay attention?" Sal growls, his thick eyebrows arched. "Our sister is about to get married."

"You don't say?" Fausto's sarcastic response isn't met with a smile from our eldest brother. He's hardly even older, born only eleven months before Fausto and me.

"Shut the fuck up," my brother, Salvatore Moretti, Don of the Outfit, whispers in the most threatening tone. As if that would scare me. I'm much too valuable for him to kill off. I have to stifle a laugh, because at times he sounds so much like Dad did. Sal thinks he's better than Dad, that he's not as heartless, but really, they are cut from the same cloth.

The priest drones on in Spanish, raising his tan hands up into the air. I catch a few words that I've somehow remembered since taking Spanish in high school, but I can't really follow along.

Lily, bound into the ugliest dress I've ever seen, is hardly paying attention. Instead of focusing on her groom and the ceremony, her eyes are fixed on the flowers in her hands, her gaze vacant.

My heart breaks for her. I know how hard this must be. Only yesterday she was planning out classes for her master's degree, and then we ripped it all away. Or should I say Dad did ten years ago. She doesn't seem to blame him though, not as much as she blames my brothers and me. I suppose she expected more loyalty, probably thinking we should have come forward and told her about this little arrangement.

But we couldn't. Dad would never have allowed that.

Even though he and Mom have been gone for five years, my brothers and I are still honor bound to see this treaty through, and he was explicit that Lily would not know until the last minute. I've considered why she was left in the dark, and I keep coming up with the same conclusion—she would have fled. Lily is smart as a whip, brave, and sure of herself. She would never have allowed this to happen had she gotten wind.

So instead of preparing to go into hiding to avoid this little marriage, she lived the last ten years of her life like normal, studying, hanging out with friends, and planning her future, unaware that it would all be torn away in one painful rip.

Sometimes I hate my dad for his choices. Giovanni Moretti might have looked like an excellent father on the outside, but the Mafia was his real family, his real love. The rest of us all came second to his position as leader. Many times I hated him for his lack of attention and lack of interest in my life or my brothers' lives for that matter.

Mafia.

Money.

Then family.

Mother was no better. If she knew and she never told Lily… well, I just hope that Lily can still love our mom after this, even though she's long gone.

"Marido y mujer."

I'm not sure exactly what the priest said, but the words he uttered seem so final, so permanent. Alejandro Hernandez leans down and kisses my sister, making me clench my fists in anger. I hate that she has to give herself over like this. I hate that she has to marry a man she doesn't even know and that he'll fuck away her innocence.

I hate that there's nothing I can do about it.

The next thing I know, Alejandro is practically pulling Lily down the aisle, her long train dragging behind her. I haven't even said goodbye or even congratulated her, and she's already out the front door.

Something in my gut tells me to rush after her, that this is my last chance to see my baby sister for a long time, so I quickly get to my feet and push past the crowd of people bustling down the long church aisle.

"Lily!" I call out. I can see her through the doors, standing between Alejandro and what could only be one of his brothers.

I know Lily hears me, because she bristles at my voice, but she doesn't even turn around. The man Alejandro hands her off to turns toward me and sneers.

Cock sucking motherfucker.

I'll wipe that grin off his fucking face so fast he'll never see straight again. The man makes a show of pushing Lily into the back of the awaiting car and climbs in after her. Alejandro shuts the door behind them.

"Lily!"

She doesn't hear me. Fausto steps up next to me, his hand clamping down on my shoulder. "She'll be alright, brother."

"How can you be so sure? Did you see the look on Alejandro's brother's face when he pushed her into the car? I didn't fucking like it."

"You don't have to like it," Sal replies, moving to my other side. "What's done is done. Her fate was sealed a decade ago. There's nothing you can do about it."

Sal has always been cold, but more so in the past six months after his girlfriend, Gianna, up and left him. He was a dick before, but now he's almost unbearable to be around. I don't even understand why he dated her in the first place, knowing his fate lies in the hands of another woman, the daughter of the infamous Don of the Cosa Nostra, Carlo Rossi.

Fausto chuckles and places his sunglasses on his face, then he turns toward Sal. "Getting excited for your own bride, are you, brother? Nice and ripe for the picking."

Sal doesn't acknowledge Fausto, still staring into the distance. "She's a child. I'm hardly excited. But who knows, I might give her to one of you and rid myself of this burden. Armani, you fuck anything that walks, so perhaps you'd like her."

I can't even argue. He's right. The brain in my dick speaks much louder than the one in my head. "Perhaps I will, and after I fuck her, I'll tell you how sweet and tight her virgin cunt was. Would you like that, Sal?"

Sal rolls his eyes and walks over to Alejandro, offering our new brother-in-law his hand to shake. Fausto and I leave him to it, and after glancing back at the cathedral one last time, we walk away, leaving behind the family we once had.

It was never perfect, a little broken even, but it was ours.
Now, the bonds we once had are likely severed forever.

CHAPTER FIVE

Valentina

I LOVE WEEKENDS. Knowing I don't have to get up for school changes my entire mood. There are no questions to answer about my childhood, and no lies I've already told about who I am that I need to remember.

I can just be me.

I have to admit, though, that my dad forcing me to take on this fake persona has caused me to be a little introverted. Sure, I like hanging out with friends when I'm allowed to, but when I do, I have to live the lie. One thing I hate is liars, yet here I am, the ultimate hypocrite.

Stretching my arms above my head, I let out a satisfied moan and slip my sleep mask off my eyes—don't judge me until you try it, it's the most wonderful creation in all of mankind. The sunlight shining through the bedroom shades lets me know it's time to get up. Rolling over, I dump my sleep mask on my nightstand and check my phone.

There's a message from Lucian. Sitting up, I unplug my phone from the charger and swipe it open to read it.

Lucian: Your date with Marco Capelli has been arranged. A car will pick you up at precisely 2:00PM. The guard will be wearing a black suit and black sunglasses. One of our men will stay with you as your chaperone. Alfonzo Capelli himself will chaperone for Marco. Enjoy your time while you can.

Enjoy my time while I can?

Why does everything Lucian says lately sound so damn cryptic?

While I can...

Maybe he's just referring to the fact that I'll be off to college in just a few short months and unable to easily see Marco during that time, but something tells me that's not the case.

Stomach grumbling, I wipe the sleep from my eyes and head downstairs to the kitchen, thankful I'm alone. Sure, I like Theresa's company, it's nice not to always be alone, but even when she's here I'm still lonely. Not being able to talk to her aside from anything food related can be maddening and frustrating beyond belief.

There's a sadness in her eyes when she looks at me, and more than once we've both almost slipped up. Asking something as normal and mundane as "How was your day?" could be enough to get her fired or worse.

Thinking about that makes me hate the Mafia and this life I have to live even more than I already do. Maybe I won't go to college. Maybe once I turn eighteen, I'll petition the courts for a name change and just disappear, start a new life somewhere.

I could do it... I think.

Grabbing a cereal bowl from a cabinet—you know the ones with the little straw attached so you can slurp up the milk—I dump a generous amount of Golden Grahams into the dark blue plastic container before I head to the fridge for milk. My mouth waters as I think about the first bite, and I quickly replace the milk and walk over to the kitchen table.

I push half of the cereal to the back of the bowl, keeping as much out of the milk as I can so it stays crunchy, and then I get to work. The sweetness of the first bite coats my tongue, and I groan as I chew. From here, I can see through the side yard and across the street. This house is on a corner lot, making views from the side of the house something other than another home's siding.

It's a gorgeous morning here in New Hampshire. The bright blue, cloudless sky is inviting, telling of the summer warmth that's already begun to settle in. The trees are nearly in full bloom, the tulips giving way to roses.

Across the street, Mr. Lampoon, a portly man with white hair in his early seventies who always has a smile on his face, is meticulously mowing his lawn. Every week it's the same pattern. First he mows from his house to the sidewalk, and then he mows it a second time across his yard. Next he will use the weed whacker around his flower beds, and finally, he'll edge around the driveway and sidewalk.

Half of me wonders if he's just bored, or if maybe he just doesn't like to be in the house with Mrs. Lampoon. Every time I see her, she's shouting something at him, her little white apron covering an old, stuffy dress. Sometimes she has faded pink rollers still pinned to her graying hair, her half-moon glasses perched on the very tip of her nose, and a wrinkled frown on her face. It's no wonder I find her so unapproachable.

As I scoop more cereal from the dry half into the pool of milk at the front of the bowl, I start to daydream about this afternoon.

I have a date with Marco!

I couldn't be more excited… or nervous… or slightly scared. I wish things didn't have to be so damn formal in the Mafia. Not a single person in Oakwood Prep has to suffer the company of a chaperone on their dates. It does me no good to complain, I know that, but sometimes I just can't help it.

It pisses me right the fuck off.

After eating the rest of my cereal and drinking the delicious sweet milk through the bowl's straw, I rinse the bowl in the sink and place it inside my dishwasher. It's only 10:00AM, leaving me a couple hours with nothing to do before I start getting ready.

I decide to open Facebook. I'm not friends with Marco Capelli because Dad insists that the Mafia can't know my fake name. Luckily for me, when I search his profile under my fake account, I find his isn't restricted.

Bingo.

I click on his profile pic with shaky fingers and open his profile. The first post I see is from only a few minutes ago. It reads, *Excited for my date today.* Tagged below it is the popular GIF of the little baby boy celebrating at a sports game.

Seeing that post does something to me. My gut flutters and my heart thumps rapidly. Marco is just as excited to see me. Wow.

And here I thought I'd have to stay single forever.

After scrolling through my feed, I get bored and play Candy Crush before I decide to get ready early. I can't sit around another second.

Stripping off my shorts and shirt, I take a long, hot shower and scrub my body, shaving my armpits and legs. It's not that I expect Marco to get close enough to touch me, but I'll feel better about myself if I'm completely prepared.

I'm one of those weird people who likes the shower water a degree cooler than the temperature needed to actually burn myself, so once my skin is all red and blotchy, I turn off the water, secure my hair in one towel, and wrap a second around my body.

Using tweezers, I carefully pluck out a few rogue eyebrow hairs then check my face for new blemishes. I'd like to get my eyebrows waxed. As an Italian woman, my brows are fuller and bulkier than I'd like, but Dad won't allow it. I'm lucky he permits me to get my hair cut four times a year, insisting that I keep it long. Sometimes I think he wants to keep me looking young so no one my age would want to date me, while other times I think he's trying to extend my youth in a desperate attempt to be a part of my life. I know that's reaching, however, because Dad is far too selfish for that.

I apply a minimal amount of makeup—a shimmery face powder, pale pink blush, soft pink shadow, and black mascara. I hardly need mascara, my lashes are long and thick, but the makeup accentuates them, making them darker, sexier. The shadow plays nicely with my pale blue eyes, the only physical characteristic I inherited from Mom that I love. Next, I brush and floss, making sure my teeth are sparkly white, and then I begin fixing my hair.

Unbinding my hair from the towel allows the long brown strands to hang past my shoulder blades, the damp locks clinging to my skin. I use a blow dryer first, then a curler, giving my hair long, loose curls with ease. That's one of the benefits to being alone, I have all the time in the world to watch hair and makeup tutorials. Too bad I don't get to show them off anywhere.

Next is the dress… Which one to wear?

My closet is filled with items, most of which I've never been given the opportunity to wear, thanks to Dad. After rifling through several hangers, I decide to stick to today's theme and choose a baby pink sundress. It's not snug, but it's form-fitting. The sleeves cover my shoulders, and the bodice is high enough to cover my breasts while leaving my collarbones exposed. It's cinched in at the waist, and the flowy skirt hits me just below the knee.

I add a pair of pearl earrings, one of the many earrings Dad has bought in an attempt to win my affection, and Mom's necklace. Pulling the gold chain from my jewelry box, I can't help but reflect. The necklace doesn't really go with my outfit, but it was hers, and it's the only thing of hers that I still have. I secure it behind my neck and finger the little Italian horn charm, remembering how it looked on her.

Damn, I can't believe she's been gone three years already.

Looking at myself in the mirror, I wonder what she would have to say about the date today. Would she have been proud of me and helped me get ready? Or would she have been too drunk by noon to give a fuck about me?

A knock raps against the front door, and I check the security cameras on my phone before answering it. As Lucian said earlier, a guard in a black suit is waiting for me.

I slather some gloss on my lips, grab my purse, and head to the front door.

CHAPTER SIX

Valentina

My hand shakes as I will it to grab the cool, metal doorknob and twist. Warm air greets me when the door swings open, but unlike the welcoming scent of summer in the air, the suited men are stoic and cold. Wearing dark sunglasses, black suits, and shiny black shoes, the men don't even acknowledge me. Words are not exchanged either, similar to my experiences with Theresa.

Instead, a large man, whose arms look as though they might burst from the confines of his suit at any moment, gestures down the porch stairs to an awaiting Mercedes, which, unsurprisingly, is also black.

Unlike the cold, hard feeling my family's guards give off, the car looks sleek. Shining under the midday sun, it oozes wealth. I almost shake my head as I close my front door, lock it, and head to the car, because if my brothers and father had wished to keep my true identity a secret, then this is not the way to go about it.

I can already see old Mrs. Lampoon pulling her drapes aside to peek out at what's going on across the street. Little Brian McCarthy stops shooting hoops in his driveway to watch, his basketball tucked casually under his arm. And let's not forget about the porch dwelling soccer moms, Sara, Jane, and Alyssa, who gossip while staring directly at me, their hands wrapped around what I know are mugs filled with spiked coffee.

I smile smugly and wave my fingers at them, acknowledging that I see them staring. Sara looks aghast and quickly says something to Alyssa, whose bright blue gaze narrows while she brings the mug to her thin lips. Jane just blatantly stares, as if she wants me to say something.

Bitches.

Part of me secretly wants to be accepted by them, to be in their inner circle. Maybe that's why I dislike them so much, because I know that can never happen.

I'm jealous of them.

Not of what they have or who they are, but of their friendship and closeness. I'd love to have a bestie to drink spiked coffee and gossip with. Payton would be my closest friend, but I have to keep her at arm's length. I'd never want to let her in and risk her life, her future, should she hear or see something she shouldn't.

Nope.

So instead, I meander through this life all alone.

The less bulky of the two guards, who so kindly greeted me at my front door, walks ahead of me and pulls open the door to the backseat. Sitting against the far side is a third man who watches me from behind his dark sunglasses as I sit on the seat opposite him. Then I feel a tap on my right arm and look up to see the bulky one motioning for me to scoot over.

Fucking A.

Really?

I have to sit bitch between these two Neanderthals?

Groaning, I scoot over and allow myself to become a Val sandwich as the large man sits and shuts the door behind him.

The driver glances over his shoulder, looking at the large man who nods once. The driver nods back and shifts the Mercedes into gear, then he begins the drive to wherever it is we're going.

I learned long ago not to ask the suited men sent by Dad or my brothers questions, because I'll only end up disappointed. They never answer. Hell, they never even speak to each other while I'm with them.

Annoyed, I pull out my phone and wait for facial recognition to unlock it before texting my oldest brother.

Me: Is this really necessary?

His reply is almost instant, as if he knew I'd be texting him.

Lucian: Is what necessary?

Me: Four guards? Is that really necessary to take me to see Marco? It's not like I'm heading into the bowels of the Russian Mafia. I'm going to lunch, for God's sake.

Lucian: Do not question what I see fit for you. You're lucky you're going on this date to begin with. Dad doesn't even know I've allowed it, so shut your fucking mouth and be grateful that you're going at all.

My heart thumps in surprise.

Me: Dad doesn't know?

Lucian: Of course not. He'd hardly allow you to see Marco Capelli again, not after the argument he and Alfonzo had at the wedding a few months back. Have some grace, sister. I'll be in touch soon.

Huffing at his condescending messages, I flip to Facebook and immediately go to Marco's profile. He posted a status update about twenty minutes ago...

Getting ready for my date today.

Knowing that I'm that date, I almost hit the like button, but when I feel the guard next to me shift, trying to look at my phone, I quickly shut it down. I know the guards have been ordered to watch my every move, and if they see a Facebook account that I'm not supposed to have, Dad or Lucian will have my ass.

I've just put my phone back in my purse when I feel it vibrate through the fabric. Pulling it back out, I see a message from Marco. Anxious, I slide it open.

Marco: I'm excited to see you today. Be there soon. XO

XO? Hugs and kisses?

Aren't those little letters kept only for someone you really like?

Me: I'm excited too!!! I'm on my way!

I hit send then wish I hadn't let my excitement drive me so hard. Were the exclamation points too much? Do I seem too eager? He did write XO, so maybe the exclamation points were necessary but not so many of them.

"So stupid," I murmur under my breath, shoving my phone back into my purse. The guards stay silent as we drive through the city, past Oakwood Prep, and merge onto the freeway.

An hour later, after I've had plenty of time to chastise myself over my excessive use of exclamation points, we exit the freeway and drive into a shopping complex. I've seen this one advertised on TV. It's called Majestic Village. Village is really too small a word to describe the vastness of this place. Tall buildings rise from the center of miles of parking lots. There are many expensive restaurants, clothing stores, high-end furniture, and gourmet coffee bars.

It looks like a pop-up book, the kind you'd read as a kid with buildings full of color. The scent of food fills the air, and Majestic Village is bustling with people as we drive slowly through the center. Moms drag their complaining kids along with a firm grip on their hands or push them in fancy strollers. A group of guys enters a place called Boyd's Beer & Burgers, all wearing Yankees gear, which makes me wonder if baseball season has already started.

I've never really followed sports, probably because I didn't grow up around them. My brothers are die-hard fans though. They have season tickets in a loge box, but I've never gone purely because I haven't been invited.

The driver makes a right turn and slips in front of a bright yellow building with a sign hanging out front that proudly reads Antonia's Bistro. I know from commercials it's a well-known Italian restaurant.

Of course.

God forbid we try something Mexican or Indian. Fuck, I could go for a taco right now. Actually, I can always go for a taco.

The bulky guard exits the car and motions for me to follow him. As I slide out, I see a familiar face I did not expect to see.

"Gabriel!"

My youngest brother rushes to greet me, pulling me into a warm embrace. I squeeze him hard. I'm so deprived of human affection, I hold onto him a little longer than normal.

Giving him one last squeeze, I pull away and tuck my hair behind my ears. "What are you doing here?"

Gabe just grins down at me. "Chaperoning your little date of course."

Relief washes over me, because I thought it might have been the guards' duty to watch over me. "Thank God it's not Lucian."

Gabe's smile falters, but only for a moment. He quickly recovers and wraps his arm around my shoulders, guiding me through a little gate on the side of the building to an outdoor seating area spread under a tall awning complete with rotating fans.

My heart hammers when I see Marco, who's texting on his phone. When he sets it down, he folds his hands on the table and casually looks around before his eyes land on us. A smile grows on his handsome face, making my stomach flip and flutter as Gabe and I head over.

Marco stands and clasps his hands behind his back. He looks amazing. Light khaki pants hang loosely on his legs, and a baby blue polo snugly encases his torso. A gray cardigan is bound around his neck, making him look so proper that I start to feel underdressed.

Gabe leans in and whispers quietly so no one else can hear. "Be careful with your heart, sis. Keep it close. Keep it guarded." He releases me and extends a hand to Marco. "Marco. Nice to see you."

Marco grips Gabe's hand. "Gabriel. It's nice to see you as well."

Gabe pulls Marco close. "Take care of my sister, understand?"

It's incredible how his tone changed from friendly to sinister in a millisecond.

Gabe pats him on the back, drops his hand, and turns to me. "Now you two have fun." Gabe winks then saunters to the back of the patio where he orders a Bloody Mary before sliding onto a barstool.

"You look beautiful," Marco says, pulling my attention from Gabe back to him.

I rub my sweaty hands down the skirt of my dress. "Thanks, you do too."

Marco's eyes widen, and I realize what I just said.

"Handsome is what you are," I blurt out. "Not pretty. I mean, you're a little pretty in the most masculine way possible. Man pretty. By man pretty I mean hot. Really hot. Did I just say that out loud?"

My cheeks are on fire with embarrassment, but Marco takes my awkward greeting in stride, laughing as he walks over to pull my chair out for me.

"I think you're hot too," he murmurs, leaning close so I can feel his breath on my neck. The feeling of him so near makes me shiver and causes my breath to lodge in my throat as I sit on the chair and scoot myself in.

I think he knows it too, judging by the smug look on his face as he sits opposite me. As soon as we are both seated, he beckons to a server who must have been waiting in the wings. Dressed in a white linen shirt and pressed black pants, the thin, pale man in his mid-thirties, with thinning black hair and an even thinner mustache pathetically trying to grow above his upper lip, bustles over. He pours us each a glass of iced tea before placing the glass pitcher on the table.

"Your menus," he adds in a sniveling voice. Handing each of us an obnoxiously long menu book with gilded edges, he stares down at us over his exceptionally large nose.

"Thank you," Marco replies politely, accepting his menu and flipping it open. I mimic him and begin perusing the lunch specials. It's been so long since I've been to an actual restaurant, months probably. I haven't been since my brothers drove me home from our cousin's wedding. The wedding, in fact, where I met Marco.

As I'm reading through the options, I notice how eerily silent it is and glance up to look around. Marco's blond brows are furrowed as he reads, and I flick my eyes away from his baby blues to the surrounding tables. There must be at least twenty, four-person tables out here, yet we are the only customers aside from Gabe, who is at the bar, and another older gentleman with short gray hair who's sitting in the far corner watching us—Marco's chaperone I assume. Funny, I thought Alfonzo would be accompanying him.

Then it dawns on me. Our families probably reserved the whole patio so we would be watched and monitored. Sometimes I hate the fucking Mafia. There's never a sense of normalcy or family. Such isolation is required for protection. Sometimes I think I'd be better off wounded or even kidnapped for a short period of time. Maybe my family would miss me then and nurse me back to health if I got hurt.

"See anything you like?"

Marco's question pulls me from the dark recesses of my mind. Regardless of what my existence has been like, I have this moment, right here, right now, where I can be Valentina Rossi, and the guy sitting across the table knows who I am and is here in spite of it. Hell, maybe he's here because of it. My brothers always say that people want to get in close with our family for their own gain, not to actually help us in any way. Maybe that's why Gabe whispered that warning before heading over to the bar.

"Umm..." I haven't even looked at the menu, and he's already closing his.

"Might I recommend the caprese salad and the veal parmesan? Both are exquisite."

Veal? Who in their right mind would eat that knowing it's made from a baby cow? But my brain just turns into goo around this boy, and I suddenly nod a little too fast. "Yes. Veal."

Marco smiles. "Good."

I close my menu and rest it on the table as Marco waves our server over again. This time I notice his nametag: Brian.

Could there be a less Italian name in the entire world?

"Are you ready to order?" Brian asks, lifting his chin into the air to look down his nose at us again. Damn, he has huge nostrils. You could fit a fucking quarter up there.

Marco orders for both of us. "Yes. Two orders of veal parmesan. Do you want to try the salad, Val?"

Marco locks his bright eyes on me, and I forget how to speak.

Salad?

What salad?

"Yes," I mutter, mentally slapping myself. I hate tomatoes, and caprese is covered in them.

I notice Brian doesn't write down our order, instead he just tries to remember.

How fancy and a little extra if you ask me. I'd rather he wrote it down so he didn't get it wrong, but whatever.

Brian nods and takes the menus off the table before departing to place our order, leaving Marco and me alone.

What do I do?

What do I say?

"I'm so glad we finally got to do this." Marco sips his tea, and I envision my lips pressing against his as he sucks the brown drink up his straw. "I haven't stopped thinking about you since the wedding."

"Me too," I admit a little too enthusiastically. "I haven't been thinking of myself, of course. I meant I've been thinking of you as well."

I cringe at my lack of couth. Are all seventeen-year-old girls this pathetic?

Or is it just my hermit lifestyle that makes peopling so challenging?

I have more mature conversations with the squirrels in my backyard and the orchid on my windowsill than this, but then again there's no pressure with them. The squirrels just ignore me while eating their acorns, and my orchid, well, she thrives under my conversation. My CO_2 ensures her survival, and trust me, nothing is worse than a wilted orchid.

Marco's eyes narrow slightly, and suddenly I feel like an amoeba being studied under a microscope. "So tell me about your plans for next year."

"Dartmouth," I blurt out, then clap my hands over my mouth and jerk toward Gabe, hoping he didn't hear. His back is turned to me as he watches the game on a TV hanging behind the bar.

"Don't worry. I won't tell Gabe or anyone else." Marco reaches across the table and slips his hand over mine, squeezing gently. "Your secret is safe with me."

God, I'd love to believe that, and although I could so easily succumb to this boy holding my hand, I know that the only secrets that remain as such are the ones you keep to yourself.

"He can't know," I whisper. "Not yet. Not until I've officially been accepted."

Marco nods and pulls his hand back as Brian approaches with a tray resting on his shoulder. He sets the tray down on a pair of collapsible legs then places two plates of caprese salad in front of us.

"Thanks," I mutter as Brian grabs a cheese grater.

"Cheese?"

"Yes, please," Marco answers, and Brian gets to work, grating cheese all over Marco's plate.

Brian finishes with Marco's salad and turns to me. "And you?"

I shake my head. "No, thank you."

Brian flares his huge nostrils disapprovingly then turns swiftly, gathers his tray and its stand, then heads back through the patio.

Marco shoves a bite of salad into his mouth, but not me. My stomach churns at the idea of having a cold, slimy wet tomato in my mouth, but I have no choice. I ordered it, so I have to eat it.

It would be rude not to.

Marco chews happily, cutting into a juicy tomato when an idea hits me like a baseball bat. While he's looking down at his plate, I pull a strand of my hair out of my head and stir it into my salad.

I've just finished hiding it when Marco looks up and sees me with my uneaten salad. "Is something wrong with your food?"

"Umm... There's a hair in it."

Marco sucks in an exasperated breath before tossing down his napkin and snatching up my plate.

"It's okay, really!" I call, but he ignores me, instead marching to the bar with the tainted salad bowl.

I watch in horror as he shouts at the bartender, demanding a fresh one be made and an apology from the cook who made it. His whole demeanor changed in an instant, reminding me of Gabe's abrupt shift earlier. What is it about the men in my life that gives them the ability to do that? Is it an Italian thing or a gift all men are blessed with?

I'm unable to look away as Brian rushes into the bar and is verbally assaulted by Marco. "How dare you feed her contaminated food! Don't you know who she is? Who I am? Don't you know what we could do to you?"

Brian's eyes widen, and he puts his hands up in a submissive manner. "I-I'm so sorry, sir. I'll take care of it right away."

"See that you do," Marco grumbles, shoving the salad into Brian's chest before returning to our table. I glance at Gabe who shrugs but has a satisfied look on his face.

Marco sits back down with a huff. "Sorry you had to see that, love. But I'll be damned if you're not taken care of. You're my woman now, I'll always protect you."

CHAPTER SEVEN

Valentina

Part of me is horrified by what's just happened, but the other part is loving it. Seeing someone get irate on my behalf over something so minuscule as a random hair in my salad was something I never thought I'd experience. Sure, I feel bad, knowing it was my hair in the first place, but it did get me out of having to eat gross fucking tomatoes.

I do wonder, though, how someone could become this outraged at something as simple as a hair in a salad. With a temper like that, one so similar to my dad's that it's almost painful, what else would set him off?

Sucking the straw into my mouth, I take a long sip of iced tea and watch Marco from across the table. When he lifts his eyes to mine, I flinch at the anger there. There is a ferocity in his gaze that would make an angry lion retreat into a den of vipers.

Swallowing my sip, I trail a finger along the condensation on my glass and clear my throat. "What about you? What are your plans for next year?"

Marco holds my gaze. There's an emptiness inside his eyes I didn't see before. A dead zone. Only a psycho could stare this long and not blink, or someone trying to intimidate.

News flash—he's succeeding.

"My sole focus is furthering myself in all ways, bettering my life, and *our* future together. I was serious, Val, when I said that you're my woman now. I mean that with all that I am. Does that scare you?"

I tense when he pushes himself up from his chair and walks around the table, taking my hand into his. He gazes down at me with a look of desire, of want, his eyes trailing from my face and over the rest of me. He makes me feel as though I'm wearing nothing at all, and I feel my cheeks heat in what I'm sure is an obvious reaction to his nearness. Marco releases my hand and cups my face, running his thumb across my cheek, and then he kisses me, and the emotion evident in the kiss takes me by surprise. Here I was thinking I liked him more than he liked me, but now I think it might be the other way around.

His kiss is dominating but a little sloppy, his tongue feeling thick and too large in my mouth. I can barely keep up as he shoves his tongue deeper, sliding his over mine, and I soon find myself pressing on his chest, worried I might not be able to breathe if he doesn't let up.

When he finally pulls away, I gasp as he looks at me with hooded eyes and a slackened jaw. "That was incredible, Val." He touches his lips as if remembering how they felt on mine. "You're panting. Did you feel it too? Our connection?"

Unable to form words, I simply nod. I don't want to hurt his ego by telling him I'm panting because he choked me with his huge tongue. I don't think we're at that point in our relationship for that kind of honesty.

"You were meant to be mine," he proclaims, crouching down before me, his hands now squeezing my thighs. "Mine in all ways possible. I didn't see it before, but now I'm sure. I've never been more sure of anything in my life."

His touch edges up under my skirt, and I glance around to see if anyone notices. Gabe is still at the bar with his back turned to us, and besides him, we are alone.

No one would ever see.

"One day, I'll make you mine forever under the eyes of God and anyone else watching. What's mine will be yours, and what's yours will be mine. We will rule New York someday, Valentina. I vow it."

Rule New York?

Grabbing his hands, I stop them from going any farther. "I won't be running New York, Marco. That job will go to my brothers someday, but not for many years. My father is far too stubborn to die."

Marco simply blinks, the serious look on his face not faltering even though I've just disputed his envisaged future. "We'll see about that," he murmurs almost to himself as he stands up and walks back to his chair.

Brian, clearly shaken by his altercation with Marco, saves me from what would absolutely be an awkward moment as he walks over to our table carrying a large tray on his shoulder.

"Your veal is served." Brian sets the tray down on a nearby table and bows deeply toward Marco before serving the warm dishes. I have a moment where I almost ask why I didn't get a bow too before shutting up. The last thing I need is another aggressive interaction with Brian and Marco. One, I don't think Brian would survive. In fact, he'd probably lose his job. And two, I kind of like this place. Another outburst could mean that we'd be kicked out of here forever and placed on the blacklist.

So I just smile politely and thank Brian for the food while avoiding his condescending nostril flaring. Brian almost runs from the table once our food is served, and my stomach growls loudly. I glance up at Marco to see if he noticed, but he's much too preoccupied with his food to note my hungry belly.

Unfolding my napkin, I place the dark cloth on my lap and pick up my silverware. The veal is like butter, making my steak knife pointless, but I had manners beaten into me as a child, so I use it anyway, cutting small portions and taking small bites.

Marco must not have had the same lessons as I did, because he eats like a starving animal, slicing his cut of meat into huge bites. He swirls spaghetti around his fork, stabs the prongs into a juicy cut of veal, then shoves the whole thing into his mouth. And damn, he has a huge fucking mouth.

Marco catches me staring, but he seems unaffected. "Something wrong?" he mumbles, that huge bite sloshing around his even huger mouth as he speaks.

I shake my head then avert my eyes to my own plate. I'd much rather swirl my spaghetti around my fork like he did, but I opt for my manners and cut the pasta into one-inch lengths before placing a bite into my mouth.

The pasta is cooked to perfection, not too chewy yet not firm either. Smooth and flavorful, the sauce is seasoned with garlic and basil, but it's not overpowering. Forcing myself to take a bite of this poor, baby cow, I have to stifle a moan. Shit, this is good. I can see how people overlook the slaughter of a baby animal to chew on this piece of meat.

And the garlic bread... Don't even get me started. I sink my teeth into the warm slice of bread in my hand. "Mmm. The garlic bread is delicious. The outer layer is crunchy and the middle is soft, just like I like it."

Marco almost chokes on his bite, then he clears his throat. "I have something hard on the outside and soft on the inside. Want to see?"

I pause for a moment, then it dawns on me. "Umm. Maybe later?"

Marco points at me, his hand in the shape of a gun that he fires. "You have yourself a rain check."

This dinner has not gone as I had anticipated, and I'm not sure how I feel about it. Thankfully, Marco is so consumed by his meal that small talk is unnecessary through the rest of my time here.

"Five minutes, guys. Time to wrap it up," Gabe calls from the bar, tapping on his watch.

"Thanks for lunch," I offer, wiping my mouth on the napkin before setting it down next to my plate.

"The pleasure is all mine, love." Marco walks over to me and offers me his hand. Not wanting to be rude, I take it and allow him to pull me up. He draws me in for a hug hard enough that a few of my vertebrae crack. "One day, you'll see," he whispers. "Just me and you ruling the world together. That's what I want. You, Val, forever. Kept safe behind a white picket fence just for me."

He kisses my head then lets go as Gabe grips my upper arm and pulls me away. "Tell your father mine will be in touch soon," Gabe tells Marco.

Marco nods and watches me almost sadly as Gabe leads me out of the restaurant to the black Mercedes.

CHAPTER EIGHT

Valentina

I HUG Gabe a little longer than normal, squeezing my brother tightly. Living alone has its perks, such as not having to wear a bra or pants, but it's also quite lonely. I miss my brothers. Well… maybe not all of them. Lucian can stay as far away as he pleases. But I miss Raph and Gabe.

"You two seemed to hit it off," Gabe notes, pulling away from me and opening the back door to the car.

I shrug. "I guess."

Gabe crosses his arms, arching one dark eyebrow at me. "You guess? Yesterday you could hardly wait to see him. What changed?"

"He… He's just not the guy I thought he was." The admission slips out so easily.

Gabe leans in and whispers, "None of us are. Keep your heart safe, sis. Hold it tight. Keep it close." He kisses my cheek and ushers me into the car, not shutting it until I'm squished between two oversized guards. "See you soon, sis," he says before slamming the door.

I'm not even five minutes from the restaurant when my phone chimes with a new message.

Marco: I had so much fun today. I hope we can do it again soon.

Me: I had fun too.

I don't know why I lie. Sure, the beginning of the date was good, but the middle and end left me wanting.

Marco: Next weekend?

Me: I'll have to ask my dad and let you know.

I don't know why I said my dad when Lucian approved this whole debacle.

Marco: I'll be thinking about you until then. Send me snaps when you can, okay?

Me: K.

Then a message from Payton buzzes through.

Payton: How was it? Tell me everything!!!

Me: Which part do you want to hear, the good or the bad?

Payton: You know I don't make decisions lol.

Me: Fine. I'll tell you when I get home.

Payton: *Heart emoji*

The ride home is over quickly. I don't know if it was my daydreams, pure mental exhaustion, or the subtle vibrations in the car, but the next thing I know, I'm being shaken awake by a silent guard.

Sitting up abruptly, I wipe the sleep from my eyes and check my chin for drool before seeing where I am.

Home.

The guard on the curb side of the car steps out, and I follow quickly after him. He watches from the sidewalk as I walk to my door, keeping my eyes down so no nosy neighbors can make eye contact and try to talk to me. I don't look up until I've entered my house and have the door safely shut behind me.

"I can't believe I fell asleep like that," I mutter to myself in disbelief, dropping my purse on the entryway table. I head over to the fridge and note that a taco casserole is waiting for me covered in plastic wrap with directions on how to cook it. Theresa must have been here earlier.

Taking a Dr. Pepper from the fridge, I crack the can open and enjoy the pleasant hiss of the carbonation before heading to my room. I need to clear my head, and one of the ways I like to do that is to get all my thoughts onto paper.

Stacks of unused journals rest on the upper left corner of my desk. It's an addiction I have, collecting journals with no intention of using them. Usually, I just enjoy the pretty bindings and colorful pages, then I close them forever.

But there are some I use.

Pulling out my current journal, I flip to the first blank page and grab my favorite purple Bic pen. I click the top over and over while I think. Sighing, I mentally make notes of all the pros and cons of the date.

Pros
*Handsome
*Well dressed
*Demands respect for me
*Demands respect for himself
*Possessive in a way I've never felt before

Cons
*Quick tempered
*Not a great kisser
*A little too forward
*Over-confident
*Chews loudly and talks with food in his mouth

I look over my lists, trying to decide what I can live with and what I'm unwilling to settle for. Hell, maybe he was just nervous today like I was, or maybe he was just trying to show off in front of me.

I was so nervous I was stumbling over my words. Heck, I told Marco he was *man pretty*. Who says shit like that?

Thinking his nerves got the better of him eases me. At the wedding, he was nothing but a gentleman, sweet and kind. Who's to say he isn't those things under less stressful circumstances? It couldn't have been easy trying to woo me—did I just actually use the word woo?—and satisfy my brother at the same time. The poor man probably didn't know how to act.

Yep. It's decided. I'm being ridiculous. I'll give him another chance, a second date. Happy with my decision and ignoring Gabe's little warning, I change out of my sundress. It always feels good to slip into comfy clothes. I exhale happily as I ease into sweat shorts and a racer-back tank, then head to my couch for much needed relaxation, binging a show on Netflix.

The hottest series on Netflix has just released season two, and fuck if I can't wait to spend some alone time with the gorgeous man whose long, white hair makes my thighs tremble.

Two episodes in, I'm screaming at the TV and pulling at my hair. The writers are fucking insane to do something like that! Grabbing my phone, I glance at the screen which I've ignored for the better part of two hours and see two calls, three texts, a snap, and a missed call from Payton, plus a snap from Marco.

My heart pitter-patters when I open his snap and grin at the sleepy look on his face.

Marco: Heading to bed, love. Sweet dreams. XO.

Knowing he likes pics, I quickly tousle my hair, add a kissy face, and find the best angle before snapping back.

Me: My dreams will be all about you tonight.

Send.

Shit.

Did I just send that corny ass snap to him?

Ugh!

Do you just ever hate yourself so damn much that you'd beat your own ass if you could? That's exactly how I'm feeling right now, like a huge fucking idiot. Sometimes—well, all the time—I need to slow the fuck down and think before I act. I'm sure some of that maturity just comes with age and experience, but my impulsive reactions are going to get me into trouble if I'm not careful.

My phone pings with Marco's pic, and I cringe when I open my phone.

Marco: Wet dreams I hope.

And there it is.

A second pic.

A *dick* pic.

My first dick pic.

And I don't really know how to feel.

Part of me is completely grossed out, but also very curious. Being the great Carlo Rossi's daughter comes with complications in regard to boys and relationships. Basically, they have not been allowed, approved, or accepted in any way, shape, or form.

You're a Rossi, Valentina. Daughter of the don. You will remain pure until I say it is time.

Talk about embarrassing. Having your father talk to you about your virtue is something I don't recommend. Thumbs down. Zero stars. I was just starting high school, with puberty in full action, my hormones raging, and so many zits on my chin you could play connect the dots.

And I wanted to die.

If there was a hole, I would have crawled in it and covered myself up with dirt to get out of that. The worst part—yes, it gets worse—is that my brothers were all there too. Gabe was making sex gestures behind my dad, shoving his finger into a circle formed by his pointer finger and thumb. Raph was doing his best to keep a straight face, but I heard him snort at least once. Lucian was stoic, as always, not even looking in my direction.

There was no one to save me, no one to help. Mom was out at the salon getting her hair and makeup done for an important dinner with the heads of the Cosa Nostra, and Dad took this opportunity to discuss the birds and the bees.

So forgive me if I zoom in on this dick pic and study it. The pale creature is poking out of his sweats and resting in his hand. It appears Marco is squeezing the life out of it as if he has a strangulation kink.

Hell, maybe he does.

Can I get down with something like that?

Only time will tell.

I don't know what the normal size of a dick is, but this one looks to be the size of an Italian sausage—no pun intended. To think that thing is supposed to fit inside of me is concerning. The girth of my tampons is a quarter of that, and toward the end of my period, even they can be a struggle to get in. Even more concerning, some women suck these down their throats or take it up their asses!

Nope.

Exit only for this girl.

Besides, why would a guy want to stick their dick in a hole that more than likely is filled with shit when the other one is perfectly usable?

I mean… is there a shit dick kink?

Dick shit?

CHAPTER NINE

Fausto Moretti

Feeling my fist slamming into the jaw of someone who's done me wrong will never get old. Neither will the sound of that jaw cracking or the scent of blood as it mists the air.

A gentle rain falls on us from the dark night sky, making the old brick under our shoes slick. Not that it matters. I won't slip, and my 9mm won't miss, even if we're lurking down here in the shadowy dead end of an old, smelly alleyway.

"Where the fuck is the product?" Sal shouts behind us. Armani slams his fist into the man's gut, and the asshole drops to his knees. I take the opportunity to chop him hard in the throat. Choking, he clutches his neck like we fucking care.

In reality, his pain fuels me and corrupts me further. There are days when my muscles ache to cause pain, and I want to revel in the sound of another's suffering and be the cause of it.

Sometimes I seek out pain, finding my way through the slums of New York to some underground cage fight or drunk bar brawl. I disguise myself, using the fake name of Tony because everyone knows at least one Tony. Leaving my watches, rings, and my grandpapi's necklace at home, I wear bloodstained jeans and a tight leather jacket, assuming my new identity. Sometimes it's nice to pretend I'm not Fausto Moretti and blend in with the lesser of our society. There, no one has expectations or rules, just the fierce will to live, to survive.

So when the back of my hand stings from slapping our captured thief, I enjoy it.

"Where… the fuck… is it?" Sal's voice is smooth and controlled, a sinister game he is able to play. His less angered tones seem to inflict more terror on our victims than when he shouts. My twin and I just stay silent, acting as the muscle to Sal's brains. Really, though, we all know I'm the brains here, but perception is everything. As the oldest Moretti brother, the one who was groomed to take over our father's position as head of the Outfit after our parents tragically died, it is his job to maintain our reputation and to ensure fear enters every room when we do.

No one fucks with the Morettis and gets away with it.

No one.

We've been referred to as the Irish triplets, which really pisses all of us off. There's no one we abhor being compared to more than the Kellys, except maybe the Russians. Just because my twin and I were born eleven months after Sal doesn't make us triplets.

But it does make us appear more threatening. Though Sal has blue eyes, while Armani and I have brown, we do look like triplets. Imagine three of the same, powerful towering men coming after you. How would you feel?

Small?

Unprepared perhaps?

Maybe you would feel like dying.

Because you could be damn sure we'd feel like killing.

The thief's sobs annoy me, and I nod to Armani. He swivels behind the man, taking one arm with him and yanking it high up his back, his free hand pressing a blade to the crying man's throat. I pull out a knife of my own and kneel on the thief's hand, pressing the sharp end against his pinkie finger.

"I'm going to ask you one more—" Sal begins, but his words are cut off as screams ring out in the dark alley.

"Oops," I murmur as I hold up a severed pinkie finger.

"Okay! Okay! I'll talk!" our victim shouts, noisily sucking in a shaky breath through his pain.

Sal nonchalantly pretends to clean his fingernails with a blade. "I'm listening."

"It was Alfonzo," he wheezes out, blood dribbling from his lips and spewing from his finger.

Sal doesn't react. In fact, none of us do. It would do our thief here no good to know how we actually feel about this. Alfonzo Capelli is the only Alfonzo I know personally. He's also Carlo Rossi's right-hand man, and in just a few short weeks, Carlo's daughter will be ours—or Sal's at the minimum. We've discussed sharing the girl between us, joint custody or some shit, as Armani joked, but this little tidbit of information is interesting.

Why would Alfonzo Capelli be trying to thwart our drug trade? He would have known we'd find out, so what could his motives possibly be?

"Kill him."

Sal's command isn't questioned, simply executed. Armani, already poised behind our victim, snuffs out his life in seconds. As his knife imbeds in the tender flesh of the thief's neck, a pang of jealousy rages through me. This could put Armani above me in our kill count, and I can't let that happen.

As the man's cries of death turn to disappointed gurgles, Armani drops him to the ground and kicks him once in the ribs for good measure before flicking his long hair out of his eyes.

"Alfonzo..." Sal growls out the name, brows furrowed in thought while heading toward us.

"What the fuck, Sal? We shouldn't have killed him so soon," I argue, cleaning the blood off my knife. "He could have had more information for us, confirmed that it was Alfonzo Capelli, or given a motive."

Sal shrugs. He's become more careless since Gianna left him, and it's getting dangerous. "Dead men can't lie."

"Neither can they rat out the living," Armani grits out. "You're fucking losing it, Sal. We need you to fucking focus now more than ever on what's in front of you and not some dipshit woman who left you in the past. Gianna isn't coming back."

My pulse speeds up. We never mention Gianna to Sal, or worse, belittle her. Just hearing her name throws him over the edge sometimes, which is both alarming and shocking. How is it possible that a woman had that much of a hold on him? My brother is strong of will and stern of heart, yet one woman had him on his knees.

Not me.

Not ever.

Sal lunges at Armani, and for a moment, I think I might have to step between my brothers. Sal grips Armani's shirt, and Armani puts a chokehold on Sal's wrist. "Never speak her name again," Sal snarls, his blue eyes glinting with a hint of madness.

"Let me fucking go," Armani demands, and Sal reluctantly releases him then jogs down the alley and out of sight.

Yep. This just confirms what I already felt in my soul. In my relationships, it will be the woman who kneels with my cock buried deep in her mouth while her delicate hands grip my ass. After seeing what Gianna has done to Sal, and how fucked up he is just because she left his ass, I've made myself a vow to never let a woman in like he did.

And when Fausto Moretti makes a vow, he keeps it.

CHAPTER TEN

Valentina

The unwelcome sound of a familiar song playing from my phone wakes me up. By the custom tone, I know it's Payton. She must have called me a dozen times yesterday and messaged me on FB, Insta, and Snapchat, but I was too tired and confused to speak.

Pulling up my sleep mask, I squint one eye at the phone, seeing her smiling, freckled face staring back at me, and decline her call, but the bitch is persistent and calls again.

And again.

And again.

Until I can no longer leave her hanging and am forced to answer it with a groggy voice. "Hello?"

"Bitch, wake up! How can you do me like that? I need details of the date. You said you'd call me, but you never did."

Rolling onto my back, I close my eyes again. "I'll call you later. Give me a few minutes to wake up." Today is Monday, but lucky for us, school is closed today due to a power outage. As soon as I saw the text, I fell right back asleep.

Payton just laughs. "It's half past noon, and I'm standing at your front door with coffee. Get your ass up." She hangs up.

Payton is here? I'm not allowed to have people here without explicit permission from my dad.

Fucking A.

While I love her, sometimes that girl puts me in a pickle. Maybe that should be my name for her—Payton Pickle or Pickle Payton. Hell, I don't think she even likes pickles. Or olives for that matter. You can't trust people who don't like olives.

Wiping the sleep from my eyes, I exit my bedroom and make my way through the house to the front door and pull it open. There she is, double fisting matching coffee cups and grinning from ear to ear. "Let's see you get out of spilling the details now," she jokes, walking inside. We could be twins with our matching outfits—baggy sweats, tight tanks, and Ugg slippers that are as awesome outside as they are inside.

Today she has her hair pulled back in double braids, a look I can't seem to pull off without looking like I'm a fucking ten-year-old girl, but she does it perfectly.

Bitch.

Payton kicks off her slippers and plops down on my couch, then hands me my drink. "Venti vanilla latte."

"Thanks," I tell her gratefully, bringing the drink to my lips. Something catches my eye before I take a sip. "You told the barista your name was Bruno?"

She nods proudly. "And when they called my name, I grabbed the drinks and said gruffly, 'Shh, we don't talk about him.'"

I almost choke on my sip, spitting the delicious drink out of my mouth in laughter. Payton joins me, making my heart feel full, but then sadness washes over me. Because of who I am, I've been denied friendships like this, denied letting good people, like Payton, get close. Although I'd consider her my best friend, there are still so many secrets I haven't told her, things I can't tell her but so desperately want to. She's someone who makes it so easy to let my guard down and just be myself, but that can also be dangerous. My ease could lead to her demise, and I'd never want to be the cause of her pain.

"So," she begins, crossing her legs and pulling a blanket down over her lap, "tell me everything."

I take a breath, ready to spill the beans, when there's a knock on the door.

"Expecting someone?" she asks, and I shake my head. Who the hell could be here now? Grabbing a blanket of my own, I wrap up my torso to hide the girls since I'm not wearing a bra and answer the door.

The same black suit and sunglasses men from yesterday are back, and the same black Mercedes is parked out front of my house.

Before I can ask what the hell they are doing here, my phone rings.

"Daddy?"

"Sweetheart," my dad says, but there's not an ounce of affection in his voice. It's cold, devoid of all warmth, and almost robotic in his delivery. "I've sent some men to come take you out for the day. Several appointments have been booked for you. You'll learn more about them at each location."

"But Dad—"

"This is not up for discussion!" he barks, raising his voice. "You have ten minutes to get ready. The clock is ticking."

He hangs up, and I almost want to cry. This started off as one of the best afternoons I've ever had, and in an instant, he crushed my happiness. He must have been watching the cameras in the living room and knew Payton was here, so he sent his goons after me. But if what he said about the appointments is true, then that might not be the case, though I'm still sus about him watching me through the cameras.

"I'll be out in ten," I mutter to the man outside before shutting the door and turning back to Payton. "I have to leave, Payton. I'm sorry."

"But I just got here," she says sadly.

"I know." I sigh. "My dad scheduled some appointments for me but didn't tell me ahead of time."

Payton nods and tosses the blanket off her lap, eyeing the suited men out the front window. "Like doctor appointments?"

I shrug my shoulders. "I wish I knew."

I think Payton can hear the sadness in my voice, even though I try to keep my emotions off my face, because she pulls me in for a hug. "Maybe he's finally going to let you get your hair done, babe."

I hug her back hard. "Doubt it."

"You never know."

She pulls away and steps into her slippers, then grabs her barely drank coffee and heads for the door. "Call me later if you want. I can always come back."

"Thanks, Payton. Maybe I will."

She smiles at me in a way that says she knows I won't, but she doesn't argue, shutting the door behind her.

THE NEXT TEN minutes are a blur.

I take the fastest shower of my life, only washing my hair once. There's just enough time left to brush and floss my teeth before there's rapping on the front door again. I slip on a sports bra, a Gryffindor shirt, a pair of black yoga pants, and some flip-flops before walking out the door, shutting and locking it behind me.

The spring air is inviting, blowing through my damp hair which I know will dry soon in the warmth, but there's nothing warm about the bulky man ushering me into the back of the Mercedes. There also isn't anything warm about sitting bitch between two men who might as well be professional wrestlers.

"Fucking A," I mutter to myself as the car takes off into the sunlit afternoon. Outside, kids are playing basketball, riding their bikes, and chasing the ice cream truck. Parents have set up lawn chairs and are happily watching their kids. Other neighbors have on their sunhats and gardening gloves, cleaning out their flower beds to prepare them for planting.

I love flowers, but I don't have any myself. Well, aside from one single orchid plant. Years ago, I bought it for Mom for Mother's Day. She had really bad allergies, so flowers were something she abhorred, but orchids give off no smell, so she was able to tolerate it. Since her death, I've somehow managed to keep that orchid alive, and interestingly enough, it always seems to bloom near her birthday. Maybe it's her way of letting me know she's here, and that even though her body has left this earth, her essence, her soul remains. I thank my faith for that belief. Knowing my deceased loved ones are resting in heaven and waiting to see me again eases my grief. I just hope she's happy now without the weight of the world on her shoulders.

My eyes mist, but I keep my head down and hide my grief. It's weird how it can crash into you out of nowhere, slamming through your chest in a wave of agonizing pain. Part of my sadness comes from never knowing what having a real mother must be like, one who takes care of you when you're sick and comes to all your sporting events or dance recitals. Half the time our roles were reversed. I took care of her when she was too drunk to find her way to her bedroom. I dispensed medicine and made soup when she was suffering from a headache and an upset stomach after another night of drowning herself in wine.

She was never like the moms I see outside today, playing with their kids. Instead, she forbade me from even going outside because she was either too lazy or too disinterested to watch me.

Letting out another sigh—something I seem to be doing a lot these days—I watch the world fly by as we head onto the freeway. I wonder what my brothers are up to today. Maybe they are catching the Yankees game and actually relaxing for once. I almost text Raph to see what he's up to when the car exits the freeway and parks in front of a medical center. Confused, I pull out my phone to ask Dad what's going on when an appointment notification shows up on my Google calendar.

Dr. Christine, Suite 233

Okay then.

As I'm helped from the car and walked to the building, I force my fingers not to rapidly type the doctor's name into Google to figure out what she is a doctor of. After entering the structure, I soon find out, spotting her name on the list displayed on the wall.

Dr. Miriam Christine, OB-GYN

Fuck.

Completely unprepared for this, I pull out my phone, and in a brave moment, call my dad.

"Yes, sweetheart?" he answers on the second ring, his tone laced with ice.

"Dad, you can't be serious right now."

"As serious as a heart attack, sweetheart. Get in there. You're already one minute late." He hangs up.

Pocketing the phone, almost shaking with anger, I trudge up to the elevator and press the button for floor two. I can't believe he's springing something as intimate as a vagina doctor on me. And to think I only took a ten-minute shower today.

Ten fucking minutes!

If I had known some stranger was going to be poking around my crotch, I would have done some grooming and washed the dirty bitch at least four or five times. I would have even done a toilet paper check to make sure there were no stragglers.

But no.

Here I am, completely unprepared, my hands sweating and heart hammering as I check in with the receptionist.

"Name?" she asks, and I blank. What name did he want me to use? My real name or my fake one? "Uhh…" I stammer, and the receptionist, Karen—oh fuck me, right?—squints at me and purses her lips.

"Name please," she repeats.

I decide to keep it short and hope it works. "Val." Since Val is the nickname for both my real and fake names, I think it should work.

She blinks at me then checks her computer. "Valeska Anthony?"

I nod. "Yep, that's me."

Karen promptly piles a mound of papers on the little counter in front of her, then she hands me a clipboard and a pen. "Fill these out. A nurse will bring you back shortly."

Grabbing the stack, which I'm sure would equate to the death of an entire tree, I find an open seat and start filling out the questionnaire. This manuscript of my sex life, perhaps the most boring one ever handed in to Dr. Christine, is so embarrassing.

Current medications: 0
Allergies: 0
Years sexually active: 0
Number of Sexual partners (male or female): 0
Pregnancies: 0
Date of last menstrual cycle:

How the hell am I supposed to remember that? What was I doing during my last period? Umm... Umm... Umm... Oh! It was Easter morning. Too bad the Easter Bunny didn't put Kotex and Midol in my basket this year. Well, I did make my own basket, so really, the only person to blame is myself.

Jotting down the date, I'm halfway finished when I hear my name called.

"Valeska Anthony."

It's almost humiliating having your name read out loud to a crowd of women who really would rather be anywhere but here. Gathering my things and my unfinished stack of killed tree, I hustle over to the nurse who's holding the back of the door open with her ass.

"Over to the scale, please," she orders, gesturing to the staple of any doctor's office—the height and weight combination machine. I slip off my flip-flops, because who wants that extra eight ounces shown on their weight, and wait for the digital number to pop up.

My weight blinks up at me in bright red numbers.

Mmm. Not too bad.

My height is next, a number unchanged since the sixth grade, unfortunately. Yep, I'm just under five feet tall, though I can nail it exactly by wearing any pair of shoes. Perhaps I should have left those flip-flops on after all.

The nurse, a stern-looking woman with black hair streaked with silver, whose name tag I haven't gotten a good look at yet, jots down all the numbers onto a slip of paper then gestures to exam room three. I frown, unhappy with the odd number. I prefer them to be even.

Inside, she closes the door behind me, then asks me a series of questions about my mental health and if I'd like a second person in the exam room with me when the doctor comes in. One person is bad enough, so I can't even imagine having a second person face-to-face with my crotch. And what if they both spoke a second language and were talking about my unkempt crotch right in front of me, but I didn't even know it? Even if they weren't, I would assume they were, so I'd feel just as embarrassed.

The nurse, Linda, hands me a tattered gown. "Take all your clothes off and leave it open in the back. Dr. Christine will be with you shortly."

She leaves, while I'm just standing here mortified that this is happening. As I reluctantly strip down, I can't help but wonder why my dad is insisting on this. I'm not sexually active, and I don't have a boyfriend. Hell, he doesn't even know about the date with Marco. Well, at least I don't think he does. I guess it would be probable that he's aware. Marco's father, Alfonzo Capelli, has a big mouth and loves to brag.

Maybe I shouldn't be so mad. Maybe Dad is doing this for my own health. Maybe he knows I like Marco and he just wants me to be prepared. Maybe I shouldn't always just assume the worst about him.

Maybe.

Maybe.

Maybe.

After I've stripped down and have the thin gown draped across my front, I step up onto the paper-covered table and wait.

And wait.

And wait.

I don't know what time my appointment was exactly, but it's been at least fifteen minutes, and now I feel like I have the fart of the century stuck up my ass. I clench my cheeks, unwilling to stink up this tiny exam room moments before the doctor peruses my crotch like a waiting room magazine.

Nope!

Not me!

Why is it that I don't have to fart until the moment I shouldn't fart, and then I have to? It's like when you're on a call and are asked to wait on hold for something, and then ten, maybe fifteen minutes in, you have to poop. It happens every fucking time. So then you take a shit with your phone on speaker, but muted, hoping to push the fucker out before someone comes back on the line.

So. Damn. Stressful.

But if I let this one rip, it will be the fart of the century.

There will be columns written in their prestigious doctor journals about the patient with the fart of doom and the doctor who survived it.

Okay, maybe I'm getting a little carried away.

It's been twenty minutes now, and I'm starting to sweat, yet I'm completely frozen at the same time. I decide to hop down and grab my phone when I hear the click of heeled shoes. There's a small knock on the door and then the doctor walks in, and she's nothing like I was expecting.

I don't know what I was expecting.

An old hag.

A banshee.

A monster with one eye and a pair of horns.

"Hi, Val, I'm Dr. Christine. It's nice to meet you." The doctor is young, mid-thirties, with beautiful curly blonde hair and kind blue eyes. Underneath her white lab coat, she has on a fantastic black dress paired with bright red pumps. She extends her hand in greeting, and I shake it.

"Hi. I'm Val. But you already knew that," I greet awkwardly.

She smiles and sits down on a rolling stool, then opens up a small laptop. "So, is this your first time?"

I nod but realize she's not looking at me. "Yes," I shout, cringing at the word vomit.

"And what brings you in today?"

How the fuck should I know? "Umm. My umm... parents thought it was time for me to come?" I shouldn't have raised my tone on "come" because now it sounds like a question instead of an answer.

"Yeah, that's all. I'll be eighteen soon and heading off to college next year so…"

Oh yeah, good save, Val. Now she just thinks you're just preparing your vagina for all the dick she's about to meet next year.

"Well, you've come to the right place." Dr. Christine closes her laptop and rolls right in front of me. On either side of the table, she pulls out a stirrup, and I gulp. It's really happening. "Scoot your butt to the end and lie back, resting your feet in the stirrups. That's it. Don't be embarrassed, honey. You can't imagine the vaginas I see on a daily basis and the crazy things people shove up them. I promise you, this is nothing but routine for me."

When my heels firmly sink into the stirrups, I lie back on the crinkly paper covering the table and just squeeze my eyes closed. "You have to open your legs for me, Val. I promise it won't hurt."

My God. Someone please save me.

I try to part my legs, but it's like they won't open.

"A little bit more. Just a bit more. There. Now, I'm going to start my internal exam just using my fingers. The jelly I use to lubricate can be a bit cold. Ready?"

"Yes?"

"Okay, here we go. Just breathe for me, Val."

As she's feeling around, she makes small talk about her son who's in high school and his baseball team, and then she asks me if I have any plans for the summer. I really appreciate her effort. Talking through the process did make it easier to get through.

But then comes the clamp of death.

I shouldn't have looked, but I did. It was a stupid decision really. Seeing the size of the metal torture device before she gently inserts it inside of me was a bad idea. Pain greets me next as this thing stretches me farther than I ever have been before. My vagina doesn't magically turn into Gumby or Stretch Armstrong just because someone wants to take a peek inside.

Dr. Christine does her best to speak in soothing tones, but my body feels paralyzed, frozen, and broken. After what feels like hours, it's finally out and I can breathe again.

"You did great, Val. Everything looks completely normal. Clean bill of health. Now for your breast exam. Does breast cancer run in your family?"

Breast exam?

Gynecologists do breast exams too? Is the vagina not enough? How greedy are these people? Then again, it's better to have a one-stop shop. I'd hate to have to schedule two appointments with different doctors when it could just be done in one. Besides, what would a breast expert even be called?

Breastologist?

I bet they'd all be cringy men too.

Nope, I'm quite happy with Dr. Christine.

With my lubricated vagina all covered up by the shitty gown, Dr. Christine asks for my permission to begin. After I say yes, she pulls the gown down, revealing my breasts, and then begins to press on all the tissue. I wouldn't say it's aggressive, but it's forceful. There's no way that woman missed anything if there's a problem.

God, my nipples are getting hard. I try to think of anything nasty and gross to make them stop, but the kiss of the cool air makes it impossible. I hope she doesn't think that I'm like… enjoying this, or that I'm into her or something.

With the exams all done and my mortification meter at one million, she covers my body and assists me back into a sitting position. Then she jots a few more things down in her laptop. "Are you interested in birth control?"

Hmm? I guess I never really thought about it. "I-I don't know?"

She smiles. "Well, how about this? I can write you a script the old-fashioned way, and if you decide you'd like it filled, just take it into your pharmacy. How does that sound?"

"Good," I respond like a normal human should.

"Excellent." She claps her hands together and stands, grabbing her laptop. "You should hear back about your pap in a few days. It was very nice to meet you, Val. Gynecological exams are done every three years, so I'll see you in a few unless you have any problems. Feel free to call or email the office with any questions you might have. Have a nice day."

And as the door shuts behind her, I clean my jelly coated crotch before dressing myself again, thinking she might be one of the nicest doctors I've ever met.

The rest of the day is filled with more appointments. I visit a dentist—which I actually love, since getting my teeth cleaned has always been euphoric—an ophthalmologist, and a general practitioner. I have blood drawn for tests which I can't even pronounce.

By the end of the day, I'm fucking drained, and I have just enough energy to bake the taco casserole Theresa left in the fridge yesterday—or was it the day before? Doesn't fucking matter.

I shower for the second time, cleaning the rest of the sticky jelly off myself and the smell of doctor off my skin. By the time I'm out, dinner is ready. I collapse onto the couch with a huge plate of Mexican food in hand and my favorite Netflix show ready to go.

Nothing takes my mind off a long day more than a gorgeous, muscular man in black, fighting terrifying monsters, and an overflowing plate of Mexican food. I consider calling Payton but decide against it. I've had enough human interaction for the day.

CHAPTER ELEVEN

Valentina

Nothing beats a short school week, except maybe an unexpected snow day. Yesterday was a bonus day off, and after spending it amidst several doctors' offices, I have to admit, I would have rather spent my Monday at school.

I still feel violated, my crotch a bit sore from the pressure of that metal spreader. If I never have to do that again it will be too soon, but I also understand how important sexual health is to overall health, and even though it was like the worst thing ever, I'll keep up with my exams.

That's not too much to ask, right?

My eyes feel heavy this morning, and my body doesn't want to respond. I stayed up way too late watching my sexy monster killer, and now I'm paying the price. Checking my phone and seeing that it's already 6:30, I force my legs to swing off the bed and stand, stretching my arms over my head while indulging in a prolonged yawn.

Walking over to the windows, I open my shades and let the

morning sunshine in, then I check my calendar—yes, I still use a wall calendar. I know it's prehistoric, but I like to see things written down.

Today is the first day of May, and as I flip the calendar over from April, I see tomorrow decorated in bright, happy colors. Tomorrow is my birthday, and not just any birthday, but the big one-eight. I'll finally be considered an adult. I'll be able to vote, which I'm very excited about. I'll also be old enough to be able to buy lottery tickets, even though I don't gamble. I could join the armed forces too and fight for our country, but I still won't be old enough to buy a bottle of wine. America is interesting sometimes.

I hurriedly throw my hair up in a messy bun, brush and floss my teeth, dress in our school's token baby blue and gray uniform, and grab a granola bar for the ride.

I toss my clutch inside the front pocket of my backpack and head into the garage, opening the garage door. It makes a god-awful screeching noise as it ascends, and I make a mental note to tell Dad about that. It must need grease or oil or something.

My BMW springs to life, and I back out of the driveway, ensuring I close the garage door and watch it shut completely. That's another paranoid part of my routine, to make sure I see it close, because if I don't, someone could run inside and be waiting for me when I get home. I'm not prepared for that kind of kidnapping scenario.

School is boring as usual. The teachers are overworked and overtired, and the students' spring fever is getting worse. Only four weeks left. That's what I keep repeating to myself during another course review and another practice exam.

It's almost over, and then my life can finally begin.

My dad can't keep me under lock and key forever. He's got to cut the cord sometime. I'm determined to make it through this summer so I can go off to college as a free woman.

AP English and government are my first two periods, followed by double chemistry which I loathe. While I have loved every science class I've ever taken, I have to admit that chemistry has almost ruined it for me. I expected it to be something like potions class, but fuck was I wrong. There wasn't even a fucking cauldron in the classroom.

Fifth period is lunch, and I head through the first floor to the cafeteria.

Today's menu consists of cheese-filled breadsticks and a chocolate milkshake.

Excited, I grab my tray and look around for Payton, finding her sitting at our usual table along with some other friends.

"You never called," she complains as I pull out my chair and sit down.

"I know, Payton. I'm such a shit. But you wouldn't believe the day I had."

Payton finishes chewing a bite of her own breadstick then takes a sip of her Vitamin Water. "You're right. I probably won't believe you since you refuse to tell me anything or let me into your life."

I close my eyes and breathe deeply. "Payton, today is not the day for this conversation."

"Fine. Then tell me a day or time that works better, and I'll be there." She speaks low so the other girls at the table don't hear her. "You're not getting out of this one, Val. Something is going on with you, and you're going to tell me, dammit."

See, this is the problem with being a mafia princess—the isolation. "I'd give anything to let you in, Payton. It's just… complicated."

Payton opens up her planner and clicks down the purple pen. "I'm waiting. I'm even going to write this in pen. That's how serious I am about not changing it."

"Okay, fine," I relent. "How about next weekend?"

"Saturday or Sunday?"

I think about that for a moment. I might need a day to recover from this. "Saturday."

Payton scribbles in her planner. "Done. Now tell me about your date with Marco."

At the word *date*, Dani, Nicole, and Kristina perk up. "Date?" they ask in unison.

Groaning, I give a brief recap while Payton gives me the stink eye. That girl knows I'm not telling the whole truth, but she lets me live my lie for now. When I feel my phone vibrate, I slip it from my backpack and see a message from Marco.

Marco: Hey, love. Any plans this week? I need to see you again.

Me: Hi, Marco! I have plans for Saturday, but I can probably do Sunday. I just have to check with my brothers first.

Marco: I can't wait that long. We'll figure it out. Talk later.

He can't wait that long?

It's strange to have a guy so interested in me. His attention makes me feel good, but I've been taught to be suspicious, and his actions aren't exactly normal for a boy my age.

A guy that good-looking could have any girl he wants, yet he's chosen me, even though I'm not easy to get to. There are so many hoops with chaperones and dates that need to be approved by the men in my family—barf—it's a wonder he stuck around after the first date.

The rest of the school day passes quickly, and I'm soon driving home, anxious to get this uniform off and put on something comfy. I wish private schools would get out of the stone age and allow girls to wear pants like the boys do.

At least I only have a month left of plaid skirts, knee-high socks, and white collared shirts. One. More. Month.

Then everything will change.

Turning down my street, my stress of the day already easing, I brake suddenly. There's a car in my driveway that I don't recognize, so I drive past it, getting a good look before turning around at the end of the street. I park and watch the car, trying to decide what to do. I could call my dad or my brothers, but I don't want to alarm them if this is something I can handle myself.

I check the security app on my phone, seeing if the alarm system went off, and notice it was manually turned off about thirty minutes ago. Only someone with the passcode can do that. I bet one of my brothers is in there.

Hoping to see either Gabe or Raph, I open the garage door and pull into the driveway, taking note of the gorgeous candy apple red color on the car next to me. I park my car, grab my backpack, and head inside.

The scent of food cooking reaches me, and I wonder if maybe Theresa got a new car. She usually drives an older Toyota Corolla.

"Hello?" I call.

"In the kitchen," a voice answers, a voice I'm surprised to hear. Dropping my backpack in shock, I head to the kitchen and confirm who I thought it was.

The question is, how did they get into my house?

CHAPTER TWELVE

Valentina

Standing at the bar, I see a man facing the stove. He wears a white apron around his waist, and he wields a black spatula in his hand.

"Marco?"

Marco turns around, grinning. "Surprise, love! I'm making you dinner," he says, and then he turns back to whatever he's making on the stove.

My brain fails to compute, and I think I might be twitching. How can he be acting so normal when this is anything but normal?

"Dinner?" I almost choke on the word.

"Yeah. You know, the last meal of the day." His nonchalance is irritating.

"I know what dinner is," I grumble. "How did you get in here?"

All the muscles in Marco's back clench, and he rocks his head side to side as if he's preparing his body for a fight. Slowly, he turns to face me with a frown on his face. "I come all the way over here to make you a special birthday dinner, and the only thing you have to say to me is 'how did you get in here?'"

Oh shit. I'm not a fighter, and I'm the last person to come up with snappy comebacks, so my brain is bereft of any response. Later, I'm sure I will be able to think of a million things to say, but all I'm able to mutter out is, "Sorry."

Marco nods sadly. "I bet you are. Come here." He spreads his arms wide and waits, so I have no choice but to walk around the corner and allow him to hug me. "But I forgive you, love." He holds me tight and kisses the top of my head while rubbing my back. "Just don't let it happen again."

I'm at a total loss. Did he just… scold me? In my own home?

"Aren't you going to hug me back? Don't be rude, Val."

I hadn't even realized my arms were hanging limply at my sides, so I quickly wrap them around him. With our height difference, my arms rest along his waistband, and I feel the impression of a gun on his right hip.

Holy shit balls.

What have I gotten myself into?

Marco's presence is feeling more and more oppressive, like the outcome of one of my worst fears. I want to press him harder and ask how he got the code to my house, but I fear his response more than I want to know the truth, so I shut my mouth.

I can get through this one night, change my passcode, and never see Marco again.

Right?

"That's a good girl." He squeezes me one last time then swats my ass. "Dinner will be ready soon! I've made you my mama's famous spicy meatballs and pasta!"

It's strange how he can be so domineering one second and downright jolly the next. The shift is alarming to say the least.

Marco hums as he opens the fridge and pulls out a bottle of wine, then he starts opening all my drawers for a wine opener. Still humming, he uncorks the wine then rolls the meatballs around the frying pan.

A timer goes off on his phone and he stops to drain the pasta—traditional spaghetti—then puts together two plates that look and smell good.

"Dinner is served. *Buon appetito.*"

Marco sets the plates on my kitchen table, which I notice is already set, then ushers me into a seat. Before I know it, a glass of wine is poured for me. He comes around behind me and places a cloth napkin across my lap—one of Mother's.

I just don't understand. He would have had to be here for at least an hour to figure out where all my stuff is. I texted him during fifth period. There's no way he could have gotten here from where he lives in that short amount of time, which means this wasn't an afterthought. He'd been planning to come here all day, so even when he asked me if I had plans, it wouldn't have mattered. Marco does what Marco wants to do, and nothing else matters.

"Dig in," he orders, gesturing at my food with the pointy end of his steak knife.

Grabbing my silverware, I slice through a meatball and bring it to my mouth, blowing gently. Marco's eyes light up when I slip it between my lips and actually taste it. As proud as he is of the meal, it isn't very good. The meatball is charred on the outside and unseasoned on the inside, something I couldn't tell with all the sauce piled on it.

The pasta is good, but what kind of Italian would he be if it wasn't? I'm not a fan of the sauce, which is clearly a premade sauce from a can and not homemade. The difference in taste is so painfully obvious.

"Well?" he asks, almost bouncing in his seat.

I lie, knowing the truth might cause one of those personality shifts again. "It's so good, Marco."

He grins. "I knew you'd love it, and that's not even the best part of the night. There are more birthday surprises in store for you."

Marco takes a sip of his wine then holds up his glass to toast. "To us."

I don't want to drink, hoping to keep all my senses intact, but I can't just not toast. "To us," I mimic, and we clink glasses before bringing the wine to our lips.

It's actually quite delicious, a brand I'd like to write down so I can get it again when I'm of age.

"Mmm, this is good, Marco. Where did you get it?'

I expect him to say he stole it from his father's well-known supply, but instead he tells me, "That little liquor store just outside of town. You know the one on Third and Center Street?"

I nod. "I know of it. I haven't been inside myself."

Marco snorts. "Oh, I'm a regular there when I'm on this side of town. Everyone in that store knows my name."

Well, that's not good when all the liquor store employees know your name. It also raises a red flag for me about his age. I guess he could have a fake ID, but now I'm wondering if he wasn't truthful about being eighteen. More than once, I've thought that he looks older than the rest of the boys in my grade. "Drink a lot, do you?"

He slams his glass down hard, spilling a bit of wine. "Why? Is that a problem?"

I shake my head fast. "No. No. Just curious. Trying to, umm... get to know you is all."

"There will be much more of that later. Drink up."

I don't like his tone, but I try to focus on the meal, eating a lot of the pasta and trying to mush around the meatballs so it looks like I ate those too. After he's had seconds and thirds, he grabs my hand and pulls me up from the chair, walking me to the couch.

He pulls me onto his lap, a move that makes me very uncomfortable, and grabs the remote, flicking on Netflix. "Why do you watch this garbage?" he scoffs, seeing what show I was watching last night.

"I like it," I answer simply. "It's entertaining."

Marco flips to the comedy section and puts on a movie I absolutely hate. I know hate is a strong word, but the humor is just so... childish, and that's coming from me, a seventeen-year-old girl.

Dick jokes don't make me laugh, yet Marco is almost rolling on the floor joke after joke, pun after pun. Somehow, I managed to scoot off his lap during one of his outbursts. Now he's relaxing with an empty bottle of wine in his hand. As the afternoon changes to night, his skin flushed with alcohol, I try to think of any excuse to get him to leave.

"You know, Marco, I have some homework I need to get done for tomorrow."

He waves his hand as if irritated. "Then do it."

Fuck, can't he get the clue?

"Umm. I really need it quiet in here to focus on my studies, and with finals coming up, each night counts. I'm sure you know exactly how I'm feeling."

Marco hiccups, his words slurring slightly. "Yeah, I remember. I fucking hated school."

I slap my hands on my knees, the token sign that the night is over. "Well, thanks for a great night. I couldn't have been more surprised than if Santa came down my chimney."

Marco narrows his eyes. "I can come down your chimney, Val. Just show me how to get inside."

I roll my eyes, unable to help myself. Do guys actually believe girls think this is funny or even remotely sexy? It's like gag worthy.

"Don't roll your eyes, Val." Marco's voice deepens as he pushes himself off the couch and leaps on top of me. I fall back, my legs hanging off the armrest, my body pressed into the soft cushions. Marco pushes himself between my legs, and I begin to panic.

This can't be happening.

This can't be happening.

"Don't you want me, Val?" he asks in a low tone, the scent of wine heavy on his breath. "I want you so fucking badly."

He presses his groin against my crotch. My thin, white cotton panties and his jeans are the only thing separating him from touching me. "I-I do. It's just…"

My words catch as he slips his hand between us and actually rubs me.

"I'm on my period!" I finally shout, and he leans back, his huge boner poking through his jeans.

"Fuck!" he shouts, kicking a decorative pillow across the room.

Scooting back on the couch, I try to distance myself from him, hugging a pillow to my chest while struggling to hold back my tears. "I'm sorry, Marco. I don't know what you want me to say." My voice shakes, but I can't help it.

I'm terrified.

Marco hears the emotion, and being as pig-headed as he is, he thinks I'm actually sad that he's not fucking me. He rushes over and tenderly cups my face. "Aww, my love. Don't be sad. I'm not going anywhere, okay? You and me, this is something real. You're mine, Val. Now. Always."

I just nod and let the tears fall, feigning dejection to protect myself.

He just holds me, the first move he's made all night that's actually nice. I can't believe what a mess this whole night is. I was so wrong about him. How didn't I see what a narcissist he is? It's no wonder he's still single. Looks aren't everything.

"Can I put you to bed, love? I want to make sure you're taken care of before I leave."

Put me to bed? How bad can that be?

"Okay," I answer shakily, and Marco scoops me up in his large arms. He stumbles a few times, tripping on absolutely nothing but his own drunk legs on his way to my bedroom.

He sets me down a little roughly on my bed. "Thanks, Marco. Goodnight."

"Well, I still have to put you to bed, now don't I?"

"I can take care of mys—"

He covers my mouth with his hand. "I won't hear of it. Now let me help you with your shirt."

He reaches for the buttons on my shirt, and I slap his hand away. "Marco, I've got it," I state firmly.

He wags his finger at me. "A man takes care of his woman, love."

This isn't care. This is lust. This is an overbearing, power hungry psycho who just wants to see my tits.

I think about how to distract him and start sniffing the air. "Marco, do you smell gas? I think you left the burners on."

He rushes from the room, and I change into a shirt, pajama pants, and an oversized hoodie for extra protection. He comes back a minute later, panting, but he seems to lose focus when he sees I've changed. Surprisingly he's not mad, instead he has a dopey look on his face. "You look so cute in your pajamas, Val."

I fake a huge yawn. "Thanks. I'm so tired. I can't wait to get my homework done so I can get into bed."

"Come here." He beckons closer and pulls me against him. I see it coming, but there's no way to stop it as he wraps his arms around me and lowers his head.

His tongue slithers into my mouth, and I'm forced to become a snake and dislocate my jaw to accommodate it. The slimy muscle chokes me, and I wonder if he learned how to kiss by watching old black and white movies where women had to churn their own butter.

When he finally pulls away, I'm breathless, and my whole face is wet with his smelly spit that I desperately want to wipe off. He gazes at me with a look of satisfaction that tells me exactly how he feels about himself—he believes he is a man's man, the kind of man any lady would beg to hang onto.

It's disgusting.

"Let me walk you out?"

He nods and holds out his arm. I reluctantly walk under it, and he drapes it across my shoulders. He collects his wallet, keys, and phone from the living room before I guide him to the door.

"Thanks again, Marco."

"Anything for my" —*hiccup*— "woman," he slurs, and then he stumbles down the front stoop and into his car. The sense of relief I feel as he drives down the road is immeasurable, like I'm finally able to breathe again after being submerged in water.

Too exhausted to even think, I lock up and head to bed. I'll have to look into changing the passcode tomorrow. For now, I just need to sleep it off, and maybe in the morning, I can forget this ever happened.

CHAPTER THIRTEEN

Salvatore

SWEAT DRIPS down my face and chest, every muscle in my body taut as I fist the jet-black hair of the woman on her knees in front of me. My hips jerk as I slam my cock into the back of her throat, trying to force myself to come.

Her oversized breasts bounce against my legs, and her fingernails dig into my ass as she tries to remain upright. I do my best to choke her, gag her, hearing her struggle to breathe, hoping it will turn me on.

Tightening my fingers in her hair, I fuck her harder, bruising her lips as her teeth scrape across my cock. The little bit of pain finally pushes me over the edge. "Swallow it all," I growl as my balls tighten and my eyes close, my cum spewing into her hot mouth.

After I finish, I slip my cock from her cum-filled fuck hole and pick up her shirt to clean myself off with. As she falls onto her back, her fake breasts heaving as she sucks in breath after breath, I dress and leave her lying alone in the damp basement of this dive bar without so much as a goodbye.

She doesn't deserve a goodbye. She's just some whore looking to make a buck or be seen with a man of my caliber, but she won't get either. I'm not paying some slut to suck my dick, any woman would consider that an honor, and I'm damned sure not letting her be seen on my arm.

That place by my side will remain empty forever. Gianna's ghost is now the only woman to truly keep me company. My heart pangs at the thought of my lost girlfriend, which pisses me off. It's been over six months. I should be over her by now, should have gotten past the grief, but I can't seem to pull myself out of it no matter how many people I kill or how many women I fuck. Nothing is working.

Simple things that used to give me so much pleasure are now boring and mundane. I go through my routine automatically, not really present for any conversation or any significant length of time. Part of it is that I don't want people to notice I've changed. My grief can be exploited as a weakness, and with Carlo Rossi's daughter being delivered in the next few days, I don't have the time or energy to be seen as weak.

Storming up the basement stairs, I push open the nearest exit and head outside, letting the cool rainfall try to cleanse me of my sins. She's dead because of who I am and my shitty choices. It's my fucking fault, and no matter how many church services I attend, how many priests I blindly confess to, or how many prayers I offer up, I can't rid myself of this guilt.

It's weighing me down and changing me into someone I don't like or recognize. It makes me worry that I'll never be myself again, that the Salvatore Moretti I once was is lost forever, buried alongside Gianna's decaying body. I not only think about her and her lost life, but also her family who will never have answers. After killing Gianna, Carlo's goons knocked me unconscious. I have no idea what they did with her after that, and knowing she's dumped somewhere in an unmarked grave or thrown away like trash hurts even more.

She deserves better than that.

She deserves to be honored and remembered with a proper funeral and burial. Instead, she's not only been denied the right to live, but also the right to die in peace as well.

And it's all my fault.

It will forever be my fault, and it will haunt me until the day I die and see her once again. Yes, recently my decisions have become less calculated and more reckless. Sometimes I think I subconsciously have a death wish I'd like to see fulfilled.

Maybe I do.

Death seems better than living most of the time, but until that day comes, I'll remain cold and guarded, an unbreakable, impenetrable statue, my heart chiseled from the hardest stone.

Even though I'm honor bound to accept this new girl into my life, the one last tie to my dead father, the pact didn't say I had to love her or even like her. I just have to take her.

And I will.

No part of her body will be off limits. Her screams will play out as the softest music as I unleash every bit of my wrath on her, imagining it is her father suffering. Carlo Rossi took from me, and soon, I will take from him.

CHAPTER FOURTEEN

Valentina

TODAY IS MY BIRTHDAY, and not just any old birthday, but my eighteenth. Turning eighteen is such a huge deal for a person, a milestone that you look forward to, especially once you start high school.

I'm determined not to ruin this moment, so when I roll out of bed, I leave the memories of last night behind with my crumpled sheets. Nothing is going to destroy this day for me.

While drinking a cup of coffee—more like half coffee, half vanilla creamer, but who's pointing fingers?—my phone won't stop buzzing. Message after message pours in from friends, family, and acquaintances, all sending well wishes and good thoughts for my big day.

I haven't heard from Dad yet, but it is early. However, he has forgotten my birthday more than once, so I wouldn't be surprised if I get a belated birthday gift in the next day or two. Mom would forget as well, often too hungover to even know what her own name was.

My brothers never forget me though. I can always count on them, even if it's just a simple text. Lucian has already sent one, but Raph sends me a video. Grinning, I hit play on my phone and the video begins.

My handsome brother, who has the same eye color as me, starts the video by singing happy birthday. I can see how hard he's trying to make this a happy moment for me, but there's something about the look in his eyes, a sadness that I don't normally see, that makes it feel off. He ends the video by blowing me a kiss, and then he says, "Enjoy it while it lasts," before ending the video.

Enjoy it while it lasts?

This isn't a breath mint, it's a birthday, and you get to have one every year, so I don't understand his need to be all fucking sad and cryptic. I shoot him off a thank you text just as my phone rings. This time it's Gabe, and I happily answer.

"Hello?"

"Happy birthday, little sis! How is your morning going so far?"

"Thanks! So far so good, but the day is only just getting started."

Gabe laughs. "I know, I know. It's too early to tell, but I just wanted to tell you how proud I am of you and the woman you are becoming."

"Aww, Gabe! Don't get all sappy on me. I've already applied my makeup."

Gabe clears his throat before speaking again, and when he talks, I can hear how emotional he is. "It's just that… everything is about to change. You're a woman now."

"Gabe, it's just a single day," I argue. "Age doesn't make me a woman, it's time and experience. I'm still the same Val I was yesterday, just twenty-four hours older."

"You'll find out soon how untrue that is, sis. Happy birthday. I'm sorry."

He hangs up, and I'm left with my jaw gaping open as I stare at my phone, wondering what the fuck just happened.

Lucian was the only normal one today, how is that possible?

Trying to shake off the bad vibes I got from Gabe and Raph, who somehow made their birthday wishes come off as a funeral eulogy, I fix my hair, adding extra conditioner to help my waves stay pretty, and spritz on my favorite perfume, a step I usually skip for school.

After slipping into my uniform and pulling up my knee-high white socks, I grab my backpack and head into the garage. As I back out into the road, the sun shining brightly and the air warm enough to have my windows down, I can't help but smile.

Last night was a disaster of epic proportions, but today is going to be amazing, even if I have to spoil myself. With thoughts of expensive coffee and pizza takeout for dinner on my mind, I park in my numbered spot at Oakwood Prep.

Somehow, the school seems less oppressive today than usual. Perhaps it's my unusually good mood. Heading to my locker, I grin when I see it down the hall. Streamers and balloons decorate the front, and when I open it up, there's a bouquet of flowers inside.

God, I really do have good friends, even if I have to keep them at a distance. They have made me feel loved and appreciated, and it makes my heart all warm and fuzzy.

Carrying around the bouquet of flowers all day long kind of makes me feel like I'm homecoming queen, but I love it. It lets others know that I'm cared about too, and in some odd way, that makes me feel good. I know I shouldn't care what others think, but I've always been such a loner—not by choice, of course—so I can't help but want to sashay a little bit when I walk.

My friends did this for me, not for themselves, with nothing expected in return. In the mafia world, that's not how things work. You do something for someone else, and now that person owes you, but that's not the case here. They simply did this for me, for my happiness, not expecting anything in response, and for that, I'm so grateful.

This is already turning out to be the best birthday ever!

The first four periods fly by. I'm a good student, paying attention to my lessons and filling in my assigned classwork until it's finally time for lunch. Today, I treat myself to cheese fries and a chocolate shake. The cheese is hot and melty, so good on my crispy salty fries, and the shake tastes extra cold and chocolaty.

Payton pulls out a chair across from me and plops down. Her hair must have been in braids last night, because it falls in gorgeous waves today, making her even more pretty than she usually is—and believe me, that girl doesn't need any help in that department.

"Happy birthday, babe!" she greets. "Do you have any birthday plans?"

I'm too embarrassed to admit that I'll be spending the night by myself, knowing that most of my friends would be sharing their birthday with their family, so I lie to hide my embarrassment. "Oh yeah, my dad and brothers are taking me out to dinner."

Payton scoops a bite of her shake into her mouth. "Oh, sounds fun. Where are you going?"

I shrug, shoving three cheesy fries into my mouth, chewing while I think of a response. "Don't know. They said they wanted to surprise me."

Payton smiles. "I love surprises. Liked your locker and flowers, did you?" she asks, nodding to the bouquet.

"I loved them! You guys are so thoughtful to do that for me."

Picking at her nails, Payton coyly asks, "And is Marco taking you out this weekend?"

Just the sound of his name has my heart skipping a beat, and not in a good way. It's the kind of racing one's heart does when walking alone in the dark and you think you hear footsteps behind you.

Yeah, that's how Marco makes me feel. The thought of him touching me again has my skin crawling as if I stepped in the center of an ant nest and pissed them the fuck off.

"He's mentioned wanting to set something up, but no official plans have been made," I offer casually, shoving another fry into my mouth.

The girls at the lunch table continue to make small talk, and every single one of them wishes me a happy birthday and gives me a great big birthday hug. I'm on cloud nine when I pull out my phone and see a text—no, eight texts have come through.

Any guesses who they are from?

Marco: Happy birthday, love.

Three minutes later.

Marco: I said happy birthday to you.

One minute after that.

Marco: AREN'T YOU GOING TO THANK ME? WHAT THE FUCK, VAL?

Ten minutes later, a giant paragraph of text.

Marco: When I text you, I expect an immediate answer. I don't know how it worked with your past boyfriends, but this shit won't work with me. Send me a picture right now of where you are and hold your thumb up in front of it so I know it's current.

Marco: Don't read that last text. I forgot you had school today. You should have reminded me of that. Anyway… I just wanted to tell you what a great time I had last night. *Three heart emojis* I think you're the best kisser, Val. I could make out with your face for an entire night, though my tongue is useful in other places, as you'll soon find out. Hope you loved my birthday surprise yesterday. I have a present for you too, I just forgot to give it to you during all the fun we were having. I'll call you later, and we can make plans for this weekend.

One minute later.

Marco: And Val… I think I'm falling for you

I think I might cry. It's just too much. The happiness of my birthday deflates like a punctured balloon, and I can literally feel my smile falling, being replaced by a trembling lower lip.

"Val?" Payton asks, rushing around the table to be by my side. "Val, what is it?"

"It's nothing," I lie. "Just, umm… missing my mom is all."

Payton frowns. "You didn't even like your mom. You must have told me so a dozen times."

Shit.

"Well, I just miss having a mom on my birthday is all. Not necessarily *her* so much as a mother figure. Does that make sense?"

Payton smiles softly. "It makes perfect sense."

Phew! Got out of that one.

I know I'm going to have to tell her soon, but right now is not the time. Well, I don't have to tell her, but I need to. I have to get this off my chest, and the details are too personal to share with my brothers—though I do plan on asking if they gave the dick who must not be named the code to my security system. That just doesn't seem like something they'd do without letting me know first. I've been protected my entire life, hence the fake name, which is why my mom and I lived in a separate house from my brothers and father. I grew up away from mafia life, protected from the hatred and violence like the mafia princess Dad claims I am. So why would they give someone the code to my house now? It just doesn't sit right with me.

The bell rings, saving me from telling more lies. I slip on my backpack and sit through my final three classes. To say I'm distracted would be an understatement. I'm falling apart and struggling to hold myself together. I just want to get through the day so I can head home and wrap myself up in a warm blanket with the new book I downloaded on my kindle.

I vaguely remember the description mentioning knotting... Maybe the heroes of this one are sailors or advanced boy scouts who are good with rope. Who else would be good at knotting?

The rest of the day is a blur. I try to focus and get my work done, but I can't concentrate, turning in what I know are half-ass papers.

When the final bell rings for the day and it's time to go home, I can't describe the relief I feel. It's almost as good as when Marco finally left my fucking house last night.

With a birthday treat of iced coffee on my mind, I head out to my car, holding the bouquet of flowers close to my chest and keeping my eyes down so no one attempts to talk to me. When I get to my spot, however, my car isn't there.

It's fucking gone.

Heart racing, I look up, searching the parking lot, hoping beyond hope that I parked in the wrong spot this morning. Then I see it. My white BMW is sitting on the back of a tow truck, which is pulling out of the school's driveway.

"No, wait!" I scream, running like a psychopath through the parking lot. In my haste to get to my car, I fail to notice the other difference in the scenery. Lined up, blocking the school's entrance, are several dark SUVs all in a row. Outside of each is a man dressed much like the men my dad sent to escort me to all the doctors' appointments.

They wear dark suits and dark sunglasses, and their faces are stoic like the soldiers who guard Buckingham Palace. They stare up at the school, searching. I'd bet my ass they are Mafia.

My stomach sinks, and my feet turn into immovable lead weights.

There is only one person they could be here for.

I beg my legs to work, and they slowly start to back up, allowing me to run around the back of the school. A friend shouts at me, asking me why I'm running, but I don't stop to answer. I have to get back inside, I have to hide. It's instinct, the innate ability to sense danger, something everyone in the Mafia has, and my danger meter is going through the fucking roof.

Slamming my body into the rear door of the gym, I shove the little metal bar, but the door doesn't open.

"Come on!" I scream, jogging to the other one about two hundred feet away, but it's locked too. "Fuck!"

I fork my fingers through my hair, seeing black suits approaching on all sides. They are herding me. Whipping my head around, I try to find somewhere to hide. The only place that jumps out to me is the large, green dumpsters.

Having flashbacks of *The Neverending Story*, I rush toward it, my backpack bouncing on my back and the flowers long abandoned. As I open the black lid and prepare to climb inside, a gunshot rings through the air.

I freeze, praying like a dumbass that they won't see me if I don't move.

"Valentina Rossi."

At the sound of my real name, a blast of ice shoots through my veins. I turn toward the voice and see four men standing not fifty feet from me. Their black suit jackets are pulled back, revealing shiny firearms attached to their hips.

A stocky man steps forward, holstering his gun, and I know he must have been the one who fired the shot I just heard. "There's no sense in running, Ms. Rossi," he says, his Italian accent thick. "Don't make a scene. Like it or not, you're coming with us."

CHAPTER FIFTEEN

Fausto

Downtown Chicago is where everything happens in this city. Sure, shit goes down in the burbs, but not like it does here. Every kind of drug you would ever want to buy, try, or sell is here and easy to access once you know the right people—and the Morettis happen to be the right people.

We run this fucking town, from the most expensive high-end stores to the dirtiest nightclubs with questionable clientele. Strip clubs, dance clubs, exclusive bars… we own it all. Our men are everywhere, the eyes and ears of our operation. So how the fuck did a lowlife thief penetrate our lines and thwart a huge drug sale worth millions of dollars?

"It has to be Alfonzo Capelli." My twin brother, Armani, downs whatever liquor is in his glass and pours himself another drink. "It just makes sense."

Sal and I are sitting in two of three leather chairs that each face a single table. We come here when there is a need to talk and discuss business. It's our own private space, complete with a bar, a couch, a TV, and these leather seats. Sal crosses his ankle over his knee and strokes the scruff on his chin. "We still lack a motive."

I motion for Armani to make me one of whatever he's drinking. "Well, maybe if you hadn't ordered us to off the only informant we had, we might have one."

Sal just glares at me. "Can't you ever just let shit go?"

"Can't you ever make a good fucking decision?" I retort. "You're so impulsive lately, and one of these days, it's going to cost us."

Heading behind the bar, Sal pours himself a glass of whiskey, his drink of choice when he wants to get fucked up and forget. "Don't be so fucking dramatic, Fausto. You're bitching like a teenage girl. Grow a fucking pair."

"You need me to knock some sense into you, brother?" I ask, punching my fist into my open hand. "Don't give me a reason to."

Squaring his shoulders, Sal takes a breath to respond, but Armani interrupts. "Shut the fuck up. Both of you. Someone has infiltrated our system here, and instead of trying to figure out who or why, you've both decided to make enemies of each other. Stop trying to compare dick sizes. It's fucking ridiculous." Sal deflates, and I do as well. Armani is right. "Besides," Armani continues with a chuckle, "we all know I have the biggest dick."

Sal grins and slams his glass down, then rushes Armani. Armani leaps over the bar, knocking over two barstools in his attempt to get away from our oldest brother. A moment later, a knock sounds on the door.

"Hey, you guys alright in there?"

It's Bernardo, the man we stationed outside to make sure no one else enters our private room in the back of one of our bars.

"Just my big dick knocking shit over again," Armani shouts as Sal puts him in a headlock.

Bernardo's deep laugh sounds through the door as Armani finally gives up—not because he can't beat Sal, but because he's laughing so hard he's about to pass out.

"Pour us another round of drinks, fuckhead," Sal orders, slapping the back of Armani's head.

"C-C-Course, boss," Armani jokes, speaking in a high, trembling voice.

I don't bring it up, but this moment was much needed and unexpected. I haven't seen Sal smile in weeks, but I won't mention it and embarrass him. I just hope it means he's finally breaking out of his funk. I don't like the man he's become since Gianna left, and I sure as fuck don't understand how a woman he'd only known six months could have this profound of an effect on him.

She's like one of those earthquakes who sends aftershocks for hours or days after its main event.

Armani hands out drinks then sinks into a leather chair. "Back to business. Can either of you think of a motive?"

Sal shakes his head, but the way he averts his eyes makes me question his answer.

"Let's pretend that it is Capelli who did this, and we know Capelli is Carlo Rossi's right-hand man," I muse, paying close attention to Sal and noticing how his fingers curl around his armrest, his knuckles blanching at the sound of Carlo's name. So there is something there… "Do you think this has anything to do with the girl?" I keep my voice cool and casual.

Sal rubs his temples. "I really don't know."

"Why do I feel like you're lying?"

"I'm with Fausto on this," Armani agrees. "There's something you're not telling us. We don't keep secrets from each other, Sal. Not since Mom and Dad died. Not since we had to raise Lily and protect her from the world, though we've done a shit job of it. And now we can't even speak to her, confined in the clutches of that Hernandez fuck. So cut the bullshit and tell us what's going on."

Sal's jaw twitches, and his eyes blaze with a hatred so potent I can almost smell it. "I wish I could," he murmurs under his breath, then he downs his drink and storms out of the room, leaving Armani and me in the dark.

I turn toward my brother. "He knows something."

Armani nods and stands. "If it wasn't obvious before, he just gave himself away. I don't fucking understand. Why hide something from us? Why now when we need to stick together most?"

"If I know Sal, then I'd say he was trying to protect us. The question is… from what?"

CHAPTER SIXTEEN

Valentina

There's no use in running, and my hiding spot was found before I even managed to get my ass inside the dumpster. Defeated, I turn to face the suited men and walk toward them.

"There's a good *piccola ragazza*," one sneers. "Keep your mouth shut until we're in the car. There's no sense in you drawing more attention to yourself than you already have."

"You're the ones kidnapping me in front of an entire school. This shit will be all over social media. The cops are probably already on their way. They'll rescue me."

A short, stocky man with a bald head laughs in the most unfriendly way, his accent thick. "The police won't come. They have already been paid to stay far away. No one is coming to save you."

I gulp, and he grins back at me as he slips his hand around my upper arm. Another man mimics him on the other side of me, while the third and fourth man walk in front and behind us. I'm surrounded in plain sight. Surrounded by the fucking Mafia.

I don't know these men from a hole in the wall, and though I'm not familiar with many of my dad's men, I'd bet my right eye these men are not from the Cosa Nostra. No. They smell of Chicago's Outfit.

"Why do you tremble, *piccola ragazza?*" the stocky man sneers. "Fear does not look good on the daughter of a mafia don."

I won't answer his questions, not until I have answers of my own, so I keep my mouth shut as they guard me like I'm some fucking murdering prisoner. A black SUV rounds the back of the school, its windows tinted so dark I can't see who's inside.

The back door swings open, and I'm marched forward.

"Get inside," they order, so I do, grateful that this mess is happening behind the school, hoping most of the students don't see.

As was the case when my dad had me chaperoned to all those doctors' appointments, I'm once again squished between two meatheads. The engine revs and the car takes off, driving through the parking lot of Oakwood Prep. I watch the school longingly, wondering if this is the last time I'll see it. It's not that I've given up. It's just that as much as it was hidden from me, I know how the Mafia works. When they want something, they take it. When they wish to hide someone, you'll never see them again.

More suited men have stopped the traffic at the end of the driveway. An escort is waiting for us there, and more SUVs drive in front and behind us. Like an ominous parade, we head off, driving onto the freeway.

"Do you guys want to tell me what's going on?" I ask, pretending to be brave.

The driver glances at me in the rearview mirror. "We're under strict orders not to tell you, but I'll tell you what. We can play a little game. If you guess your reason for our... little trip, I'll tell you all about it."

"Can I have my phone first?"

"Not on your life."

Grumbling, I cross my arms and try to think of what this could be about. "Is this about my dad?"

He merges onto another freeway, one we only take when we're heading to the airport. "Getting close."

"My brothers then? Did they get into some kind of trouble?"

He laughs. "I am sure your *fratelli* are into more trouble than they can handle, but no."

I think for a moment, wondering if perhaps I've done something bad or made anyone mad at me. Then it hits me.

"It's Marco, isn't it?"

The man sitting in the passenger seat turns around, his face pulled into a grimace as he pushes his glasses back up his rather large nose. "Who the fuck is Marco?"

"Okay, so not Marco then," I offer, trying to deflect. "I can't think of anything I've done to warrant this kind of umm… treatment."

"You think this is bad, kid? I promise we can make things much worse for you," the man beside me says.

I've had quite enough of this. "You do know who I am, don't you? When I tell my father about this—"

The driver slaps the steering wheel, laughing as if I just told the funniest joke. "Your father knows! He's always known. Your fate was sealed when you were still a little girl, a *piccola ragazza*."

"You've said too much already," the front passenger warns.

The driver nods, and no words are exchanged the rest of the way. It's not until we pull into the airport that I start to get nervous. Not only am I being whisked away to an unknown location, but I also have to take a flight to get there. Maybe that's a good thing. I can pretend to need the bathroom in the airport and sneak away.

With that plan in mind, I sit back and try to relax, but we turn away from the terminal and parking structures, maneuvering to a section of the airport I've never been to before.

We stop at a gate, the top coiled with barbed wire. The driver presents a piece of paper to a man working a kiosk before the gate opens and we can pass through.

I watch as we drive by the large, commercial airplanes and finally come to stop before a small jet.

Holy shit.

Whoever wants me has money, that's one thing I know for certain.

My escorts pull me from the car and take me up a short flight of stairs. The wind is a bitch, making my skirt fly up and display my cotton panties covered in little red and pink hearts. I know the men climbing the stairs behind me are getting a good view, and my face heats with embarrassment. I just hope these ones don't have period stains on them. I should have fucking looked before I just threw them on today, though I never thought a stranger in a black suit with a gun would be getting an eyeful of them. Hell, maybe he's too distracted by my peeking butt cheeks to even notice a stain. Then again, maybe he's not an ass man. Which begs the question—do breast men dislike the ass or just prefer the tits?

Hmm...

A question for another day.

Once inside the jet, I'm ushered into a seat. Unlike the car ride, this time I'm given a little bit of space, with men sitting in the seats in front of and behind me, and across the little aisle. I take a peek around and count only ten seats in the whole aircraft.

A sweet, southern female voice rings out in the cabin through staticky speakers. "This is your pilot speaking. Buckle up as we begin our ascent. When the seat belt lights turn off, feel free to unbuckle and move about the cabin. This will be a short flight today of about one hour. The weather in Chicago is a brisk sixty-five degrees and partly cloudy. Enjoy your flight."

Chicago?

My mouth dries, and I'm suddenly desperate for some water as I secure my seat belt. I don't know anyone in Chicago. Then it hits me—the Outfit is from there, but I have no beef with them, at least not personally. The driver alluded to this having something to do with my father. I guess in about an hour, I'll get to find out how.

CHAPTER SEVENTEEN

Valentina

THE FLIGHT IS QUICK. After I've had a bottle of water and a bag of peanuts, we start to descend into an airport. By the sheer size, I'd guess it's O'Hare, but I have no idea, and I don't think the black suits guarding me would tell me even if I asked.

Staring out the window, I wonder what my friends are thinking. It's one thing to see my car being towed away, that much alone will alarm them, but if any of them actually saw me being escorted into the back of that SUV... well... let's just say the police will be getting more than just one call.

They told me the police had been paid off, so I guess all calls made to them would be pointless, but it would still make me feel good knowing they tried. Then again, maybe no one did. Maybe I'm not important enough to anyone to actually merit a call to the police.

They did decorate my locker...

Still, I'm sure Payton organized all of that and the rest of the girls just took credit. She's really the only one who cares, the only one I've let get close, even if it's the slightest bit, and only because she's so damn persistent. If it had been my choice, I would have kept her at arm's length. Not only because my father demanded it, but because it made me feel like I did my job protecting her. I know how the Mafia can be, hurting those closest to you to get what they want. So, in a way, having no friends protects them from things that could happen, even things that aren't probable.

It's better this way.

The lies get harder the older I get, especially as my friends turn eighteen and start doing grown-up things. Payton and the girls actually went on a spring break trip to Punta Cana this year. Of course I couldn't go, but they did. I could barely look at the pictures, even though I tried to be excited. Really, all their tan skin and smiles just made me feel bad for myself, and I just felt... sad.

I'm sick of feeling sad and alone. This was supposed to be my year of freedom. I was going to graduate high school and find the new me in college. I might be held back from accomplishing those goals right now by powers unknown, but I'm not going to lie down and just let someone take my life from me—especially the Outfit, if that's who's behind my abduction.

I know what you're thinking. The word *abduction* might be a little dramatic, but what else can I call it?

Kidnapping? No... Is kidnapping just for children? I mean, it is called *kid*napping. Okay, I don't want to think about that anymore.

Abduction kind of has an alien ring to it though... If we were doing a word association game and someone said *abduction*, I'd shout *alien* for sure, followed quickly by *butt stuff*.

I've had poops big enough to hurt my little booty hole, so I don't want any little green men sticking their probes up there, that's for sure.

Maybe I could make an exception for Brad Pitt or Henry Cavill when he's dressed as the witcher.

Maybe...

With my seat belt locked firmly around my lap, the pilot takes the plane—jet, whatever the fuck it is, down to land. I have to say, after flying in larger commercial planes, it's a hell of a lot scarier in a smaller one.

I shut my eyes, not wanting to see how fast the ground is hurtling up toward us before the rear wheels touch down with a skid, then the nose drops as softly as a feather falling to the floor.

Wow… I'm impressed.

It's the woman's touch, I'm sure of it. Men pilots just want to get the job done fast, whereas women want to do it a little slower, but safer and more pleasurable.

I wonder if that's true for sex…

I'm not really experienced, and my most recent sexual encounter was the slobbery kiss of one Marco Capelli. If his kisses were that messy, I can't imagine how gross he'd be in bed. There are so many sticky body fluids, and I'm sure all he cares about is himself.

The only lucky thing about my little *abduction-napping* is that I'll never have to find out.

After the pilot steers the small plane into a docking area, the black suits come to claim me again. With firm grips on my upper arms, I'm led into another black SUV, and I almost do a double take. It's the exact same car that brought me to the airport. I glance back at the plane, wondering if they were somehow able to take it with us on the flight, but I quickly realize how ridiculous that is. There's no way a huge SUV could fit on a ten-passenger plane. The one huge black suit hardly fit in the seats, let alone an eight-passenger vehicle.

Sitting bitch again, I'm squished in spite of my thin frame as the SUV starts driving through the airport and out of a gated exit. I don't pay attention to the overhead signs on the freeway telling us which exit is approaching, though, since I have no idea where the hell I am anyway.

"I don't suppose you could give me my purse now?" I mutter, keeping my eyes focused out the front window.

The man sitting to my left pats my leg and squeezes my thigh to the point that it becomes uncomfortable. "It isn't yours anymore."

My eyes roll on their own. This is really starting to get annoying. "Well, can you tell me where we're going then?"

Another black suit sitting in the third row just laughs. "You could say you're going home."

I can't hold back my snort. "You do know I live in New Hampshire, right? I mean… you guys did abduct me from my school."

They fall silent. The gangsters must feel bad about what they did, even if they don't say it. I can see their emotions in the way they all shift uncomfortably in their seats. "Yeah, that's right, assholes. Whatever is about to happen to me is all your fault."

This lights a fuse, because the stocky driver actually screeches the car to a sudden stop and turns around to face me. "You should watch your mouth, *piccola ragazza*. Where you're going, insubordination is not tolerated. They will cut out your tongue if you don't learn to mind it."

I gulp, eyes wide, as I try my best not to cower and shake in my seat. He just grins at me, and I see one of his canines is actually a gold cap. I won't forget that, I have a thing about teeth. I might not remember faces, but if someone has a snaggle tooth, I won't forget it.

When he turns back around and shifts the car into gear, I decide to keep my mouth shut. These black suits don't really make for good conversation, and it seems every time I open my mouth, something snarky comes out of it. Snarky comebacks lead to trouble.

But he did offer me a clue. He said "they will cut out your tongue."

Not he or she.

They.

So where I'm going, I'll be with more than one person.

The more I think about it, the more I think this has to be my brothers' doing. I bet this is a birthday surprise they have arranged just for me—a trip with them. They know how hard it is on me to be away from them all the time. I bet they have been planning this for months, but just wanted to scare their little sister before the big surprise.

That thought calms me and eases my racing heart.

I'll tell you what though, I'm going to let them fucking have it when I see them—after I hug the shit out of them.

To pass the time, I try to get lost in the houses we pass, reciting entire movies in my head while attempting not to think about where I'm headed. After an hour or so, we pull off an exit and head through an upscale community to an even more upscale development.

The houses grow larger, and their grounds become more expansive. I've never seen homes like this. Huge mansions sprawl across well-manicured lawns, with spurting fountains of angels, dolphins, and cherubs adding movement to the front yards.

Spring flowers are blooming, and the scent of lilac reaches me, even inside the car. Expensive cars are parked in the driveways to show off the ample amount of money they cost, each one polished and shiny in the late afternoon light.

We pull into a long driveway with large, stone pillars on either side. An iron gate swings open as we enter, and a towering mansion comes into view. It's surprisingly modern for this community. Dark gray stone, a black tin roof, and hints of wood give off a masculine, contemporary vibe.

I count six garage doors, and those are just the ones I can see. Two tall flagpoles fly both the American and Italian flags, which wave proudly in the wind.

We park, and I'm led up to the front door, but before the black suits can knock, the door swings open and a kind-looking man greets us. Sparse, bright white hair covers his rather pink head. He has gentle blue eyes and a friendly smile. With the uniform he wears, I know he's a butler, one whose family has probably served this one for generations. "Good evening. I'm Joseph. You must be Valentina. They have been waiting for you."

Joseph offers me his arm, and the black suits release me into his care. Joseph guides me inside, and as the door closes behind me, it feels like closing a book after a good chapter for the final time. I just hope when the next chapter of my life begins, it doesn't start in a horror story.

CHAPTER EIGHTEEN

Armani

My phone vibrates in my pocket, so I pull it out and swipe the message open.

James: She's here. Joseph is bringing her inside.

Me: Good. Take her to the dining hall.

My heart thumps, but not because I'm anxious. I don't usually get anxious. It's because the girl who will be ours forever is in our home right this very moment.

"She's here," I tell my brothers. Sal doesn't react, still bent over his desk, rifling through the notes sent over from her recent doctor exams.

Fausto looks up from his phone and grins. "I've got our security cameras pulled up. Come take a look at her."

I walk across the office, leaving Sal to muse over her entire medical history, and pull a chair over next to Fausto. He turns his phone sideways to make the footage larger.

"There she is," he says, pointing as if I couldn't see her, but how could I possibly miss her? Even on the security footage, I can tell she'd turn heads when she walks into a room. "We've been waiting ten years for this."

Kinky thoughts race through my mind when I get my first look at her. "Holy shit, is she wearing a school uniform?" My cock thickens as I imagine pretending to be her teacher and needing to discipline her when she's naughty.

"Fuck. They didn't make them like that when we were in school, did they?" Fausto remarks.

I adjust myself so my erection isn't as obvious. "Fuck no they didn't. Our school was riddled with nerds and headhunters."

"Look at the legs on her. Shit."

I laugh. "Look at all of her, brother. And she's all ours." I turn toward Sal. "Unless, of course, you'd like a piece of her too? Her mouth perhaps? I know your cock doesn't like hot cunts anymore."

Sal flicks his eyes up to me with a penetrating look that reminds me so much of our father. "Keep thoughts of my cock out of your sick mind, Armani."

"Sheesh," I reply, holding up my hands in a placating gesture. "Take that stick out of your ass while you're reading over her medical history."

"It's important to know if she has any—"

"Any what? Diseases? We know she's led a sheltered life, Sal. The only things that girl has that we should be concerned with are a virgin cunt and an untrained mouth." The look of disgust that crosses Sal's face is exactly what I wanted from him—a reaction. Any reaction. "Oh, find me sickening, do you? And here I thought your face had turned to stone."

Sal doesn't react this time, instead, he lowers his eyes to the desktop. Meanwhile, Fausto and I continue to check out our new girl. Her long, light brown hair hangs in loose waves, hitting below her shoulder blades, and her bright eyes flick up to the security camera. I see her lips part and can almost hear her gasp as she registers that we're watching her. Joseph leads her through the foyer and into the dining hall.

She's small and thin, with olive skin that makes the color of her eyes seem to pop. Somehow, the knee-high socks and short plaid skirt make her appear so vulnerable, so innocent. If there's one thing I love, it's collecting innocence and corrupting it.

Valentina

JOSEPH GUIDES me through an elaborate foyer, gently patting my hand where it's clutched onto his upper arm. Marble tiles spread across the floor in an elaborate pattern that had to take an artist hours to create, and the soft cream walls are decorated with ornate picture frames housing expensive artwork.

I think I see an original Rembrandt. How the hell is it displayed here instead of in a museum for the whole world to enjoy? I bet it's stolen, along with many other things. In this world, some people earn their own money, while others steal it from the wealthy and try to justify their wrongs by saying the wealthy don't need it, even though they earned it.

Hanging low on a silver chain is a massive crystal chandelier, which casts a white glow over everything. Vases filled with fresh flowers give color to the foyer, their soft scent calming.

We walk slowly to a set of double doors on the left, our footsteps echoing off the walls as cameras follow our every move. "It's okay, dear," Joseph reassures me as he pushes them open, and we move into an elaborate dining hall.

Who the hell lives here?

And what do they want with me?

A long, deep mahogany table occupies the center of the room. At least twenty chairs surround it, enough to seat an entire family and then some. A painted mural of the Last Supper spreads across one wall, and a statue of the Blessed Mother stands tall in one corner, next to a large bay window overlooking the front yard. A ring of wilted flowers surrounds her head from her May crowning.

Joseph guides me to a chair in the middle of one side and pulls it out for me. As I move to sit down, he pushes the chair in under me like a real gentleman. I turn to look at him. "Thank you, Joseph."

He smiles kindly. "Of course, my dear. Sit tight, and they will be with you soon."

They…

There's that word again.

"Umm, Joseph. May I ask you a question?"

He turns to face me, his gloved hands joined in a relaxed manner, and arches a white brow at me.

"Umm… Can you tell me who 'they' are?"

Joseph doesn't even blink, but his Adam's apple bobs up and down, the only sign of anxiety he's shown me. "I'm afraid I cannot. They prefer to introduce themselves. You'll meet them in just a moment."

Joseph offers me a slight bow and exits the room, leaving me alone in the huge dining room with only my racing thoughts, grumbling stomach, and pounding heart to keep me company.

I wish I was given a seat on the other side of the table or at the far end, then I could have at least gotten lost in the mural or had a good view of outside. Instead, my seat faces a wall with a set of double doors just like the ones Joseph brought me through.

I begin to make a mental map of this place in case there's any chance I can escape. I'm not here of my own free will, and no one sent me an invitation. Instead, I was taken from my school's parking lot in broad daylight by armed men who weren't willing to provide any information.

A chill sets in, and the tiny hairs on my arms rise even as I hug myself to try and keep warm. Each minute that ticks by is agonizingly slow, and I wonder how long they are going to keep me here.

Pushing away from the table, I walk over to the doors I entered through and give them a slight push, but they don't budge. Shit. I don't dare try the others yet, because getting lost inside a place like this is worse than being stuck in a single room. At least here I have my bearings.

Outside the bay window, I notice the sun is setting, so I walk over to look at the colorful sky. There's nothing like a spring sunset, the smattering of colors pierced by white, puffy clouds. It even has a scent to it, a warmth that's welcome after a long, cold winter.

The grounds of this place are so pretty, the grass bright green and freshly cut, the lines from the lawnmower crisscrossing over each other in a diagonal pattern. I run my hands along the window seams, searching for a latch, but I can't find one. These windows must not open.

Feeling sad for myself at having the shittiest birthday ever, I stare at the crystal water spraying from the fountain, hoping today can't possibly get any worse than this.

CHAPTER NINETEEN

Armani

Fausto slaps my back in excitement. "Let's go and pay our guest a visit."

"Are we playing good twin, bad twin?" I ask.

Fausto shrugs as I pull my hair up into a bun, wrapping it in a tie. "Only if she's feisty. Come on."

Standing, I straighten my blazer and check my face in the mirror before we head downstairs. I don't want to seem too eager or too excited, though my cock says otherwise.

"You coming?" Fausto asks Sal.

He answers without even looking up. "I'll be there in a moment. You two go ahead."

Without another word, I push through the office door and walk down the spiral staircase with Fausto by my side. We stride through the foyer and over to the dining hall doors. Joseph is standing outside it, waiting for us to arrive.

"First impressions?" Fausto asks, keeping his voice low.

"She seems like a sweet girl, boys." Joseph turns to me. "Be gentle with her, won't you?"

I clap Joseph on the shoulder. "Gentle? When have you known me to be anything but gentle?"

A grin pulls at Joseph's lips. "Only your whole lives."

"Hey, don't you pull me into this," Fausto jokes. "Everyone knows I'm the sweet twin."

I scoff. "Even sweet things turn sour with enough poison. Now if we're done here, I'd like to go check out our girl."

Fausto and I exchange a grin then push open the doors.

Valentina

I FEEL a sudden warmth behind me, and I wonder if I'm standing over a vent. I take a step back to look when I bump into something.

My entire body freezes, and that's when the scent of a man's cologne washes over me.

I'm not alone anymore.

I move to turn around when a deep voice warns, "Don't fucking move."

Frozen, I struggle to inhale a single breath as the man behind me runs his hand through my hair, the gentle tugging sending tingles through my body. I feel him bring my hair upwards then hear him sniff it. He's… smelling me?

When my limbs finally remember how to work, I step away, taking my hair with me. I turn to face him, not wanting him at my back for another moment. The man who stares back at me is nothing like I expected.

With one hand still raised to his nose as if he's still clutching a handful of my hair, he flicks his dark gaze to me. My heart skips a beat, and my lips part on a gasp. He's gorgeous in a threatening way.

Someone who is evil enough to abduction-nap me shouldn't be allowed to be this attractive.

He's tall and bulky, and I'd guess around thirty years old. His navy blue blazer hangs open, revealing a cream-colored, V-neck shirt that hugs his form and makes his tan skin look darker than it probably is. His hair is gathered on top of his head in a man bun that accentuates his high cheekbones and piercing dark brown eyes.

A thick beard covers his face, but unlike the bushy nightmares you see on TV, this one is neat and trimmed, cut at sharp angles that highlight his face instead of hiding it.

He drops his hand and takes a step forward. "You disobeyed me, kitten," he purrs, his voice a deep, melodic rumble. "Since you didn't know the rules yet, I'll let this little slipup slide." He edges closer, and I take a step back. "When we tell you to do something, you do it. You don't question it. You don't consider your options. You just comply. That's the first rule."

He advances again, and I raise my hands in front of me for protection as I back away and run into something hard. I gulp, knowing I'm not close enough to the wall to hit it.

A smug grin tugs at the lips of the man facing me as the man behind me leans down close to my ear. "Yes. You'd do well to mind rule number one. It will make all the other rules much easier to obey if you do."

His voice sounds identical to the first man's timbre, though a little less playful and a bit more forceful. "Now, be a good girl and hold still."

The first man stops before me, and I gaze up into his face, refusing to lower my eyes and let them know how scared I really am. The guy behind me runs his hands down my sides, and I can feel his heat through my uniform.

The man before me, who I will call Ponytail, reaches toward me, and I flinch slightly. He pauses for half a second, and I wonder if he might stop, but he doesn't. Behind me, the man dips his fingers under the top of my skirt, sliding them around the edge as Ponytail grips my chin and lifts my face. "She is very beautiful, brother. So young and… untouched."

Brother?

"Mmm," the other man hums. "So delicate, like the petals of a newly bloomed flower, isn't she?"

Ponytail turns my face left and right as if studying me, his dark brown eyes roaming over my face. "That's the thing with flowers though. If they aren't fed and watered, they will eventually begin to wilt."

The second man's wandering hands curl around my waist and squeeze. "Then we shall feed her, brother, and fill that sweet mouth up with something to keep her—"

The far door crashes open, and a third man walks in, interrupting the man behind me. He looks a lot like Ponytail, but although he has the same color hair, his is cut short and styled, and unlike Ponytail's thick beard, this third man's face is covered in a five o'clock shadow. It's his eyes, however, that are so vastly different. Instead of the dark, sultry gaze of Ponytail, bright blue beams stare across the room—they aren't looking at me though. "Will you two cut this shit out?" His voice holds an air of authority, a man whose demands are always met and whose orders are always fulfilled.

Men in power have certain mannerisms, and their demeanor is almost identical. They walk with puffed chests and their chins raised as if normal people are so far beneath them they don't even deserve to lock eyes with them. Their voices are stern, and their words are spoken harshly and abruptly so that you'd never think to question them, simply following instructions because the ramifications are too great to risk.

I know who this man is, this man of power, of control. This man who reminds me so much of my dad.

Ponytail releases me and looks at this new man. "Jesus, Sal. We're just having a little fun with our new… possession."

"I'm not your fucking possession," I growl, throwing off the wandering hands still clutching my body and turning to see what the man behind me looks like. My eyes widen when I see his face is a mirror image of Ponytail's.

They have the same facial features, same eyes, and same hair color. The second man wears his hair longer than the third man, Sal, does. His face is clean-shaven, accentuating his full lips and a set of gleaming white teeth. His dark brown hair reaches just below his ears, and he runs his fingers through it like a model might while posing for a camera.

I glance back at Ponytail, and a knowing look crosses his face. "What? Haven't you ever seen twins before?"

"Enough." Sal walks farther into the room, rolling the sleeves of his white dress shirt up. A thick, gold watch gleams on his left wrist, shining against his tan skin. He pulls out the chair usually designated for the head of the family, the one at the very end, and gestures toward it. "Sit."

I look over at Ponytail, thinking Sal was addressing him, when the second man leans down and whispers, "You were given an order. Don't forget to obey the first rule. It will piss off Sal, and you don't want to fuck with Sal."

He smacks my ass a little harder than I would have preferred, but I get the hint and walk over to the chair. Before I get there, Sal turns his back on me and moves halfway down the table. Ponytail pulls out the chair directly to my right, and his twin mimics him on my left.

Sal paces, moving around the length of the room in a slow gait while the twins simply focus on me. There's a palpable tension in the room. It's like when your parents were in an argument, but then you walk into the room and they fall silent—that's how uncomfortable it is in here.

Sal squares his shoulders in front of the bay window, and though he's looking in my direction, he won't make eye contact with me. It's like he's staring at my forehead. "You made a comment earlier. Something about not being Armani's possession."

Armani, so that's Ponytail's name.

"I believe her exact words were, 'I'm not your fucking possession,'" the man whose name I still don't know repeats. I want to slap the fucker.

Sal almost smiles, but it's like he catches himself before it can actually happen. "Thank you, Fausto." So that's his name. "No matter how much you believe that to be true, your statement is a lie."

I shake my head in disbelief. Who the fuck does he think he is? Feeling brave, I push my chair back and try to stand tall. "No. I'm a person, not some dog you just plucked off the streets. I have a life. A family. You can't own me no matter how much money you have."

Sal slams his fists down on the table, and I jump back. My legs crash into my chair, and I fall back down on my ass. "Don't raise your voice with me, Valentina." Sal speaks slowly and carefully, as if he's trying to harness an anger he's afraid to unleash. "You don't want to be on my bad side."

"I didn't know you had a good side," Armani jokes. Fausto laughs but tries to hide it. Okay, so the twins have a pleasant side, even though they want to seem tough. I can work with that.

Sal begins pacing again, this time stopping just next to Fausto. "Money has nothing to do with it, but your family does."

"I fucking knew it," I grumble, throwing my hands in the air in frustration. "Which brother was it? Gabe? Raph? What did they do?"

Fausto speaks this time. "Not your brothers. It was your father."

I feel the blood drain from my face. "My f-father?"

"Yes, kitten," Armani adds. "He sold your soul to the devil."

I shake my head. "No. He—He wouldn't."

"Oh, wouldn't he?" Sal struts around the table again, brushing past me but still not looking at me. "Ten years ago, you were how old?"

"Eight," I reply. "Why?"

Sal stops to stare out the window. "Because that's how long you've been promised to us." My heart drops as he turns back around and looks at the mural. I glance from Armani to Fausto, and they both grin back, but it's not a friendly grin. It's the kind of smile you save for your enemies right before you off them.

"Ten years ago, the leaders of the six most powerful mafias took part in a legendary meeting," Sal continues. "The Cosa Nostra was there, represented by none other than the infamous Carlo Rossi."

There's something about the way Sal grits out my father's name that has the hair on my body standing on end. It's the way you'd utter someone's name if you hated them, if you wished them dead, as if their name is almost painful to say.

Fausto picks up where Sal left off. "Dons from London's Firm, Boston's Irish Mafia, Russia's Bratva, Mexico's Cartel."

Armani steps in. "Your father was there, of course, as leader of New York's Cosa Nostra, and the last don present was our father, Giovanni Moretti, Don of Chicago's Outfit."

My limbs go numb. Dad spoke about the Morettis from time to time and never had anything nice to say. The rivalry between the Cosa Nostra and the Outfit goes back generations. There's no love lost between them, and now here I am, sitting at a table with people Dad would call enemies.

"I still don't understand why I'm here. Our families have hated each other since the Outfit began. Why put us together now?"

Sal scrubs at the scruff on his face, then crosses his arms over his chest. "We weren't *put together,* Valentina. You were given to us by your father in exchange for peace."

"Well, I'm not staying." I push my seat back and make a break for the door leading into the foyer, but Fausto intercepts me.

He seizes me around the middle before slamming my back into the wall. One hand grips my wrists, and he pins them above my head, while his other hand ensnares my chin, forcing me to look at him. No matter how hard I pull, I can't shake his grip. "You are ours, Valentina." His voice is low and deep, a fearsome growl. "A decade ago, a pact was made, forged with the blood of our fathers. A blood pact like that can never be broken. What you want no longer matters. It's what *I* want, what *we* want, that concerns you now."

In one quick movement, Fausto spins me around and shoves me back down in a chair, his large hands holding my shoulders to ensure I can't get up again.

Armani watches casually from his seat across from me while Sal continues his relentless pacing. "A pact was made, Valentina," Sal repeats for what must be like the fifth time. "Six daughters were exchanged for peace, with six marriages to ensure war between us never happens again. You now belong to the Morettis, and one day soon, under the watchful eyes of God, you will make a vow to be ours until the day you die."

My mind is reeling with all of this. "It doesn't seem real. Why didn't he ever tell me?" I think back on the last ten years, trying to see if something changed, but there's nothing.

"Some things are best kept secret," Armani offers. "But us? We've always known. We were children ourselves when our dear old pop told us."

"And my brothers?" I stutter out. "D-Do they—"

Sal nods. "Yes, they have a female of their own now. A British woman. But you? You're just a child. A spoiled little brat. It's no wonder you can't get a fucking grip on things. Your filthy Rossi blood is staining my dining hall."

My stress and anxiety give way to potent anger. "Excuse me? I've sat here and listened to all your bullshit. You've talked down to me, bossed me around, and even hurt me." I glance at Fausto, and he holds his chin high, proud of what he did. "But I will not sit here and have you insult my family."

"Then stand if you must, but the results will be the same," Sal shouts, his control fading. "Your presence is unwanted but necessary. You never asked for this, but neither did we. I would have chosen any of those girls, any single one, besides you. Your family is a disgrace to all Italians. The thought of having to marry you sickens me, and the thought of your blood running through my family churns my stomach. I don't want you here, Valentina, but my father made a pact, and regardless of how I feel, I will see it through. Because Moretti men are men of their word, unlike the Rossis. You're all fucking cowards."

I'm at a loss for words, my brain flatlining. Never in my life have I been talked to like this or insulted just for being part of a family I had no choice to belong to. Tears well in my eyes, and for the first time since I've been here, I drop my head, not wanting them to see any weakness.

Sal storms from the room, the door slamming shut behind him. Fausto and Armani don't say a word to me either, getting up from their chairs and leaving through the same door Sal did.

Joseph comes in to collect me and leads me from the room. I don't take note of the hallways we walk through, the stairs we climb, or the rooms we pass. Nothing matters in this moment.

Finally, we reach a closed door, and Joseph ushers me inside. "You'll be staying here unless they tell me otherwise. There are clothes in the closet, and your bathroom is stocked. You'll be collected in the morning. Sleep well, my dear."

The door shuts, and I collapse onto the ground in a crumpled heap, letting the emotions flow through me. My shoulders shake, and tears drip down my face as I try to comprehend what just happened and what this all means. Even though I'm stuck inside a lavish room in a large mansion, it just feels like a prison.

My life as I know it is over, and I'm terrified to see what's going to happen next.

CHAPTER TWENTY

Fausto

Armani is pissed, and so am I, though he's the first one to voice it.

"Was that fucking necessary?"

We chased Sal through the house to the back patio where a covered bar overlooks an unfilled pool, still closed for winter. He doesn't even bristle at Armani's words, just slams back a glass of whiskey then pours himself another. "You guys don't understand," he murmurs after finishing the second glass.

"Then help us understand, Sal," Armani pleads. "Or do you want her to fucking hate us before she even gets a chance to know us?"

Sal unfastens the top few buttons of his shirt then takes a sip of his third drink. "There are things as don that I keep to myself. Things that you two don't need to fucking know."

"Oh, don't give me that shit," I grit out, walking over to my older brother. "You act like we're fucking children instead of your partners. You're not the only one who runs the Outfit. Not since Dad died. It's been the three of us. We made a promise to stick together and look out for each other, but here you are, sabotaging our future."

Sal scoffs and downs his drink. "Don't be so fucking dramatic, Armani. She's pissed at me, not you two."

I raise my hand. "I think she's pissed at me too. I did slam her little ass against that wall."

"Yeah, that was hot, bro," Armani commends, slapping me on the back. "I thought you might take her right then and there."

I can't help but laugh. "I almost fucking did, to tell you the truth. If old fuckface hadn't still been in the room, we could have shared her."

"Aww. Like old times," Armani jokes. "Not this girl. She's different. I will deflower her petals first."

I choke on my own spit. "Her petals? Seriously, Armani?"

He nods. "Yeah. Sounds better than meat flaps or cum dumpster."

"You could just say cunt and be done with it," I shoot back.

"Pfft," my twin scoffs. "What's the fun in that? Everyone calls it a cunt these days. I'm thinking about bringing snatch back."

I shake my head. "Nope. Snatch sounds like the latest app all the kids are playing."

Even Sal reacts to this one, making him choke on his drink. "I think cunt is appropriate. All the other names have too many synonyms."

Armani shoots me a *can you believe this guy* look. "Synonyms, Sal? Who the fuck are you? Webster's fucking dictionary?"

"Just because you don't know what words are doesn't mean I don't," Sal retorts before taking another sip of whiskey.

Armani grabs the bottle from him and pulls two glasses down from the shelf. "Shit. You're going to drink this whole bottle before I even get one sip."

"Because you're too slow," Sal begins, and then he pauses and looks at me, waiting for our brother's reaction. There's a split second where neither of them moves before Armani lunges for him. Sal twists out of the way and leaps over the bar, running out into the backyard.

Armani gives chase, but only for a moment. "You're fucking lucky the pool is still empty, or I would have thrown your ass in it," Armani yells, cupping his hands around his mouth.

Sal just raises his glass and keeps jogging around the side of the house, leaving Armani and me alone.

I pull up a barstool and sit down on it. He takes the drink I hand him and twists the glass on the bar top.

"In all seriousness," I murmur, "what do you think that outburst was about?"

Armani lets out a frustrated sigh. "I wish I fucking knew. One moment he's all proper mafia don, telling her how it is, and the next—"

"It's like he was possessed," I finish. "I thought the veins in his fucking face were going to burst."

"And that poor girl just had to sit there and take it."

I think for a moment. "Armani, have we had any interaction with the Cosa Nostra recently that might have caused Sal to act out like that? I mean, he wasn't just spewing dislike for her family, it was pure hatred."

He considers my question and shrugs. "I can't think of anything. They have pretty much stayed out of our way." I can see him working through the problem before his eyes widen and he looks at me with a knowing gaze. "At least they did until—"

The lightbulb goes off for me, and I interject, "Until that dead fuck sabotaged our last deal and incriminated a man named Alfonzo."

Armani bites his lip. "Yep. Alfonzo with no last name."

"You think it's the Capellis then?" I ask, sipping my drink.

"It makes sense. We know he's Carlo Rossi's right-hand man, right? The timelines match up. Our deal got fucked the same week we got Valentina. You really think that's a coincidence?"

I stare out at a line of trees enclosing the perimeter of our property and the six-acre pond that's filled with fish. "It just doesn't make sense though. Why sign the pact in blood if you were never willing to fulfill it?"

"And didn't Dad tell us that Carlo is the one who organized it all?" Fausto adds, and I nod.

"I remember that. We were surprised to say the least."

Armani runs his hand through his hair, something he always does when he's thinking hard. "So if Carlo Rossi wanted this peace deal more than anyone, what happened in the last month that caused him to change his mind? When did the shift happen?"

I take the last gulp of my drink and set my glass down. "I wish I knew, brother. I wish I knew."

CHAPTER TWENTY-ONE

Valentina

The lavish furnishings and lush, imported fabrics don't make this room feel any less cold. Lying in the middle of a huge, four-poster bed with a canopy spread across it, I can't even bring myself to look around. After I picked myself up off the floor, I collapsed onto the bed.

I'd be lying if I said it wasn't the most comfortable thing I've ever lain on, but I still hate it. Plush blankets and decorative pillows in soft grays and pale pinks surround me, and there are at least four layers of bedding I'm lying on.

Four!

Who has that many layers and doesn't sweat their ass off when sleeping under them? What am I, a fucking onion? Do I need to be peeled? And where the hell is my fan? I can't sleep without a fan, or at the very minimum a white noise app. I can't take this silence. Hearing my stuttered breaths and racing pulse is making me more stressed, and there's nothing to relieve my anxiety or the pressure in my chest.

There is a wall of windows to my right, four across. I can hear shouting through them, but I don't have enough energy left in me to even bother to see what the fuss is about.

Deciding I've had enough of a pity party, I slip off the bed and actually take a look around. Nightstands rest on either side of the bed, tall and gray, with three drawers each. Instead of lamps, crystal sconces hang over the nightstands, though I have no idea how to turn them on.

Next to the bed, right as you enter the room, is what you might call a little living room. A gray suede couch with fluffy pink pillows rests against the wall, and a huge mirror hangs above it. Across from the couch, a massive TV is mounted over an electric fireplace. The remotes for both are resting on a small round coffee table.

Passing the TV, I walk to the door and grip the handle, but it won't budge. I thought I heard a lock sound when Joseph shut me in here, but I wasn't sure until now.

I'm fucking trapped like some fairy-tale princess.

"Fucking bullshit," I grumble, turning back to the room. Well, at least I have a TV to watch. Hopefully I can log into my Netflix account to pass the time.

Wanting to explore more, I walk past the TV to a huge, white bookcase that sits across from the bed. Knickknacks and trinkets fill the shelves, but there's not a single fucking book. How can there be no books on a bookshelf? Why not just have shelves then? This is clearly a bookcase, and bookcases need books.

This should be called a bookless case or a knickknack display area. Beyond the bookless case is a door, so I push it open to find a large bathroom. Silver and crystal chandeliers hang over the double sinks of gray and white marble. Huge planks of marble make up the floor and continue into the glass shower. However, this bathroom has something I haven't seen before—the soaker tub is actually inside the shower.

How fucking genius is that?

Seriously, how many times have you been in the bath and realized how fucking dirty the water was so you had to do the wet tiptoe trot from the tub to the shower to actually feel clean? Or you shower first, then get into the tub, but realize if you rinsed the shampoo from your hair while still in the tub, you'd make a huge fucking mess that you'd have to clean up?

Okay so maybe this room isn't so bad. Now if I just had a good book or two to pass the time.

At the far end, across from the door I just entered, is a second door leading to a closet. It's not like the closet I'm used to having, but a giant walk-in closet. Hanging from matching hangers—who actually has matching hangers anyway?—are my clothes.

Which means…

Maybe the Moretti brothers are telling the truth. Without the passcode to my house, there's no way they could have gotten inside.

That means it was given to them, and no one knows my security system's passcode besides my brothers and my dad.

Well… and Marco. I was so sure my family would have never given him the passcode, since he's someone I barely know, but he did have it, and boy did he use it.

I feel so alone, so isolated from life. Isn't there anyone in my corner to fight for me? Am I really all by myself? Sal said my dad sold me to the devil. Was he referring to himself?

I feel faint. The truth is so glaringly obvious. Maybe that's why I've been kept isolated for all these years. Dad told me it was for my protection, but it was really because I had a destiny he needed to fulfill for his own nefarious reasons.

Ten years, they said. Ten years ago, this blood pact was made, and no one told me. Not even Raph. When Mom died, he came home and took care of me, and he didn't even have the balls to tell me.

My sadness is quickly replaced with anger. I'm fucking furious and want to bitch, scream, yell at anyone who will listen, but I'm stuck in this stupid fucking gorgeous room without a soul to talk to.

Hoping my phone might be hiding in here, I open all the drawers and look through all the shelves. I find my purse sitting on a shelf and snatch it down only to find it mostly empty. My wallet is missing. It contained my ID, cash, and credit and debit cards. My phone is gone too. All that's left are some black hair ties, because you always need extra—one for now, and one in case the first one breaks because they always break at the worst fucking time—and my collection of lip balms.

What am I going to do with fucking hair ties and lip gloss?

Feeling defeated, I shove my purse back on its pretty little shelf and resign myself to defeat. They didn't even fucking feed me when I got here, other than their loads of bullshit.

I'm starving, my belly rumbling to the point that it's uncomfortable. Leaving the closet, I decide that a bath might make me forget about my empty stomach. I head over to the huge glass structure and check out all the levers and buttons to control it. Fucking thing has so many gizmos I need a YouTube video to learn how to work it.

With my hand on the control panel of buttons, I start pushing them until I finally have the water running, but my excitement is cut short when a man's voice cuts through the sound of rushing water.

"We need to talk."

I jump at the sound, not expecting anyone to be in the bathroom with me, and I accidentally smash my hand into the control panel. The shower springs to life, and I learn that it has not one, not two, but three showerheads. There's one on each wall, and a rainfall head in the ceiling. I'm the lucky bitch who put them all on.

Bottom line—I'm fucking drenched.

Sad, starving, and embarrassed, I frantically hit the buttons, trying to get it to turn off, when the glass door swings open and in walks none other than the devil himself—Sal. Just being near him makes my skin crawl.

"Move out of the way," he orders before pushing me out of the shower. My school shoes aren't made for wet surfaces, so I slip on the tiles and fall hard on my tailbone.

"Oww," I moan, rolling onto my side, trying to relieve some of the pain.

"You're a fucking hopeless child, a little baby girl, aren't you?" Sal accuses, swiftly shutting off the shower. "You can't even work a shower by yourself. Do you have servants run your bath for you, hmm?"

"Oh, fuck off already," I retort. "Why are you even here? I have nothing to say to you."

I try and fail to stand up, my feet slipping in the pool my wet clothes created. Sal doesn't try to help me in any way. Instead, he leans against the wall with his arms crossed over his chest, watching me struggle.

Pissed, I pull off my shoe and throw it at him. He swats it away with ease. I throw my second shoe, then strip off my sock and aim for his face. One hits him square in the cheek, and I watch his demeanor immediately change from somewhat calm to pissed.

It's the grimace that pulls at his lips, the way his muscles tighten under his shirt, and the crazy look in his eye that makes my fear escalate.

I scoot backwards on my ass as he prowls toward me, his hands clenched in fists.

"Get away from me!" I shout, finally finding my footing. I slam the bathroom door, but he's there before it even shuts. He lunges for me, and I try to leap across the bed, only to have him land on top of me.

My face is smashed into the bedding as he sits on the backs of my legs, one hand pressed firmly onto my back, holding me down.

He lifts up my skirt, baring my soaked white panties, and smacks my ass hard. I yelp and try to wriggle away, but I can't fight him. He leans down, his chest pressed to my back, his lips right next to my ear.

He squeezes my ass and then his hand drifts slowly inward. I start to die inside. "I could take you now," he warns, his finger trailing up and down my panties. "I could take you hard and long, and no one would come to save you. No one would fucking care. Don't you get that? You're all alone now."

Sal's erection presses against my leg as he slips a finger under the edge of my panties and tugs on my pubic hair. I knew I should have shaved that shit off weeks ago. "You were given to me, to us, and if I choose to use my gift, then I fucking will."

He releases me and flips me onto my back. I lift my legs to kick his chest, but he catches my ankles and presses them down into the bed on either side of his thighs.

"So fucking weak, so undeserving."

"Get the fuck off me!" I shout as he presses between my legs, then leans down and captures my wrists. There's no doubting he's strong as he restrains both my wrists in one hand.

"Keep shouting, Valentina. I like it. It turns me on." Sal deftly unfastens the top button of my uniform, then the second, and I arch my back, trying to get away. "Yes! Fight back," he urges as the third button goes, and I know my bra is on full display. "A filthy Rossi like you shouldn't have a body like this. You make me want to do bad things to you." My wrists scream in pain as his free hand curls around my neck. "You make me want to hurt you until you beg me to stop with tearstained cheeks." His grip on my neck tightens, and I struggle to suck in air as he runs his nose along my cheek, his dick pressing between my spread legs. "You come into my home wearing this little schoolgirl outfit, then get your clothes fucking soaked. It's like you're asking for me to take you."

"You stole me from school, asshole!" I choke out. "This is my fucking uniform!"

Something flickers in his eyes, and he shakes his head as if he's trying to rid himself of some feeling or thought. For a moment, he doesn't move, staring through me instead of at me.

He blinks and sits up, releasing me, and I gasp for breath.

"You're nothing," he spits as he moves off the bed. "Nothing but a sheltered brat, a little baby girl." He walks toward the door, adjusting his pants and shirt as he does. "The Cosa Nostra has always thought they were better than us, and now here you are. Your life is mine now. Consider yourself my prisoner, a new plaything for my brothers and me."

"I'm not your plaything," I argue, pulling the covers over myself as he knocks twice on the door. It opens, and he's about to walk through it when he turns to face me, his calm demeanor back in place.

"Not yet," he warns before he closes the door and locks it behind him.

CHAPTER TWENTY-TWO

Armani

B̲e̲l̲i̲e̲v̲e̲ ̲i̲t̲ ̲o̲r̲ ̲n̲o̲t̲, I'm a morning person. Even if I stay out all night partying or fucking, I still get up before seven. There's something about the early morning sun and watching the world come alive that excites me, especially if I have a hot cup of coffee in my hands.

The view today is especially good as I check the security cameras and see Joseph gently knocking on Valentina's door. He's going to invite her down for breakfast. Italian women can be very stubborn when they want to be. Sometimes there's no budging them, but with the temptation of good food on the line, they usually cave.

So I'm not surprised when she opens the door and allows Joseph to lead her down the hall. Hell, I don't think she's eaten a single thing since lunchtime yesterday. I switch cameras and watch her grip Joseph's arm so tightly that I worry about the old man's circulation.

He escorts her down the main stairs and through the foyer to the kitchen—the room I'm in. Relaxing in a little breakfast nook that overlooks the backyard, I sip on a very hot cup of coffee and watch her enter. At first she doesn't see me, and I get it. The kitchen is massive, with two wide, stainless steel freezers, an eight burner cooktop, double islands, extra sinks, and more cabinetry than we could ever possibly need.

The upper cabinets are stark white, and the islands are dark gray. Huge slabs of marble twisted with white and silver spread along all the countertops and islands. Recessed lighting usually brightens the whole place, but I find it a little offensive in the morning and prefer just the natural light, which pours in through all the windows.

When her eyes finally land on me, I simply wink and raise my cup before taking a noisy sip—the fucker is still hot, don't judge me.

"Mr. Moretti will be joining you," Joseph says as he walks her over to my table and plucks her clutching fingers off his arm. He heads back through the main kitchen doors, and Valentina just stands there, looking down at the table.

"Would you like a cup of coffee?" I ask, and she lifts her eyes. There's something captivating about the bright blue orbs that makes my skin tingle. There's a knowing there, but also such innocence, an innocence I want to take and fuck and shatter and own.

She chews on her lower lip then nods, her messy light brown hair falling around her face.

"Well, good. Let's get you one." I scoot out from the bench seat and stand next to her, realizing for the first time just how short she is. "How tall are you?"

"Umm..." She looks away again and starts picking at her nails. "Just under five feet." It's easy to see she's a little uncomfortable with my closeness. After the shit that went down yesterday, I can understand why, but I'm the only one who didn't yell at her or touch her, so I hope she'll feel safer with me.

Gently, I lift her chin up so I can see her face. "It's adorable."

The little thing blushes in the sweetest way, crimson running through her cheeks and down her neck. My gaze dips lower to the tight baby blue tank top hugging her breasts, her pert nipples pressed temptingly against the fabric. Her breasts aren't large, but fuck are they perky. My fingers itch to pull down the fabric and take one into my mouth, so I can scrape my teeth across her hard little nub and feel her lithe body tremble under my own.

I wonder what color they are. Pale pink or more rose in color? One thing's for sure, I can't fucking wait to find out.

The tank top ends just above her belly button, displaying her flat stomach and the sexy dip of her hips. A short pair of loose running shorts makes her legs look lean and long, even though she's just a tiny little thing.

Fuck, I'm getting an erection.

Now is not the time, soldier.

Needing to distance myself before I bend her over the table, pull her fucking pants down, fist her hair, and slam into her, I move to the coffee pot. "Come on, I won't bite."

She watches me with interest as I turn and lean against the counter—then I realize the reason she's probably so uncomfortable is because I'm naked.

Well, only half naked, though not by choice. I sleep in the nude, but I did put on a pair of dark green pajama pants before I came downstairs. That's all I have on though. Her eyes drift from my hair to my chest and abs. I make sure to flex as her gaze roams down my body. It's so intense that I can almost feel her touching me where she looks.

I work hard in the gym to look the way I do, we all do. The Morettis pride themselves on their looks and their power, both power of the mind and power of the body. It's the intimidation factor. No matter which one of us you're with, it's clear that we're strong and can manhandle anyone who fucks with us.

Fausto and I, being twins, are almost the exact same size in every way—and I mean every way. Salvatore is slightly less bulky than us, but you'd never be able to tell unless you took a measuring tape to our biceps. When we stand together, our frames look identical, three powerhouses of muscle, might, and strength.

I run my hand over my abs. "Like what you see?" This throws her completely off guard. She stumbles as if she's been struck and shakes her head. "I caught you looking."

"I'm sorry. It's just..."

"Just what?" I run my fingers through my hair, which is still down from when I slept. I don't like to sleep with it up. Her eyes widen, and I watch her struggle to find something to say. "Yes?" I roll my hand, encouraging her to continue.

"Umm." She looks so small and fragile, so pure and unsure. It's endearing to see someone like that. As the right-hand man of the mafia don, it's rare that I meet people like her. Normally the men are hard, arrogant assholes and the women are even harder. The catty bitches rip each other apart to climb to the top, to get by our sides, and to sleep in our beds.

There was a time when I loved that kind of attention, when I yearned for it. I've slept with so many women I've lost count. Each night was someone new. I'd do anything to get my dick wet, but the ramifications of each encounter were cumbersome. They wanted to exchange numbers and plot out our entire lives, when all I wanted was to bust a load and be done.

I found them snooping through my things while I slept and taking pictures of me as blackmail. Now, I make it a point to take their phones away until our time together is over. I don't have time for that shit.

"I've just never seen anyone like you before," she finally blurts out.

Her comment takes me by surprise. "Oh? Is it the beard? The hair maybe?"

Her cheeks turn crimson again, so I know it's something more than that. How sheltered has her life been that she's never seen anyone like me? She's the daughter of a powerful mafia don, so surely she's met similar men or at least seen them. She's back to picking at her fingers, so I decide to drop it. There's no sense in wasting a perfect, sunny morning. "Do you still want that cup of coffee?"

She nods, raising only her eyes. My heart pangs, and the twitch is so powerful, it shocks me. I didn't know it could do that. What is it about her that affects me so much? Her innocence or her lack of interest?

No.

She's interested, she's just too scared to admit it to me or herself.

"Come here then. Let me show you how to work the French press."

Slowly, she comes closer, and I grab a coffee cup for her, setting it on the counter. "First, you—"

"I know how to use a French press, thank you." And she does, pouring herself a steaming cup of coffee.

"Would you like sugar or cream?"

"Both if you have them."

She waits patiently while I hand her the sugar, but I pause at the fridge. "Regular or flavored creamer?"

She stirs sugar into her drink. "French vanilla if you have it, otherwise regular is fine."

"French vanilla it is then," I say, grabbing the creamer for her. She adds that too and stirs it in. The methodical way she does such a simple task tells me this is something she does routinely for herself.

I press my hand against her lower back and guide her to the breakfast table. My fingers tingle where they touch her skin, and I have the urge to grip her hips firmly and tug her down onto my lap, but I resist.

My brothers have fucked this up enough that I need to work hard to gain any sort of trust. There's enough tension in this house between Sal, Fausto, and me, and I don't want it between her and me as well.

The breakfast table is a small circle that comfortably seats six people. The custom-made bench curves along with the windows. She takes a seat on the bench, and I sit opposite her, really wanting to see her face and study her reactions. That's one thing I've gotten good at over the years, noticing people's reactions. It's become second nature for me to understand when someone is lying or hiding something.

I'm just about to start up a conversation when Fausto barges into the kitchen. "Morning."

Unlike me, he's already fully dressed in black slacks, a burgundy dress shirt, and buffed shiny black shoes. I flick my gaze to Val and see she instantly looks away from him, pretending to be interested in something out the window. Her fingers clench around her cup, her knuckles blanching. I can't tell if it's fear or anger causing this reaction.

Fausto pours himself a cup of coffee with a splash of cream and walks in our direction. "Aren't you going to say good morning back?" he asks Val. "Consider this rule number two—you speak when spoken to. If we ask you a question, you'd better be damn sure we expect an answer."

"Morning," she mumbles, staring hard into her coffee cup.

"There, that wasn't so hard, was it? Now scoot over." She darts her eyes up at me, and the look on her face is so helpless. I nod once, encouraging her to listen to Fausto, and she scoots over, her small breasts bouncing as she moves.

Fuck, this girl is going to kill me.

Or kill my dick.

One of the two.

She's so sexy, and what makes her so sexy is her complete lack of awareness of how gorgeous she is. It's clear by how she holds herself that she has no idea what her body does to men. She's completely oblivious.

The kitchen doors swing open again, and in walks Matilda, our morning help and a woman of many talents. "Good morning, sirs, ma'am," she greets before getting started in the kitchen. Matilda is Joseph's wife, an older woman with gray and white hair, which she always wears pinned to the top of her head. She wears—completely by choice—a long black maid's dress, complete with a white apron. She bustles about, pulling out pans and ingredients, and soon the smell of bacon fills the kitchen.

Valentina watches Matilda like a lion stalking its prey, her little pink tongue darting out to lick her lips.

"So," Fausto starts, spinning in his seat to face her while simultaneously blocking her from leaving the table. She's stuck between us. "Tell me about Alfonzo Capelli."

This was not a conversation we previously discussed having, but one that's important nonetheless. I've been so caught up in her closeness this morning that I forgot about the bigger picture—who she is and what she means for our future.

She runs her fingers through her hair then holds her cup tightly, her hands shaking. "Umm. He's my dad's friend."

Fausto slides his hand over her shoulder and around the back of her neck, gripping her tightly. The gesture makes me jealous, because he's touching her and I'm not. "I'm sure there's more to it than that, isn't there, kitten?"

Kitten?

That's what I fucking call her.

She winces as his fingers tighten, and her shoulders scrunch up. "I don't know what you want me to say. I only just met him for the first time a few months ago at my cousin's wedding."

Fausto releases her neck and strokes her hair. "Very good. Did anything about his personality jump out at you as strange or unusual?"

"No. We didn't even talk. He was sitting by my dad, and I was sitting by… by…"

"Yes? Fausto prompts, urging her to continue.

"My brothers," she finishes, but the tone in her voice sounds like a lie. "He never said a word to me, too busy drinking whiskey and smoking cigars with my dad."

Fausto wraps his arm around her shoulders and pulls her into his side. "Was anyone else from his family there that night?"

I see her shutting down minute by minute. I had her relaxed and talking until he came in. "Just drop it for now, Fausto. Let the girl have something to eat, you can interrogate her later."

Fausto purses his lips. "Fine. I'm hungry anyway."

Matilda brings over a tray filled with crispy bacon, a bowl of strawberries, syrup, whipped cream, and a pile of waffles. "Breakfast, sirs, ma'am."

I take a heated plate with an oversized waffle. "Thanks, Matilda. You're dismissed."

Matilda offers us a small curtsy as Fausto grabs a waffle as well. "You need to eat," he says, sliding the plate in front of Val.

"I'm not hungry."

"You have to be," I argue. "I know you haven't eaten since yesterday."

"Yeah, thanks for dinner," she mumbles, then claps her hands to her mouth, realizing she said that out loud.

Fausto, ignoring her outburst, coats her waffle with syrup and strawberries, and adds a squirt of whipped cream. "If you had behaved earlier, you would have been fed. I told you to be a good girl and you didn't listen." He cuts her a bite of waffle and holds it up to her lips. "Open."

She moves to take the fork. "I can feed myself."

"But you're not," he counters. "I gave you a chance to feed yourself and you made the decision to fucking starve. Since you clearly are incapable of doing something as simple as feeding yourself, it's now up to us to see that you eat. We have plans for you, so we can't have you withering away. You're small enough as it is."

"But I—"

Fausto cuts her off. "It's not up for discussion. Open your fucking mouth or I'll open it for you."

Valentina parts her pink lips, and my brother slips the bite of waffle inside. I have visions of her mouth opening for something larger before she sucks my cock down her throat as I tangle my fingers in her long hair.

She chews, and Fausto cuts off another bite. She tries to take it, but he swats her hand away and bumps the bite into her lips.

"You should listen to Fausto," I urge, finishing my first waffle and grabbing a second. "He just wants to make sure you eat."

She glares and accepts the bite. He grins back, then cuts off a bite and eats it himself. She looks at him incredulously for using her fork.

Before he can cut her another bite, she picks up the dripping waffle with her fingers and takes a bite as if it were a big, juicy burger.

I can't help but laugh. "Well, that's one way to beat the system."

"I'll be damned," Fausto says with a hint of humor while grabbing his own plate of food.

The rest of the meal is silent. Val munches on her waffle while my twin and I grab seconds and thirds. When she finishes, she sits back, resting her forearms on the table to hold up her sticky hands.

Fausto grabs a napkin. "Let me help you with that." He takes her left hand and wraps the napkin around her pinkie, but before she can pull away, he slips her pointer finger into his mouth and sucks the syrup off.

Val's eyes widen, and she gasps, that blush creeping up her neck again.

"Fausto can't have all the fun," I complain, grabbing her right hand and doing the same. I work methodically, gently sucking the syrup off each tiny finger while keeping an eye on her reaction. Her pupils dilate, her chest rises and falls faster, and her little nipples become more defined as they harden.

Whether her mind wants to like us or not, her body does, and her response has my dick thickening.

Fausto moans as I finish cleaning her last finger. "We could lick syrup off other places, kitten. Just give us the word and we will rock your world." He grabs the pitcher of syrup and pours some on her chest. Val doesn't move. With her hands captured by Fausto and me, and her exits blocked, she has nowhere else to go.

But she also doesn't try to stop us.

The syrup drips down between her breasts and over her tank top. I lock eyes with my twin, and a knowing look passes between us. We've shared dozens of women over the years. We're experts at this.

Pressing her hands against the back cushion of the bench, Fausto and I lower our heads and lap at her chest. I start at the top, licking along her skin before moving down to her nipple. I lap at the hard tip, soaking her shirt as little gasps leave her mouth. Fausto mimics me, and we work her nipples simultaneously until she begins to shake.

"Oh God," she whispers as we pull down her tank and bare her perfect breasts.

"Fuck," Fausto groans as he grabs the whipped cream.

"Fuck," I agree, taking her in. Her breasts are perfect, just more than a handful with plump, dark pink nipples that beg me for a taste.

My brother squirts whipped cream on each nipple, and then we feast, licking and sucking. I slide my teeth along the tight bud to see how hard I can make it. Valentina's head falls back as she gives in to the sensations, her mouth open and eyes closed as she shivers from the pleasure.

"Well, I wasn't expecting to see this when I woke up today."

Sal's voice rumbles through the kitchen. Fausto and I exchange an annoyed look, her nipples still sucked between our lips.

Sal walks farther into the kitchen, stopping about five feet from us. "Don't stop on my account. By all means, continue. Let's see what the little Rossi whore has to offer."

My blood begins to boil at his blatant disdain. He hasn't even tried to get to know her or see who she really is, instead judging her for being part of a family she didn't ask to be born into.

Fausto and I release her, and I move to fix her shirt when I hear Sal cock his gun. I freeze and put my hands up to placate him, but that's not enough. Sal's switch has flipped. "I said don't stop. Go on, touch our new plaything. Squeeze her breasts and pinch those little nipples until the whore winces in pain." The sights of his firearm are aimed at Val. "That's what you are, right?" he taunts. "A little whore flashing her titties at the first man to look at her."

"It wasn't like that," I defend.

"Oh?" Sal tilts his head to the side, his eyes fixed on Val's chest. "Then tell me, what was it like, because I'd very much like to know. Go on. Touch her."

"I'm not doing this," Fausto grumbles, pushing away from the bench. "You're out of line, Sal."

Sal shifts the gun, now aiming it at my twin, and looks at him incredulously. "You're the one pleasuring a filthy Rossi, and I'm the one out of line?"

Tears well in Val's eyes and drip down her cheeks, though she keeps her cries silent. It's pitiful, her sitting here with her tits out while three grown men argue over her.

Fuck it.

I pull Valentina behind me and block her while I fix her tank top. "I'm sorry about this," I whisper as I grab her hand and pull her out of the bench. I know Sal won't shoot us, this is all for show to incite fear in Val, and it's fucking working.

Her shoulders shake as I lead her through the kitchen and hand her off to Joseph. "Help her run a bath, please."

Joseph looks at Val sadly, his lips pulled down in a disapproving manner. He's not disappointed in her, but in me, and I hate that.

"Come along, dear," he says softly, offering her his arm. This time, though, she doesn't take it. Instead, she hugs herself as she shuffles behind Joseph, and my chest clenches at the sight.

Once she's safely upstairs and out of view, I barge back into the kitchen. I'm fucking pissed.

"What the fuck are you doing, Sal?" I can't contain my anger, my frustration.

He cuts up a waffle and carefully chews a bite. "You were out of line, I was just bringing you back in."

"Oh, cut the shit," Fausto yells, snatching Sal's plate and slamming it into the nearest wall. Sal fumes as Fausto shouts at him. "The hate you have for her is next level. What has that poor girl ever done to you to deserve this?"

I'm shocked by Fausto's reaction, but I agree with it.

"Because she's hiding something," Sal replies calmly. Sometimes I hate how calm he can be. I want him to shout back, to fight with us and stand his ground instead of putting up the front he's been hiding behind for so long. "I've been watching this whole interaction on the security cameras. I watched her deflect when you asked about Alfonzo Capelli. She's hiding something and we're about to find out what."

Sal reaches into his pocket and pulls out a cellphone. By the pink glittery case, I already know whose it is.

"Val's phone," I say, and Sal dips his head.

"Precisely." He wags it in the air then pockets it again. "It's dead, but in an hour or two, it will be charged, and then we'll get some answers. In the meantime, you two keep your cocks in your pants. Understand?"

"You can't tell me what to do with my cock, Sal," Fausto argues.

"I can't," Sal agrees. "But I'm asking you to wait until we see what's on this phone. After that you can fuck her as often as you want."

Fausto and I lock eyes before I answer. "Fine. Then no more of your bullshit. The girl is ours, and if we want to play with her, you're not going to stop us."

Sal pushes up from the table. "Fine." He checks his watch and looks toward the kitchen doors. "I have a meeting to attend. We'll check in later." He leaves, and Fausto and I stare at each other, completely at a loss.

Our brother is losing it. Can we help him find himself again, or are we on the verge of losing him forever?

CHAPTER TWENTY-THREE

Valentina

W<small>HAT THE HELL</small> was I thinking?

I cover my face with my hands, shaking my head in disbelief and embarrassment as Joseph locks the door to my bedroom behind me.

I'm so fucking stupid, letting them touch me like that, and then to have Sal walk in with my shirt pulled down and both his brothers licking my chest…

It was so embarrassing.

I should know better, be stronger, and find my voice to say no, but the thing is, I didn't want to say no. I wanted to say yes. I wanted to say more. I've never had a man's lips on my body like that, and I didn't know how good it could feel to have my nipples kissed. It was incredible. My body came alive, trembling uncontrollably, while my clit fucking ached.

It still aches, even minutes after leaving the kitchen. I was almost desperate for someone to touch it, either the twins or myself, and that's not something I've ever wanted before. I've never masturbated, but fuck… Those twins switched something inside of me and awakened a part of me that has been asleep my whole life.

Maybe it has something to do with turning eighteen. Gabe even said that everything was going to change. He said I'm a woman now, so maybe this is what he meant.

I can't think about that now, it's too confusing. Yesterday, I hated them all—well, maybe not Armani, but I definitely didn't like him—and today he was… different. He wasn't sweet, but he wasn't mean either. And fuck… Armani's body is so unbelievable I had to do a double take. He is all tan skin with defined muscles, muscles I didn't know men could even have. I thought Marco was built, but he looks like a small French fry compared to Armani. And not just Armani, they are all around the same size, though I've only seen Armani without his shirt on.

The way those pajama pants hung low on his hips with the little line of dark hair leading from his belly button down… It made me want to explore him. I wanted to let my fingers roam over his skin and feel him. I wanted to taste him like he was tasting me.

And to think I thought Marco was a real man.

Speaking of Marco…

I don't know why I didn't tell them about him. I don't know why I lied. The mere mention of his name makes me feel sick. I just didn't want to relive what he put me through, what he did to me, and what he promised he would do in the future. I almost mentioned the meeting Alfonzo and my father had at the wedding, and how disgruntled Alfonzo appeared when they returned to the table, but it didn't seem relevant.

Marco isn't a man they need to be worried about. He's not a man, he's a child, a big fucking child. The way these men act, though I don't like all their behavior, is not comparable to what Marco did. Yes, Sal had a gun pointed at my head, but Marco had a gun too, he was just too drunk to brandish it about. I'm grateful for that.

Part of me wasn't even scared of Sal's gun, maybe because Fausto and Armani were there. I knew they wouldn't let anything happen to me, not after what we just did together. It opened a door that I thought was sealed shut, and it makes me realize that maybe there can be something between us in the future. Maybe I won't be locked in this room for years to come.

Maybe.

Maybe.

Maybe.

That word churns around in my head like the violent winds of a tornado, crashing through every possible outcome to every fucking scenario. It's exhausting.

Dropping my hands, I walk through my room and into the bathroom. It's time to take a shower and rinse the remnants of syrup and the twins' lips off my body.

Instead of turning on the light, I open the large window and let the cool morning air and sunlight pour inside before stripping down. After fiddling with the buttons again, I get the tub to fill and decide to soak in there for a bit. It's not like I have a lot going on today.

I can't find any bubble bath, so I drizzle some body wash into the tub to create bubbles then slip inside. It's been so long since I've taken a bath that I've forgotten how relaxing it is. The warm water laps gently at my body, and when I close my eyes, I almost forget where I am.

I duck under the water once, wetting all my hair, before resting my arms along the back of the tub and lying my head back. Shit, I might stay in here for the rest of the day and just keep filling up the tub until I'm one giant walking prune.

Splashing some soapy water over my chest, I rub at what's left of the syrup. My fingers glide over my nipples, which harden under my touch. I've never really played with them before, but after what the twins did…

With my bottom lip gripped tightly between my teeth, I play with them, rolling them between my fingers, tugging them away from my body. They get harder, longer, and my clit starts to throb again.

I slide one hand down my belly and under the water, spreading my legs to explore myself.

"Do you always have men fight your battles for you, baby girl?"

I freeze, my eyes flying open to see Sal standing just outside the glass.

"What the fuck are you doing in here?" I shout, sinking low under the bubbles to hide myself. "I don't have anything to say to you."

Sal pulls out his gun again, studying it as if it were an item he's never seen before. "I like you better when you're not talking anyway. Some women should be seen and not heard. In a few years, when you're not a little baby girl anymore, that will be the life you lead."

I struggle to gather the fleeting bubbles, pushing them back over myself. "Didn't your mother teach you that if you have nothing nice to say, then don't say anything at all?"

Sal starts to pace the length of the bathroom. "Don't talk about my mom. Your filthy Rossi lips don't deserve to speak her name."

My blood begins to boil. "I'm not keeping you captive in here. Feel free to leave at any time so I can finish my bath."

Sal laughs and spins to face me, looking at the wall above me. "Your bath... Just like a little baby girl. Speaking of babies..." Sal reaches inside his suit coat and pulls out a folded piece of paper. "This is from your doctor. Dr. Christine, was it?"

My stomach plummets. Why would he have paperwork from there?

He rolls up the paper and slaps it against his hand. "She said your vagina is in perfect health. Let's keep her that way. See these?" He holds up a little purple case about the size of a credit card. "These are birth control pills. You will take them every day from now on. If you're going to be a whore, then I'll have to take proper precautions so that my brothers or any other man doesn't impregnate you before I marry you off. It would be... embarrassing for the Morettis."

Is he fucking serious right now? "I'm not a whore," I grit out.

"We'll see about that. Hell, maybe you're right. A protected little princess like you probably has no real-world experience. You probably don't even know how to use your own cunt, much less a man's cock. Tell me, have you ever had a man inside of you before?" He moves closer to the glass, pressing his hands on the outside, the gun still clutched in one of them. "Have you ever had a man fuck you senseless or choke you with his cum?"

"That's none of your business," I retort, folding my hands over my chest as the last of the bubbles retreats. "Please stop looking at me."

"You think I want to look at your disgusting Rossi body? You think it does anything for me?" The look on his face is pure disdain, and his eyes turn wild. "You might have won over my brothers by flaunting your perfect body, but I won't be enticed by you. Not now. Not ever."

Does he even realize he just said I have a perfect body? "You say you don't want to look, but then why sneak into my bathroom, not once, but twice? Stop lying to yourself."

I don't know where this is coming from. Salvatore Moretti is a terrifying man, and yet here I am, completely at his mercy but standing up to him. I'm proud of myself.

"Don't believe me? I'll prove it. Get out of the tub."

Sal takes a step back then starts undressing. First he removes his suit jacket, then his shirt. I'm distracted by his sculpted body, which is decorated almost completely by tattoos, and by the shock of him stripping in front of me.

"I'm not getting out."

He unfastens his belt, then lets his pants drop to the floor, leaving him only in a pair of tight boxer briefs. "Get out of the fucking tub, or I'll come in there and get you."

There's no way out of this. There's no door for me to run to and no one to come help me if I shout. I don't know what to do. The look in his eyes makes me want to listen, fearful of the ramifications of pissing him off when his gaze appears soulless, like empty sockets vacant of emotion. Even his brothers seem to coddle him, making me more inclined to listen.

"Fine. Then hand me a towel."

By now, the water is cold and I'm shivering a little bit, causing goosebumps to cover my arms. Sal opens a lower cabinet and pulls out a towel, then he throws it two feet in front of him. "Come and get it."

I shake my head. "Sal, what are you trying to prove here? That you don't want me? That's fine. I believe you."

"You don't." Sal slips his fingers under the band of his boxers and slides them down his body. The man is well manicured. He's not totally shaven, but neatly trimmed, making me feel self-conscious about my own crotch. I've still never trimmed or done anything because I've never had a need to. Sure, I've shaved my inner thighs on the few occasions I've worn a bathing suit in public, but the main bush is still intact. Now I realize how right he is. I don't know how to use my own... cunt.

There.

I said it.

Cunt.

Cunt.

Cunt.

If I'm going to be a big girl, then I need to use big girl words.

"Now who's looking?" he accuses with a hint of humor in his tone.

"Why are you naked, Sal?" I ask, ignoring him, forcing my eyes to look anywhere else.

"To prove your body does nothing for me. Now get the fuck out of that tub and stand in front of me. My cock won't even jerk at the sight of you."

I can't believe this is happening. I really can't believe it. Never in my life have I wanted to hide so badly and to become a shadow in the dark.

But here I am, stuck in a bathroom with a naked man who is ordering me to stand naked before him. What choice do I really have? Either I comply, or I deal with what might happen if I don't, and I'm not willing to take that risk.

Besides, it's just skin, right? Everyone has a body.

Oh, who am I kidding? This is mortifying on the lowest level.

"Now, Valentina." His voice is low and threatening. "You have five seconds to stand up, or I'm coming in to get you, and I can promise you that you won't like what happens when I do."

With tears welling in my eyes and my lower lip trembling, I grip the sides of the tub with my hands and pull myself up. I attempt to cover myself, one hand cupping my crotch and the other draped across my chest.

"Out of the shower too," he orders. "Come get this towel before I take it away."

Holding back my tears, I swallow hard, push at the glass door with the side of my body, and slowly walk over to him. I keep my head down and eyes lowered as I force myself to move step by step.

I stop at the towel and move to pick it up, but he steps on it with his foot. "I didn't say you could pick it up. Didn't your mother teach you to respect your elders and listen to grown-ups?" He says the last bit in a voice to mimic my own, and a part of me dies inside.

"Drop your hands. Let me have a look at your disgusting Rossi body while you watch my dick. Come on. Eyes up. I want you to memorize every fucking vein in my limp fucking cock."

"Please," I whisper, tears flowing freely down my cheeks as my shoulders shake. "You wouldn't want this happening to your sister, would you?"

He pauses for a moment at the mention of his sister, but he shakes off any empathy he might have felt, and then his next words are firm. "Drop your hands."

I choke out a sob. Defeated, I uncover myself. I don't look up to see his reaction. I don't want to see his perception of me.

"Good. Now you'll pose for me so I can get a better look at you. I want you to brush your hair behind your shoulders, then lock your hands behind your head, and part your legs about two feet."

It's so hard to move. The tremors in my body even make breathing hard. I've never been more ashamed or more humiliated than I am in this moment as I move my hair and lock my hands behind my head, my breasts completely exposed.

He prowls toward me, a snarl on his lips as he walks behind me. "No, like this." He pulls my elbows back and presses on my upper back, forcing my chest out, then he kicks at my ankles until I spread my legs far enough for him.

Please, Lord, take me now.

"Why are you doing this?" I ask on a soft cry.

"To prove how little you mean to me." He runs his hands up and down my sides then grips my ass hard. "To prove your body has no effect on me." He slides his hands up to my breasts, gently brushing his fingers over my nipples. "To prove that no matter how sexy you think you are, no matter how much your body reacts to mine, I'll never want you. I'll never love you. I'm just doing my duty to my family."

He pinches my nipples, and I cry out, dropping my hands to pull him off. He pushes me forward, and I stumble into the countertop, but he's on me in a second, his chest pressed to my back. He seizes my arms behind my back with one strong hand, and with the other, he grips one of my legs behind my knee and lifts my foot onto the countertop, the movement spreading my lower lips open wide.

"There she is!" he exclaims, licking his lips. "Every inch of you is exposed and displayed for me. Today you were hiding something, some information you don't want us to know. Now you recognize you can't hide from me. Not when I have you pinned in your own bathroom, stripped naked and vulnerable, your fucking cunt open for me if I wanted it." He moves his hand over my crotch and pats it. "See all this?" He tugs on my pubic hair. "Just like I said, you're a sheltered baby girl. You have no idea how to use your own cunt. You can't even take care of yourself. Has this thing ever had a haircut?"

My words are lost on soft sobs as he releases me, and I collapse onto the ground. I was so strong just a moment ago, so proud of sticking up for myself, but this man has torn me down and crushed my spirit because part of what he says is true.

"Look at me," he growls. "Look at my limp fucking dick. I can't even get hard for you, can't even get hard for free fucking pussy."

While I hug myself and cry, Sal gets dressed. "I'll have answers soon, and for your sake, they had better be the answers I want to hear."

He storms out of the bathroom, leaving me in shambles. I thought I'd hit rock bottom before, but this is an all-time low. The humiliation he makes me feel with such ease is something I'm not sure I can ever recover from.

CHAPTER TWENTY-FOUR

Fausto

I MOAN SOFTLY, my cock fisted in my hand as I jerk myself rapidly. I can't get her out of my head. I can't stop thinking about the way her skin tasted, how her nipple felt rolling over my tongue, and how her body began to shake from the pleasure.

I can't stop thinking about the soft gasps expelled from her perfect lips, and the way she submitted to Armani and me so beautifully.

Squeezing myself tighter, I pretend my cock is slipping in and out of her cunt and imagine what it might look like spread open for me, her little clit swollen as I fuck her senseless. I visualize what she looks like when she comes, the flush of her skin and the sounds she might make.

And then I come, grunting louder than I wanted to, shooting my cum into the tissue.

I need to get the fuck out of here.

Being near that girl is fucking with my head and twisting my emotions. A dark part of me wants to follow Sal and fuck with the girl. For as long as the Outfit has been assembled, the Cosa Nostra has been our most hated enemy. It's easy to understand why. The pampered fucks think they are better than us, the true Italian Mafia.

Now here we are, proud owners of the Cosa Nostra princess, and a princess she is. Armani and I agree she's not a savage like her dad is known to be, but so far, Sal can't be swayed. He thinks she's just as violent and that her sweet demeanor is hiding a monster within. He can't see, and doesn't realize, that he's the monster. He's turning into the man he hates most in the world—Carlo Rossi.

As I exchange my suit for my disguise of tight faded jeans, an 80s band shirt paired with a leather vest, and black leather boots, I think about what happened this morning in the kitchen.

The little pistol melted under our touch. Surprisingly, if I hadn't been there, I don't think Armani would have made the move like I did, but he sure followed suit. Dripping syrup over Valentina's breasts and sucking them off made my cock so fucking hard that I had to jerk off.

It's rare that I have to step away from my day to masturbate, because I can usually control myself, but Val… she's driving me wild.

Zipping up my jeans, I try to wash the sexy image of her from my mind. I turn toward the mirror and transform from Fausto Moretti to Tony Caruso, cage fighter. Using dark eye liner, I trace my eyes then smear it, giving me a haunted look, and then I grease my hair with baby oil to make it look like I haven't showered in days.

I take black eyeshadow and drag my nails across it, forcing the black to slip under them. My watch, rings, and necklaces all come off and sit inside a little box within my closet.

I'm ready.

Taking a rear elevator, I head down into the garage and select Tony's car—a souped up Jeep Wrangler Rubicon with a lift kit and subwoofers that make your ass feel like it's in the middle of an earthquake's aftershock.

The engine revs to life, and I shift my electric blue Jeep into gear, driving up and out of my garage. Turning up the volume, I blast old-school grunge music to get myself in the headspace for a fight, beating on my steering wheel to the tune of each song.

WILTED ORCHID

Exiting the suburbs and heading into the city makes my whole body come alive. The sights and sounds, the stink of people, the exhaust fumes, the food stands, and the neon blinking lights, it's all part of the experience. Tony loves this shit, he lives for this shit.

And right now, I'm ready for a battle.

I drive through the gritty part of Chicago, the parts travelers do their best to stay far away from, where homes are boarded up, basketball courts have broken hoops with chain nets, and gangs try to hustle drugs on every corner.

Tony lets them move their product, because more than likely, it came from us. The people here know me, and when they see my blue Jeep coming down their road, they give me looks of respect. Everyone knows what kind of fighter I am and the list of opponents I've taken down.

Money is thrown my way as bets are placed and won, because I use my fists to crush anyone who steps into the ring with me. I don't lose. I never lose.

I swing left and head to the old steel factory that's long since been abandoned by once hard-working men and women. Charred smokestacks rise toward the sky, no longer expelling pollution into the world. Instead, they have become the favorite resting place for ravens and crows, who squawk at us as we head inside.

Graffiti covers the outer walls in a colorful display. One image is of Jimi Hendrix absolutely shredding on a guitar with a joint hanging from his lips. Another has a pair of women kissing. Both are bare chested with heavy breasts and defined nipples.

Driving slowly over the potholes and gravel that make up the long driveway, I swing the Jeep into a parking spot and shift her into park. A crowd has already gathered, and cars litter the parking lot. Blaring music pounds from inside the factory, the deep bass rumbling my chest as I pull open the door and step inside.

You'd never know this wasn't built to be a nightclub. Black paint covers the high windows, making it permanently nighttime inside. A makeshift bar spreads across the back wall, where the barstools are filled with people drinking and smoking, even though it's only midafternoon. Black lights shine from above, causing the white on people's outfits to glow, accentuating more graffiti splattered across the walls. On the right side of the old factory is a boxing ring. Folding chairs are lined up around it in rows, where the crowd will gather to watch the night's fights.

Across the looming, cinder block wall are the words "The Crater," which glow in the black light. That's exactly what this place is, a huge fucking hole in the ground where some venture and never return from.

We don't just fight within these walls, we battle. Sometimes our very lives are on the line if the prize money is high enough and the fighters are desperate. Death matches are rare, but they do happen, and the money passed around for them is unimaginable, especially for people of this level in society.

Traditionally, the lowlifes are poor, but it's my belief that there are those with money, people like me, who come here wearing their own disguises, pretending to be someone new.

I HEAD around the bar to the back corner where a bookie named Fast Stan, who is quick with words and even quicker with cash, is taking money and making matchups. Whispers follow me as I walk, and people turn their heads and point at the infamous Tony Caruso.

"Tony!" Fast Stan greets with excitement, a freshly lit cigarette hanging from his lips. "I was beginning to think you might not be coming back."

I shove my hands deep into my pockets and lower my voice. "I always come back, don't I?"

Fast Stan licks his thumb then counts a stack of twenty-dollar bills. "It's been a few weeks. People have been talking."

I'm not surprised. After our last batch of product was stolen by the long dead thief, I needed to take out some aggression. Naturally, I came here and threw myself into a death match. I didn't do it for the money, but for the adrenaline rush that came with it. I craved the rush and the euphoria it brought me, allowing me to forget everything else happening in my life.

I didn't just fight the man who stepped in the ring with me, though, I destroyed him. Blood was everywhere, splattering the people sitting in the first couple rows. His beaten, lifeless body was left on display while I rubbed his blood into my skin, shouting out my victory like I'd lost my mind. "And what have they been saying exactly?"

Fast Stan flicks his dark eyes up to mine and takes a long drag from his cigarette, blowing the smoke right in my face. "That you have lost it, Tony."

Fausto Moretti would have shot a man for doing something like that. Tony, on the other hand, has to play it cool, so I shrug it off. "I had a bad day and took it out on my opponent. I didn't force him to enter a death match. He chose his own fate."

"And how has your day been today?" he asks, counting another stack, hundreds this time.

I think back on this morning, on the little pistol of a girl's sweet breasts, remembering how sexy she was while Armani and I licked whipped cream off her nipples. "Good actually. Now enough with the bullshit, Stan. Do you have a fight for me or not?"

Fast Stan flips through his books, running his finger down a list of names. "Ahh, here's a good match. You'll be fighting Dagmar Sullivan in the third round."

I nod once, accepting the fight, and head off to the bar. My routine is always the same, I perch my ass on the very last barstool, making whoever is sitting there move. Some of the newer clients who don't know Tony Caruso try to tell me to fuck off, but they learn my name fast when I throw them to the ground and dump their drink over their heads. Everyone knows you don't fuck with Tony Caruso.

Luckily, the man sitting in my seat recognizes me as I walk over and steps off when I'm a few feet from him. The brownnosing fuck even offers to buy my first drink. I let him, not even saying thanks as a whiskey on the rocks slides into my hand.

The barmaid is a woman named Crystal who's in her mid-fifties, with crazy permed hair still stuck in 1985 and a pair of huge fake tits shoved into a leather vest. Her skin so severely weathered from years of tanning beds that I think I could wear it through a hike in the Himalayas and not freeze to death. Her dark eyeliner makes her look mean and unapproachable, putting even these dogs in their place.

Deep down, however, I know she's a sweetheart. She puts up a front like I do in order to survive a place like this. Plus, the men here love her. Not only is she a great bartender, but for a price, she'll flash you her tits.

I've seen them, and I'm not impressed, but the dogs here will do anything for a close look at a pair of titties.

There's not a lot to choose from in The Crater. Men don't bring their women here unless they are new and don't know any better. You can bet she'll be hit on and groped right in front of you if you're not careful.

There are no limits here, no rules, and no police to force you to stop. There's just liquor, money, and blood. That's it.

Static emits from speakers mounted high in the rafters, and the crowd grows silent as they turn to the ring. "Introducing our first fight of the night," the announcer's voice blares. "Tristin Montague versus Johnny Bear."

Oh, Tristin and Johnny. This will be a good fight. I've met Johnny in the ring only once, and he nearly took me down. I blame my performance on too much whiskey, but I'm not sure that's entirely accurate. Johnny is a trained fighter who's been boxing since his youth. The only reason he didn't go professional is because he suffered a coma shortly after his last underground match, and not because he didn't win, but because he got so fucking black-out drunk in celebration that he wrecked his car. His lack of a seat belt caused him to be launched through his windshield like a missile. He was down for several weeks and had to work his way back.

Now, like me, he takes his aggression, his failures, out on the man standing in the ring across from him.

Johnny and Tristin enter from the back room where fighters prepare for their battles and climb into the ring. Tristin is new to the scene and doesn't have a lot of supporters. Johnny is well loved, a sure bet for those gambling, and the crowd cheers loudly in support of him.

I haven't even finished my second drink when Tristin connects hard with Johnny's face. Blood flies from Johnny's lips, but like a good fighter, he turns his pain into aggression.

Spinning, Johnny lands a kick to Tristin's temple, and just like that, the match is over. After a quick ten count, it's clear Tristin isn't getting up. The fucker is knocked out cold.

Celebrations can be heard throughout The Crater and money is exchanged. Tristin's limp body is extracted from the ring and the mat is cleaned while the second pairing is announced.

The speakers crackle again as the announcer speaks. "For our next fight, please welcome Gary Robinson and Ferdinand Carmona."

Oh, please. Both Gary and Ferdinand are full-time losers. Gary usually shows up drunk with puke covering his already stained shirts, and Ferdinand is a known slime bag who's always on the hunt for a new prostitute to fuck.

My money would be on Ferdinand, though, because he won't be as drunk as Gary.

The bell chimes and the fight begins. Gary holds his own, taking blow after blow but rising back up. Ferdinand gasses out, his chest rising and falling fast as he circles Gary. Gary sees an opportunity and swipes at Ferdinand's legs, striking his ankles. Ferdinand falls to the ground and Gary leaps behind Ferdinand, seizing him around the neck and executing a surprisingly good sleep hold.

Too exhausted to fight, Ferdinand swings his arms and bats at the air. When he finally hangs his head, Gary lets him go and begins to celebrate, pumping his fists into the air, but the joke is on Gary, because Ferdinand wasn't down—he was playing dead. Now the corpse is rising from his grave.

Ferdinand stands behind Gary and taps him once on the shoulder. Gary spins around and meets Ferdinand's right fist. Gary flies across the mat, blood seeping from his nose and mouth. The ref begins the ten count, and Gary tries to pull himself up, but he doesn't make it farther than his knees before he's falling back over.

I don't watch the end of the match, finishing my second drink and tipping Crystal a crisp Benjamin. It's my time to get ready, to get in the right mindset to take on the poor fuck assigned to me. In the back room, I shed my leather vest and jeans for a pair of boxing shorts and a mouthguard. I lather up my skin with oil until I'm shiny and slippery, and then I begin to stretch.

It's not long before my name's called. Tony Caruso doesn't lose, and that poor bastard is about to learn his lesson taught by my fists and feet.

It's the perfect distraction.

Here, I don't think about the information Val is withholding from us.

Here, I don't miss my sister, Lily, and worry that Alejandro Hernandez isn't taking care of her like he should.

Here, I'm not concerned about Sal, who's spiraling out of control.

Here, all that matters is blood, sweat, and the sweet taste of victory.

CHAPTER TWENTY-FIVE

Salvatore

Pacing.
　Pacing.
　Pacing.
　Back and forth, I weave through my wing of the house. I stride through the bedroom, across the living room, into the bathroom, and back again. I can't sit still because the moment I do, all I see is her.
　I see her gorgeous blue eyes.
　I see her lithe body.
　I see the fear and pain in her gaze.
　And I'm the one who put it there.
　But I can't stop. I must continue this front and keep these walls fortified with the strongest steel and thickest concrete. I can't let her in, I won't let her in. Even if I am to marry this girl, I'll remain steadfast in my determination to never let another woman into my heart for as long as I live. I've promised myself I won't.
　There are times when the mere thought of her makes my skin

crawl with disgust. How can someone born with Rossi blood look and sound like her? How can someone whose lineage is tainted with the spilled blood of others have such an innocence about them?

She's submissive in the most perfect way. The quiet sobs that escaped her lips when I put her in her place almost did me in. Though I try to deny it, my cock was rock fucking hard when I left her.

Rock. Fucking. Hard.

I came straight up to my room to rub one out, yet it did nothing to alleviate the pain, craving, and desire I feel for this girl.

My future wife…

Maybe I'll let Fausto have her, or Armani.

The treaty never said which one of us had to marry her. It was always assumed it would be me because I'm the oldest, but how much older am I really? Eleven months is nothing. Hell, for three weeks each year, my brothers and I are the same age.

The Irish triplets…

I fucking hate that moniker. I've hated it ever since I can remember. What Italian man wouldn't? I immediately associate any Irish word with the Kellys, and believe me, there's not much worse scum on the earth than Tiernan fucking Kelly and his goons, Colin and Shay.

I could count my blessings, but I'd rather tally my sins.

Pausing in front of the bathroom mirror, I stare at my reflection with pure fucking hatred. I hate who I am, who I've allowed myself to become. I feel like I'm drowning without a life vest, my wrists split open and my blood pouring out of my heart and into the world around me.

I'm losing myself.

A stranger stares back at me in the mirror. A stranger with wild eyes and a racing heart that doesn't know how to feel. My reality is skewed, I know that. I've lied to myself about how I really feel for so long that I now believe the lie, living a life of deception because the real world is too much to process.

I fucking hate myself.

Hate. Hate. Hate.

And I hate her…

Or is my hatred another fabrication of the truth, something I force myself to believe in order to thwart the potential for pain? What happened to Gianna broke me, changed me. I'll never be that man again, and I refuse to be the cause of someone else's death, someone innocent.

I re-fucking-fuse.

Unable to look at myself another moment, I head back into the living room and over to the end table where Valentina's cell phone charges. It's been charging for an hour, and I forced myself not to look. There are answers there, I'm sure of it. I'm just not sure I want to know them just yet because I don't know how I'll react to what I'll find.

When the madness takes over, I become blind to the world around me. I don't think, I react, allowing my anger and hostility to take control. It's easier that way. I don't have to think or feel. Anger is easier to tolerate than heartache and pain. I'd rather be pissed at the world than let my heart beat for someone else once more, so I've become stone, an empty shell casing whose shots have long since been fired.

I'm a wild animal, deranged and hungry, relying on instinct instead of rational thought. Starving and feral, the only way to satiate myself now is to cause pain in others. I focus on their agony, and it allows me to bury my own deep inside me.

And I've chosen my victim.

I try not to think about my sister, Lily, as I unplug Valentina's phone and glance at the background on her screen. It's a picture of her and her brothers that must have been taken years ago when they were all still kids. Palm trees cast shadows over the four smiling kids, each one wearing a floral bathing suit, the blue ocean glistening behind them.

It's hard to imagine Valentina and her brothers as children this young, children who knew nothing of the hatred and lies fueled by the mafia wars. I wonder if the treaty had already been sealed when this was taken, if her future and fate had been decided for her before she even learned how to write in cursive.

Seeing her young face reminds me so much of Lily, my heart softens for a moment, but then I remember how everything has changed. Lily is now the bride of Alejandro Hernandez, a soulless monster. I can only pray that he spares her his malice, his anger.

I think about Val's brothers and how they must care for her like I do for Lily, and I hate myself even more. Our fathers swore to protect the daughters given to their sons. We swore to keep them safe, and here I am shitting on the treaty.

I preach about how it's my fucking duty to have her here, but I'm not really holding up the Moretti's side of the bargain. Sure, she has food and a roof over her head, but I'm not really taking care of her. None of us are.

She's been sent to a lion's den, a den with three hungry males thirsting for a bite. We all want a piece of her, but we want to treat that piece very differently.

I'm sure she's confused and scared, and I'd be fucking furious to know Lily felt the same way. Yet here I am, unable to move past the, well, past, and unable to see through the blinders I've placed over my eyes.

I can't live like that, wondering, worrying, and feeling unsure. Instead, I've willed my heart to turn to stone and forced my face not to show emotion. I can't look at the girl because if I do, *I* feel, and I don't like what feelings emerge.

Valentina's phone warms in my hand as I stare at her family photo. I try to open it several times, but she's got a facial recognition lock in place. The only way I'm getting into this thing is by shoving it in her face. The issue is, I don't want her to know I have it, not until I know all the secrets hiding within.

Her phone shows the time is 4:30PM, just before dinner.

Dinner…

That could be my key to unlocking the secrets on her phone. Matilda should be in the kitchen now preparing something wonderful for dinner. I miss her cooking, not because I don't eat it anymore, but because food has no pleasure for me these days. It's purely a requirement in life so my body doesn't shut down.

I don't enjoy it, which is a shame because that woman can cook her ass off.

I head back into the bathroom and fix myself, straightening the collar of my shirt, styling my hair, and ensuring my face is devoid of emotion before heading downstairs.

The scents of tomato and basil filter through the house, and my mouth begins to water.

"What's on the menu for dinner, Matilda?" I ask kindly as she bustles about the kitchen.

"Good afternoon, sir," she greets, moving between several pots that are cooking on the stove. "Tonight, I'm making my famous lasagna."

"It smells amazing," I praise. "Will Joseph be bringing our guest her dinner?"

Matilda grabs a tablespoon and tastes her sauce, then adds more seasoning. "That's up to you, sir."

I ponder my situation for a moment, fingering the sleeping pills in my pocket. If I bring her dinner, she might not eat it just to spite me, especially after I bared her little ass this morning.

If I slip the pills into her food, however, she might eat enough of them to fall peacefully asleep. "I'd like to prepare her plate myself. Let me know when it's ready."

Matilda begins layering her lasagna into a baking dish. "Of course, sir. It will be ready in exactly fifty-five minutes, if you'd like to set a timer."

Hmph, a timer. Not a bad idea.

"Will do. See you then."

Back up in my suite, I take the pills and crush them up with the bottom of a whiskey glass. I intend to spread the powder all over her food so that she can't choose not to eat it. This afternoon, I ordered Matilda not to send up lunch, therefore, I know she's extra hungry tonight.

There's no way she's not eating her dinner. No fucking way.

Fifty-five minutes is a long time when you're feeling anxious, but when my timer goes off, I head downstairs again and find Armani sitting at the table, waiting for Matilda to serve him.

"Hey, Sal, joining me for dinner?" Armani asks a little too cheerfully, tearing into a chunk of garlic bread.

I grab a plate and spread the powdered pills along the bottom, then place a generous scoop of lasagna on top of it. As if I were adding a pinch of salt, I sprinkle more over the top, add some to her glass of milk, then toss some on a piece of garlic bread. "In a moment. First I'm going to bring our guest her dinner."

My brother's eyes widen in surprise. "Why not have Joseph do it?"

I pause at the kitchen door and realize he's right. Even my bringing the food up could be enough for her to refuse it. "Actually, I think I will have him bring it up. Joseph," I call, and he walks over from his station at the front door, taking the plate I hand him. "Bring this up to Valentina."

He offers me a curt bow. "Of course, sir."

Matilda already has a plate fixed for me sitting at the table along with a glass of red wine. I scoot in across from Armani and pull up our security feed, wanting to make sure Valentina takes the food from Joseph.

I watch him knock on the door and unlock it. She accepts the food from him and steps back into her room. Joseph dutifully locks it behind her.

Now, all I have to do is wait.

Matilda's lasagna never disappoints. I eat my meal slowly, trying to pass the time one bite after another, wondering how long it takes for sleeping pills to take effect.

Armani tells me that Fausto has run off to his little fight club or whatever he calls it. It pisses me off that he takes such risks. All it would take is one single person to recognize him and his life could end. One. Fucking. Person.

That's it.

Game over.

The bragging rights for offing a Moretti would be unimaginable, and yet he still delves into the darkness, submitting to his depraved desires.

"I drugged Val," I mutter casually, stuffing a bite of lasagna into my mouth.

Armani almost chokes on his wine. "You what?"

I swallow my bite and stab another. "You heard me."

Armani runs his fingers through his hair. "I thought perhaps you misspoke, brother. Why drug your future wife when you can freely take all she has to offer?"

The corner of my mouth twitches, but I force it to still and hold up her phone. "Because I have this."

"It's… a phone," he retorts, completely uninterested.

"Not just any phone, jackass, her phone."

Armani swallows his bite and reaches for the phone, but I tug it away. "Not so fast, brother. She has a facial recognition lock on it."

"So let's go shove the damn thing in her face and unlock it," he says, shifting in his seat.

I shake my head and pocket the phone. "Not yet. I'd rather keep my possession of it a secret for now and learn all about her, then spring it on her all at once."

Armani takes a long drink of wine. "Sounds like you're planning on an interrogation."

"Only if she forces me to."

Armani scoffs and rolls his eyes. "With the way you treat that girl, she'll do anything you ask. She's terrified of you now."

"That's not the point. The point is she's hiding something. We've all agreed on that. And in about an hour's time, we're going to learn what."

Armani and I spend the next hour in our office, pouring over shipments and paperwork, trying to keep ourselves busy. When I feel enough time has passed, I close my computer and slap my knees.

"You ready?"

Armani tosses down his pen and pushes away from his chair. "Do bears shit in the woods?"

I'm confused by his answer. "I would assume they do. Everything shits."

Armani laughs at my confusion. "No, brother. It means yes. Yes, bears shit in the woods, so yes, I'm ready."

"Then why didn't you just say yes?"

My brother rolls his eyes and steps out of the office. With Valentina's phone in hand, we head upstairs and to her door. Armani knocks gently. "Valentina, it's Armani. I just wanted to check in on you."

No response.

Armani gives me a fucking thumbs-up, and I push him aside while he laughs and use my skeleton key to unlock it. Upon entering the room, there are a few things I notice. First is the terrible reality show playing on the TV. Second is the half eaten plate of food and empty glass of milk. Third is Valentina.

Passed out flat on her back in the center of the bed, Valentina is nothing short of stunning, and I hate her for it. She's sprawled out on top of the covers with her arms up over her head, her legs slightly parted. The loose, pink cotton tank top she wears does nothing to hide what's below it. Cut deep under her arms, the thing is almost transparent. Loved, worn, and washed too many times, it makes the anatomy of her breasts clearly visible.

She wears pink pajama pants of the same material on her legs. It must be a set. And like her top, her pants leave little to the imagination.

My mind immediately goes back to the bathroom when I forced her to stand naked before me, and I quickly have to shake that image from my mind. I insulted her body and humiliated her, but only because I crave her so much.

"Holy shit," Armani murmurs beside me, voicing what I refuse to say.

"She can be all yours soon," I respond, taking the phone from my pocket. "As soon as I have answers, you and Fausto can do whatever you like with her."

Armani leans over her and gently rubs his fingers across her cheek. "Don't tell me you don't plan to partake. How can you deny yourself access to this stunning creature?"

"Easy," I offer, turning the phone to face her. "She's a Rossi. It's as simple as that."

"She's so much more than that, Sal," Armani defends, his stance on her a little surprising. "She deserves better."

"Let's just see about that," I respond, opening her now unlocked phone. First thing I do is open up her messages, since there are over seventy notifications. Dozens of messages are from a guy named Marco and a girl named Payton.

I scroll through Payton's first and realize she must be one of Val's good friends because of the concern in her texts. Every message is her checking in to see how Val is, begging her to respond. She said she keeps going to her house but never gets an answer.

Then I open the chat with Marco, my anger brewing. The thought of another man texting her, of her answering him back, pisses me off even though I know it shouldn't. Whoever this guy is, he was in her life before we were, before I was.

But my brain doesn't seem to give a fuck.

Marco: I miss you.

Marco: Where are you?

Marco: ANSWER ME!

Marco: I'm at your house. Where is your stuff, love?

Marco: YOU'RE MINE, VALENTINA! MINE!

Marco: I swear to fucking God, if you don't call me back soon, I'm going to lose my shit.

His messages are all the same. Maybe he's her concerned boyfriend, a boyfriend she was forbidden to have. Maybe he's something else. At this point, I don't know for sure.

I open up his information and take a screenshot of his number then send it to all of our phones for reference. When I close the message thread and open her photos, however, red coats my vision. Whoever this Marco guy is, she saved a picture of him, a very intimate picture of him.

"Is that some guy's dick?" Armani asks, looking over my shoulder, and I begin to tremble with uncontrollable rage. The screen cracks and breaks in my hand as I crush it to death. Pieces of glass embed into my palm, but I don't feel the pain. I'm fucking numb.

"Find out who the fuck Marco is, and do it now," I order my brother as I drop the phone and lunge for Valentina, gripping her flimsy shirt in my hands.

Armani, sensing my anger, leaps in front of her to block me, yanking my hand off her tank, but not before it stretches out, revealing one perfect breast and rosy nipple. "Not like this, brother," he grits out, holding me back. "Take this out in the gym."

"She has to pay," I growl, wanting to rip all her fucking clothes off and bite her pretty skin until she cries. I want to clamp those pert little nipples until she's writhing in pain and shove my dick so far up her cunt that she fucking chokes on it.

When Armani slaps me across the face, I stop fighting, the desire to hurt her fading for a moment. "She will. Now get the fuck out of her room before you do something you can't undo. Understand? Don't be the reason this treaty fails and the mafia wars resumes."

I nod once and take slow steps backwards until I'm out of her room. Then I run, and I don't stop running until I break down the door of our gym and attack the nearest punching bag.

It seems like I've gotten my answers after all. Now it's time for the repercussions.

CHAPTER TWENTY-SIX

Valentina

I don't know how long I slept, but it feels like hours. Perhaps I'm catching up for all the sleep I've lost since I've been here.

Groggily, I push myself up on my elbows and open one eye, glancing around the room. Everything is exactly as it was when I went to bed. The TV is still on, my plate of half eaten dinner is on the coffee table, and I'm here on the bed.

It's funny, I don't even remember falling asleep. It felt more like passing out from utter exhaustion after I chugged half a bottle of NyQuil or something.

Swinging my legs off the bed, I slip to the ground and head into the bathroom, desperate to brush this awful taste out of my mouth. That's when I realize how fucked my shirt is. I pull at the flimsy thing, trying to fix how it lies, but it won't cover me anymore.

It's like a person ten sizes larger than me wore it and gave it back. I almost laugh, looking at myself in the mirror. The worthless fabric is so stretched out it doesn't even cover my tits.

It fit when I went to bed. I wonder if I had a nightmare or something and tugged at it in my sleep. That wouldn't really be a shocker considering my situation.

Rubbing the sleep from my eyes, I open the drawer with my floss and electric brush, then clean the shit out of my teeth, finishing with my tongue scraper. It's really disgusting what a good tongue scraper will pull off your tongue, even when you do it every day.

Fucking nasty.

I change into a more fitted shirt, my powderpuff shirt, and sadness washes over me with a side of anxiety because it reminds me of something I have to address with the Morettis—my education.

Plucked right from the final month of my senior year, I haven't been told a single thing about graduation or any option to finish my classes online.

Nothing.

Zilch.

Nada.

It's like they are ignoring each and every part of my personal life while imposing every single bit of theirs. It's just not fair. If I'm to marry one of them, you'd think that they'd want a… a wife—eww that sounds so gross to say—who is educated, not some high school dropout.

Yet here I am, missing my what… third day? I haven't called out absent. I've simply not shown up. And what about next year? I have plans to attend Dartmouth, plans to better myself and prepare for the future. Now, with my destiny sealed as the wife of a top tier mafia man, what does that mean for further education?

Most degrees can be done online nowadays, so I wouldn't even have to leave their house to complete it. I have my own money in an account from my dad to pay for it, so they wouldn't have to give me a dime. I don't see how they could say no.

Pfft. Who am I kidding? Of course they can say no. Sal was very vocal about using the word "own" when it comes to me, but maybe I won't ask Sal. Armani seems like the most likely of the three to tell me yes to something like this. Maybe I'll ask him.

Or maybe I'll succumb to my fear, not say anything to anyone, and accept my fate as a wife and nothing more.

I spit out my toothpaste and rinse my mouth, gazing at myself in the mirror. Determination sets in, and I make a promise to myself to ask. I owe myself that much. If I'm to be locked away in some mafia mansion, then at least my studies could keep me busy and pass the time. As much as I love to watch TV, I'm getting a feeling I'll soon run out of shows and movies on Netflix with the amount of time I'm forced to stay inside this room.

My room.

I might as well admit it to myself, because that's what this is, right?

Unless it was their sister Lily's space, but I don't think it was. There's not a whisper of personality in the room. No, this place was just a spare room they threw a bed in so I'd have somewhere to sleep. I guess I should be grateful for that.

I could be sleeping on a blow-up mattress, or even worse, the floor.

I'm just putting my toothbrush back in its drawer when there's a knock on my door. It must be Joseph. "Come in."

Padding across the cool tile, I round the corner of the bathroom and find none other than Fausto Moretti leaning casually against the door in my bedroom. He's wearing a long-sleeved, dark green shirt with the sleeves pulled up and loose gray sweats—and he looks like shit.

"What happened to you?" I ask, looking from his bloody lip to his wrapped knuckles.

He pushes off the wall and struts—yes, that's how he walks—into my room, standing in front of the TV. "Fight club."

"But... the first rule of fight club is that you don't talk about fight club."

Fausto smiles, and his whole face lights up. He's handsome when he scowls, but when the man fucking smiles, panties all over the place must catch on fire. "Are you hungry?"

"Not for waffles," I joke with an embarrassing snort, but he doesn't laugh.

Instead, he bites his lower lip and shuffles closer, his eyes flashing with mischief as he shoves his hands into his front pockets. Fucking men and their pockets, I'll never stop being jealous. "We could skip the waffles and just grab the syrup."

My face flushes red at his suggestion, and I can actually feel myself heating up. "Umm..."

Fausto closes the distance between us and tilts my chin up with his finger. "I've been wanting to do this for a long time."

I lick my lips, my pulse stuttering at his nearness, at the ferocity of his gaze. "Do what?"

His dark eyes flick between mine, the scent of male body wash invading my nose. "This."

Fausto crushes his lips against mine, and I don't stop him. In fact, I welcome it. His hands snake around my back, running up my shirt, while mine grip his shoulders for dear life. I part my lips for his prodding tongue, and when our tongues collide, we both moan. The kiss deepens, and all my worries melt away as my body comes alive, shivering and needy.

Fausto picks me up under my ass and walks over to the bed, tossing me on it. I squeal in midair, but as soon as I land, he's crawling on top of me. "I want you so fucking badly, little pistol," he growls before capturing my mouth again. He works his way across my jaw, planting small kisses as he goes, and then he licks down my neck and sucks on the tender skin.

"Holy shit," I mumble, not believing something like this can feel so good.

Fausto sits up for a moment and rips his shirt over his head, showing off his body. Perfection is the word that comes to mind—chiseled abs, defined pecs, and arms ripped with thick muscle. He could crush me in an instant if he wanted to, yet somehow his power increases my excitement.

I grow damp between my legs as he grips the hem of my shirt and glances up at me for permission. My nerves kick in, and I almost say no, embarrassed about my body even though I shouldn't be. I saw the way they looked at me in the kitchen, and I felt their desire, so I decide to live in this moment and nod eagerly.

Fausto licks his lips as he lifts up my shirt, revealing my breasts. My immediate reaction is to cover them up with my hands. As I do, Fausto seizes my wrists and pins them down next to my head.

He leans down and captures my nipple between his warm lips. I groan as he nibbles on it, sucking and pulling and flicking the hard nub with his tongue before shifting to my other side. I can feel my insides clenching and arousal soaking my pajama pants.

"You are fucking gorgeous, Valentina. A flower amongst the thorns." My ability to speak is lost as he kisses me again, releasing one hand and dragging it down over my body before cupping me through my pants. He lets out a low moan as he discovers I've soaked the fabric. "Wet for me already, little pistol? I'm just getting started."

I groan as Fausto kisses down my belly and bites the hem of my pants with his teeth, but as soon as he does, I freeze, Sal's snide remark playing through my mind.

Has this thing ever had a haircut?

I'm suddenly mortified, and I'm about to stop him when there's another knock on my door. Fausto's eyes narrow as a playful voice says, "Got room for one more?"

With Fausto distracted, I pull myself away and fix my shirt, rolling over to see Armani in my doorway wearing basketball shorts and nothing else. He leans against the doorframe with his arms crossed, tossing his long hair behind one shoulder. "And here I was inviting you to breakfast, but I see Fausto was too hungry to wait."

"Starving," Fausto replies with a grin, scooting off the bed and finding his shirt.

Armani lifts an eyebrow and smacks his lips. "Matilda is making a bacon, egg, and cheese frittata, and she has a loaf of fresh bread in the oven. You two coming down?"

"I am," I respond immediately, needing to remove myself from temptation. "Can I change first?"

The devilish grin that crosses Armani's face would have women either swooning or running. "Only if I can pick it out."

I gesture toward my bathroom. "Have at it but don't expect a lot of variety in there. I'm a simple girl with simple tastes."

"We'll see about that." Armani almost skips into my room and disappears through the bathroom door. He comes out a moment later holding the sundress I wore on my date with Marco. I shake my head, and Armani frowns in disappointment. The last thing I want is to be reminded of that asshole. I'll probably donate that dress to Goodwill.

Armani steps out dangling a sparkly red gown from a cloth hanger. I shake my head. "That's my homecoming dress. Try again."

The third option is a charm, a cute workout outfit from Lululemon. "I love it," I say, taking the outfit from him and heading into the bathroom.

Fausto looks at me pointedly. "I want to watch."

"Yeah, I think that's rule number three," Armani jokes.

"Not today, guys." I push a disappointed Armani out of my bathroom. Just to be sure they can't see me, I also hide inside my closet. You know, extra walls and all that.

The teal, racerback tank top is one of my favorites. Its straps connect between my shoulder blades, and it hugs my boobs together without needing a bra. This particular tank is cropped, so it exposes my belly. Matching black pants with a teal stripe running up the sides and a pair of Nike flip-flops complete the outfit.

Back in the bathroom, I gather all my hair and put it into a messy bun, pulling a few strands in front of my ears before heading back into the bedroom. Fausto is draped across my bed, while Armani looks casually out the window.

"I'm ready," I announce, feeling more comfortable with them than I have previously.

"You look adorable, kitten," Armani comments.

My shoulders scrunch up in response. "Thanks."

Fausto slips off the bed and heads to the door. "Let's get some food. I'm feeling ravenous."

Armani follows him, and they both pause at the door to look at me. "Aren't you coming?" Armani asks.

I pick at my fingers. "Umm. Is Sal going to be there?"

Armani runs his fingers through his hair. "He shouldn't be. Last I checked, he was taking his aggression out in the gym."

Good enough for me. "Okay."

I let the twins lead me downstairs and through the kitchen to the back patio where our breakfast is ready for us on an outdoor table. There's a fresh pitcher of iced tea complete with lemon slices and a silver cloche covers what I'm guessing is the main course. Strawberries, blackberries, pineapple, and mango make up the delicious-looking fruit salad, and there's also a carafe of coffee.

As I sit down and eagerly await my breakfast, I think that perhaps this isn't so bad after all.

But hurricanes often strike right after the calm, and if I'm not careful, I might drown in the sea of Moretti men.

CHAPTER TWENTY-SEVEN

Armani

It's been over a week since Valentina came into our lives and turned them upside down. Every chance I get, I spend time with her, and the more I do, the more I like her.

She brings out a side of myself that I've always tried to smother, a goofy, silly side. We joke, laugh, and make fun of each other in the most natural of ways.

Sometimes I catch her staring at me when she thinks I'm not looking, and it makes my chest clench. If I'm being honest here, I do the same thing to her.

Valentina is pure, like spring water caught fresh from a frozen mountain, or morning dew glistening on flower petals. It's impossible to be around someone like that and not be affected. She changes the atmosphere in the house, affecting the whole dynamic.

Well, until Sal comes around. He's been darker and meaner than ever, snapping at her for the littlest things, like cutting her food too loudly or watching too much TV, yet he won't give her more freedom to roam around.

What else is the girl supposed to do locked away in her room aside from watch TV? Her phone is damn near broken, not that he would have given it back anyway. When he's around, her personality dies like an insect under a sunlit microscope.

I hate that about him, I hate the effect he has on her, and I hate that he doesn't give a fuck. He seems almost proud of it as he gloats. Other times he fixes his gaze on her and glowers in the most menacing of ways. It would be impossible for her not to sense or feel it, especially when he takes great care in letting her know.

I've asked him when we're going to bring up the conversation about Marco after learning who he is, but he just offers me a sinister grin and says, "Soon."

Knowing what we know, and the battle that is looming between Sal and Val, is enough to make even me anxious, and I'm a pretty chill guy most of the time.

Val can sense something is up too, her anxiety increasing these days, which is why we're here in the gym to work off some of that stress.

Fausto is busy on the treadmill, getting his miles in for the day. I'm more of a bike guy, riding my calories away, and today, Valentina is joining me.

"Select program five," I tell her, scrolling through the various workouts we can choose from.

"Aww, I don't like five," she whines. "Let's do ten again."

"Ten? Why?"

She scrolls to ten and looks over at me, her finger resting on the start button. "It's not as hard."

"Don't you want it hard, kitten?"

Val blushes and looks away, but not before selecting track number ten on my bike. "It depends on how I'm feeling. Track five killed me yesterday. My ass still hurts."

There are so many sick things I can say to that, and so many sexual innuendos she just set herself up for, but I let it go just this once.

We ride hard. Val kicks some serious ass on her bike, sweat pouring down her face. As she pumps her legs, her whole body tightens, causing every movement she makes to look glorious. Her arms are defined, her legs are toned, her abs are flat, and her waist is narrow.

She's the perfect package.

Fausto ends his jog and says goodbye to us before leaving the gym. Val and I ride in comfortable silence, which consists of her riding hard and me staring at her ass when she stands up to pump harder when the bike takes us uphill.

She drapes a towel over her neck and puffs out an exhausted breath. "I need to take a shower."

The little thing walked right into this one. "Me too. What do you say we conserve water and take one together?"

My sweet kitten rolls her eyes at me and heads toward the gym door. As we pass other machines, I think about how I could drape Val across each one and use it for new and interesting sex positions.

Yep.

That's happening.

As we exit the gym and head down the hallway, Sal comes rushing toward us. Valentina's shoulders stiffen and she steps in close to me.

Sal pauses a few feet away, blocking our exit. "There you two are, I've been looking all over for you."

"You could have texted me," I suggest.

I'm not sure he even hears me, his blue eyes fixed on Valentina in an almost robotic stare. "There's something we need to talk about. I'll see you both in the conference room in one hour."

Sal shifts his gaze to me then back to her before turning on his heel and walking away. Val glances up at me. "I wonder what that's about. Did he seem more on edge than usual?"

I scrub at my face. The stress of Sal's mental state is really starting to wear me down. "Nope. He seems like his usual, charming self." I shoot a sly grin at Valentina, hoping she'll let it drop, because I know there's only one thing Salvatore would want to speak to us about.

He's figured out who Marco is.

CHAPTER TWENTY-EIGHT

Valentina

Sitting on the cold floor of my bathroom, I stare hard at the hand mirror placed across from me, contemplating how to tame this mess of pubic hair.

I glance down at myself then up at the counter where I have a few items set out—an electric razor, my normal razor, and a pair of scissors.

Has that thing ever had a haircut?

I grumble at Sal's crass words, but at least they motivated me. Well, along with the twins' advances. I'm ready to take the next step sexually. Maybe not full-blown intercourse, but I'm ready for them to… to… *touch me.*

It's a weird thought for me to ponder, but at this point, there have been too many close calls for me not to be prepared anymore. It's time to tame this beast.

Spreading my legs wider, I scoot closer to the mirror and grab the scissors first, giving the longer hairs a trim. This is such a weird feeling. There's been hair down there for years, obscuring my view of what my vagina actually looks like, but not having hair there is clearly what men want, and I don't want to suffer another embarrassing episode like I did with Sal.

Next, I try the electric razor, switching it on. The damned thing is louder than my toothbrush and can probably be heard from miles away. At first, I hold it away from my skin, and just like, take off more length. As the hair gets shorter, I touch the razor to my skin. I expected it to bite into me, but it doesn't, and as I move it along my inner thighs and lower lips, the hair trims nicely. I pull my skin with my free hand, gently shaving off as much as I can before shutting the razor off.

I feel so strange with a bald vagina, but it's also kind of sexy to actually see what she looks like. Grabbing the mirror, I hold it closer and spread my pussy lips apart with my fingers. The skin inside is a darker pink and wet. I imagine the twins' tongues tasting me, and my clit starts to throb. I prop the mirror up on my ankle and gently tap my clit, moaning at how good it feels.

I picture my hands threaded through Armani's hair as his tongue flickers over my clit, his dark eyes fixed on me, and my pussy clenches. I watch arousal leak from inside me, so I slip my finger in it. It's warm and slippery. I gather more wetness on my fingertip before dragging it back up to my clit.

Gliding my finger over the hard little nub, I watch it swell and grow, the pleasure making my heart race and my thighs shake. I remember Fausto's lips on my nipples, his teeth dragging across them just on the edge of pain, and move my finger faster. And faster. A deep heat grows within me, and my breaths become short and raspy. It feels like my whole body is on fire.

I recall my time in the kitchen with the twins, when both of the gorgeous, powerful men were licking syrup off my breasts, and it throws me over the edge.

Moaning loudly, I come all over my fingers, my pussy covered in the milky white liquid. Slowly, I reduce my pace until I'm fucking spent and fall backwards onto the cold floor, still trying to catch my breath.

Soon, I'm going to let one of the twins touch me there. I wonder if they can do it as well as I can.

When my legs aren't feeling as wobbly, I pick myself up off the tile, clean the mess of hair, and head into the shower, grooming my vagina for the final time with a straight razor. It's hard work trying not to nick that soft skin with a razor, and the angles I have to move my hands at to complete the job are insane and take me forever. It's no wonder some women opt to have this shit waxed off. I'm lucky I didn't lose a pussy lip in the process, or at the minimum, severely maim my damn self.

With the hot water cascading over me, I wash my hair and body then towel dry off. I grab the hand mirror again and lift one leg up on the counter, really checking out my business. I feel around my pussy lips, which are surprisingly soft, and make sure I didn't miss any stray hairs.

Satisfied with my handiwork, I lower my leg and slip into a bathrobe to air dry, then I brush out my long hair, scrub my teeth, and head into my closet. Sal said we're having a meeting, and for the life of me, I don't know how to dress.

I wish I had my fucking phone so I could ask one of them.

Maybe I'll ask for it back at their meeting. All they can do is say no.

It doesn't hurt to ask.

Right?

CHAPTER TWENTY-NINE

Salvatore

I ALMOST CAN'T WAIT for this.

As the minutes tick by, I become more and more excited. This is it. I have all the facts in front of me. Now it's time for the little whore to own up to what—no, *who* she's been doing.

It all makes sense, her connection to Alfonzo and his relationship with her dad—Carlo fucking Rossi.

Let's see her deny it when I shove the evidence in her face. I can't wait to watch her squirm under my scrutinizing gaze.

I've been sitting on this information for a week, stewing over it and coming to my own conclusions. She acts like she had no idea we were coming to collect her, but I beg to differ. She knew all along, and her dirtbag father planted seeds to corrupt my entire syndicate.

But he won't.

Oh no, he won't.

Because I've caught onto his little game, and I'll show him I'm a better player than he'll ever be.

Checkmate, motherfucker.

He sent me a mafia princess with intentions of making her my queen, but soon, he'll learn I've transformed her into the ultimate pawn. Easily disposable.

As I stand outside Valentina's door, my heart slams against my ribs. I unlock the door and enter without knocking.

"Time's up," I call loudly, looking around the room for her as I walk farther inside.

"I'll be right out," she answers from the bathroom.

Nope. Fuck that. I won't wait another second.

"I said time's up," I growl, storming into the bathroom to find her inside her closet, looking through clothes.

She pauses and stares at me like a deer in the headlights, her big doe eyes wide and frightened as she stands there wearing nothing but a bathrobe. Her fear is so potent, I could taste it if I licked the air.

She pulls an item off a hanger. "I heard you, just give me two minutes to change, Sal. Please."

Even though I like it when she begs, I shake my head and close the distance between us. "Time is fucking up. The baby girl can't even get herself dressed in time. Pity."

Lunging for her, I grab her upper arm, drag her out of her closet, and pull her out of the door.

"Let go of me," she says, tugging on her arm, but I ignore her little outburst and pull her along, her bare feet slapping against the stone stairs. I march her little ass through the first floor to a room adjacent to our office.

Jerking her to a stop, I grip her chin and lean close to her face, my warning and intentions clear. "If you don't stop fighting me so hard, I might have to drape you over my lap right now and spank your bare ass for disobeying me." I don't focus on her eyes, instead, I watch her lips and see the lower one tremble. "Good girl."

I drop her chin, and she immediately stops struggling, following along beside me like a good, obedient dog. Inside the conference room, I have the main table pushed against the back wall and all the chairs shoved aside except for a single one.

"Sit," I order, tossing her toward the chair. She stumbles then levels me with a glare while tucking her hair behind her ear, but she listens, adjusting the belt on her robe before lowering her ass down.

Heading over to the controls, I dim all the lights except the one shining on her and lower the temperature to a cool forty-five degrees. I want her as uncomfortable as possible and as vulnerable as I can make her.

My brothers aren't here yet, which gives me time to prep. "I want you to think long and hard before you answer this question," I begin, circling her like a bloodthirsty shark. She folds her arms over her chest and crosses her legs, trying to comfort herself. It won't work, especially when they are handcuffed to the chair.

"What do you know about Alfonzo Capelli?" I make a show of rolling up the sleeves of my dress shirt, making sure the tattoos covering me are on display. "Consider your answer before speaking."

She chews on her lip, her head lowered as her foot bobs up and down. "I told you everything I know about him."

"You lie," I seethe, reaching into my pants pocket and pulling out two sets of handcuffs. Quickly but methodically, I secure one of her arms to the chair, and then the other. "There are ramifications for lying to me, baby girl. Try again."

"I-I don't know," she stutters. "I only met him one time at my cousin's wedding. I already told you about that."

I reach into my back pocket and tug out a third set of cuffs, twirling them on my finger. "Do you think I'd be asking you the same question if I wanted the same answer? There's more, and you're hiding it from me."

Dropping to my knees, I pull her legs apart, securing her ankles to the curved legs of the chair. As the handcuff around her ankle clicks into place, the door opens, and in walk my twin brothers. I don't need to look at them to know their reaction to the predicament I've put their new plaything in. I heard them gasp when they entered the room.

I stand back and appraise my handiwork, cupping my chin. "Now, let's try this again. Tell me everything you know about Alfonzo Capelli."

A fat tear leaks from her eye as she shifts uncomfortably in her seat. "I don't know what you want me to say. I only met him that one time. My dad kept me isolated from the family business. Whatever answers you're looking for, I don't have them for you."

"Lies. Lies. Lies," I snarl, pacing back and forth in front of her. My brothers sit on top of the table across from her. "Is it a trait of the Rossi family to lie so much, or are you simply too stupid to know the truth?"

"I'm not stupid," she grits out, tugging on the cuffs binding her wrists, her blue eyes flashing.

"Then you must be a liar, because I have proof that you've been dishonest with us, with me. I just hope you're ready for the repercussions."

She swallows hard but holds her resolve as I pull my phone out of my pocket, open up the photos I sent from her phone, and select the dick pic.

I turn my phone to face her. "Mind telling us whose dick you have a picture of on your phone, Valentina?"

Her reaction is perfect. Her lips part, her hands clench into fists, and her eyes widen in terror. Redness creeps up her neck and down her chest, and her breathing quickens. All token signs of a liar. "He's no one."

She's got guts of steel, I can give her that.

"Tsk. Tsk. Tsk," I scold, walking slowly in front of her. "That's not the entire truth, is it? Because he must be someone, or else this photo wouldn't exist at all."

"Tell him what he wants to know," Armani urges, and I shoot him an angry glare. There's sympathy in his eyes, a sadness that shouldn't be there. He's *my* brother. He should be on *my* side, not hers.

I begin to unfasten my tie and pull it off my neck. "This is the last time I'm going to ask nicely, Valentina. Tell me who it is. I already know the answer."

"I-I..." She looks toward my brothers for help.

I charge at her, grasping her shoulders and shaking her hard. "Don't look at them for your answers! They are my brothers. Mine!" I swing around to her back, securing my tie over her eyes. "There. I won't have you fucking with my brothers by batting your eyelashes at them. No. Now it's just you and me."

I lean down close and whisper in her ear, slipping my hand inside the front of her robe. "Do not forget, baby girl, that I will strip you bare in an instant to ensure you have nowhere to hide." Her breathing stutters as my fingers whisper over her nipple before I pull my hand free.

"His name is Marco," she admits.

"Very good, Valentina. It seems a Rossi can tell the truth, at least when persuaded. And does Marco have a last name?"

I can see the gears turning in her head. "Capelli." She speaks it so low, I almost can't hear it.

I start clapping, and Valentina jerks with each slam of my hands. "Marco Capelli is Alfonzo Capelli's son, is he not?"

"Y-Yes."

"And you didn't think that was important information to share?"

Valentina licks her lips and takes a breath. "Marco Capelli is not important."

The laugh that expels from my lungs surprises me. "Then why the fuck do you have a picture of his dick on your fucking phone, Valentina?"

The girl begins to whimper, her shoulders shaking. The robe is precariously close to falling down one arm. "It's a long story." She sniffs pathetically, but her effort won't work on me.

"Tell him the CliffsNotes, Valentina," Fausto urges. "His patience is wearing thin."

I toss my hands up in the air in frustration, glowering at my brothers. "I see I have to do this interrogation myself. Fine." Turning back to the girl, I capture her throat in one hand and trail a single finger down the center of her chest. "Are you fucking Marco Capelli? Have you had his cock shoved deep inside you, whore?"

"No!" She shakes her head violently. "But even if I was, it's none of your fucking business."

I tighten my grip on her neck, and her nostrils flare. "How dare you speak to me like that? You are our business now."

"Fine," she snaps, her blind face turned toward my voice. "Then why don't you drop me lists of all the women you've fucked so we're even?"

The rage that fills me is insatiable. I feel it dripping from my head through my limbs as the potent anger brews to the point of no control. "You little bitch!" Blind with fury, I tear open the sides of her robe.

"No!" she cries out, trying to shift her body away from me, but she's fucking cuffed and has nowhere to go.

The scream that follows is like music as I seize her pert nipples between my fingers and twist. Fausto and Armani are on me fast, screaming obscenities at me that I can't hear. It's like I'm at the far end of a tunnel listening to whispers of their echoes. My brothers pull me off the little fucking whore, but not before I squeeze those little nubs harder than I've ever pinched anything in my life.

Her shrieks echo through my chest as she arches her back into my touch, and a sinister grin grows on my face. I can feel it etching itself into my skin. Her body shakes as she cries, each sob making her breasts jiggle in the most delectable way that infuriates me. Her reddened nipples point at me, hard and erect from my abuse, begging for another pinch or an even stronger bite. How I'd love another moment alone with her to paint her tits red with my handprints and leave stripes across her ass.

"You're dating him!" I holler. "Admit it! You're plotting to take us down! Tell the fucking truth, or I'll leave you sitting there all night with your tits out, handcuffed to the fucking chair."

"Did you even read the texts?" she screams through her sobs, her chest burning with anger and embarrassment. "Or did you just find the dick pic and assume I asked for it? I didn't ask for it. I didn't. H-He's a fucking psycho, Sal. No different from how you're acting right now." Her words grip my insides and twist. Am I no different? "He somehow got the passcode to my house and broke in. He… He was trying to force himself on me, and there was nothing I could do about it." She sniffs and hangs her head in defeat, her fighting spirit leaving. "It was the worst night of my life until now."

"That's enough," Fausto growls, pushing past me to Valentina. "Give me the fucking keys, Sal. We're done here."

Armani helps Fausto fix her robe, covering up her tits, and holds out his hand for the keys. "You've gone too far this time, Sal."

Have I gone too far? My anger evaporates, and I really see my situation. I see my angry brothers and a sad, broken girl.

"The keys," Fausto demands louder, his rage aimed at me.

I take a step back as the horror at what I did to her sinks in. A vindictive part of me is proud that I've broken the daughter of the infamous Carlo Rossi, while another part of me is riddled with guilt, knowing if this happened to Lily, then I'd be the one who broke. "They are keyless. Just push the button by the keyhole and they'll pop open."

As Armani and Fausto take off her blindfold and remove her restraints, my phone vibrates in my pocket. I do a double take as the name Gabriel Rossi blinks across my screen.

"Quiet," I order as I answer my phone. "Gabriel Rossi, to what do I owe this pleasure?"

At the mention of her brother's name, Valentina freezes and wipes her tearstained cheeks, staring at me with bloodshot but hopeful eyes.

"I need to speak to my sister. It's urgent."

I almost hang up the phone, but there's something in his voice that makes me stop. "Fine. I'll put you on speaker."

Clicking the speaker button, I walk over to Valentina and hold my phone in front of her. "Gabe?" she murmurs.

"It's me, little sister. How are you?"

A sad smile crosses her face. "Oh my God, Gabe. I miss you guys so fucking much. How are you? How are Lucian and Raph?"

"We're good, sis. Listen…" Gabe lets out a long sigh. "I have some bad news to tell you about Dad."

Her little nose scrunches in confusion. "Dad? Okay… What's going on with him?"

Gabe sighs again. "There's no easy way to say this. Dad's dead, Val. He's gone."

CHAPTER THIRTY

Valentina

My whole world implodes.

The chaos shredding its way through my heart feels like two freight trains crashed together head-on. My head pounds, and despair rips through me, causing an insufferable weight to press on my chest, making it hard to breathe.

I try to suck in air, but the room spins as blackness creeps into my vision. How can one person's suffering not be shared with another? How can the world continue on as if nothing has happened, completely oblivious to my pain?

Does the world not suffer as a whole? Does the destruction of one person not affect another?

My legs shake and give way, and I fall through the blackness, ready to give in, to say fuck it, and enter the darkness with my dad.

But someone catches me, and I'm lifted into the air, held tightly against a strong, hard chest. I hear people talking, but their voices are a low whisper, and their words are incomprehensible and muffled.

The arms surrounding me tighten as the person carrying me walks in a slow and steady pace. I sink into him, into the lull of his gait, wishing that sleep would take me so I don't have to think about what I've learned.

A soft kiss is planted on my head, and the subtle sweet gesture has me spiraling once more. Sobs rack my body, the grief so painful and potent that I clutch my chest, wishing to rip out my own heart if it would prevent me from having to feel.

I don't want to feel.

I want to be numb.

A door creaks open, and I'm carefully placed down on cool leather. I curl up into a ball, trying to wrap my robe tighter around me as relentless tears roll down my cheeks.

A blanket is placed over me, and a low, soothing voice pulls me from my sorrow. "Val... I'm... I'm so sorry."

Armani.

I just nod slowly, unable to look at him. I can't bear to raise my head, exhaustion weighing me down. He gently tugs at my hair, pulls it away from my face, and ties it up on top of my head, then he presses something cool against my swollen eyes and my throat clogs again at the kindness.

I almost wish he'd just let me be and leave me to rot in my own sorrow rather than show me this compassion. It makes the pain that much harder to bear when someone sees it. I can hold myself together in my own pain, but with just one look of empathy, I'll shatter.

I'll break.

And right now, pieces of me are chipping off, lost forever in the cacophony of life.

Armani removes the cold cloth from my eyes, and I find the energy to open them. I'm in a living room I've never been in before. Wood floors give way to slate walls that rise to tall ceilings. Sports memorabilia is displayed proudly in glass frames, covering almost every inch of wall space. Beneath me is a large, black leather couch that curves along the corner of the wall. It even has built-in cup holders. Across from me is the largest TV I've ever seen, projecting an image of the Moretti family crest.

The sound of a cork popping pulls my attention, and I glance to my right and see Armani pouring red wine into two stemmed glasses. He's standing at an island in a simple kitchen with dark cabinetry accented with white and gray countertops.

Large glass pendant lights shine down on him, somehow making his outfit of jeans and a tight heather gray shirt seem more grand. He glances up and sees me looking his way, giving me a small smile.

With the wineglasses safely in his hands, he walks over to me and sits down, offering me one. "Here. It will help take the edge off."

I accept the glass and bring it to my lips, taking two big gulps. I know tradition would have me sniff and swirl the wine, but right now, I don't fucking want to enjoy it as much as I need its effects.

Armani takes a sip of his own and smacks his lips while running his fingers through his hair. "Are you okay?"

I shrug. "I don't know how I am. He was the only parent I had left." At that admission, the tears start back up, and I hang my head in my hands. The wave of grief slamming into me is so powerful it sucks the air from my lungs.

Armani wraps his arm around my shoulders and pulls me into him. "I know how that feels. Both of our parents were killed during a freak boating accident over five years ago now. It's hard enough to grieve for them, but it's more crushing to know they aren't there for you anymore."

I sniff hard, wiping my face on the sleeve of my robe. "That's how I'm feeling. Totally alone. Like I'm drowning and there is no one to save me. I'm drowning, Armani."

Armani squeezes me tight, and I rest my head on his chest while he trails his fingers up and down my back. "You're not alone, kitten. We're here for you."

"You call what happened down in that conference room as being *here for me?*" I scoff. "No. You have your brothers. But me, I am alone. I'm all alone. In some ways, I guess it's not a huge change for me. I've been alone for years now. I don't know why Dad's death should make me feel any different."

"Tell me about him," Armani suggests as he urges my wineglass back up to my lips. "But drink this first."

I sit up and hold the glass between both hands, chugging the wine as if it were water and I just crossed an entire desert.

He plucks the empty wineglass from my hands and heads into the kitchen, refilling both.

"There's not much to tell. I barely know the man."

More silent tears fall, and I blink them away. God, I sound so pitiful, pouring my heart out to this man I hardly know, a man brought up hating my father and me purely for being born Rossis.

Armani hands my full glass back to me and sits down. "Surely you had to know him a little bit."

"Not really," I admit. "Mom and I… We lived separately from Dad and my brothers. He… He even forgot my birthday this year." Sadness pummels through me again, and I croak out a sob. "It's like… I don't know if I'm sad that he's gone or if I'm mourning the possibility of having him in my life, a possibility that can never happen now. He wasn't a good father, but he was still my dad."

"Drink," Armani orders, and I lift the glass to my mouth, not even tasting the wine as it passes over my tongue.

I drink hard and long until I feel the change in my head, the slight dizziness of a buzz. "I, uhh… I don't drink much, so I apologize in advance for anything stupid I might say."

Armani takes a drink and sets his glass down on the coffee table. "You don't have to apologize. Sometimes we all need to get lost in the crimson liquid, and sometimes we all say stupid things."

I take another gulp. "I just don't want to feel anymore, Armani. I want to forget." I glance up at him, feeling the liquid courage brewing and wondering if he can sense what I need from him.

His dark eyes flicker between my blue ones, and his lips part. He cups my face in his hand, wiping away my tears with his thumb. "What are you asking me to do? I'll do anything."

With two glasses of wine simmering in my veins, I make a bold move that I would never consider when sober. "Help me," I whisper, climbing onto his lap and straddling him. I place my hands on his chest then slide them up his body before gripping his shoulders. "Help me forget." Rising up on my knees, I thread my fingers through the back of his hair and guide his handsome face toward mine.

His eyes focus on my lips, and his breathing picks up as our mouths gently brush against one another.

"Are you sure you want this?" he asks breathlessly, his arms around my back, pressing my chest into his.

I nod and close the distance between us, placing a soft kiss on his lips. I pull back, looking up at his face to see his reaction. Desire sparkles in his eyes, and I know he wants me just as badly as I want him.

"Kitten," he purrs before crushing his mouth against mine. I tug at his hair as our lips part and our tongues collide. Armani's hands drag up and down my back, then grip my waist hard, squeezing. I slide my hands down his chest and abs, tugging at the hem of his shirt. He pulls away for a moment, stripping his shirt off, and my mouth actually waters.

He is flawless, a paragon of what it means to be a man. Tan and chiseled, his body is a work of fucking art created by thick, corded muscle. "Your turn," he tells me, nodding at my robe.

I hesitate for just a moment then slowly slide the robe off my shoulders until it falls to my waist. My nipples harden under his gaze, still sore from the abuse they took from Sal.

"You're fucking perfect," he mutters before lowering his head, taking my nipple into his mouth as his free hand massages my other breast. "Mmm," he hums as he sucks, and my core clenches while heat simmers low in my belly. He switches sides, and I gasp at the pleasure, at the ache of my clit as it begs to be touched.

I run my hand through his hair, pressing him against my chest, needing more, needing all of him.

His hands slip to my waist, and suddenly I'm airborne as he spins us around, tossing me back against the couch. He pushes the coffee table away and falls to his knees in front of me. "Robe. Off. Now." He grunts out each word while pulling at the cloth tie securing it.

This is it, I'm about to be naked in front of a man for the second time. I inhale deeply as he tears my robe open and just stares. Embarrassment heats my skin, and for a moment, I wonder if this was a bad idea, but when he grabs my knees and wrenches them apart, he *groans*.

The man fucking groans.

He mutters something in Italian, and I catch *bellissima*, which means beautiful, so I relax. He finds me beautiful. Armani closes his eyes and plants tiny kisses up my inner thigh, inch by agonizing inch. He stops at my pussy, his breath fanning my skin, and the air catches in my lungs.

He looks up at me, extends his tongue, and licks. I inhale sharply, my pussy clenching and my clit tingling with need. "Mmm," he hums, squeezing my hips while he strokes the length of my slit with his tongue.

I gasp when he growls and grabs my knees with his hands. He wrenches my thighs apart, spreading my pussy open for him. "Keep your fucking legs open," he orders, spanking my inner thighs with the backs of his hands when I close them slightly. "I said keep them open," he grits out, slapping my pussy. I had no idea I'd find that so hot, but the moment he spanks me there, I feel arousal gushing out of me. "I need to see this perfect fucking pussy."

Armani lowers his gaze again and uses his thumbs to spread my lower lips. Cool air flickers over my sensitive skin, and I wriggle at this position. It's hard not to feel so vulnerable with him mere inches from my most private area. "Tell me, kitten. Am I the first man to taste you? Will I be the first man to have your sweet cream coat his tongue?"

Holy shit.

I nod, and all my insecurities vanish as he strokes my clit with his tongue. I moan loudly, my body on fire, needing more of him.

"Fuck," he curses. "Valentina, this is the prettiest fucking pussy I've ever seen." He dives in, and the sensations consume me. His tongue circles my clit like a predator stalking its prey. Every few strokes, he swipes over the hard nub and my thighs jerk at the feeling.

It's overwhelming.

I squeeze my breasts as I watch him. My breaths become shorter, and my moans grow louder. Heat builds in my core, and I almost can't take it. Desperate for a harder touch, I reach down and grab a handful of his hair, pressing him against me.

Armani doesn't like that, however, so he pulls away from my pussy, spanking me there again. My body twitches in pleasure, and my legs fall open all on their own now even as my skin tingles from the slap. "You have a naughty little pussy, don't you, kitten?" He taps lightly on my clit, and I almost fucking come. "Tell me how naughty you are. I want to hear you say it."

"I-I'm naughty."

He shakes his head. "Louder."

"Please," I beg, sliding my hand down my body, but he clutches my wrist before I can touch myself.

He squeezes my wrist to the point of pain then slams it against the back of the couch. "I'm in charge here. I'm the one who gets to make you come. I will see you unravel at *my* touch, not yours. Understand?"

I nod, unable to speak, my pussy throbbing, aching, and desperate.

"You'd better. Keep your arms up. You come when I'm done tasting you."

Armani's hair shrouds his face, making him look like a fallen angel who's ready to punish me for my sins. He slides his hands down my arms and over my chest, capturing my breasts. He squeezes and kneads them, and I'm moaning all over again.

His thumbs gently press on my nipples and move them in small circles. Even sore, it feels so good. Too good.

"Please," I beg again, arching my back into his touch.

I'm not ready for the slap that lands on my breast, and I scream out when the second one lands on the other. "I told you not to fucking move," Armani scolds. "Maybe you don't want to come all over my face? Maybe you don't want my tongue buried in your dirty little cunt? Is that it?"

"I want you so badly," I sob out, doing my best not to move.

He flicks both my nipples with his fingers, and I screech again, the pain morphing into something erotic, a pleasure of unbelievable proportions. "I know these plump little buds are still sore, or they'd be taking a beating too," he promises darkly, gently massaging them again.

Wetness pours from within me, caused by his actions, his pain, and the depravity of his words. I know I've soaked his couch.

"Please," I implore again, body trembling. "Armani…"

"Put your hands under your knees and spread your legs as far apart as you can." He fondles himself through his jeans as I hold my legs open for him, then he lowers himself back to the ground. "Just look at this wet fucking pussy," he rasps, running a single finger up and down my slit, circling my clit then my entrance over and over again. "Are you wet just for me, kitten?"

"Oh God, yes!" I groan.

He lowers his face and licks me once, then traces lazy circles around my swollen bud with his finger. "Are you going to come hard for me?"

My core pulses, every bit of me on edge. "Yes. So hard, I promise."

A serious look glazes over his eyes, and he stops touching me. He lifts his finger to my mouth, running the wetness over my lips. "Suck," he orders.

I moan as his finger slips over my tongue, the taste of myself coating my mouth. "I want you to cover my face with your cream. Understand? I want to smell you on my skin for days."

He removes his finger and lowers his face once more. My eyes roll into the back of my head as he flicks his tongue over my clit in rapid succession. Heat builds, and my whole body turns molten. My breaths stutter, and my muscles become rigid.

Then I see stars.

I cry out and come hard, gushing all over Armani's face while he laps at my pussy like a starving man. When he doesn't stop, I try to push him off, but he slaps me away like a bad kid touching something they shouldn't. "Armani," I whine, the sensitivity too much.

Until it isn't.

I don't know how he does it, but another orgasm approaches. This one takes me by surprise, slamming into me with so much force that I almost can't take it. The pleasure is immeasurable, and the sensations rush through every inch of my body thanks to Armani's skilled lips and tongue.

I feel like I'm floating in the air, basking in sunlight, and drifting through the clouds. It's like an out-of-body experience.

By the time he comes up for air, I'm gasping for a breath, exhausted, and unable to move.

"Armani," I murmur, trying to reach for him.

He stands up and kisses my forehead. "You did amazing, kitten. You were glorious."

He scoops my naked body into his arms, and I snuggle into his chest. He's so warm and smells amazing. He carries me through the kitchen and into a bedroom. "What about you?" I ask, tracing circles on his skin. "Let me take care of you."

He kisses the top of my head. "Another time. This night is all about you. Now get some rest."

Armani settles me down into his sheets, and I nestle in. He leaves for a moment and comes back with a rag. He doesn't even ask, just opens my legs again and cleans me up ever so gently with the warm cloth.

The action is tender.

Loving even.

He covers me up and kisses me again. "Sleep well, Valentina. I'll be back soon." Then he's gone.

He gave me such a gift tonight.

With him, I was able to let go.

With him, I was able to forget.

But when I wake up tomorrow, nothing will have changed. I'll still be a prisoner here, and my father will still be dead.

I push the thought from my mind as I roll over onto my side.

I'll deal with that tomorrow. For now, I'll bask in the exquisite soreness all over my body, compliments of the most gorgeous man I've ever met.

My mortal enemy.

Armani Moretti.

CHAPTER THIRTY-ONE

Valentina

The next several days are a blur, my body running on autopilot. I don't remember daytime or night, my exhaustion and utter sadness causing me to sleep at all hours just to forget.

I'd give fucking anything to be out of this house, to be out of Chicago and with my brothers while the grief is fresh. Sure, Armani and Fausto have been there for me through this, offering me comfort and a distraction if I'm ready for it, but the end result is the same. Once I'm alone again, the despair rains down on me like a torrential storm.

Sal didn't come to see me until last night. That was the first time I'd seen him since the moment I found out I no longer had parents. He's kept his distance from me. I don't know if he's letting all that bullshit about Marco slide out of kindness while I grieve, or if the sight of my sadness makes him uncomfortable.

I couldn't even bother to cower before him, wondering what abuse he was ready to throw my way this time. Surprisingly, our visit was short. He simply told me to pack for the funeral and that we'd be flying out to New York tomorrow.

Funeral…

That word bangs around my head like a ping-pong ball crashing around an old arcade machine.

Funeral…

It opens up memories I try so hard to forget of Mom's burial. Dad couldn't have been more disinterested, taking calls and writing emails during the sermon. I seemed to be the only one who gave a fuck that she died.

Maybe I was.

My brothers had virtually no relationship with her, and my dad was a shitty husband. Mom cried all the time about it, lamenting how he was never there and how she got word he cheated on her again. And again.

The bottle became her husband. Pills or alcohol, it didn't matter to her. The only criteria was that it would alter her reality so she didn't have to feel. I get that now. I get why she sought comfort in endless bottles of wine. For her, it was better to be numb all the time, even if her only daughter suffered. She was so depressed that my happiness no longer mattered.

In spite of all her shortcomings, she was still my mom, and I'll never get another one. Just like my dad. He was a shitty father, but he was still mine.

My hands clench into fists, grabbing onto the air as if it could bring me comfort. It doesn't. Not until Fausto unravels my fingers and threads his with mine. There it is again, that kindness I'm not used to. It seems to be the trigger to the tidal wave of emotions, and the floodgates behind my eyes open at the gesture.

He brings our hands to his lips, planting a kiss on my knuckles before lowering it back down onto the plane's armrest. I appreciate the gesture, really I do, but my exhausted mind starts to question everything that's happened since I got here.

Do these Moretti men actually want me, or are they just using me for their own nefarious reasons? Part of me wonders if Sal's distance, if his detestation, comes from something darker than hatred of my family. Sometimes, I think he's plotting to kill me.

The history of the mafia wars doesn't just get erased overnight. It doesn't just go away because six sacrificial lambs were sent out to slaughter in kill pens across the world. It sounds nice when you see it on paper, but really, who's to say the lines blur for only a moment? Anger festers, and sometimes old wounds never heal, then the taste of revenge is too sweet to pass up.

Lambs to slaughter...

That's what the six of us are—women with no fucking choice, used as pawns in a masterful game of chess played by the six reigning mafia families. One thing I know for sure is that as damaged as my brothers are, they will take care of the girl given to them. I just know it. Even Raph will be good to her, because deep down, they are good men.

Are the twins good men? Or are they just trying to fatten me up before they eat me alive? Sometimes I'm not so sure. Their sweet kisses cause a visceral reaction in me. I can feel it rush through my body and tingle my skin whenever they touch me. My response could be pure lust and nothing more. At least that's what I try to tell myself, but when I look into their eyes, I see more than just pure desire. There's something else there, though I can't say what just yet.

I consider the lies I've told and know they have held back as well. Those secrets, when unburied, could crush us all. In the end, I won't be the one who will survive it. I don't stand a chance against the strong, powerful Moretti men. They'll eat me for dinner then forget I ever even existed.

Fausto squeezes my hand and brings me back to the present. I blink and notice the plane has begun its descent. Blankets of clouds rise up from below, and soon we fly through them as if moving through a dense fog.

A city emerges once we pass through them, a city so familiar yet not at the same time. Everyone in the world knows what New York

City looks like from movies and magazines, so even if they haven't been here in person, they kind of feel like they have.

Tall skyscrapers rule the sky, the concrete jungle below more vast than I ever imagined. My heart pangs when we pass over the monument for the twin towers, and I send up a silent prayer for all the men and women who died that day.

It's a stark reminder of the cruelty so potent in this world, of how one person's deranged views can affect thousands of people even decades later.

Some wounds never heal.

I rub my chest, feeling too much. My heart suffocates as if a vise has captured it and is squeezing relentlessly.

Sal's voice sounds from across the cabin. "How are we on time?"

Fausto releases my hand to check his watch. "Mass starts in a little over an hour. We're right on schedule."

An hour…

That's all that's left until I'm reunited with my family one member short. I can't even be excited to see my brothers or meet Lucian's new wife. I can't get past the barriers in my brain, the walls I've erected to protect what's left of myself. Right now, it's all about self-preservation, nothing more, nothing less.

The plane lands uneventfully, the seasoned pilot setting her down with ease. Fausto helps me from my seat and escorts me down the short flight of stairs where a black limo awaits us. Armani takes me next, his hand lacing with mine as he pulls me into the limo and fits me snugly against his side.

Much to my chagrin, Sal enters and sits to my right, leaving Fausto out of reach. Having him so close, with his leg pressed against mine, has my anxiety flaring. What might he do to humiliate me today? Or will he allow me one more reprieve from his hatred to bury my dad?

I'll find out soon.

The door shuts on the limo and the driver shifts into gear. I'm reminded of my arrival in Chicago, crushed between those two Neanderthal black suits while on my way to an unknown location. That's kind of how this feels, except the men I'm squished between are far more imposing than the black suits could ever be.

Fausto grabs the bottle of champagne chilling for us and pours four equal glasses. While I'm not one to drink much, especially before mass, I welcome the cool beverage. The sweet carbonation fizzles past my tongue and down my throat with ease, and I extend my empty glass to Fausto, wanting a refill.

Sal takes the glass from my hand before Fausto can grab it. "No more, Valentina. That's enough for you."

Annoyed, I huff out a breath and roll my eyes, scooting as close to Armani as I can get so I'm not touching even a smidge of Salvatore Moretti. God, he can be a fucking prick sometimes.

Sensing my frustration, Armani squeezes my knee in an affectionate gesture as I cast my gaze out the front windows, my arms folded across my chest.

In less than an hour, we arrive at St. Patrick's Cathedral. The tall, white stone building, with its harsh angles and pointed peaks, resembles a gothic castle more than a church. It is almost too big to behold, taking up an entire block. I've never seen another one like it in my life.

Many memories exist in the place. This is where every Rossi is baptized, celebrates their first communion, is confirmed, and married. It's also where we come to say our goodbyes. Funerals are always held here. In fact, the last time I was in this place was to say goodbye to Mom. Here I am again, saying goodbye once more.

The limo parks right out front, and the driver steps out so he can open our door. Fausto emerges first, then Sal. To my surprise, Sal offers me his hand to exit, so I slip my gloved hand into his and allow him to help. As I slide out of the car, I realize why—the paparazzi are here. This is part of the mafia experience I've never had to live through. Having a fake name and a fake persona has kept me out of the media. This is probably the first time they have even seen me.

Leave it to them to take something as sad as a funeral and exploit it. The death of the great Carlo Rossi will stay in the headlines as long as the hungry readers continue to beg for more information, soaking up every detail of my father's demise.

From what the twins shared, it was a fire that killed him. Dad was caught inside the bowels of a company building and never made it out.

What an awful way to go.

Standing tall, I run my hands down my little black dress and steady myself in the pair of heels I'm not used to wearing. Sal rests his hand on my shoulder and guides me through the main doors and into the church. Even though I've been in here hundreds of times, the sight still takes my breath away.

Thick white pillars stretch from floor to ceiling, holding up the three-story building. Rows of dark pews run the entire length, split down the middle by a gold accented walkway. High, stained glass windows run around the entire upper portion, depicting angels, prophets, and saints, their unblinking gazes casting judgment down on the people gathered below.

The architecture is incredible. Severe arches meet polished gold accents and red carpet, and the altar itself is staggering in its presence. The massive, gold structure is as elegant as it is bold, covering a golden cross like a gilded trellis.

Behind the altar, the grand organ plays a soulful melody, its pipes mourning as much as the people filling the pews. Sal holds me tightly to his side, and my body goes rigid from being this close to him. Family and friends fill the pews, and many curious gazes drift from me to the men shrouding me. Armani takes his post on my right side, with Fausto next to him, making a formidable line of men as we walk down the aisle. In their dark suits, wearing even darker glowers, they startle those caught in their path.

I search for my brothers, scouring the people, but I don't see them anywhere as we take our place in the front pew. The skin on the back of my neck prickles, and I turn to see Gabriel and Lucian walking down the aisle with a gorgeous blonde woman between them.

I was wrong when I thought seeing my brothers wouldn't excite me. I wriggle out from between Fausto and Sal, practically leaping into Lucian's outstretched arms. *"La sorella,"* he whispers, wrapping his arms around me.

My eyes well with emotion. I haven't heard him call me that in so damn long. Releasing Lucian, I walk right to Gabe who brushes a kiss over my forehead. "Have you gotten taller?" he jokes, and I roll my eyes, punching him lightly in the shoulder.

When Gabe lets me go, I turn to the beautiful woman with them. "And you must be Dahlia." Her beauty is almost indescribable. With soft blonde hair and bright blue eyes, she is a white blossom amongst the wilted, thorny flowers of my brothers. I don't know this woman from a hole in the ground, but I feel a sense of kinship with her. We've both been plucked from our lives and thrust into the menacing hands of the enemy. We are both entirely alone.

I pull her in for a hug and squeeze tightly. "I always wanted a sister." She pats my back when I hear Sal clearing his throat, and I roll my eyes. "Idiots," I mouth at her, and she giggles before I take my place back at Sal's side.

Well, not just Sal.

Armani and Fausto surround me too, and part of me hopes no one notices the affection I'm receiving from the twins when Sal is the only one who should be doting on me. At least, that's how it should appear to the outside world. Fuck, if they only knew the truth.

When the organ switches songs, playing the sorrowful hymn "On Eagle's Wings," the entire congregation turns toward the back of the church as the doors open and Dad's casket is carried inside. It should be my brothers carrying him in. Hell, Raph isn't even here yet.

Six strong men, a few I recognize from my trip to the doctors' offices, have the honor. His casket is a dark mahogany that gleams under the soft lighting inside the church. As the priest passes us, he glances at Lucian. The terror on his face has me turning to look at my brother, wondering what the hell he did to this man of the cloth.

Dad's casket is settled at the base of the altar and the priest, Fr. William Sullivan, turns to address the congregation, but before he can get out a word, the church doors fly open again, and in stumbles my brother, Raphael. He's completely disheveled. His hair is a mess, and his suit is in tatters like he just crawled out of a bar fight.

Raphael pushes his way next to Dahlia and slurs, "Sorry I'm late."

"Raphael, what the fuck are you doing?" Lucian hisses loud enough that everyone near us can hear. Raph just laughs then glances in my direction.

He salutes me as if I were his commanding officer. "Oh hey, sis. Fancy seeing you here."

I give him a small, confused wave. I can't say I'm surprised that he showed up to Dad's funeral drunk, but I'm definitely disappointed about it.

Fr. William clears his throat and begins his eulogy. He talks about what a great man my dad was, how influential he was in our community, and how much he will be missed. When he spoke about how kindhearted Dad was, Raph began to laugh. I know no love was lost between Dad and my brothers, but I had no idea until now how deep the wounds were.

Armani, forgoing all formalities, grips my hand tightly, sharing in my grief as the mass continues on. It's not so much the scripture or the eulogy that gets me as much as the music. It speaks to my soul, each hymn ripping a new piece of my heart right out of my chest.

As mass ends and Dad's casket is carried out of the cathedral, "Be Not Afraid" wails from the organ. Part of me just shatters in that moment, praying that my dad was good enough to make it to heaven.

Outside, under the warm morning sun, friends and family approach me, and formal introductions are made. I'm so uncomfortable with all the people forcing their handshakes upon me and the Morettis that for a minute, I forget I'm even at Dad's funeral.

I keep glancing at my brothers, checking in on Raph. It's apparent that Gabe has his hold on Raph to keep him from trying to dip out early. Raph was never good with his emotions, drowning them out like Mom used to. Lucian gains most of the attention. With Dad gone, he now is the leader of the infamous Cosa Nostra, and people are begging to be recognized by the powerful mob boss.

It is strange to see my brothers in this kind of limelight when I've always observed from a distance. Finally, Sal has had enough of the pleasantries and introductions. "We're leaving. Now," he grumbles, gripping my upper arm.

"But I'm not ready to go yet," I complain, but it's not like it matters. He practically drags me into the back of the limo, the twins filing in behind us.

Fausto cracks open a second bottle of champagne, and I snag it from his hands, drinking right from the bottle before Sal can stop me. I exhale loudly after a few gulps and wipe my lips with the back of my hand.

No one tries to stop me.

The procession is long, with dozens of cars lined up with little purple flags marking them as mourners. The hearse leads the way, followed by my brother's limo, then ours.

The entrance to Green Wood Cemetery is like a smaller, darker version of the front of St. Patrick's Cathedral. They could be siblings.

Our driver weaves down the narrow roads, passing through the headstones until we reach the Rossi plot where all my relatives have been laid for their eternal rest.

All happiness escapes me as we exit the limo once more and walk behind my brothers to the open gravesite, passing monuments dedicated to great Rossi men and women of the past. As people exit their cars and surround my family, I can feel how uncomfortable the Morettis are. They must feel like small fish in a whirlpool of sharks, but we must be here, if nothing more than to uphold the image expected of them, of us.

A large, green tent was erected and lined with chairs, Dad's casket just in front of it. The mayor stands up from the crowd and walks to a wooden podium just beyond Dad's casket and begins to speak about how much Dad meant to him. I had no idea they were even close. That's how far removed I've been from my family.

The realization saddens me further as Lucian thanks the mayor and takes his place behind the podium. My shoulders begin to shake at seeing him standing there, now the head of the Rossi family, knowing how daunting of a task that is.

He takes a breath and begins to speak. "Thank you all for coming to be with us on this very sad occasion. My father..." He clears his throat. "My father was a man that the world, and his family, will not soon forget. His influence will no doubt last for generations, and I know that he would be so honored to have all you here saying goodbye to him."

He plucks a rose from a rather oversized display and tosses the flower on top of the casket as Dad is lowered into the earth, but then he does something I did not expect—he spits on the casket. It happens so fast that if I hadn't been watching him closely, I might have missed it.

Horrified, I glance around at the people gathered, but no one reacts, meaning no one saw it. Relief washes over me, but then a wave of pain hits. How horrible of a man was he that Raphael came to his funeral drunk and Lucian spat on the dead man's grave?

Dahlia, Gabe, and Raph join Lucian, grabbing roses too. Dahlia utters something I can't hear before tossing hers in as I move to grab two roses of my own. Tears pour down my cheeks as I run my eyes over the wood casket, grieving for the man I knew and the man I never will.

"Goodbye, Dad. Rest in peace. Give Mom a kiss for me." I take one final look and toss my rose on top of the others, then walk over to a place I haven't visited in the past three years—Mother's grave.

So many words come to the tip of my tongue, but I'm unable to voice them, each sentiment clogging in my throat. Fausto steps up next to me, placing his own flower on Mom's grave. After a few minutes pass, he places his hand on my lower back. "It's time to go."

I nod and turn to find my brothers. Gabe looks anything but mournful. If anything, I'd say he was annoyed. "I can't believe we still have hours to go at the funeral reception."

Lucian grabs Dahlia's hand. "I'm going to leave you to handle all of that, brother. You and Valentina can take the reins, right?"

I can't stop the shock that spreads across my face at the thought of him not coming. He has to come. "Where are you going?"

"Anywhere but here," he shouts over his shoulder, not even

glancing back as he leads Dahlia to a black convertible. Before I know it, Lucian and Dahlia are gone, speeding off through the cemetery.

I glance at Gabe who just shrugs. "You know how Lucian is."

The sad thing is... I don't.

"Come on, kitten. Back to the limo," Armani urges, gripping my hand in his, uncaring who sees. I appreciate that he's not embarrassed to be with me or to show affection. It's refreshing.

The four of us pile into the limo again, and as we drive away from my mom and dad, I feel lighter than I have in days. It's hard to breathe with a looming funeral, just knowing all the emotions you'll be forced to feel, but now that it's behind me, I can finally inhale deeply again.

Yes, I'll miss Dad in my own way, but with the initial trauma over, I hope I can begin to piece myself back together.

The reception flies by in a blur. I don't taste the food or enjoy the drinks. I don't smile and reminisce about my dad with family and friends, because really, I have no happy memories of him.

Gabe takes the lead, for which I'm grateful. Having never been given a single family responsibility, I felt like a deer in the headlights when Lucian suggested I help, how did he put it... take the reins.

Gabe puts on his friendly smile and mingles with everyone, stopping at every table as if this were his wedding. Sal and the twins do a great job of holding up the wall behind a table filled with food while I stand just in front of them.

"Can you guys excuse me for a moment? I have to use the ladies' room."

"I'll escort you," Sal insists, grabbing my upper arm.

I jerk away from his grip. "I'll be fine. We're surrounded by my family, not yours. I'll be back before you know it."

When I walk away, I feel three glares following me out of the hall. I quicken my pace toward the bathrooms and head inside. After I've finished, I wash my hands at the sink, but when I go to pull a piece of paper towel off the electric distributor, I find a message scrawled across the piece in black marker.

Val, meet me outside. Go through the back door.

I glance around, peeking under the doors to see if anyone else is in here, but I'm alone.

Who the hell?

I should go right back to the Morettis, or at least take Gabe with me, but curiosity gets the best of me. I crumple up the towel and toss it into the garbage before heading out. Keeping my head down, I make a beeline for the back door, hoping no one sees me.

When I step outside, it appears as if I'm alone aside from a man I don't know, who's sitting on a bench smoking a cigarette with a black cowboy hat perched on his head and a thick, black beard covering his face. I sigh into the soft breeze and tap my foot on the ground. Rolling my eyes at my own idiocy, I wonder if perhaps I imagined the whole thing.

Then I hear a familiar voice.

"We need to talk."

I look around and see the man with the cowboy hat stand up and pull down his dark sunglasses.

"Marco?" I gasp in surprise.

He saunters closer, his eyes blazing. "I've missed you, Val. You left me."

"I-I…" I take two steps back, but he continues his advance until my back is pressed against the cool brick exterior.

He cages me with his hands on either side of my head. "You're mine, Valentina. Mine! God himself can't keep me from you."

I consider screaming for help when he captures my cry with his lips. I pound on his chest as he presses against me, his hands seizing my own as he chokes me with his tongue. I can't think or breathe, horrified and terrified at the same moment. I should have listened to Sal. I should have let him come with me.

"Mmm, your lips taste so fucking good, Valentina. They'll look so beautiful wrapped around my cock. I can't wait to see your belly swollen with my child and your breasts heavy with milk."

"Marco, stop it," I grit out as he grinds his crotch against me.

"I know you want it too. I know you felt it that day at your house.

We belong together, Val. With your dad dead, our time has come. Together, we will rise to the top. You'll see."

I'm saved when the back door squeaks open and a funeral director emerges to light a smoke. Marco's hands are off me before the man even glances our way, his back turned toward the newcomer.

Marco lowers his voice, blocking my view of the man. "Soon, Val, I'll have you in my arms again. Once I get you back, I'm never letting you go. You're mine. Never forget that."

He walks away and I run. I run like my fucking life depends on it, and I don't stop until I'm back in the reception hall, standing in front of the Morettis.

"Val?" Fausto questions, concern on his face as I gasp for breath. "Val, what's wrong?"

I flick my eyes to Sal, worried what his reaction will be. "Marco Capelli. He's here."

To my shock, Sal rolls his eyes, an annoyed look on his face. "There's not a chance in hell that sleazeball got in here, not past—"

"Not past what?" I argue. "All the people here know him. Fuck, his dad is—was my dad's best friend. Who would think anything of it?"

Sal gestures toward the people. "Then where is he?"

I tell them what happened, about the note in the bathroom and how he cornered me outside, but they just brush it off.

Sal shakes his head and rests his hands on his hips. "I think you're hallucinating, Valentina. This has been an emotional day for you."

"He was here," I growl, looking at the twins for support, my hands balled into fists, but they look as confused as I feel.

"You… You don't believe me either?" I ask, feeling completely invalidated.

Armani runs his fingers through his hair and sighs. "I don't know what to believe."

"I'll tell you what," Fausto says, glancing up at the corners of the room. "I'm sure this place has security cameras. If they do, then we'll have an answer for sure. Until then, don't stress about it, okay? Besides, he has to go through the three of us to get to you."

I don't respond, too angry for words, knowing I'll regret whatever

I say. Fausto does have a point though. It would be almost impossible for Marco to get to me when I'm sealed tightly inside the Moretti compound.

If there's one lesson I've learned in life, however, it's to never underestimate those who are desperate and have nothing to lose. Desperation changes people, and if I'm not vigilant, I'll become its next victim.

CHAPTER THIRTY-TWO

Valentina

THE JOURNEY back to Chicago is as much of a blur as the trip to New York. Limo rides, private jets, black suits, and escorts. I'm fucking over it. I'm over it all, ready to put it behind me and try to make sense out of my new life.

We travel back to the Moretti manor in separate cars. Sal and Armani had to make a side trip to take care of a business issue. Not like I'd fucking miss Sal. His unwavering arrogance is exhausting. I mean, how big of an ego can one man have?

But I do miss Armani, and that realization surprises me. I've been alone for so long that in a way, I've trained myself not to need emotional support, and now that my reality has changed, so has my perception.

Thoughts of Marco have smothered my sadness. I guess I really shouldn't have been surprised to see him at Dad's funeral, but in a way, I was. Maybe it was the disguise—the clear, undeniable evidence that he had been trying to be someone else—that unsettled me. Perhaps he thought I told the Morettis about what he tried to do to me that night, but knowing Marco, he sees nothing wrong with his actions.

You're mine, Valentina. God himself can't keep me from you.

He meant it, every fucking word.

I haven't brought Marco back up to the Morettis, knowing that just the mention of a Capelli will cause a personality switch in Sal. I'm not too keen on him handcuffing my naked body to a chair again while he tortures my nipples.

Nope.

Pass.

Thumbs down.

Our limo comes to a stop in front of the grand staircase leading up to their house. Fausto doesn't wait for the driver to open our door, impatiently doing it himself. He's as ready to get out of this fucking thing as I am. All I can think about is a long bath, a fresh pair of pajamas, and binging a new series on Netflix.

Outside the car, Fausto takes my hand and leads me up to the house.

Joseph is there to greet us with a soft smile on his face. "Welcome home, sir, Valentina. I pray your trip was uneventful. Matilda has a light lunch prepared for you should you be hungry."

My stomach rumbles audibly, and I cringe, hoping no one heard. "Thank you, Joseph. I could use a snack."

Fausto claps Joseph on the shoulder as we walk past and head inside. I make a beeline for the kitchen, finding a platter filled with tiny sandwiches and a salad. I load up the empty plates Matilda left out for us then grab a bottle of water from the fridge before heading out of the kitchen.

Fausto is nowhere to be seen, and Joseph is off tending to some other matter. I'm actually alone in the house for once, and I'm not confined to my room. It figures the day I'm too exhausted to care is my first opportunity to taste freedom.

It's strange to be excited to see my own little apartment inside this mansion. I climb the stairs, glancing around to ensure I'm still alone as I make my way to my room.

Sure enough, the door is unlocked. Maids have been in because my bed is made, the trash is taken out, and it smells of fresh lilacs. I scoot right past the door, place my plate down on the coffee table, and head to the bathroom. The opportunity for a bath and clean clothes is too seductive to pass up. I'd rather clean up now then relax for the rest of the day.

I start to strip off my shirt when I notice something on my bed that I didn't see when I first walked in. Dropping the hem, I walk over to the bed and grab the little stuffed bear sitting amongst the abundance of pillows. He's light brown with black eyes, and he has on a red sweater with "I love you" scrawled across it.

Turning it over, I search the bear for a note identifying who this could possibly be from. My immediate thought is Payton. She's sweet and thoughtful enough to do something like this, but my old friend has no idea where I am, not a fucking clue. That thought causes a pang in my chest, and I add her name to the list of things I wish to ask the Morettis about, right under graduation.

Then I notice a little heart on his paw that says, "Push me." I almost feel like Alice in her episodes in Wonderland as I press the paw and a voice starts to speak. I expected it to be some high-pitched, recorded voice repeating the message on the shirt, but instead the voice is much more sinister.

"I love you. I have always loved you. We'll be together soon."

My hands tremble, and I almost drop the bear.

"It's fucking Marco," I mutter out loud in disbelief. I play it again and again, listening hard to make sure there's no doubt in my mind that it's him. I've never been more sure of anything.

But how did it get up here?

Unending questions seem to plague me as I grip the bear hard in my hands and head into the bathroom. I even take it with me into the tub after the water is filled and the bubbles are plentiful. Stripping out of my travel clothes is glorious. With gusto, I kick the constricting bra and even tighter jeans across the floor then step inside the bath.

The water is warm and wonderful, lapping at my body like summer ocean waves. I splash some on myself and place the little bear on the teak bath caddy stretching across from one side to the other.

For the sixth time, I press the button, the voice still the same.

"I love you. I have always loved you. We'll be together soon."

It's bad enough he showed up at the funeral in disguise. Now he's somehow infiltrated the Moretti house. I have to tell them.

Sitting up in the tub, I grab the bear and rip off its little red sweater, looking to see if some tracking device or camera has been placed inside it.

"Valentina."

Fausto's deep, booming voice echoes across the bathroom. Not expecting anyone to barge in here—stupid of me really, considering my past history of bathroom privacy issues—I jump at the sound and drop the bear in the water.

"Shit, shit, shit," I grumble, losing the bear in the bubbles as it sinks to the bottom of the tub. Jerking my head toward the man in question, I make sure he can hear the annoyance in my voice. "What the fuck are you doing in here, Fausto?"

Fausto walks farther into the room, his hands clasped behind his back. He's still wearing black slacks and a burgundy polo. "Can't a guy sneak a peek at his girl in the tub every once in a while?"

"First of all, I'm not your girl. Second of all, you made me drop a crucial piece of evidence."

I fish out the soggy teddy bear and hold it up for him to see.

"Evidence you say?" he asks from beyond the glass.

I nod, wringing out the wet bear. "Evidence about Marco. He's coming for me."

Fausto rolls his eyes. "He can't get to you, little pistol."

"That's what you think," I murmur under my breath.

"If you're so sure he can get past all of our guards, our security systems, and us, then please, share this evidence you have."

I press on the soaked wet paw, feeling the little button under the fabric, but nothing happens. "You fucked it up," I tell him. "You scared me and made me drop it. Now the voice recording won't work."

Fausto's eyes darken. "Raise your voice to me again, Valentina, and I might have to throw your naked ass across my lap for a round of discipline. It's long overdue anyway."

My core clenches at the thought of me draped across his legs, his hand spanking my ass. What would that feel like? Would I enjoy it? I consider snarking, but I'm too tired for all that right now. This week has depleted me.

I decide to ignore him, looking away and lowering myself deep into the tub. "Valentina," he growls, opening the glass door.

"Can't I just take a bath by myself for once?" I complain, lifting my eyes to his. He squats down and grabs a fistful of hair, yanking my head back. I gasp, reaching up to my hair as my torso lifts from the water, exposing my sudsy breasts.

He turns my head, our faces only inches apart. "You might not think of yourself as my girl yet, pistol, but I do. Every glorious inch of your exquisite body belongs to the Morettis, and if I chose, I could just take you now."

Fausto drags his free hand down my body, playing with the bubbles over each breast before plucking my nipples. My breath stutters and a low heat begins to grow within me, because dammit, it feels good. Fausto's eyes become hooded, noticing my reaction. "You like when I boss you around and play with your body, don't you, pistol?"

His hand sinks under the water, slipping down my belly before cupping my pussy. He squeezes my pussy, and a wanton groan escapes my lips.

"Fuck," he groans, dipping a digit between my lower lips. Feeling horny, I part my thighs for him. "You're playing with fire," he warns, tightening his grip on my hair while tapping my clit.

"Maybe I want to get burned," I retort breathlessly, all thoughts of Marco far from my mind. "Burn me, Fausto. Brand me with your touch."

"Fuck!" he shouts, releasing me. I fall back into the water, his fingers combing through his own hair. "You're not ready for the things I want to do to you. Finish your bath and get dressed. We're going out tonight."

I feel the exhaustion in my limbs and how heavy my eyes are. "Fausto, I'm really tired. Can—"

Fausto slams his fist against the glass. "I don't give a fuck. We are going out. Finish your bath and get ready. I even bought you an outfit for the occasion. I expect you to wear every fucking thing in that bag. Understand? I'm on edge, Val. Remember rule one."

With that, he leaves the bathroom, and I'm left with an aching pussy and a soggy teddy bear.

CHAPTER THIRTY-THREE

Fausto

I LEFT HER DOOR UNLOCKED, sick of Sal's needless control over Val. This girl is no threat. She's often meek and undeniably submissive in the sweetest ways. It took every ounce of willpower I had not to strip my clothes off and enter that bathtub with her.

The sight of her soapy body will stay with me forever, a memory to jerk my cock to when the mood strikes, and as I pace back and forth down the hallway in front of her room, my desire for this girl elevates to an entirely new level.

Her door opens, and out walks a dark goddess here to claim my soul. Fuck, I'd give it to her. "Holy shit," I exclaim as she timidly walks toward me, her head lowered ever so slightly. "You wore it."

Valentina slides her hands down the leather outfit, tugging at the hem of the very short skirt. "You basically demanded that I do."

She's right.

I grip my chin and blatantly appraise her, dirty thoughts of things

I'd like to do to her running through my mind. "And what a damn fine decision that was. Do a slow little twirl for me, pistol."

Val's hands clench as she rotates, allowing me to take in every sexy angle of her body encased in black leather. Her breasts are pressed together by the short, snug leather top, which zips up the front. Her midriff is bare, displaying her flat belly, narrow waist, and the little dimples on either side of her lower back, making my cock harden.

The skirt—holy shit. Short and sexy, it barely touches her upper thighs, and it hugs her ass so tightly that I'm oddly jealous. To complete the outfit, thigh-high boots lace up the backs of her legs on a two-inch heel. She's styled her hair in loose waves with the front pulled back. Her dark makeup somehow makes her blue eyes seem brighter, and a deep red lipstick is painted over her lips, a color I plan to see smeared over my cock one day when I finally give her a taste.

"Wow," I murmur, unable to believe this is the same girl I first met what feels like only days ago.

"Yeah?" she says, unsure of herself. "You like it?"

"Pistol…" I close the distance between us and press my lips to hers, trailing my hands down her back to cup her leather-clad ass. "Are you wearing the panties I left you?" I ask, releasing her mouth. Her cheeks flush and she nods. "Show me." Valentina shudders against me before I back away and spin my finger in the air, ordering her to turn around. She licks her lips nervously before twisting away, her fingers latching onto the bottom of her skirt. "Part your legs and lift it up, Valentina." I leave no room for argument as she moves her legs apart and slides the leather skirt up, blessing me with a view I was not prepared for.

The sheer, black lace thong dips between her ass cheeks then wraps around them in the most seductive way. Her pussy lips are clad in the same material, and I know if I had her bend forward, I'd be able to see their outline through the gossamer material. If I did that, though, I'd be forced to fuck her right here in the hallway, and I have other plans for my pistol tonight.

I drag my fingers down her ass and slide a digit over her pussy, making her gasp. "You have no idea how sexy you are, do you, pistol?"

She responds with breathy moans as I squeeze her hips and slam her ass into my groin. "So fucking sexy," I murmur, brushing her hair off her shoulder and planting a kiss on her soft skin.

My cock thickens, and I force myself to stop, pulling her skirt down before spinning her to face me. "So fucking sexy," I reiterate, grasping the zipper on her top and pulling it down so it displays the swell of her tits. "These shouldn't be hidden."

"My nipples are going to slip out if you undo my zipper any farther," she complains, grabbing her chest.

"I don't see a problem."

She scoffs and rolls her eyes, pushing my hands away. "Okay, enough fiddling with my outfit. I'm uncomfortable enough without you making it even more revealing."

"Be careful, pistol, or I'll have you walk around topless tonight."

Her lips part, and she inhales sharply, her eyes wide and a little afraid. "You wouldn't."

She's right, I wouldn't, but only because no other man deserves to lay their eyes on this perfect creature, on my woman. However, she doesn't need to know that.

"Wouldn't I?" I counter, tugging at my leather vest.

She appraises me as she considers my words, running her gaze up and down my body. She pauses on my eyes. "Are you wearing eyeliner?"

"The shade is called charcoal, if you must know, and yes I am, because tonight, where we're going, Fausto Moretti doesn't exist." I do a little spin and run my hand through my oiled hair. "Tonight, I'm going to introduce you to my friend, Tony Caruso."

Grabbing her hand, I lead her down to the garage and over to my electric blue Jeep. I've already taken the hardtop and the doors off. Hopping into the driver's seat, I pat the passenger seat. "Get in."

She walks around to the other side, her heels clicking on the concrete, then stops and stares, looking more confused than ever. "I can't even reach the seat, Fausto."

"Didn't you ever climb trees as a kid?"

"Not in a leather outfit and high heels," she counters, placing her hands on her hips.

I nod. "Okay, you have a point."

She looks very pleased with herself as I slip out of my seat and walk over to her, grip her waist in my hands, and lift. She's so little she's like air, effortless to move. With her ass so close to my face, I have visions of yanking her panties to the side and tasting her right now.

Instead, I set her gently in her seat and even help her with her seat belt. She looks at me gratefully as I walk back over to my side and buckle myself in.

"So," she begins as I start the engine and shift the Jeep into drive, "want to tell me where we're going?"

"It's a surprise."

She frowns. "I don't like surprises."

Now that's surprising. Every girl likes surprises. "Why not?"

She folds her arms over her chest and looks away as we exit the driveway. "In my world, surprises are never happy things. They are coming home to find a man you barely know has broken into your home, learning your parents are dead, or having black suits show up at your school to abduction-nap you."

"Abduction-nap?" I question.

"Yeah, it's my version of abduction and kidnapping. Like what you guys did to me."

I startle at her words but don't let it show on my face, placing sunglasses over my eyes. "You can't kidnap what's already yours."

She shakes her head, and I can feel her annoyance. "You can if the victim isn't made aware ahead of time. It seems like everyone knew about this treaty but me. I was left in the dark while you all had time to plot and prepare. You can't imagine what that day was like for me. What it's still like."

"What is it like?" I ask curiously.

She pauses for a moment. "It's like a bad dream that you can't wake up from no matter how hard you try. It's like being stuck in a dark hole with no way to climb out. It's suffocating at times. I feel more like your pet than I do an actual human. You and Armani both tell me that

I'm your girl, yet you treat me as so much less than that. It's confusing, Fausto."

I think about all our interactions since she's come to our home. "I'm sorry for that, Valentina. I'm not going to make excuses for how I act because this is how I am. My words are not intended to make you feel like less than the incredible woman you are, even if it comes across that way." I pull onto the freeway and consider how much to tell her. "Growing up in the Mafia, part of you withers and dies. Endless death, destruction, backstabbing, and killing changes a person, especially a kid who's exposed to such things. I've become used to shouting orders and even more accustomed to having those demands obeyed. That part of my life has spilled over to what I have with you, and I don't know how to change that."

I glance to my right and see I have her full attention. She's shifted in her seat to face me and is holding her hair in one hand so it doesn't blow away in the wind. "And I don't know how to change my perception of being treated this way. You talk of how the Mafia changed you, well, it has changed me too. I've been alone for years, fending for myself, even though I was kept away from the bloodshed. I've had no family and no support. My brothers and Dad lived in a different state than me, for fuck's sake. Imagine having all that freedom, then having your family's mortal enemy strip that from you. A part of me wishes I knew ahead of time what Mafia life was really like, then maybe this wouldn't be such a hard pill to swallow."

We drive the rest of the way to The Crater in silence, both lost in our thoughts, my mood switching from excited to pissed. Tonight was supposed to be an adventure for us, a way for her to forget Carlo's death and focus on something new and exhilarating.

As we exit the freeway and make our way through the slums, catcalls and other sexual comments are thrown her way. Fausto would have lost his shit, but tonight I'm Tony, and he just goes with it. Val shifts in her seat, keeping her eyes straight ahead as she tries to ignore them.

Turning into the old factory, I glance over to see Val looking up at the tall, abandoned smokestacks. "We're going to a factory?" she asks, appearing more grim than I feel.

My Jeep sinks into a pothole and Val shrieks, bouncing in her seat while she clutches her seat belt for dear life. "This place is so much more than its appearance. Just like you, pistol."

Shifting the Jeep into park, I swing out and round the hood, knowing she'll need help to get down.

"God, this is embarrassing," she mutters, as I lift her off her seat and set her on the torn asphalt.

"I think it's cute," I tell her, bopping her on the nose before taking her hand in mind.

She smiles but it doesn't reach her eyes. There's an unease there, and she leans into my side as we walk up to the rusted metal door, the bass from the music blasting inside growing louder.

"You ready?" I ask, gripping the cool handle.

"I guess," she answers, looking up at me.

"Get ready for a night you will never forget." With that statement, I pull the door open.

Blacklights shine and neon paint glows. The Crater is already packed to the brim with people.

Val's grip on my hand tightens. "What is this place?"

I gesture around us. "This is The Crater. An underground bar and fighting ring."

She casts a nervous glance at the currently empty ring before swallowing hard. I hold in a laugh and pull her around the ring to the man at the back.

Fast Stan lights up a cigarette, blowing out a cloud of smoke as he runs his eyes up and down Valentina. "Tony, I see you brought a guest today. Will she be fighting too? You know how good female matches pay."

Val bristles against my side, and I wrap my arm around her shoulders. "Not today I'm afraid. The little vixen needs a bit more training before I unleash her."

Fast Stan lets his disappointment show, his gaze traveling up her legs and pausing on her chest. "That breaks my heart, Tony. A body like hers needs to be seen, not hidden away."

I grab Val's hand and spin her around. "Does her body look hidden to you?"

Fast Stan groans. "She looks like a leather present I want to unwrap."

Unable to help myself, I pull out the Sig Sauer I had tucked in the back of my pants and aim it at Fast Stan, racking the slide loudly. "You touch her, you die. Understand?"

He holds his hands up in surrender. "The fuck, Tony? Can't you take a fucking joke?"

I shake my head. "Not when she's the brunt of it. Now, why don't you be a good little bookie and tell me who's on the roster tonight."

Fast Stan flips through the pages of his books, muttering the names of each man ready to enter the ring. When he mentions Brennan "the beast" Gallagher, I tilt Fast Stan's chin up with my weapon. "I want him."

Fast Stan blinks. "He's yours. Second round."

"Third round, and make sure he knows I'm coming for him."

The bookie nods, and I holster my gun before taking Valentina's hand again. "Nice talking to you, Fast Stan."

He just glowers at me as I walk away, taking Val to my corner of the bar. Crystal, wearing her patented leather vest and black cowboy hat, sees me and showers me with a smile. "Tony! Nice to see you back so soon." She turns to the man sitting in my seat. "Move your fuckin' ass, Tony's here."

The man takes one look at me, slips graciously from the barstool, and offers me a drunk grin. "It's all yours, Tony man."

I turn to Val and pat the seat. "Sit and order yourself a drink."

She climbs up and perches carefully in the chair, her lean legs crossed. She immediately becomes the envy of every single man in here, and probably a few of the women too. "But F—"

I stop her with a powerful kiss, one that forces her off balance so she clutches my shoulders. When I pull away, I lean close to her ear. "In here, I'm Tony, and you are—"

"Naomi," she finishes with a wry grin. "But I don't have an ID. I can't order a drink." She lowers her voice. "Besides, I'm not even twenty-one yet."

"In here, pistol, dirty money replaces IDs. The sight of blood pays better than most jobs, and a leather ensemble like yours will get you whatever the fuck you want."

Crystal walks over as the announcer introduces the men battling in the first fight and slides a whiskey in my direction. She nods at Val. "Girlfriend?"

"Fuckbuddy," I answer quickly, shocking Val.

Crystal just laughs and swivels her head toward Val. "Pick your poison, sweetheart. I don't have all night."

Val taps her chin with a single finger. "Umm. I guess I'll have a glass of wine."

Crystal smacks her lips. "Got no wine in here besides the ones comin' from the ring after a good ass whooping."

Val stumbles over her words as she watches Jimmy "the rat" Richards and Jerome James begin to fight, so I order for her. "She'll take a screwdriver and a wet pussy." Val looks over at me, stunned. "Make that two wet pussies."

Crystal tips her hat. "You got it, Tony."

"A wet pussy?" Val inquires, transfixed by the fight. "What the hell is that?"

I lean back against the bar and face my girl. "That is what happens, *Naomi*, when you slip those skimpy little panties off and finally let me lick that sweet cunt of yours."

Her eyebrows arch, and her mouth gapes as Crystal comes back with my order. She hands Val her drink, then slides two pink shots in front of us. I offer Crystal my gratitude and place a shot in Valentina's hand. "This is a wet pussy. It's pink and tastes delicious, much like I know you will. Bottoms up."

Her cheeks turn crimson, and she bites her lip at my words. Raising my shot, I clink our glasses before gulping mine down. When she hesitates, the rim resting on her lower lip, I tip up the bottom, forcing her to drink it all. She grimaces only slightly as she sets the empty shot glass down on the bar. "That wasn't too bad actually."

"Great. I'll order us another round."

She presses a hand on my chest. "Tony, that's not what I—"

I place my finger on her lips. "Shh. Let loose a little bit and stop worrying about everything. This night was supposed to be a getaway for us, a place where we don't have to be what the world demands us to be. Now tell me, what would Naomi do if her man offered her a shot?"

Val chews on her lip and blinks her gorgeous eyes up at me. "She'd drink it."

"There's my girl," I say with a smile.

We down a second round of shots and sip on our drinks as Jerome pummels Jimmy. Jerome raises his bloody hands in victory after delivering a particularly hard blow to the side of Jimmy's face. The ref counts to ten and boom, the match is over, chants for Jerome resounding through The Crater.

"That was intense," Val notes, sucking seductively on her straw.

"They get better as the night wears on. They'll announce round two soon. Let's change seats for a better view. Come on."

After Crystal refills our drinks and shots, Val and I walk over to the stands and perch ourselves in the top row overlooking the ring. We toast and take our third shot, Val grinning happily as the next fight is announced.

"How are you feeling?" I ask as Brian "the brain" Harvey lands a loud kick to the side of Tyron "the teeth" Johnson.

Val meets my eyes, her features softening. "I feel good. Thanks for this."

I kiss her lips softly. "Don't thank me yet. The night is still young."

The fight wears on, and I place my hand on her bare leg, slowly inching upwards until my finger rubs her slit through her panties. "Fausto, what are you doing?" she asks, and it's her tone that gets me. It's not angry or condescending, it's… playful. If other viewers were closer, I'd have to scold her for forgetting to call me Tony, but no one can hear us where we're sitting.

"Open your legs, pistol. Let me play with that sweet pussy of yours."

Val shifts, her eyes darting around as I press harder. "People are watching."

"You worry too much. No one can see us up here. We're in the last row where the lights don't reach. Now spread those thighs apart for me."

"Fausto," she moans.

"Do it. I want to make you come in front of all these oblivious people. Don't tell me you don't want it too."

Val blinks up at me, her eyes darkening, the alcohol giving her the courage to do what she might not have done sober. "Okay."

"That's a good girl. Now lean back and drape your left leg over my lap." She's so fucking gorgeous. She listens to my directions, even though she's nervous. I grab her knee and yank her leg wider, dragging my hands down her bare thigh to her panties.

She gasps when I cup her pussy over the lace, squeezing hard, and then I pat her cunt, making her jerk, before sliding my hand under the fabric and finding her slick with arousal. "Fucking wet already," I tease, tracing her slit with the pad of my finger. "You like it when others watch, don't you?"

Her words are lost when I sink my finger between her lower lips, pressing against her entrance. She sucks in a loud breath, her hands clenched around the armrests as I sink that finger inside her and slowly fuck her. "Can you hear how wet you are, pistol, as I fuck you with just my finger?"

She moans, and her legs start to tremble as I slip my finger out of her and drag it up to her clit, circling the engorged little bud. "So sensitive, aren't you?" I murmur, dipping back inside her.

I repeat this pattern, fucking her hole then teasing her clit until her body jerks with every soft touch. "Do you want to come, Valentina? Do you want to come with your thighs spread wide while a man you barely know plays with your pussy where others will hear your cries of pleasure?"

"God, yes," she breathes out, her chest rising and falling rapidly.

I stroke her clit faster, feeling the little bud roll around my fingertip. "Then come for me, Valentina. Take your pleasure."

Her breaths shorten and her eyes squeeze shut. In a burst, she comes, my finger covered in her cream as I work her clit until she's pushing my hand away.

I fix her panties and lower her leg back down, letting her rest and enjoy the feeling. "Rest easy, pistol. Keep your eyes on the ring, and I'll be back before you know it."

As the bell chimes, indicating Jerome's victory, I head down the stairs and into the back room.

It's time to show Val how a real man fights his battles.

CHAPTER THIRTY-FOUR

Valentina

I CAN'T BELIEVE I let him do that.

My body still shakes from the pleasure, my own wetness coating my inner thighs. Finally, when I open my eyes and look around, I expect to be the focus of many men's eyes, but Fausto was right, we must have been hidden enough in the shadows, lost in the loud violence in the ring.

What's crazy is… I want more.

I want his hand to play with me again. I want to come three or four more times until I can't take it another second. My hand clenches, and I glance around, wondering if anyone would see me if I did it myself.

Inside the ring, workers spray cleaner and scrub the fresh blood off the mat, and fresh towels are stacked on stools behind the corners of the ring. Fausto said to keep watching, and I do, especially when I hear the staticky speakers announce the next fight. Brennan "the beast" Gallagher is announced first, and cheers erupt, but when Tony

Caruso's name is spoken, the crowd goes crazy, and I realize that's Fausto's fake name.

The need to touch myself flees, and I sit up taller, focusing on the ring as I sip my drink. What did he call it? Some kind of tool... The hammer maybe, or the hacksaw.

Fuck if I know.

Alcohol churns in my system, washing away my sadness and enhancing my mood. With my blood heated, I watch Fausto climb into the ring, his hair greased back and muscles glistening with oil. He's only wearing boxing shorts, and his sculpted body calls to me. His muscles flex with every move, displaying his defined physique.

He is fucking gorgeous.

His opponent is a big man, taller and broader than Fausto, but he has more of a weight lifter's build. With strong arms and a bigger belly, one might not think he has the body of a fighter.

The men shake hands, and Fausto starts bouncing around on his toes. Brennan beats on his chest, howling like a madman, then throws a punch at Fausto who ducks to his right with ease. Fausto sidesteps and lands a punch on Brennan's belly, but the punch doesn't faze the big man at all.

He lunges for Fausto, landing a blow to the side of his head. Fausto spins, retaliating with an attack of his own, his foot landing on Brennan's throat. The big man stumbles backwards, his arms catching on the ropes as Fausto leaps into the air. Before Fausto can land his attack, however, Brennan spins out of the way, so Fausto alters his trajectory, twisting to face Brennan before he touches the ground.

The two men circle each other, feinting kicks and punches, making me perch on the end of my seat and shout, "Get him, Tony!"

I think he hears me, though he keeps his eyes focused on the menacing man snarling before him. Fausto feints right then drops to the ground, sweeping a leg under Brennan's unstable feet, forcing the big man to fall on his ass.

Brennan struggles to get up, his big belly now causing a severe disadvantage. Fausto takes control, leaping onto Brennan and pounding the man's face. Brennan flails, trying and failing to land a hard hit, crashing into Fausto's arms instead of his head.

Blood drips from Brennan's eye and mouth, his red teeth bared at Fausto. When the ref pulls Fausto back, he bounces around the ring on ready feet as the ref begins his ten count. Brennan rolls onto his side, breathing heavily and shaking his head as if trying to bring himself back to reality.

"Five. Six. Seven."

Brennan pulls himself up on eight and raises his fists. Fausto jumps high into the air, kicking both legs into Brennan's chest. Brennan flies backwards. Off balance, he tips over the ropes and falls out of the ring. The ref begins his count again, and I scream Fausto's fake name, cheering and pumping my fists.

Brennan smashed his head against the ground when he fell from the ring, and blood pours from a laceration on his face while men surround him, shouting at him to get up.

"Five. Six. Seven."

Fausto already begins celebrating, throwing his hands up in the air, knowing there's no fucking chance in hell Brennan can get his big ass into the ring in the next three seconds.

With the ref raising his hand, Tony Caruso is declared the winner of the match. Cheers ring out as men celebrate not only Tony's win, but the exchange of money coming in their direction.

I continue to celebrate, jumping around like a crazy person. Fausto points at me then curls his finger, beckoning me to him. Giddy with excitement, I race down the stairs and climb into the ring, uncaring that I've flashed half the audience my lace thong. Fausto scoops me up and kisses me. I wrap my legs around his waist while he grips my ass in his hands, demanding more from my mouth.

I tilt my head back to catch a breath. "You were amazing!"

Fausto arches an eyebrow while people on the side of the ring dump a bucket of water on Brennan's head. "Yeah? Watching your man fight turned you on, didn't it?"

"Maybe," I tease, biting my lip.

"Good enough for me." He grins, setting me down on my feet.

"Looks like your hands are empty. Best fill them up with a couple glasses before you get too thirsty."

Laughing, Fausto and I exit the ring and take up our position at the corner of the bar as we did before. This time, though, he sits in the chair and pulls me onto his lap. It's a little awkward but I enjoy being this close to him. It makes me feel good.

Within an hour, The Crater dies down, money is counted, and winners are paid. Poor Brennan had to be taken out in a wheelchair. It took four men to lift him into the damn thing. Fast Stan made an even faster exit when Fausto caught him looking in my direction.

"Sheesh, you're so possessive," I joke.

"This ain't nothing, darlin'," Fausto responds in his best southern drawl.

Crystal, overhearing us, just smiles, cleaning the remaining few glasses left on the bar top. My buzz is still kicking, leaving a perma-grin plastered on my face. Fausto kisses my shoulder or my neck between taking sips of his drink.

When the final guest has left, Fausto calls Crystal over. "Can I close up for you? I've got something I need to do before I go."

Crystal's eyes dart from me to Fausto. "Whatever you need, Tony. Just shut off the lights and lock the front door behind ya. And don't let the door hit ya where the good Lord split ya."

Fausto tips his imaginary hat. "Yes, ma'am."

Crystal drains her sink and wipes down her counter, then grabs a beat-up old purse and heads out the front door. "I'll lock it behind me." She winks at Fausto then leaves.

I turn in my seat to face Fausto. "Mind telling me why we're staying here so late?"

Fausto drops his eyes to my chest, and he runs a finger between my breasts. "I'd rather show you than tell you."

His insinuations make me squirm on his lap. "Oh? I forgot to bring something for show and tell today."

"Don't worry," he says, brushing his lips over mine. "I've got something for the both of us."

He kisses me, dragging his tongue across mine as he scoops me out of the chair and carries me back to the ring. "Fuck, I've been waiting to do this all night," he growls. I'm about to ask him what when he grabs my thong and rips it in half.

"Fausto!" I scream as he sets me down and points at the ring.

"Climb in there, pistol, nice and slow, so I can get a good view of that sweet pussy."

His words make my cheeks heat, and for a moment, I'm embarrassed, but I channel my fake persona, Naomi, and do what I think she would do. She's a strong, confident person, and right now, so am I.

"Of course, Tony," I say seductively, turning to face the ring.

Fausto growls and grabs himself, squeezing his cock through his shorts. "Going to be a bad girl, are you, Naomi?"

I grab the bottom rope and lift one knee onto the ring, bending my torso down so he can get a good look at my pussy. The cool air wafts against my wetness, and I glance over my shoulder at Fausto who has his hand shoved down his shorts.

"Fuck, pistol." He moans, and I moan right back. Watching him rub himself while he's staring at me is turning me on.

"Around here, I'm called Naomi," I correct, flashing him a sultry grin. I climb all the way up and crawl to the center of the ring, making sure my legs are wide enough for him to see every move, then I turn back to face him, perched on my knees with my thighs slightly parted.

Fausto leaps into the ring, rolling under the ropes in one suave move. "And does Naomi do as she's told?" he asks, standing tall and placing a finger under my chin.

"Depends on who's giving the order," I retort quickly.

Fausto's eyes heat, and he drops my chin, nodding at my shirt. "Pull that zipper down and free those titties. Breasts as perfect as yours should never be hidden."

Gripping the zipper on my shirt, I tug it down slowly, tooth by tooth. When my breasts pop free, Fausto drops to his knees and seizes them in his hands, squeezing hard before plucking my nipples into twin peaks. "Lock your arms behind your back, gorgeous," he orders.

I moan, following his demand. My head drops back as he works my chest like an expert masseuse, making wetness pool between my legs.

Then suddenly, he's gone, and I open my eyes, missing his touch. Fausto walks around the perimeter of the ring, dragging his hand along the top rope. "Here, in this ring, I've conquered dozens of opponents, but tonight is my greatest victory."

"Brennan put up a good fight," I agree, confused at the change of subject, my core aching for him.

Fausto shakes his head, his eyes locked on my breasts. "Not Brennan. You."

"Me?"

Fausto nods. "Ever since you came into my house, you've not only taken over my thoughts, but you've mended a broken part of me, a part I didn't think could be fixed." He continues walking, his forceful strides causing my breasts to softly jiggle with each step. I swallow hard, taking in his every word.

"All I ever wanted in life was power and money, and to have a higher kill count than my brothers."

"You—You have a kill count?" I stutter out, crossing my hands over my chest, feeling vulnerable.

"I am second-in-command of the Outfit. Surely you didn't think my hands were clean." He stops pacing, his jaw muscles working. "You moved."

"Sorry," I squeak, latching my arms behind me again.

He begins walking once more. "But you, Valentina. You've made me feel things I've forgotten I could, things I buried so deeply inside me that I thought they were lost forever, and I want to return the favor. I want to make you feel good, even if I have to boss you around in my own way to do it."

Fausto jumps out of the ring and ducks down below the edge, and I crane my neck to see what he's doing. When a cord of rope is tossed up on the ring, my nerves fire and my heart begins to race.

"What are you going to do to me?"

I hate the fear in my question and how shaky my voice sounds.

Fausto climbs back in, grabbing the rope and unbinding it. "I'm going to make you feel good, Valentina. Now stand up and strip for me. I want nothing keeping me from every inch of your skin."

Trembling in equal parts fear and desire, I stand up and face him, dipping my hands under my skirt before easing it down over my ass, leaving me in nothing but my thigh-high boots. I point at the boots. "These too?"

"No," he grits out, his eyes fixed on my pussy. "Leave those on. Now walk toward me with confidence, pistol. You're drop-dead fucking gorgeous. It's time you acted like it."

I lick my lips and head his way, swaying my hips as I walk.

"That's a good girl," he praises, biting his lower lip. I stop two feet in front of him as he drags his eyes all over my naked flesh. "So fucking perfect." His gaze captures mine. "Do you trust me?"

Do I? I ponder his question as his eyes search mine for the answer. "Yes."

I can almost see his shoulders sag with relief, but that emotion quickly gives way to the dominating man yanking on the rope before me. Fausto brushes my hair behind my shoulders, and just the slight contact of his skin against mine makes me shiver. He nods toward the ropes. "Sit on the middle rope for me."

Taking a few steps to my left, I turn and attempt to sit on the rope, but it's no easy task, my body wobbling precariously. Fausto is there immediately, holding me steady. "Wrap your arms around the top rope like this." He snags my left arm, showing me how to wrap it through the rope for support, and I repeat it with my right. "So fucking perfect."

I watch with curiosity as he picks up the coil of blue rope and stands before me. "Don't be afraid, pistol."

"I'm not," I respond more confidently than I feel. Fausto takes me at my word and begins tying the blue rope around the top rope surrounding the ring, entwining my arm within its wicked web. He spins the rope around my arm, around my neck, and down my other arm until I'm completely bound to the top rope.

Fausto takes this opportunity to tease my nipples with his calloused hands, rolling them between his fingers and plucking them so hard it makes my breasts jiggle as they bounce against my chest. I moan as he plays with them, arching forward for his touch, somehow feeling each pinch in my clit.

"So receptive, aren't you, pistol?" He flicks my hardened tips, and I jerk, moaning at how good it feels. "The gentlest touch sets you off, the harder ones even more so. I can smell your excitement in the air, and I haven't even used my tongue yet."

I whine when he steps back, needing him, wanting him.

"The next step is going to be tricky, pistol, but I think we can do it." He kneels down before me, pressing my thighs apart, a length of rope around his shoulder. "Lift your leg up on the rope. That's it."

It's a balancing act. When I have one leg draped across the middle rope, he secures it like he did with my arms, starting at my knee and working all the way up to my thigh. He wraps the rope around my belly, then up my back, and across my chest, repeating the same steps on the other side. His lip is caught between his teeth as he works, looking like a mad artist desperately trying to finish his masterpiece.

Finally, he wraps my other thigh and ties it off, leaving my legs wide open and bound, my pussy spread and vulnerable. Even my breasts are surrounded with rope, causing a squeezing sensation.

He steps back, admiring his work, and I can't help but squirm under his blatant stare. "I've been waiting for this moment since I first laid eyes on you, Valentina. I've dreamed of tying you up in the ring since that first day when I tossed your sassy ass against the wall in my dining hall for trying to leave. Do you remember?"

"Yes," I mutter, the act which scared me so much then would make me so hot now.

"And now here we are, a few weeks later, and you've submitted to me completely, trusting me with your body. You're helpless and vulnerable, your pussy is spread wide, your tits are bound, and you're wearing nothing but a pair of fuck-me boots. You are giving me this ultimate gift, a gift I don't deserve."

Fausto drops to his knees in front of me, using his thumbs to spread my pussy lips even farther.

"Fausto," I whine as he extends his tongue and flicks my clit. I jerk in the ropes but am unable to move even an inch, forced to feel every lick and suck.

"Fuck, you taste so good," he growls, sucking my pussy lips this time. It feels so good but leaves my clit aching and my forgotten nipples throbbing. It's like I need two of him to satisfy everything my needy body craves.

"So wet, so sweet," he purrs, adding a finger to the game and pressing it inside of me. He finger fucks me gently, and I hiss when he adds a second finger. "Look how pretty your cunt stretches for me, Val. You're doing so good. So good."

He continues his praise as he sinks his fingers deep, twisting them as he pulls them out. He kisses my clit then wraps his soft lips around it, sucking gently while his fingers keep a steady pace.

I'm unraveling.

He sucks harder and pumps his fingers faster, the sound of my wetness filling my ears. Then he backs off, removing his lips and fingers, leaving me gasping and aching.

"Your cunt is throbbing for me, Val. I can see your little hole clenching. So fucking sexy."

He flicks his tongue at me then traces my entrance before sinking his tongue inside of me. "Fuck!" I cry out, his fingers pinching my clit gently. He keeps me right on the edge but unable to plummet. "More. Please."

Fausto lifts up on his knees, his face close to mine, his lips and chin covered in my arousal. "More what? More of this?"

His fingers whisper over my nipples, tracing around the nubs but not touching them, then he teases my clit the same way.

"Fausto, please," I beg, trembling. My clit throbs so hard I want to fucking scream and cry.

"More of this?" he asks, sucking my nipple into his mouth and biting hard.

"Yes!" I shriek, thrashing my head from side to side as he takes my other nipple between his teeth while I gasp for air.

He chuckles deeply when it finally slips from between his teeth, and I half cry, half whine, confused by how my body responds to the pain. "Perfect fucking titties deserve to be abused."

I suck in a breath when his hand connects with my breast. Fausto spanks my tits, one after the other, my orgasm threatening to burst with each searing smack. I almost can't take it.

"Or did you mean more of this?" he taunts, dragging his hand down to my pussy and strumming my clit once, almost sending me over.

"Fausto!" I shout, more frustrated and horny than I've ever been in my whole fucking life.

"What?" he asks as if he's oblivious. "Tell me what you want me to do and I'll do it."

"Don't make me say it."

Fausto circles my clit again and plays with my breast. "I won't make you do anything, pistol."

I blink hard, pain etched on my face. "I... I..."

"Yes?" he prompts, continuing his torment.

"Ugh! Fine! Lick me, please!"

"I'm sorry, Val. You're going to need to be more specific."

I feel like I'm going crazy, like I've lost my damn mind. This must be what purgatory feels like. "Lick my clit and fuck me with your fingers."

Fausto grins with victory, slipping his finger over my clit as if rewarding me for answering. "Anything else?"

I swallow hard. "And when you're done, I want you to fuck me with your cock."

Fausto's eyes grow hooded as he lowers his head down to my pussy and feasts with a seductive mix of his lips, teeth, and tongue. His fingers drive into me in a relentless pace, the tip of his tongue flicking rapidly against my engorged clit.

"Yes. Yes. Yes!"

My screams bounce off the cement walls as my orgasm overtakes me like a flash flood. I'm drowning and suffocating while also sucking in more air than I ever have before. My limbs twitch, my cunt pulses, and my vision turns white until I can't see, only left to feel.

I don't know when his hands leave me as I hang here limply, but I feel my left leg release from the rope. I can't look, my body depleted as he lifts my freed leg up higher, and that's when I realize he's securing it to the top rope against my arm.

With my pussy open wide and aching, Fausto's breath fans across my core. He spreads my entrance with his fingers. "I can see inside you, Val. Do you have any idea how hot that is?"

I'd squirm, but his ropes are too tight, and all I can do is shake my head. "Look at me," he orders, and I raise my head, shocked to find him naked and fisting his thick cock. His body hair is trimmed and neat, enhancing his size. He steps on the first rope and taps his dick against my lips. "Open wide and suck me past those full lips, Val. Coat my cock with your saliva while I fuck your mouth."

Too tired to argue, I part my lips. Fausto presses forward, sliding his cock over my tongue. I wrap my lips around him as he pulls out then presses in again, deeper this time. My gag reflex forces me to choke on his cock.

"That's a good girl. Choke on it if you must."

I moan as his hips move faster and faster. I can't even suck anymore, concentrating on pulling in a breath when he exits my mouth for a second. Fausto grips my hair, holding my head still as spit dribbles down my chin and onto my breasts, tears streaming from my eyes. My nostrils flare when I get my first taste of him. The saltiness coats my mouth as his smooth cock drags along my tongue, pounding my lips.

He shouts as he releases my hair and jumps down to the mat, and I drag in a breath. My lungs barely fill before he's gripping my hips and lining himself up with my wet hole.

"Are you sure, Val?" he asks, nudging my entrance.

"I'm sure," I rasp. "Fuck me, Fausto. I need it."

He doesn't ask twice, dragging his cock along my slick pussy before pressing inside. I wince as he pushes harder, sinking deeper. I look down and watch his cock disappear inside of me, my cunt feeling so full it might burst.

He cups my cheek in one hand. "You're so fucking perfect, Val. So perfect." Then he fixes his gaze where we're joined, watching himself slip out and sink back inside. It's so erotic, my swollen pussy lips giving way to my engorged clit as Fausto's cock takes me slowly, filling me up like I've never been filled before.

It doesn't hurt like I thought it would. I expected pain and blood when I lost my virginity, but there's nothing but pleasure, a different pleasure than I had when his lips kissed my clit.

No, this is deeper, stronger. The thrum of my heartbeat pounds through my entire body as a new orgasm grows, different than the last one.

Fausto wraps his arm under the top rope and lowers his body.

"Holy fuck," I cry out at the new angle, his cock hitting a spot inside me that has my body spasming.

Fausto's moans become louder as his pace quickens. He pinches my nipple, tweaking the sore peak hard as he fucks me faster. I wail out a constant scream, my voice bouncing with each thrust as this feeling grows. My body floods with pleasure, and lava fills my veins.

Fausto slams into me, my tits bouncing and pussy aching even as my cream drips from inside me. "Oh God," I scream as the orgasm takes me down, every muscle seizing. It's like the Fourth of July when the fireworks blast proudly during their grand finale. It's everything, every emotion all at once, as the world around me explodes.

He shouts, his lips pulled back and teeth bared. Fausto's body turns rigid, every muscle flexing as he pulls his dick out and aims for my chest. Wet spurts of warm cum drizzle all over my tits as he grunts out his release, our bodies covered in sweat.

Spent, Fausto falls to the ground, lying flat on his back. I hang from the ropes, content in my euphoria, even as every muscle aches and every joint cries to be freed from these bindings.

I think I must have fallen asleep for a moment, because the next thing I know, I'm lying on the mat with Fausto between my legs, wiping me clean.

"You okay?" he asks, helping me sit up. He attends to me with care, helping me back into my top and zipping it up for me.

"I am... amazing," I answer, and he kisses the top of my head before assisting me to my feet. I grab the rope while he holds my skirt out for me and helps me step inside it on unbalanced, heeled feet. He even shimmies it up my legs for me.

We don't bother to look for the thong he ripped off me, since the fucking thing wouldn't cover me anyway.

Fausto guides me down from the ring and scoops me into his arms. "Come on, pistol. Let's get you home."

I curl into him as we leave The Crater and he sets me down in his Jeep, buckling me in. We ride home in comfortable silence, holding hands the entire time. I wear the marks from his ropes proudly, reveling in the pain from my chafed nipples, the burning of my spanked tits, and the ache from my sore, fucked pussy.

Every inch of me hurts, but I wouldn't have it any other way.

CHAPTER THIRTY-FIVE

Salvatore

Watching the cameras, I flick between feeds on the security system. That seems to be all I do anymore, checking each screen to see what she's up to, to see what *they* are up to.

My brothers are fucking smitten and it's irritating as shit. Can't they see what happened to me when I lost Gianna? Can't they see how weak they become if they fall to their knees for a woman, or a girl, in this case?

A little baby girl.

That's all she is, and my brothers are trying to fucking play house with her. A motion sensor pings and I switch to channel eight—the garage. Fausto is parking his blue Jeep, the one he takes over to his grimy fucking fight club. I almost switch back, but then I see him take something out of the passenger side, and I realize it's her.

He took her with him.

Dressed in leather from head to toe, the little whore looks more like a slut than she ever has. Her thigh-high boots, dark makeup, and wild hair only add to my low opinion of her.

She can barely walk, wobbling on her tall heels, clutching onto Fausto's arm while he smiles down at her. They laugh at something, and he pulls her into his chest, her back facing the camera. As he bends down to kiss her, he grasps her leather-clad ass and lifts up her short skirt.

When her bare cheeks are exposed, my cock jerks, but my anger won't allow me to enjoy this view. I can't like her. I owe it to myself, to my family, to let my anger fuel my reactions. He smacks her ass, and Valentina crumbles in his arms, seeming to enjoy the action.

I fade out, recalling that time in her bedroom when I held her down and spanked her ass for acting out. She didn't enjoy it then. What's changed? Fausto spins her around, her back pressed to his front, and kisses along the side of her neck. He lifts the front of her skirt and gently rubs her bare cunt while her head lolls back against his chest.

She shaved her pussy...

I can't fucking watch this anymore.

Switching off the screen, I slam my fists onto my desk and push off my chair, pacing my office. How can they let her do this? She is the enemy, the enemy of all enemies. She is from the one family we loathe above all others... and my brothers are fucking her?

No.

They wouldn't go that far yet, not without running it past me.

But a voice in my head questions that. There has been a shift in our relationship at work since she wedged herself between us.

I have to fix this.

I won't lose them to that little whore. The fact that she left the house in that skimpy little outfit, with her bare cunt displayed for the world to see if she shifted the wrong way or bent down, tells me what kind of woman she is.

She's just like the rest of the power thirsty, money hungry bitches I have suck my cock when I don't feel like fisting myself. She'll do anything to get under their skin, anything to blind them from seeing what she truly is—a spy.

She has to be, it's the only thing that makes sense.

Marco isn't coming after her like she claims. She's meeting him intentionally and trying to cover her tracks by saying false things about their relationship.

Fausto checked the security footage at the funeral home, and surprise, surprise, the camera where she claims he assaulted her was not functional. Does she really think I'm dense enough not to see through that? I'm the fucking Don of the Outfit, for Christ's sake. It's my job to plan ahead, to make sure I'm not seen.

I have my guys on high alert, guarding our product and making sure shipping goes smoothly. I will not have another batch fucked up under my watch.

She may think she has the upper hand, but she has another thing coming. Salvatore doesn't just bring the storm, I am the fucking storm, and I will come down so hard on her ass when I can prove her disloyalty that she won't be able to sit for days.

My cock agrees, excited to dish out her punishment.

I'll continue to dig and claw my way through her life until I can find my proof. I can't wait to see the look in her eyes when I catch her, and the look on my brothers' faces when they realize I was right the whole time.

A Rossi can't be trusted.

My father beat that into my brain. Armani and Fausto lost that memory somewhere along the way, clouded by an eighteen-year-old whore who can barely take care of herself.

She shaved her pussy...

I saw her naked, I know her cunt was covered in dark hair. When did she manage to do that?

When my brothers started fucking her...

No!

I need to get out of this house. I need to smell the fresh air and release some of this festering anger into the world. I need to cleanse my soul from the madness leaking inside of it.

My phone vibrates in my pocket, and I pull it out to see a text come through.

Joseph: Sir, can you come out back for a moment? The pool crew just arrived and are awaiting your instructions.

Me: I'll be right down.

Grabbing my suit jacket, I slip my arms into the sleeves and head through the first floor to the backyard. With June approaching, it's time to tear off the winter cover and get our pool in working order. The foreman waves and walks over to me, discussing his plans for the day and the cost involved.

After giving him the go-ahead to start working, I leave him to it and head into the garage. Knowing where I plan on heading, I take a less conspicuous car, a white Mercedes E-Class.

The engine revs to life, and I shift it into sport mode, the engine becoming a low rumble. I drive with my music blasting, trying to keep my mind off her.

Twenty minutes later, I arrive at my destination, parking my car in the back of the lot even though every spot is open.

St. Luke's Catholic Church is set smack dab in the middle of a working-class community. Of all the churches in the area, this one is my favorite. Not only is the parish small, but no one here knows who I am. Here, I'm just a fellow parishioner showing my love for God.

Fr. Castiglione is an ancient man, his bushy eyebrows as white as his hair. The soft-spoken man is loved by everyone. Unlike most priests, Fr. Castiglione has a knack for his sermons. He makes them short and sweet and easy to understand and implement into your life.

He's been leading St. Luke's all my life, but even as a boy, he looked just as he does now. As I enter through the old, wooden front doors, part of me waits for God to strike me down with lightning. A sinner such as me shouldn't be welcome in a holy place like this. Fr. Castiglione would disagree. He would tell me all sinners are welcome in God's house as he has in the past.

I haven't kept my secrets from Father. I've let him in, confessed my sins, and exposed my soul during confession. He knows exactly who I am, yet he doesn't shame me for it or cower in my presence. He accepts me, looks past my flaws, and does his best to help me bear them.

No penance exists that will absolve me of my sins. There aren't enough Hail Marys or Our Fathers that I could utter to cleanse the darkness spreading within me.

As the years have passed, my ticket to heaven seems less and less attainable. Too much blood coats my hands, and too much death and suffering has been inflicted on my command.

Maybe I should abandon my love of God and start making deals with the devil.

St. Luke's is an old church that's had an update. Low arching stained glass windows depicting the Stations of the Cross surround the perimeter. A fountain of the Virgin Mary stands vigil at the entrance, the holy water flowing gently. The pews have been stripped and stained, the dark wood varnish replaced by lighter tones.

The altar itself is simple. Fr. Castiglione's chair is made from wood, the stain matching the pews. Then there's Jesus Christ himself rising from the back of the altar, forever cursed to hang from the cross. At times I can't even bring myself to gaze up at Jesus, unable to see his pained face etched forever into stone as he endures his crucifixion.

He suffered so much for our sins and gave his life in the most terrible of deaths, yet something so simple as walking away from an argument can seem impossible to me at times.

Shame swallows me whole again as I walk down the aisle of the empty church and sit in the second pew, my hands clasped together and head bowed in prayer.

Not long after I sit, the slow, steady gait of Fr. Castiglione shuffling down the aisle reaches my ears. He pauses next to me, his friendly hand offering me comfort as he squeezes my shoulder.

"Sal, my boy. It's nice to see you."

Father's Italian accent is thick, unchanged through his years of living in America. It reminds me of my nonno, God rest his soul.

"Thank you, Father."

Like Jesus, it's hard for me to lock eyes with Fr. Castiglione. The kindness in his gaze is hard to accept. Fury and hatred are much easier for me to embrace because that's my language. It's been many years since I've felt much else, because in my world, it's easier to be numb and to forget how to feel.

He pats my back as I stare hard at the ground ahead of me.

"I sense your distress. Tell me what ails you, son. Would you like to join me in the confessional?"

"I am nobody's son," I mutter back, instantly regretting lashing out.

Father is not perturbed by my words. "Ahh, that might be true outside these halls, but here, under this roof, surrounded by God's love, we are all his children."

I blink hard and turn to face him. "How do you do it, Father? How do you stay here year after year with the sins and sorrows of an entire community placed on your shoulders? How do you withstand the pressure when your knees threaten to buckle?"

Father's eyes soften, and his wrinkled face offers me a friendly smile. "I turn to God. He shares my burden and reminds me there are consequences of having such power. Heavy is the crown, my son. Scoot down, let an old man sit beside you."

I slide down, allowing Father to rest his old bones next to me. He gazes up at Jesus with such love in his eyes that it almost makes me uncomfortable. "There are times in our lives when the pressure seems like too much. Times when we want to take the easier path even if it's not the right one. It's those times when we need God most, when we need to stop and listen. Chaos often drowns us in its icy grip, freezing our hearts and numbing our minds. The devil sees opportunity to strike when we are at our weakest. He thrives in our anguish, clawing his way into our souls and urging us to take the easy road."

I consider his words. "And what happens if we've already taken the low path? What if his grip on you is too hard to shake?"

Father twists the handle of his cane. "It is never too late to change the course of your life, son. It is never too late to let go of your anger, share your burdens with those who love you, and allow happiness back inside your heart."

Emotion clogs my throat, but I swallow it down, forcing the burning in my eyes to retreat.

"It's a girl, isn't it?" Father asks pointedly.

Letting out a sigh, I turn to face him. "How did you know?"

He smiles at me. "An old man can tell these things after years and years of sharing the burdens of his community. Tell me about her. What's the first word you think of when you see her face?"

"Enemy," I blurt out, and Father arches his bushy eyebrows. "She is the daughter of my greatest adversary, a girl I shouldn't allow myself to care for because of who she is."

"*She* isn't your adversary, you just said so yourself. You can't fault a girl for being born any more than you can be angry at a flower for growing. She had no control over that. She didn't choose her father any more than the flower chose for its seeds to be planted. Don't you see? It's all part of God's plan. This is your test, Salvatore. This is your chance. There are no coincidences in life. Everything happens for a reason, and it's up to you to take the hard path and make the hard choices. You'll be a better man for them."

Anger has been such a crutch for me. It's easier to hate everything and everyone than to open myself to love again. I tried that once, and losing that has nearly broken me. "I've been drowning in hatred and pain for years. I don't know if I can see past it anymore."

Father clasps my shoulder again. "You don't have to be the man people expect you to be. You can choose to become something else, a better version of yourself, something more than a name that evokes fear. Ask yourself, who is Salvatore Moretti? If you don't like the answer, be strong enough to change it. The right path is never easy, son, but if you head down the wrong road for too long, you might lose yourself forever."

My chest clenches as I consider all my wrongs and how bad I've hurt this girl for something out of her control, then my thoughts shift to Lily who's suffering the same fate as Valentina. I realize I've become the monster in my own story. I'm no better than Carlo Rossi. "I'm just lost, Father," I confess.

Father Castiglione pats my shoulder then grips his cane to help him stand. He slips from the pew and faces me. "Then let her help you find your way. Let her be the light that guides you from the darkness. God suffered for our sins, it's time you atone for yours."

With that, he shuffles down the aisle, leaving me to think hard about my next move. I only see two choices.

Either I can continue on this path of death and destruction, my heart an impenetrable fortress, or I can let the crack in my wall grow and allow myself to feel again, risking a broken heart for a chance at salvation.

The question is, am I brave enough to choose the hard path?

If I'm not, I need to be brave enough to suffer the consequences.

CHAPTER THIRTY-SIX

Valentina

The telltale ache low in my belly has me groaning. I didn't want to wake up to this, even though I knew it was coming because the birth control pills this week are placebos. Armani is expecting me in the gym later this morning, our ride all planned out.

Running into the bathroom, I shove my pants down and wipe, checking the toilet paper.

Yep.

I've got my period.

I get off the toilet, pull out every drawer, and open every cabinet in my bathroom, not finding a single pad or tampon anywhere.

"Fuck!" I shout in frustration, sitting back down on the toilet to make a toilet paper pad. I shove it in my panties and adjust myself, pressing the paper up near my bleeding hole in hope that my flow doesn't start off heavy.

But who am I kidding? It's always heavy.

Embarrassment washes over me as I realize I need to ask one of the guys to take me to the store. Maybe one of them would loan me a car so I could drive myself.

I laugh at how absurd that sounds. It's barely been a week since I've been allowed to wander around the Moretti mansion without a fucking escort, so they damn sure aren't going to let me leave alone.

Rifling through my closet, I pull out my favorite pair of sweats that I've had since eighth grade. The elastic around the waist is nonexistent after years of use, making them perfect period pants.

I toss on an old sports bra, a baggy Hogwarts shirt, and my favorite Nike flip-flops before exiting my room. I trod down the hallway to the stairs, trying to avoid all the staff as I look for one of the guys.

It chaps my ass that the first one I run into is Sal—the man who hates me more than anything in this world.

Things have always been awkward between us, but for some unknown reason, things have been slightly better since my dad's funeral. He's not quite as mean as usual, though he still avoids me like the plague, which is fair enough, because I avoid him too.

I can't run away from him today though, because I need help.

Sal sits in the breakfast nook, holding a fresh cup of coffee in his hand while he flicks through his phone. I stop a few feet from him, and he doesn't even look up from his phone.

"Hey, umm… Have you seen either of the twins?" I ask, shifting my weight.

"Nope."

That's helpful. "Okay, uh… Do you know where they are or can you text one of them or something?"

Sal sips his coffee, keeping his eyes fixed on his phone. "What they do with their time is not my business. Neither is it yours. Is there something I can help you with?"

Fuck me. He's such an arrogant asshole. "I need to go to the drug store."

Sal waves me off. "Check with Matilda. We have every medication you could possibly need."

"I don't need medication," I snap. "Well, that's not all I need."

"I'm sure Matilda—"

Frustrated, I don't let him finish his sentence. "Unless she has a fucking tampon I can borrow, I don't think Matilda can help me!"

Sal finishes his coffee, exhaling loudly. "I'll take you."

I can't hide the shock in my voice. "You—You will?"

In the most shocking gesture of the year, Sal walks over to me and ruffles my hair, his gaze focused on my shirt. "Can't have you bleeding all over my house, now can I?"

I can't tell if he's joking or serious. "Umm, can we go now?"

Sal types rapidly on his phone. "Yep. Follow me."

He walks through the house and into the first-floor garage. I follow behind him, keeping some distance between us as he decides which car he'd like to take.

He pauses with his back toward me. "Which one do you want to ride in, Valentina?"

Wait, what?

Sal is giving me a choice?

"Umm…" I glance around at all the sports cars. Though they are fun to drive in, my body hurts too bad to be jostled around that much. "Which one has the smoothest ride?"

Sal points to a big Ford truck. "This one. Hop in."

Hop in?

Who is this guy?

Casting a suspicious glance his way, I walk to the passenger side and open the door, relieved when a running board swings out from under the truck.

"Can I turn on the heated seats for you?" he asks.

"Sure. It will feel good on my lower back."

He switches the car on and opens the garage door. "Did you hurt your back?"

I narrow my eyes on him. Is this his version of small talk? "No. But it aches when I'm on my period."

"Hmm. I didn't know that." Sal pulls out of the driveway and heads down the street. "So where do you need to go?"

I keep my eyes focused out my window. "Any pharmacy or drugstore will be fine, thanks."

The truck drives like a dream, taking bumps with ease. I kick off my flip-flops and curl up in the seat, my cramps becoming more painful. We arrive at a drugstore less than ten minutes later, and then I realize I have a second problem. "Umm, Sal? Can I borrow like twenty bucks? I forgot to bring my wallet."

He pulls his wallet out of his back pocket. "I don't have any twenties, but here." He hands me a crisp one-hundred-dollar bill.

I clutch the money in my hand and climb down from the truck. "Thanks. I'll pay you back when we get home." I slam the door shut before he can say anything else.

I guess I shouldn't be surprised when I hear his door open and close, his footsteps rushing up behind me. "You can't go in there yourself."

"I am perfectly capable of finding my own period products and paying for them," I say rather haughtily.

He shoves his hands in his jeans, keeping pace with me. "I just want to make sure trouble doesn't find you while you're in there. That's all."

"Aww, Sal, I didn't know you cared." I laugh at my own sarcasm, and to my utter shock, he chuckles. He actually chuckles. I stare at him, wide-eyed. "Are you feeling okay? You seem... different."

He shrugs. "Let's just say I've had a change of perspective."

"Who are you and what have you done with Sal?" I tease.

"Maybe the monster has been slayed, *Valentina*."

He speaks my name like a whispered prayer offered up moments before death, and I shudder when I hear it.

I refuse to acknowledge that and scurry through the store, trying to lose him. I have to crane my neck toward the ceiling to read the signs overhead to see which items are in each aisle.

12-B Feminine Hygiene

Oh goody.

I duck down the aisle and find my favorite brand of tampons and those horrible, long overnight pads. I've been wanting to try those cup things I see all over social media, but I'm terrified that damn thing will get stuck inside of me and I'll have to go see the doctor to have it taken out. I can guarantee that will be my luck.

Can you even imagine the mortification?

Receptionist: Hey Dr. Christine's office, how can I help you?

Me: Oh just have a menstrual cup stuck up my cunt and need help fishing it out.

I'll stick with tampons for now.

After grabbing two boxes of regulars, two boxes of supers, and the box of pads, my hands are full.

Then Sal is there, taking my boxes from my arms. "Here, let me help."

"You don't mind carrying around tampons?" I ask, surprised.

"Not really. Every g—*woman* needs them, right?"

Did he just stop himself from calling me a girl? That's his favorite insult—little baby girl.

"Yes?" I murmur cautiously, moving to the medicine aisle. I scoop up a box of Advil Liqui-Gels and a bottle of Midol then head for the register, but then a thought pops into my mind.

Snacks!

Yes. I need snacks. If I'm going to suffer for the next two to three days bleeding, cramping, and suffering from period diarrhea—my favorite—then I might as well have some comfort food.

Sal follows behind me as I scour the candy aisle, but then I feel it...

The gush.

You know, the one where you frantically try to find a bathroom because you need to change your tampon—except I haven't bought any yet.

Abandoning the candy aisle, I rush to the counter and toss my medication on it. Sal stacks my boxes of supplies for the cashier to scan. Unfortunately for me, a pimply kid whose name tag identifies him as Jeff is ringing me up, sneering at my tampons. He chews on his gum loudly, his yellow teeth surrounded by inflamed red gums.

Gingivitis much?

"Is all this really necessary? Can't you just like, hold it in and not bleed for one month?"

Is he serious?

I'm taken aback by his ignorance. "Umm, no, I can't hold it in. Don't you think I would if I could? Or do you think girls like to bleed out of parts of their body for several days every month?"

He looks me up and down, chewing louder. "I think there might be, uhh… some alternative reasons to use the" —he holds up my super boxes— "extra-large tampons." He laughs like a crazed, cracked out chicken and slaps Sal in the chest. "Am I right, my man?"

I glance at Sal, expecting him to laugh right along with this kid. He's always taken every opportunity to shoot me down and drag me through the mud, but it's not amusement I see on his face—it's fury.

Sal unholsters a gun and aims it at Jeff. "Apologize. Now. Or I'll blow every pimple off your ugly fucking face."

Jeff's gum falls out of his mouth, and he raises his hands, looking at me in terror. "S-Sorry, miss. I-I was only joking."

"Jokes on you, motherfucker," Sal grumbles, stowing away his weapon. "Expect a meeting with your manager. I'll be filing a formal complaint with your place of employment and with the police for sexual harassment."

Sal takes the hundred from my hand, tosses it onto the counter, and grabs the loaded bags of supplies. "Come on, Val. We're getting out of here."

Sal practically jogs to the car, but I have to kind of waddle, praying my toilet paper pad is still working. I dread having to part my legs to climb into the huge truck, so I awkwardly try to clench my thighs together as I get in and buckle myself.

Thankfully Sal doesn't notice, the tires on his truck screeching as he pulls into traffic. I groan as we hit a bumpy patch, holding my knees close to my chest.

Glancing at the man driving, I try to do what he said he's doing and look at him from a new perspective. I associate his face with anger and hate, so it's strange to see him any other way.

But right now, he's just a man.

A gorgeous man.

Sal is always put together and well groomed. His shirts never have wrinkles, his shoes are always shiny, and his hair is always styled. His five o'clock shadow is always the perfect length, allowing others to see how handsome he is without hiding behind a full beard. But it's his eyes that make him different from his brothers.

Unlike the twins' dark irises, Sal's are bright blue, though I've never gotten to look at them properly. Sal never looks me in my eyes. Never.

I've only been awake an hour, yet today is a fucking whirlwind. Sal has been kind, and he hasn't raised his voice or insulted me. Usually I walk on eggshells around him, trying hard to pretend I don't exist and that my filthy Rossi breath isn't tainting his air.

Today, he's different. I just hope that the monster who lurks within him doesn't resurrect itself.

I want to acknowledge what he did for me back there, but the words keep lodging in my throat. Part of me still fears speaking to him, wondering which Salvatore Moretti will appear.

I decide to keep it short. "Thanks for sticking up for me, Sal."

Sal merges off the highway. "No need to thank me. That little prick had it coming."

"Yes, I do need to thank you," I insist, shifting to face him. "You've gone above and beyond for me today, and I want you to know I appreciate it."

"I hardly think driving you to the pharmacy for essentials is going above and beyond for anyone," he scoffs. "But… you're welcome."

I know what he's doing, he's trying not to make a big deal out of the obvious changes in his personality, so I let it go. Sitting in silence, I rest my head against the seat while keeping my thighs pressed tightly together.

Sal breaks the silence. "Why didn't you get any snacks?"

"Back at the pharmacy?" I ask, keeping my eyes closed.

"Yeah. You walked down the snack aisle, then you bolted."

It's time to think up a quick lie, because the truth is mortifying.

Oh, I just had a big clot of blood drop out of my vagina, and I'm terrified it's soaked through my makeshift toilet paper pad.

"I felt bad spending your money." Yeah. That sounds better.

"Don't be silly, Valentina. You said you were going to pay me back anyway. Besides, if we're to get married in the very near future, it's time we begin sharing things, like money."

I'm pretty sure my jaw unhinged itself from my face and flew out the window. "Married?" I gulp.

Sal locks eyes with me, but only for half a second before deciding to focus on my lips, but that half second was everything. I saw *him*. I felt him. A connection sizzled between us before he cut it short, and it took my breath away. "It's expected of us to keep the peace and all that. Unless you want to be the reason the mafia wars begin again?" A wry smile crosses his lips.

"Salvatore Moretti, did you just make a joke?"

His smile grows, and he turns back to the road. "It's been known to happen." We drive in silence once more, my mind reeling from the quite normal and easy conversation we've been having.

"So, Valentina, what's your favorite candy bar? If you are to be my wife, I should know these things about you."

My response is immediate. "Snickers. Not even a real question. And you?"

"Take 5 bar."

My belly rumbles. "Oh, those are good too."

"Potato chips or Doritos?" he asks.

"Doritos."

"Cool ranch or nacho cheese?"

My brows furrow. "Nacho cheese all the way. I can't even stand the breath of a person who ate cool ranch Doritos."

He laughs again, and the sound is quite pleasant, his smile etching away some of the anger lines distorting his face. "Okay, next question. Pop or soda?"

I glare at him. "Pop. Soda isn't even a real word unless it comes right after cream."

I realize how that sentence could be turned into something sexual and my cheeks heat.

Comes right after cream...

Kill me.

"Pepsi or Coke?" he questions.

I stick out my tongue in disgust. "Neither. It's Dr. Pepper or bust."

He smacks his lips and turns down our street.

Did I say *our*?

What is happening to me?

Back inside the garage, Sal helps me down from the truck and even carries my bags. He follows along next to me as I hike up to my room. "I'll take those, thanks," I tell him, taking the bags before entering my room.

Sal stays in the hallway with a sad look on his face. "Anytime. I hope you feel better soon."

And then he's gone.

I quickly dispose of the saturated pad imposter and hop in the shower. I don't do a full shower, just one round of shampoo and a quick body scrub, needing to feel clean after all that.

After I get out of the shower, I slip in a tampon and down three Advil, angry at myself for wearing my favorite comfy outfit for only an hour. Luckily I spend most of my days in comfy clothes when I'm not in my uniform, so my closet is filled with loose items. I shove my legs into a pair of dark blue cotton panties and go for a pair of pajama pants that my brother had left at my house years ago. The forest green plaid pants are loose on me, and I pair them with a Quidditch shirt.

Today is a no bra kind of day.

I give my hair and teeth a quick brush, pulling my hair into a French braid, then walk out into the main room. Someone's been in here, and not only have they been in here, but they have brought me my favorite snacks.

On my coffee table is a bag of Snickers minis, a family-sized bag of nacho cheese Doritos, and a six pack of Dr. Pepper. There's also a travel mug. I lift the lid and smell delicious coffee, so I take a sip.

It's perfect.

I collapse onto my couch in disbelief. After our conversation, he must have gone back to the store—well, probably not that store—and gotten my favorite things.

I'm just baffled.

The rest of the day passes with me curled on my couch eating all the snacks. Around lunchtime, Fausto sends me a bag from Nordstrom with a big, cozy blanket inside and a soup and salad from Panera. Armani visits me for dinner, bringing me a soft bunny plushie and a pepperoni pizza. He even stays to watch a movie and massages my shoulders, expecting nothing in return.

If this is how good life can be with the Morettis, then count me in.

But as wonderful as the twins have been to me today, my thoughts keep drifting back to Sal. Maybe he really is changing.

The question is, can I let my guard down yet?

I think I already am.

CHAPTER THIRTY-SEVEN

Valentina

Fausto holds up the skimpy bikini he chose. "Well, you have to pick one."

I cup my chin in thought, biting my lower lip as my eyes trail over the pale pink, barely there triangles that are nothing more than nipple shields.

Today is opening day for the pool. Since we've all had a trying week, we decided we're all chilling poolside for the entire day. Because I didn't have a bathing suit, each man decided to buy me a set and let me choose which one I want to wear.

Armani elbows him in the ribs and dangles his in front of me before tossing it into my lap. "Yeah, and our girl deserves the best one. Not that piece of shit you call clothing."

Fausto looks aghast, dramatically placing his hand on his chest as if Armani severely wounded him. Armani's pick isn't much better. The material is shiny silver, but as I hold it up, I realize I only see the bottoms.

"Where the fuck is the top?" I ask him, and he just grins.

"Our pool is a topless pool, kitten. None of us will be wearing tops either."

I take his pick and throw it in his face as he laughs.

Sal pushes off my bed and grabs his bag, planting himself right in front of the twins. "A real woman wears a real bathing suit." With that, he pulls out a small box with a red bow bound around it and hands it to me.

I take it eagerly, tearing the ribbon off and opening the top. Inside is a dark red one-piece suit. Taking the fabric in my hands, I hold it up in front of me. I'd never considered wearing a one piece, and though it's risqué, it will cover more of me than the twins' choices.

The straps are thick and wrap around the neck like a halter, and the neckline plummets far below my breasts. It's still my best option.

"Sal wins," I announce, and he celebrates by pumping his fists into the air.

It's been a strange week when it comes to him. He's gradually attempted to insert himself back into the twins' and my dynamic. He's been home for breakfasts and dinners, and we've all sat together like a little fucked up family.

They even taught me how to play Texas Hold'em one night, and damn that was fun, even though I lost all the money I started with. Apparently I have what they call a tell. Basically, my entire chest flushes red when I have a good hand. I'll be sure to invest in a thick turtleneck for the next game of cards.

"Now get out so a girl can change without six ogling eyes," I demand, standing and putting my hands on my waist.

Armani pouts, and Sal has to push him out of my bathroom and into the hallway.

"I'll meet you guys down there when I'm done. Give me ten minutes," I tell them, then I shut the door in their faces.

With my back against the door, I take a deep breath, my mind still spinning from all the changes happening between us. When I hear the sound of their feet walking down the hall, I push off the door and head into my closet.

Grabbing the red suit, I hold it against my body and look at myself in the full-length mirror, wondering if I can pull something like this off. I don't have the hugest boobs, and I don't want the material to look empty. He got me a small, so hopefully it won't look frumpy. I grab Fausto's choice as a backup and begin to strip off my pajamas.

As I step into the suit and pull the straps over my shoulders, I thank myself for shaving my pussy yesterday, because this suit is much more revealing than I thought when I first saw it.

The neckline stops just above my belly button. Thankfully, my B cups fill out the suit nicely. The lower half is cut high over my hips, accentuating my hip bones in a very sexy way. It's only the crotch area that I'm not sure about. It reminds me of this outfit I once saw on social media where everyone wondered how the model could have tucked her "taco shell" inside the skimpy material. There was another one about "meat flaps," but I can't remember the exact wording. All the comments were hilarious, but it's not as funny now that I'm wearing something similar.

I squat down, testing the limits of the crotch covering, and sure as shit, it slides between my pussy lips like a piece of dental floss.

"Welp. That's not going to work," I grumble, standing up and pulling the material back where it should be. "Note to self, no squatting."

I try walking next, and as long as my strides are short, the suit stays in place, though I look like a damn robot taking these little steps. Hopefully once I'm outside, I won't have to walk…

Or squat.

Or move at all.

I glance at Fausto's choice one more time, but I think I've chosen the better option.

Tossing my hair up into a messy bun, I grab my sunglasses and head out, conscious of how I walk and move. I know how I must look, because every single staff member I come across stops to stare at me.

I want to yell at them to do their job, but they have no loyalty to me, so I pretend they aren't there as I head through the kitchen and out to the back patio.

Four lounge chairs are set up facing the pool, and two are occupied by Armani and Fausto. Both men are stretched out on their chairs, their bodies glistening with tanning oil as I exit through the French doors and carefully walk over to them. Fausto lifts his head, lowers his sunglasses down his nose to see me better, and reaches over to tap his twin.

"What?" Armani asks his brother, sitting up, and then Fausto points at me. "Fuck me, Val."

"Fuck me too," Fausto chimes in. "You look amazing, pistol."

My embarrassment melts away, replaced with empowerment by their looks and words. "Thank you."

Fausto pats the open chair between them. "Saved you a spot."

I stop in front of the chair and look around for the missing brother. "Where's Sal?"

Armani sips from a glass containing a delicious-looking blue drink. "He apologized, but he was called away on business."

"And neither of you had to go with him?"

Fausto leans forward and runs his hand up the side of my leg, dipping his finger under to grab my ass. "And miss this?"

I push his hand off, laughing as I slowly turn and lower myself into the chair, my legs pressed together to keep my vagina hidden.

It's not quite midmorning, and the sun is already beating down on us, warming my skin. The pool is filled, the blue water calm and ready for its first swimmer of the season. A slow trickle runs down the waterslide, sounding like a tranquil fountain, and a gentle breeze blows, cooling my skin.

Basically, this is heaven, a perfect morning.

I can smell summer in the air. Oh, and dirt.

Across from us, the landscaping team is busy planting flowers and adding dirt and mulch to the flower beds. I pay them no mind, closing my eyes and just relaxing.

Matilda's voice rings out. "Feeling thirsty, kids?" She bustles over with a tray filled with drinks.

Fausto and Armani snag a blue beverage. I choose a glass of her delicious iced tea and take a sip. The cool drink is just what I needed, and I sigh loudly. "Thank you, Matilda."

She smiles softly, tucking the tray under her arm. "Anything for you, dears. I'll be out soon with snacks. Ring if you need anything before then."

I set my glass down and lower the back of my chair to recline farther. "Could this morning be any more amazing?"

A gentle touch between my breasts has me opening my eyes. Armani traces his finger over my nipple, and it tightens at his touch, pressing against the thin material of my suit. "I can think of many things to enhance our morning. How about you, brother?"

Fausto hums. "Yes, I can think of two somethings that would make my fucking day." I inhale sharply as Fausto mimics his brother, gently running his finger over my other peaked bud. Though their touch is soft, it ignites my body, that familiar deep heat already growing.

Then a sharp noise pulls me from the sensations. One of the gardeners dropped his shovel and is blatantly staring at us. "They are looking," I hiss, shoving their hands away.

"Let them look and give them something to masturbate to later. Besides, we take their phones before they can enter the grounds." Fausto lowers his head. He licks and bites my nipple through my suit, and soon my head lolls back as I bask in how good it feels. "Mine is harder than yours," Fausto says to Armani, who has my other nipple clamped between his teeth.

Armani pulls off my breast and taps my erect bud. "There's no way, look how hard this one is."

Irritated and a little embarrassed that the gardeners are watching, I push both of their heads away. "It's not a fucking challenge."

Armani just laughs. "Everything is a challenge when you have a twin. Come on, Val. Let me see your titties naked in the summer sun."

"You had no problem when I fingered you in the stands at the fight," Fausto adds. "People could have seen us then."

I hold my hands over my breasts. "But I had a few drinks that night, and we were in the dark. Here, it's like a fucking spotlight is shining right on us."

Armani grabs his crotch and squeezes. "I think it's hot knowing they can see how sexy you are but can't touch you, knowing I'm the lucky man who gets to taste you whenever I want."

"*We* are the lucky men," Fausto corrects. "Just a taste, Val. Then we'll drop it."

"Please," Armani begs, pushing out his lower lip and batting his eyes.

I groan. "Fuck, you two are bad influences."

Armani claps. "Does that mean yes?"

I hold up a single finger. "You have one minute, not a second more."

Fausto gets up and pushes his chair flush against mine, Armani doing the same. He takes my left arm and rests it underneath him, waiting for his twin to copy the movement.

With my arms captured under their bodies, the twins drag my suit over my breasts, exposing them to the watchful eyes of the gardeners. I can hear them whispering amongst themselves but can't make out what they are saying. Honestly, I try to tune them out completely, feeling mortified that I've agreed to do this, but as the twins capture my nipples in their warm mouths, I forget all about the gardeners.

It feels amazing having two men playing with my breasts, teasing my nipples into gemstones. "Fuck," I murmur as they moan against my skin, and I lower my head to watch. Fausto drags his teeth across one, making me hiss, while Armani flicks his tongue over the other.

Wetness gathers between my legs, my clit coming alive at their ministrations. "Time's up," I whisper, tugging at my arms.

Neither twin moves a muscle. In fact, they have added their hands now, squeezing my tits as they attack my nipples. Fausto drags his hand down my body, rubbing his finger along my slit, even as I keep my thighs firmly pressed together. It's one thing to expose my breasts, it's a whole other level to let them see my pussy.

"She's wet," Fausto tells his brother. "Feel."

Fausto's hand trails back up my body, wrapping around my neck while Armani pries at my thigh. When I don't budge, he groans, slipping his finger inside my suit to gain access to my pussy.

Armani moans. "Fuck, she's drenched." Armani gathers the fabric covering my pussy and tugs it between my pussy lips, making me gasp. "Fuck, you're so sexy, kitten. Just look at those plump little pussy lips." He tugs hard and repeatedly, rubbing the suit against my sensitive clit, making me groan. "She likes it when we play with her while others watch. Our woman is kinky."

Fausto slips my nipple from his mouth. "Then she'll like it even more when we fuck her at the same time."

"What?" I practically shout, but Armani is there to cover my lips with his. His tongue stifles my words as he tugs on my suit, my pussy clamping down and clit firing.

Armani breaks the kiss and wiggles his eyebrows. "Ever heard of a twin sammich?"

I look from him to his brother, breathing hard.

"Let's take this inside," Fausto growls, his voice deepening.

I squeal when I'm tossed over his shoulder, my front draped across his back and my ass high in the air. He swats my cheeks as he walks toward the house. I shove my breasts back inside my suit then lift my head up to see where we're going. I lock eyes with one of the gardeners wearing a wide-brimmed gardening hat and a pair of cheap sunglasses.

He strokes his thick, black beard and lowers his glasses, and I gasp.

It's Marco.

Too stunned to speak, I can only watch from my perch across Fausto's shoulder as Marco squares his body to me and bares his teeth. Then he slices his thumb over his neck, letting me know exactly what his intentions are.

He can't be here, he just can't.

I rub my eyes and look again, but he's nowhere to be found.

Maybe I imagined the whole thing, seeing illusions in the bright sunlight. My worries are forgotten as Armani runs ahead and opens the door, Fausto charging in behind him. "My room or yours?"

"Whichever one is closest," Fausto grits out, his grip on me tightening.

"I can walk, you know," I yell at him, but he ignores me, running up the stairs two at a time as if he wasn't carrying me at all.

We rush through a door, and I immediately recognize Armani's room. I glance toward the couch where he ate my pussy like a dying man whose life depended on it, but we don't stop there, moving through the kitchen to his bedroom.

"Stop for a second," Armani says. "There's something I need to do."

I try to look behind me to see what he's up to when I feel my bathing suit being pulled aside before his tongue licks my core.

"Holy shit," I rasp as he moans, but then I'm airborne. I land on his bed, my chest pressed against his messy bedding.

Fausto is right behind me, lifting my ass into the air and yanking my suit aside. "I'm going to taste this pretty little pink cunt while you suck my brother's cock. Understand, pistol?"

Armani crawls on the bed, already naked, his dick bobbing proudly in front of my face while Fausto flips onto his back and scoots between my legs. "Lower yourself, pistol. Sit on my fucking face."

"Oh God," I moan, spreading my knees to lower myself. Fausto yanks my bathing suit to the side and feeds on my pussy, devouring me with his lips and tongue.

"Open your mouth, kitten," Armani urges, fisting his thick cock. I lick my lips and open for him. Armani drags his fingers through my hair and grips firmly, rocking his hips. He starts slowly at first, the softness of his cock sliding across my tongue. I swirl my tongue around him and suck hard. He pulls out of my mouth with a pop then shoves it back in.

Fausto adds a finger, sinking it inside me while he kisses my clit. I moan around Armani's dick, which urges him on. His grip on my hair tightens, and I wince, the pain fueling us both.

"Harder, kitten," he demands, so I hollow my cheeks and suck until my lips go numb. His cock fills my throat, choking me as Fausto adds a second finger, fucking me in time with his brother who's taking my mouth.

I quickly begin to unravel.

I glance up at Armani. Pleasure is etched into his features, his hair cascades over one eye, and every muscle in his body is tight as he watches me take him in my mouth.

Armani picks up speed, and Fausto intensifies the pressure on my clit, sucking harder then licking fast. My legs begin to tremble, saliva dripping from my lips.

"I'm going to come," Armani shouts, and then he groans, his salty cum filling my mouth as I struggle to swallow it all. Armani falls back on the bed as my own orgasm roars to life. With my hands clutching the sheets, I cry out, coming all over Fausto's face and fingers.

"Mmm," he groans, lapping me up until I fall to my side and roll onto my back, breathing hard.

"Well, that was fun," Armani says, shifting to my side.

"Fun is just getting started," Fausto replies darkly. "I don't know whether to tie her up or throw her around. What do you think, brother?"

Armani puckers his lips, one finger toying with my nipple. "First, we need to get this bathing suit off, and then we can get out my box of toys."

"Toys?" I question, sitting up.

Armani bites his lip. "Mm-hmm. Want to see?"

He doesn't wait for me to respond before rolling off the bed, his dick at half-mast. He enters his closet and comes out with a beat-up looking cardboard box and tosses it onto the bed. I sit up on my knees, tucking my hair behind my ears as he tears it open.

My eyes widen at all the items inside—dildos of all colors, vibrators, rope, feathers, and metal egg-shaped looking things. "I don't know what half this stuff is."

Fausto scoots behind me and kisses my shoulder. "Luckily for you, you're about to find out."

CHAPTER THIRTY-EIGHT

Armani

My little kitten purrs loudly as my brother strips her of her bathing suit, her pert nipples already puckered. The sight of them has my mouth watering, and I reach into the box, knowing exactly what to use first.

I hold up the two nipple clamps, linked together by a length of black chain. A little purple bell is attached to each one, and I jingle them in front of her eyes. "Do you know what these are, kitten?"

Her shoulders shrink, and she looks down at her chest where I rub a clamp over a peaked bud. "You wear them here." I hand one to Fausto, and together, we pluck her nipples into twin chips of ice. "Don't move while we put them on." I clutch her breast in my hand.

Her breaths stutter as we line up her rosy nipple between the clamps and gently close them. "It's not so bad," she says, easing up.

Fausto shoots me a knowing grin, and we turn the little knob on the side, tightening the force.

"Oh," she murmurs, her back arching. "It hurts a little."

Fausto drags his finger down the end of her nipple, rubbing it gently as she gasps. "Good. Let me see those titties bounce, pistol. I want to hear you jingle a mile away."

We ease back from our girl, and she looks at us sheepishly. I shoo her with my hands. "Go on. Jingle for us."

Val's cheeks flame bright red, and she shakes her chest, the little bells tinkling happily. "Again," Fausto urges, grabbing both of her breasts and jiggling them himself. The clamps jostle her nipples, and she mewls, biting her lip. The sound of the bells ringing in tune with her hiss makes my cock thicken again.

I brush my hand through her hair. "Are you ready for the next toy, kitten?" She nods, and I look to Fausto. "Your pick."

My twin pulls out a bullet vibrator and flips it on. It buzzes, and Val's eyes go wide as he presses it against one of the clamps.

"Oh God!" she shrieks, jumping back, the bells chiming.

Fausto points to the spot on the bed where she just was. "Get your ass back here now." Val's breathing picks up as she inches forward. "Up on your knees, legs apart." He looks at me. "Grab the handcuffs."

She laughs nervously as I pull a pair out of the box. "You don't need those. I won't move this time."

Fausto flicks one of the clamps, and she cries out again. "But you look so sexy in restraints, pistol. Armani, secure her."

I take no time pulling her arms behind her back and cuffing her wrists. "You need to listen to Fausto," I tell her, whispering in her ear. "He told you to rise up on your knees."

"Oh," she murmurs, lifting her ass off the bed.

Fausto pushes at her knees, spreading her thighs open. "Such a pretty pussy." I crawl around to her front as Fausto rubs her cunt, then out of nowhere, he spanks her right between her legs.

Val howls, the bells jingling as her body trembles. The soft skin of her pussy lips reddens, and I see the desire grow in her eyes.

She likes this.

I dip my hand between her legs. Val whimpers when I find her wet and wanting.

Smack!

Val moans, bouncing on her knees and tugging at the cuffs. She's fucking glorious, a damned goddess.

"You're doing so good," I praise her, rubbing the sting away, her lower lips flowering open for me. "So good."

Val licks her lips nervously, watching Fausto as he brings the vibrating bullet near her again. This time he starts low, tracing up her inner thigh, around her pussy, and back down the other leg. Knowing I have a second bullet, I grab it and flip it on, tracing along the underside of her breasts.

"Fuck," she grits out, trying to hold still as my brother and I run our bullets along the apex of her body, right where her thighs meet her pussy.

Fausto drags his over her clit for a moment and she jerks, breathing hard, but stays put. "How does it feel, pistol?"

"G-Good," she stutters as Fausto does it again. "Ugh!" He keeps it on her clit this time as I drag mine down her slit to her tight little hole and sink it inside of her.

Her head falls back, and she pants hard, her thighs shaking. Fausto rubs his over her clit, which is fully engorged from the vibrations. I pull mine out and shove it back in her, repeating it over and over.

"Oh God. Oh God. Oh God!"

Valentina's body goes rigid, and she cries out, clamping her legs together as she comes hard from the little bullet.

Val collapses onto the bed and Fausto rubs her back. "You're so beautiful when you come, isn't she, Armani?"

I gently ease the bullet out and take my brother's too, setting them on my nightstand to clean later. "Gorgeous."

Fausto reaches into the box and pulls out something I'm not sure our girl can tolerate yet—an ass plug—and a bottle of lubricant. He looks at me and I nod, ready to own every fucking hole on her body.

"Pistol, we're going to try something new while you catch your breath. I just want you to relax for us, okay?"

She doesn't respond. Her eyes are closed, sweat coats her skin, and her hands are still cuffed. Fausto throws me the lubricant, and I reposition her with her face pressed to the bed and her ass in the air.

When I drizzle the cold lubricant on her, she attempts to sit up, but Fausto presses between her shoulders. "Hold still, pistol."

"Not there," she mumbles as I rub circles around her little puckered hole.

I press gently, edging the tip in. "Everywhere, Val. Every hole is ours, even this one."

My kitten whines, her juicy pussy on display as I push the tip of my finger inside her ass. I ease out and add more lube, then press in again. She screams for me to stop, but I don't, knowing she can take something as little as my finger.

Fausto holds the plug in front of her face. "Open. Suck on this before we sheathe it in your ass." Her hands clench behind her back, but she lets my brother shove it past her lips. I pull my finger out and press it in again, her little hole relaxing.

"Please," she begs when he pulls out the plug and hands it to me.

Fausto rubs her back. "Please what?"

Val's cries grow louder and louder as I exchange my finger for the plug. It's the smallest one I own, maybe the size of a man's thumb, and on the back is a little purple jewel the same color as her jingle bells. I inch it forward and her body twitches. Fausto reaches under her and plays with her clit, and her body relaxes. I add more lube, coating her ass and pressing the plug deeper.

Finally, her asshole sucks it inside. "It's in, kitten. Fuck, you look so hot."

"Okay," she whispers.

"How does it feel?" I ask.

She shifts her weight, moving her ass side to side. "Umm. Like I have a big poo in my ass."

Fausto and I laugh, and he takes the cuffs off her wrists.

She sits on her knees and reaches for the clamps, but I swat her hands away. "Can't we take these off yet?"

"Not yet, sweet girl," I coo. "Are your nipples getting sore?"

"They ache," she whines, and though I don't say it out loud, her pain is part of my pleasure. I know Fausto is like me too. Hurting her nipples, her clit, and her ass turns us both on. My kitten tries to twist her body to see the ass plug. "Can you take this out at least?"

I shake my head. "No."

Fausto grips her chin, bringing her face close to his. "Not until I've fucked you with it in. Every hole, pistol. Every fucking one."

He kisses her hard, and I sandwich her between us, tapping on her nipples, the bells jingling. She moans into him as I squeeze her breasts and sweep my thumbs over the clamps. I run my hands down her body, gently pulling on the plug.

She shrieks, her tits bouncing as I move my hand between her pussy lips and strum her clit lightly. "I want you to model for us, kitten," I whisper, gliding my finger up and down her clit. "Come on. Off the bed."

Fausto and I release her, and she slowly climbs down, lying on her belly before sliding down to the ground. "What do you want me to do?"

"Walk for us, kitten. Walk all the way to the bathroom door then come back."

As she walks away, the little purple plug shines in the light, and her plump ass jiggles. Fuck, she's so hot. At my bathroom, she spins to face us and heads back, her breasts swaying on her chest, the bells from her clamps chiming. But then I realize... "You're missing a clamp, kitten."

Fausto looks around and finds it on the bed and holds it up, arching an eyebrow at her. She raises her hands submissively and takes a step back. "It fell off when I got off the bed. I swear I didn't take it off myself."

Fausto beckons her forward, and my cock gets more excited, knowing what he'll do next. He points to the front of the bed. "Lie down on your back with your arms above your head and thighs spread wide."

She chews on her lip and nods, moving into position. She tries to lie down gently, but I know the action presses on the plug.

I climb up next to her and grip her hands, pressing them down above her head. "Do you have any idea how gorgeous you are right now? Draped over my bed like a damned seductress. Your body flushed from coming. I'd give you my fucking soul if you asked it of me."

Val gazes into my eyes and smiles, but her eyes grow wide when she feels Fausto moving between her legs. "Wider," he growls, slapping her thighs until they are lying flat on the bed. "Armani, come here."

"Don't move your arms, kitten," I warn, sliding down to help Fausto.

I get lost in every view of this girl, every fucking angle. "Spread her lips for me."

"Yes," I growl, spreading them with my fingers while he lines up the nipple clamp she lost.

Val can feel the clamp pressing on the sides of her swollen little clit, and her body begins to shake. "Oh!" she shrieks, her back arching as Fausto releases the clamp. She blows out through her lips. "I can't. I can't."

I crawl up her body, caging her with my arms. "You will. You'll wear it while I fuck your hot little cunt and my brother fucks your mouth. Every hole, Valentina. We told you once that you were ours, and we meant it." Her eyes search mine. There's pain within her gaze, but there's also lust. I suck her freed nipple into my mouth and pop it out, rolling the bud between my fingers then drifting my hand between her legs. I dip my fingers inside her pussy, preparing her for my cock. "How does it feel to have the Moretti men own every inch of your body?"

Valentina's eyes grow more hooded as Fausto moves to play with her nipple while I sink my fingers into her wetness. "It feels... amazing."

Fausto smiles down at this perfect woman and captures her lips, kissing her hard.

Unable to help myself, with my fingers buried deep, I extend my tongue and flick her clamped little clit.

She screams and her thighs tremble, so I do it again, sliding my hand up to play with her tits. Fausto flicks her clamped nipple, then seizes the other between his fingers as I taste her clit again.

There's something sweet about watching her shiver. It awakens a carnal desire within me, knowing the trembling of her thighs and soft, breathy moans are the result of my own talented hands, lips, and tongue.

This girl is fire.

This girl is an uncontrollable storm raging through me. I keep working her until her body twitches wildly and I know she's right on edge.

I lift my head and look at her swollen pussy coated with her cream. "She's glistening, brother. It's time."

He nods and barks out an order. "Onto your hands and knees, pistol. Keep that ass up."

She moans and tries to shift her body as gently as she can, the purple bells tolling as she moves. "Fuck, you're incredible," I praise. "You've done amazing. This is the last little bit, okay?"

She nods and blinks hard. "I'm ready. I want this."

I spank her ass and she hisses, but she presses her ass toward me, glancing over her shoulder to watch. I drag my cock along her dripping cunt then line up, my head nudging her wet hole. I fist my cock, enjoying my view of her ass and wet cunt. Fausto does the same, edging closer to her mouth.

Val turns back to face Fausto, her eyes on his cock as she licks her lips, then she opens wide and sucks him in. Fausto grips her hair hard, sliding past her lips with a moan of pleasure, and I seize her hips and press inside.

There are no words to describe how this feels. I'm finally with her, claiming her, and taking her cunt with my cock. She clamps down on me as I begin to move, humming around my brother's cock.

She licks down the length of him as if he were her favorite treat and she wants every drop. Fausto takes his time, enjoying each thrust. I spank her ass, the bells on her nipple and cunt chiming with every movement, every plunge inside her.

Fausto wraps her hair around his hand and guides her down to the base of his cock. "Fuck, you're so sweet, baby, sucking my cock like a good little girl while my brother fucks your greedy little cunt."

Valentina likes the dirty talk, because she moans and plants kisses along his shaft before taking him down her throat again. My balls tighten as I dig my fingers into her skin, my thrusts growing harder as I bury my cock in her wet heat.

Fausto looks to me and nods, and we find our rhythm, a talent we've learned over the years from sharing other women. He slips his cock to the edge of her lips as I slam into her cunt, and when I pull back, he thrusts his cock down her throat.

We do this in tandem, finding our rhythm, while Valentina moans, groans, and shakes.

"I'm going to come, pistol. Suck harder," Fausto shouts, and she doubles her efforts, her soft lips drinking him down. Fausto groans, thrusting fast as he finds his release, and cum drips from her mouth.

I keep moving my hips as he finishes in her throat.

"Fuck!" I groan, getting close, my teeth bared as I slam into her.

Val moans, clenching the sheets. She lowers her torso, and I drop to my ass, shifting angles. "Mmm, so close," she says, her moans growing higher.

I know just what will get her there.

I flip her in one quick movement, pulling my cock out of her and sinking back inside within a second. Lying on her back with her tits bouncing and my cock thrusting inside her, Val comes undone. Fausto sucks her nipple in his mouth, lapping at it with his tongue while tapping on her clit.

"Yes. Yes. Yes!"

Val shudders, and I rip off the clamps. The screech that emits from her lips could shatter glass. Her whole body convulses, her skin burns red, and her toes curl as I hook her legs in my arms and fuck her relentlessly. Soon my orgasm overtakes me, and I'm shouting her name and painting her body with my cum.

We all collapse, the scent of cum and sweat profound in the air, hearing only the sounds of our heavy breathing.

"If that wasn't heaven, then I don't know what is," I rasp, reaching for my kitten's hand. After a few minutes, I get up and grab us some towels. Fausto and I take great care in cleaning her as gently as possible while telling her how amazing she is.

Val's breathing grows faint, and I know she's fallen asleep. We wrap her in a blanket and throw on some shorts, walking down to her room where we strip once again. I lay her between us, and we crawl into bed.

My heart is so full.

This is quite possibly the best day of my life.

CHAPTER THIRTY-NINE

Valentina

I'VE BEEN CAMPED out in my room for the past couple days. My anxiety is getting the best of me. My time with the twins was amazing, and parts of me still ache in the best way, but I'm having a hard time thinking about anything aside from him.

Marco.

He was there, in the garden. I'm sure of it.

I've picked my cuticles raw and bit my nails into nonexistent nubs, and my chest hurts from the stress he's causing me. He's found me here, in a place that I expected to be some secret compound. It was foolish of me, I guess, because mafia men don't ever stop until they get what they want.

He's obsessed. Anyone can see that. So today I'm going to throw all my cards on the table and let these boys hear what I have to say.

It's morning, and I'm lying in my bed with a pair of scissors clutched in my hands. I've mutilated the teddy bear Marco set up, cutting it into pieces in hopes I can recover and fix the voice box.

I pull out the white plastic box and spin it in my hands. It reminds me of one of those drains you put in the bottom of your shower to catch hair as it sheds off your head. I turn it over in my hands and find a little latch. Unclipping it, I watch as a flat, circular button battery falls out.

"Yes," I hiss, already celebrating my victory. If all I need to fix this is a new battery, then maybe they'll finally believe me. Maybe they'll realize the Moretti men are just as mortal as the rest of humanity.

After brushing my teeth and pulling my hair up into two matching pigtail buns, I slip on a cute pink sundress and check myself out in the mirror. It hugs me tight in all the right places. Short, ruffled sleeves hang just over my shoulders, and the neckline is modest, the cotton material gathered around my chest. The skirt is loose and flowy.

I add a light shade of pink to my eyelids and beef up my lashes with thick black mascara, then I coat my lips with clear gloss.

Feeling cute, I grab the voice box and head downstairs for breakfast. Matilda has set our meal out on the patio today. I've come to love having meals outside. I don't know why, but something about being out in the open makes the meal more enjoyable somehow. Perhaps it's the scenery or the fresh air. Regardless, it makes me instantly happy.

As usual, Sal is there first, flicking through an iPad he has propped up on a little stand. Wearing a short-sleeved, white polo and a pair of thick-rimmed glasses, he looks like one of those sexy nerds I read about in my dirty romance books. "Morning," he mutters, not looking up from his screen.

I pull out the chair across from him and sit. "Morning." Grabbing a mug, I pour myself a cup of coffee from the carafe and stir in sugar and creamer. My hands warm on the mug as I bring the delicious smelling drink to my lips, inhaling its potent and decadent aroma. The coffee is glorious, smooth, and strong, warming my body as it filters down my throat.

The French doors open behind me, and out walks Armani, still clad in pajamas, his long hair tousled. Fausto is right behind him, his hair styled. He wears a black, button-up shirt with the sleeves rolled, dark jeans, and dark brown boots.

Honestly, they both look hot. I love the comfy boy who scoots in next to me as much as I love the look of the well-dressed man who sits on my other side.

Armani plants a kiss on my cheek, smiling demurely. "Damn, you look cute today, kitten."

Fausto plucks at my messy pigtail buns. "Fucking adorable. You need to wear your hair like that more often."

At the praise, Sal flicks his gaze up at me. The man still won't make eye contact with me, always focusing on my head or my lips. I wonder if I'll find out why someday.

The boys all start talking about their plans for the day. Sal dishes out orders, letting them know items that need to be accomplished. Matilda brings out a breakfast casserole made of eggs, potatoes, cheese, and bacon that is out of this world. She also sets out a fruit salad of strawberries, blackberries, pineapple, and mango.

One of the reasons I love Matilda so much is her absolute disdain for cantaloupe and honeydew melon. I mean, is there anyone in the world that eats that shit in fruit salad? And if they do, can they be trusted?

The only melon worth eating is watermelon. Tell me I'm wrong. I put the questionable cantaloupe and honeydew eaters in the same distrustful category as people who don't like olives.

Can't. Fucking. Trust them.

I stay quiet as the guys eat, munching on my food until I find a moment to strike.

"We need to talk about Marco," I state loudly and clearly, the boys looking up at me from their phones.

"Not this again," Sal gripes. "We've talked about this, and everyone sitting here knows what a sore subject it is. Why bring up those uncomfortable memories?"

I twist the voice box in my hands. "Because you guys need to fucking listen to me instead of just brushing me off. You don't know him like I do."

"I mean... we've all seen his dick pic," Armani teases.

I punch him right in the arm. "It's not funny." Armani rubs his arm while I glare at all three men. "Would it alarm you all to know that he was here, at your house, only a few days ago?"

Fausto shakes his head, massaging his temples. "Pistol, our home is guarded. Every person that works here has clearance, and people who are hired for odd jobs are stripped of their phones and scanned for devices before stepping foot on our property. You're safe here."

I shake my head. "That's where you're wrong. He was here that morning we were sitting outside at the pool."

"Then why didn't you say anything?" Armani asks.

Sighing, I fold my hands on the table. "I didn't notice him until we were, umm… entering the house. He was dressed as a gardener. He dyed his hair, you guys, and he threatened me like this." I make the same movement across my throat that Marco had done.

Sal casts his eyes back onto his iPad. "Maybe the light struck your eyes wrong and that's what you think you saw, Valentina."

"No. No. No!" I shout loudly, letting my anger show. "I'm sick of you guys not believing me. I'm sick of you making constant excuses for what I know to be true. He's coming for me."

"Valentina," Fausto starts, but I hold up my hand to stop him.

"No. You'll listen to me. You all will." I'm even so bold to reach over the table and pluck Sal's iPad away from him. "You too. I will not be disregarded anymore. You don't know what kind of boy he is."

Sal is not perturbed, instead leaning back in his chair. "He's hardly a boy, Val. We investigated him. He's twenty-five years old."

"Twenty-five!" I exclaim. "He lied to me! He told me he was only eighteen!"

Sal leans forward, resting his elbows on the table as he steeples his fingers. "What eighteen-year-old do you know that can grow a full beard like you say he has?"

"Exactly!" I'm so frustrated I don't even know what to say and scrub my face with my hands. "Why would he lie? What would he gain from it?"

The twins look at each other and shrug. "Maybe he thought you'd be more interested in him if he was your age?" Armani suggests.

"Exactly. He tricked me just to get close to me. Who knows what he'd do to get me back. You guys don't know what he was like. Didn't you read the texts he sent me? Can't you see what it was like for me?"

"I deleted them from your phone," Sal admits. "I was furious that day when... you know." Oh, how could I possibly forget Sal tying my naked body up to the interrogation chair. "I was so fucking angry that I deleted everything from your phone. I even blocked his number."

My shoulders sag. "So all those texts are gone? All the evidence of his madness is erased?"

Sal nods, and I sigh deeply. "He's lied about his age, and he's even dyed his blond hair to disguise himself." I hold up three fingers. "Three times he's shown up since I've been here." I count on my fingers. "My dad's funeral reception, pretending to be a gardener at your fucking house, and the teddy bear."

Fausto refills his coffee cup. "You can't prove the teddy bear was him."

A smug grin crawls over my lips. "Actually, maybe I can." I hold up the white voice box. "I pulled this out of the teddy bear. The battery isn't working since the plushie drowned in the tub, but if we replaced it, I could prove it was him. You could hear it's Marco's voice." I slip the battery on the table and push it toward Sal. "Find a battery, listen to the message, then tell me I'm wrong."

Sal picks up the battery and examines it, checking to see which one he needs. "I still think you're overreacting. We're almost untouchable. He is no one, the bratty child of your late father's friend. He has no resources, no men at his back. This is like chasing a ghost."

I push back from the table, needing to leave before I say something I regret. As I pull open the French door to head inside, I turn back to face them and toss the voice box to Sal. I take a deep breath to calm myself and speak my next words with a steady voice and resolve in my expression. "He's coming for me, and by the time you believe me, it will be too late."

CHAPTER FORTY

Valentina

I HAD a hard time sleeping last night, my anger not allowing my brain to shut off. Every time I replayed my conversation with the guys, I just got angrier and angrier. How can they be so blasé with something I feel so strongly about?

I roll onto my back, lift my sleep mask from my eyes, and gaze out the window. Bloated gray clouds hover in the sky, sprinkling a gentle spring rain. I've never been one to mind rainy days. They are the perfect excuse to hide away inside your house, grab a comfy blanket, and curl up with a cup of coffee and a good book.

Yep, that's what I'm doing today.

I throw off my covers, and my feet just touch the floor when a knock sounds on my door. "Valentina. It's Joseph. I have a little something for you."

I wrap my robe around myself, not needing to embarrass Joseph with my thin tank top, and pull the door open. Joseph smiles down at me, holding a large silver platter. "May I come in?"

"Of course." I swing the door open and gesture inside. "What is all that?"

Joseph sets the tray down on the coffee table and turns to me. "In my many years, I've noticed a gift like this is usually the start of an apology. You'll have to let me know if it's good enough." He winks at me and leaves, shutting the door behind him.

I truly don't know where to begin, because the tray is loaded with items. There's a pale purple vase filled with pink and red tulips, and the token white and green Starbucks cup is filled with my favorite drink. A silver lid hides what I know will be a yummy dish from Matilda, and there's also a small pink gift bag with colorful tissue paper poking out of the top.

I spot an envelope, my name scrawled across the front in perfect cursive handwriting, and I pluck it off the tray.

Inside is a card. The outside has a picture of a sad cookie sitting in a pile of crumbs. Inside it says, "Sorry I've been acting so crummy," but the *I've* is crossed off and *we've* is written in its place.

A note at the bottom reads:

We're sorry we haven't listened or taken you seriously. We promise to look into what you've said about Marco. Enjoy breakfast and your gift, and be ready for a huge surprise too. You're going out shopping today. A limo will pick you up at noon. Be ready.

XOXO

I close the card, dumbfounded. I never expected the Moretti men to actually apologize for how they have been treating me. Feeling better, I take a sip of my latte and lift the silver lid, revealing a plate filled with breakfast food—eggs, bacon, hash browns, and rye toast.

While munching on the food, I pluck out the tissue paper and pull out my present. It's a brand-new iPhone, the latest model. I open the box and lift it out, finding the phone already on.

I open it up and immediately go to my text messages. They are all gone, so are my photos. It's a completely new phone with a new number too. While I'm happy to have access to my accounts, I'm sad that I've lost all my history. Every snap I've ever sent, every picture, and every last message from my dead parents are all gone.

Perhaps that's a good thing. My memories of them never make me happy, not really. They are a sad reminder of what life was like for me growing up, my parents more sperm and egg donors than actual parents.

The real problem is that I don't know anyone's number. Not my brothers', not my friends'. No one. So even though I got a new phone, I can't really use the damn thing yet.

I open the contacts and see that Sal, Fausto, and Armani have their numbers programmed in, so I guess that's a start.

It's ten by the time I finish my breakfast and jump in the shower. I actually take time to fix my hair, blow drying and curling it before applying a light coat of makeup.

In my closet, I select a short-sleeved, gray sundress with light pink flowers on it. I've learned it's easier to not have to deal with taking pants on and off when shopping.

I slip my feet into a pair of pink flats with a little bow on the top, grab my old purse, and check its contents. Inside is my wallet, a beat-up pack of dental floss, a pen, a half eaten pack of sugarless gum, and my trusty chap stick.

Grabbing the lip gloss I used today, I toss it in, along with my new phone, and lift the purse onto my shoulder. It feels good to have it on, like a piece of the old me that I haven't seen in so long. Feeling light and happy, I leave my room and jog down the stairs.

Joseph is waiting at the front door, and he opens it when he sees me coming. He sweeps his arm toward the outside. "Your limo awaits, my dear."

"Thanks, Joseph," I say, standing up on my tiptoes to plant a kiss on his cheek.

"Oh!" he exclaims in surprise, chuckling warmly as he waves goodbye. I'm practically skipping down the stairs, basking in the freedom I once took for granted.

The limo driver tips his hat to me and opens the door. "Valeska Maria Anthony." Valeska? No one here knows me by that name. Cautiously, I lower my head inside, and I see a ghost from my past.

"Payton?" I squeal, my eyes watering.

"Val!" she shrieks as I crash into her arms, a waterfall of tears ruining my makeup.

I squeeze her hard. "I've missed you so much."

"I've missed you too. I've been so worried."

I pull away and look her up and down. "How did you find me?"

She smiles, and a smug look crosses her face. "Well, a very handsome man by the name of Fausto came by my house yesterday looking for me. He practically begged my parents to let me come out today. He was very charming, very convincing, and very—"

"Gorgeous?"

Payton slaps her knee. "Girl, he's like… stunning. Like one of those Gucci models on the covers of magazines. How did you like… get him?"

I laugh as the driver pulls out of the driveway. "You wouldn't believe me if I told you."

Payton folds her arms over her chest. "No more secrets, Val."

I release a long sigh. "Some things are better left unsaid. It's for your protection. Just forget about all that, and let's enjoy this day together. Okay?"

She narrows her eyes, and I think she's going to fight me on this, but then her shoulders deflate and she grins. "Okay. But you're not getting away with it forever." She juts her chin toward the opposite side of the limo. "How about we open those?"

I look and see two envelopes perched on the bar, one addressed to each of us. Grabbing them both, I hand Payton hers and tear mine open, finding cash inside.

Payton counts hers quickly, looking at me with her jaw open. "It's two fucking thousand dollars, Valeska. How?"

I shrug with nonchalance, putting my money in my wallet. "I know people."

"Don't give me that shit." She runs her eyes up and down me with a suspicious look on her face. "You're not like… some secret princess or something are you?"

"No." I laugh.

She taps on her lips. "Not a princess, hmm? A secret inheritance from a long-lost rich relative?"

"Not even close."

"Hmm," she hums. "Not a relative either." She rests her chin in her hand, tapping her fingers on her cheek. "But we picked you up from a huge fucking mansion, and like the most handsome Italian man I've ever seen came begging my parents for my company, wearing more gold than I could ever imagine owning. We've been given like four thousand dollars to blow on shopping, so there's only one option left."

I swallow hard. "Yeah? And what's that?"

She points at me. "You are the daughter of someone famous. Oh! Maybe the daughter of some high rolling mafia boss! Tell me I'm wrong."

I feign laughter, cupping my hands over my mouth while forcing out a giggle. "You've lost your mind, Payton."

"Maybe."

"Totally."

Payton shrugs. "Guess it doesn't really matter. I have two grand to spend on whatever I want. What the fuck do I care where the money came from? Even if it is... *blood money.*"

We both laugh and spend the rest of the ride talking and laughing until tears roll down our cheeks and we're clutching our bellies.

Yep.

This is going to be the best day ever.

CHAPTER FORTY-ONE

Salvatore

STANDING a good ten feet from my windows, I fold my arms over my chest and watch the limo drive away. My heart flutters and anxiety rips through me, knowing what I'm about to do.

Can I do this?

Can I pull it off?

And will she forgive me for it?

Fr. Castiglione told me the greater man would choose the harder road, and the path I've chosen will be the most difficult one I've fought to get through.

You see, no one knows what I know. My nonchalance is a disguise for the turmoil I've found inside of me. Valentina is correct in her assumptions that Marco Capelli is stalking her. The evidence is profound, even if I pretend it's not.

Part of being a mafia don is making these hard decisions, keeping others in the dark regarding knowledge only I am privy to. Half of it is because I am trying to protect them, allowing them their innocence by corrupting my own soul further, but half of it is also about the control, the power, in knowing I brought this whole thing crashing down.

I wasn't even surprised when I placed a new battery in the voice box and played the ominous recording inside.

"I love you. I have always loved you. We'll be together soon."

I've listened to it over and over, cross referencing it with voice-mails he left on Valentina's phone. The voices are identical, meaning there's no way that bear could have been sent by anyone else.

He knows where we are, and worse, he's gotten through our security. Maybe Val is right, and my own arrogance has blinded me to my potential flaws. The Outfit is untouchable, yet this poor excuse for a man has found a way through.

I'm embarrassed and angry, and that's why I'm taking things into my own hands. I can't ask my brothers to help me do this. They'd probably tell me no anyway and warn her about my plans, but they don't understand. I have to do this. It's my pathway to redemption, to righteousness.

Or is it my doom?

Only God knows.

I walk back to my desk and open up my laptop, selecting security footage from our backyard the day Val says Marco showed up here. I've watched it several times, starting with the moment my brothers thought it was a good idea to expose her breasts and suck on her nipples in front of the landscaping crew. If they were anyone but my brothers, I'd have them strung up and beaten for such a thing.

The man Val described is there, groping his crotch as he watches my brothers part her thighs and tug her meager bathing suit between her pussy lips. What the fuck were they thinking?

She's our girl.

Ours!

How dare they share a view only meant for us?

My fingers clench. I'm itching to dole out violence and hear the pained cries of my next victim.

Soon, I tell myself, trying to soothe the rage churning inside me.

The man with the thick black beard does a great job of keeping his back to the cameras, hiding his face. That's a natural gift to anyone in the Mafia. I see that being part of the Cosa Nostra, no matter how small, has taught Marco the fundamentals of how to stay unnoticed, but he clearly didn't listen to the lesson of ensuring no evidence is left behind.

After the funeral, I dug through the trash myself and found the note Val said was scrawled on a paper towel. I found the broken camera, its glass still scattered on the ground before it.

And now I have the voice box.

I've been trying to find him for a week, but his trail is always cold. I can't understand it. How can my men not locate a single fucking person? Well, two persons. I'm searching for Alfonzo Capelli too. One thing I'm certain of is that Marco is too fucking stupid to pull this off on his own, but Alfonzo is not.

He's a calculating man who spent many years at Carlo Rossi's side, offering advice and receiving rewards for loyalty. He knows too much, he's trained, and he's thirsty for power.

My desperation to find them came to an end last night when a phone call came through my phone. I recognized the number but couldn't place it.

The conversation that followed had my blood pumping. I've replayed it over and over since the call ended, unable to get an ounce of sleep knowing what is coming, what has to be done.

I DON'T EVEN SAY hello, just accept the call and press the phone to my ear. Heavy breathing greets me as I strain to hear anything to give away who the caller might be.

"Salvatore Moretti, I know you're there," the voice croons in a singsong tone. "I have a proposition for you."

I grip my phone tightly. "I'm listening."

A haunting laugh invades my ear, the heavy breathing picking up again. "I know you don't love the bitch, and I also know how hard it would make your dick to take down the Rossi family. Your... dislike for them is known throughout the Cosa Nostra, and I want you to know the feeling is mutual. What if I told you I can help you bring them down? All I need is her."

Anger roars through me when he calls her a bitch, but I want to hear him out and learn all I can about this plan to bring down the Rossis. I'd be lying if I said the thought wasn't tempting. The demise of the Rossi family is something I've dreamed about every night for the past six months. Since...

I refuse to let my mind go back to that dark place. I need to focus and be present, not succumb to the allure of uncontrollable rage.

"They are tyrants," he continues. "Tyrants who need to be dethroned, and who better to do it than their arch nemesis—you."

It's true. Like it or not, my hatred has been evident, more so than ever before. "It all sounds appealing, but words mean nothing without action. You claim you're able to take them down, but how? You have no army at your back, no real power."

He laughs again. "I am not the only one involved, Salvatore. Think about it. There are more people, more disciples of the late Carlo Rossi who would love nothing more than to see their entire family rotting in the ground. He wasn't a leader, he was a dictator, a self-proclaimed warlord who couldn't see farther than the end of his tiny little dick."

Everything he said about Carlo is true, but Marco is too thick to consider any of this. He's not the one pulling the strings. "Before I commit to anything, I need more information. Who else is involved? I need names."

"Not yet, Salvatore. You'll see when you get there."

"When I get where?"

The phone goes silent, and I glance at my phone to make sure he's still on the line. After a minute, he barks out directions. "There's an old factory near Chapel Hill. Perhaps you know it?"

I swallow hard. I know it well. That very factory is the same place where Carlo took Gianna from me. Her blood will taint its floors forever. "I do."

He chuckles as if he already knew my answer. "Of course you do. Your job is to kidnap Valentina and bring her to said location. Tell no one of our plans. We'll take it from there."

I hum in thought. "That doesn't work for me. I need to be part of what happens next, or you can kidnap her yourself."

There's a clatter in the background, and then he yells like a madman.

"Don't you think I would have done that by now if it was possible? I can't fucking get to her. That's why we need you. Hand over my love, let me marry her, and together, the Capellis and the Morettis can join forces. With me at the head of the Cosa Nostra, we can combine our powers and take down everyone who entered that bullshit pact for peace, starting with Carlo's three sons. Made men don't live in peace, we crave destruction too much."

My blood boils at his knowledge of the pact, knowing full well it had to have been Carlo who spilled to Alfonzo, but it makes no sense, considering Carlo was the one who organized the cease-fire in the first place. Perhaps he thought Alfonzo's loyalty was unquestionable, but that's the thing about leading a mafia—you can't trust anyone who gains from your demise.

"If I do this, if I kidnap the girl and bring her to the factory, Alfonzo needs to be there."

He laughs. "Oh, he will be, and many more too. Everyone is anxious to watch the tyranny of the Rossis fall and the reign of the Capellis begin."

It's too good of an opportunity to pass up. "What time?"

"Anytime. We'll be there soon, and we'll be waiting."

I PACE MY SUITE, knowing it all comes down to power, and right now, the power is all mine. I could do what he wants, kidnap her and help him bring down the Rossi family. I've dreamed of nothing but hurting them like Carlo hurt me.

I could harden my heart, hand her over, and let him have her. As I've grown closer to her over the past week, I've felt myself soften. I've felt feelings that I thought I'd buried deep inside and shudder at my weakness. Her body calls to me, and her lips beg for mine to be pressed against them. My cock thickens when I imagine her luscious form sprawled across my bed and writhing under mine as I take her over and over again.

Am I willing to get lost in all that is Valentina and become who I once was for her? For a girl that, at times, I can't even look at?

It's easier to give in to the darkness again, but I know that if I do, I won't be able to claw my way back out. This is my final chance. The choices are clear, and the ramifications will change the course of my life.

I can choose the light and become vulnerable again, avenge those who hurt Val, and give myself to her completely.

Or I can choose darkness and submit to the evil side that lurks within me. I can hand her over to a man who's obsessed with her and seek my vengeance on Carlo Rossi. I can bring her whole family down if I choose to do so.

Both options are alluring.

But my path is clear.

I just hope, when it's directly in front of me, the choice I make is the right one.

CHAPTER FORTY-TWO

Valentina

I FORGOT how much I missed having a girl in my life, someone to giggle at dumb shit and talk about boys with. Payton is like a little light in my life, the constant spot of happiness. I never have to worry that I've said the wrong thing or that she'll become a catty bitch and not be there for me. She's always here, always has been, even despite how hard I've tried to push her away.

We just finished a cup of coffee and a scone at a cute little coffee shop, and now we're heading into a rather expensive boutique. I walk through the aisles and pluck a pale pink dress off the wall, holding it out to Payton. "Oh, this one would look great on you."

She frowns and backs away. "You know I don't wear pink."

I toss the dress at her, and she's forced to catch it. "Just because you don't doesn't mean you can't. Try the fucking thing on." I bat my eyelashes at her. "For me?"

She scoffs, relenting. "Fine. But then I get to pick one out for you."

"Deal."

I grin at her victoriously while she rolls her eyes and strolls down an aisle of white gowns. "You can't be serious," I gripe when she pulls one off a display and drapes it over her clothes for me to see. "White?"

"You're getting married soon, right? Might as well see how you look in virginal white." Payton laughs at her own joke, and I swallow. She doesn't know how true that statement is.

"Fine." I look around the store and find the changing rooms. "Come on. Let's get this over with and go shop for purses! Mine is becoming an antique artifact at this point."

"You know I don't use purses," Payton says as we weave our way to the dressing rooms.

I jingle the lanyard around her neck holding her wallet and keys. "Well, you should. This thing is fucking tragic."

She holds her lanyard possessively. "Back up, woman. Don't knock it until you try it."

I look at it disapprovingly. "It's like the world's worst necklace. You should call the *Guinness Book of World Records* to see if you qualify."

Payton shoves me into a rack of dresses before running inside a changing room. Laughing, I enter one at the end, right across from hers. I like the ones at the end because they are the closest to the triple mirror that always seems to sit on the back wall of all changing rooms, allowing you to see yourself from every angle.

As I strip off my sundress and take Payton's choice off the hanger, I can hear her grumbling from across the hall.

"I hate it!" she shrieks. "And I hate you for making me try it on."

"It can't be that bad," I call back, knowing Payton looks gorgeous in everything she wears. "I'm getting mine on now, then we can come out at the same time."

"Ugh, fine."

Giggling to myself, I gather the bottom of the dress and dive in. I imagine this is what it's like for a groundhog clawing its way out of the earth. Emerging on the other side, I slip the dress into place. "Hmph," I mutter, swinging my body left and right. It actually looks good.

It's not exactly a wedding dress, but it could be something a bride might wear to her rehearsal dinner, or better yet, her bachelorette party.

Glittery, white, and short, the tight dress is covered in sparkling sequins. One thin strap reaches over my shoulder, holding the entire thing up, leaving my other shoulder bare. It's tight across my chest. Hell, it's tight across my whole body, ending mid-thigh. There's even a little cutout on my right thigh, showing more leg.

This would look great with a pair of high heels, and I immediately chastise myself for thinking that.

"Ready yet?" Payton calls.

"Yep! On three!"

I unlock the door and grip the handle. "One. Two. Three."

Lurching out, Payton slams her hands to her cheeks. "Val, you look amazing in that!"

"Thanks!" I say, spinning around for her to see the back.

"Girl, your ass looks amazing. Are you even wearing a bra?"

I turn back to face her and put my hand on my hip. "Strapless. Now let me get a better look at you. Give me a little twirl."

Payton's dress is modest. It's pale pink with long sleeves and a high neckline. The dress hugs her torso and flares out at her hips. "I really like it, Payton. I think you're crazy not to wear pink."

She grabs the hem of her dress, holding out her skirt. "You think?"

"I do. You're buying it. Now let's change and get the hell out of here."

"Fine. But you're buying that one then."

I just shake my head and smile. "You are something else, you know that?"

She tosses her hair behind her shoulder and walks back into the dressing room, but when I enter mine, I realize I'm not alone.

A scream lodges in my throat as a man with a black ski mask captures me and presses a cloth to my face. His hand covers my mouth and nose, forcing me to breathe in the chemicals saturating the rag, even as I struggle against him.

"I'm really sorry," he breathes, his voice familiar as blackness clouds my vision. "I hope you can forgive me someday." My mind reels, realizing who it is. I hope when I wake up that this will all just be a bad dream, that it isn't true. "I'm sorry," he mutters one more time as I succumb to the drug and pass out in his arms.

Groggy, my head pounding, I wake up with a cramp in my neck. I try to rub out the ache, but my arm won't move, and I rouse immediately. I'm in total blackness, not a light to be found, and my arms and legs are bound tightly to a chair.

It's cold in here, so cold, and it smells of old oil and rusty metal. I shiver, realizing I'm still in the white dress, the sequins itching my skin.

"Hello?"

My heart hammers as I wait for a response, terror coursing through me and twisting my gut into knots.

It isn't true. It isn't true. It isn't true.

I chant it over and over, squeezing my eyes shut and praying for God to help me.

Music plays in the distance, the pounding beat thrumming through my chest. After a few minutes, the music pauses and a bell rings three times, the sound familiar.

I forget all about it, though, when I hear footsteps echo from behind me. I'm frozen, barely able to breathe as I strain to listen. "I told you we belong together, that you were mine. I placed a tracker inside your purse the day I made you dinner, love. It was so easy to find you."

My mouth goes dry. "Marco?"

The steps pause in front of me, and a light turns on, blinding me at first. "Yes, love. It's me. We can be together again."

Dressed in all black, his beard gone, he bends down and pinches my chin. "I've been waiting so long for this." Marco slams his mouth onto mine, his thick tongue invading my mouth. I try to scream, try to move, but I'm stuck choking on his tongue as it prods the back of my throat.

"Fuck, you make me so hard," he growls, grabbing his dick with one hand while rubbing his finger across my lower lip with the other. "Tonight, in front of everyone who supports us, we will consummate our bond and begin our rise to the top. I'm going to fuck you so hard, Val."

"What?" My voice breaks and tears burn in my eyes.

"It's always been us. Don't you feel that? Ever since your cousin's wedding, I haven't been able to stop thinking about you, about us. It was so easy to intercept the call your brother Lucian made to the Morettis and get the access code to your house. So easy to let myself in. I almost took you then, but your bleeding cunt stopped me."

"Marco, you have to let me go. If you let me go, maybe I can convince the Morettis to let you live."

Marco belts out a crazed laugh, his head tipped back as he howls at the ceiling. "They don't care about you, Valentina! They helped me kidnap you, for fuck's sake." He waves at someone hovering in the darkness behind him. "Show her."

My fears are realized when none other than Salvatore Moretti walks out of the shadows.

My tears fall freely as I glare at the man I'd started to give my heart to. "How could you do this? You bastard!"

Sal's face remains stoic even as I cry, his arms folded over his broad chest. "You made it so easy. It was like taking candy from a little baby girl."

My chest clenches and my eyes close when I hear the term he used to belittle me, a term I haven't heard for days. "I trusted you, Sal. Your brothers trusted you."

"Then you're all fools," he counters, lowering his hands.

"Why, Sal? Why? What about the treaty? What about peace? Are you willing to throw all that away for him?" I nod my chin toward Marco.

Marco steps in front of Sal, blocking my view. "Don't worry about him, love. He doesn't want you like I do."

"His brothers will fight for me if he won't," I spit.

Marco scolds me. "Tsk, tsk, tsk. You need to ditch those Moretti fucks." He's breathing hard, and there's madness gleaming in his eyes. "They don't even love you! No one loves you like I do." He charges forward and gets in my face, clutching my upper arms. "Watch, you'll see. I'll send them a video of us. Once they see how in love we are, they'll leave us alone. You'll see."

"I don't love you!" I shout in his face. "I'll never love you, you crazy fuck!"

Marco grins maniacally and stands up. "Maybe not, but it will make taking you that much sweeter."

I watch in horror as he steps into the shadows. A red blinking light comes to life as the bell tolls again. Marco emerges from the dark and pulls a blade out of his pocket. He licks the edge of the blade then slips it under the single strap of my dress. "The time to claim you as mine has come."

As the fabric tears, screams launch from my lungs as I realize what he's going to do.

And the worst part?

Sal just stands there, doing nothing about it.

CHAPTER FORTY-THREE

Fausto

Armani combs his fingers through his hair, pacing back and forth across the office. "She should have been back by now."

I open my phone. "I'll text Sal again."

Armani pauses and shakes his head. "He hasn't answered a single fucking one."

Just then, my phone rings, and the limo driver's number flashes across the screen. "It's the limo driver," I tell Armani before answering, "Hello?"

It's not his voice that answers. "She's gone!"

A woman's cries penetrate my ears as my body numbs in fear. "Who's gone? Who is this?"

"Val! She's gone!" the woman repeats. "This is Payton. I don't know what to do."

I look up at Armani who's staring at me with wide eyes. "Val's missing." I put the phone on speaker. "Okay, Payton, tell me what happened."

Try as I might to stay calm, my heart races and my fingers shake with adrenaline.

Payton sobs. "Oh God," she says, then she starts crying again.

Armani lowers his face to the phone. "Payton, we're going to need you to calm down and tell us what happened."

She sniffles and takes a deep breath. "We were at Charlene's Dress Emporium trying on dresses. We went into the changing room, changed into dresses, and modeled them for each other. I went back into my changing room to put my regular clothes back on, but she never came out of hers." Her voice begins to break again. "I called her and called her and crawled under her door, but she wasn't there. Just her purse and her clothes."

Armani is already on his phone, designating a team of our men to head there and search for clues. "Thank you, Payton, for all your information. I'll have the driver take you home now."

"The fuck you will!" she shouts back. "I'm staying to help."

"Payton, I really don't think—"

"I don't care what you think," she cuts in. "She is my best friend and I'll be fucking damned if I do nothing while a group of men she hardly knows looks for her without me."

There's no time to argue. "Fine. I'll have the driver bring you back here."

"Fuck!" Armani shouts, slamming his fists into the nearest wall as I hang up the phone. "How could this fucking happen?"

I scrub my hands up and down my face. "We never should have agreed with Sal when he suggested we allow her to go off on her own. Every single time she's by herself, shit goes down, but I know one thing for sure—we're going to find whoever took her and we're going to kill them."

"I'm trying Sal again," Armani says, lifting his phone to his ear and lowering it quickly. "Dammit. It's going straight to voicemail."

I shake my head. "Why would he turn his phone off?"

Armani freezes. "What if they took him too, Fausto? What if they have both been taken?"

Is it possible? Salvatore Moretti is one of the smartest fucking men

I've ever known. He's also proven to be quite reckless as of late. "That would mean he had to be with her at the dress shop."

Armani swings behind the desk, sliding into the chair and waking the computer. "I'm going to check the security footage and see which car he took."

I stand behind my brother as he brings up the live feed. "It's the truck," I say, seeing a big open space in our garage where the large, white Ford should be parked. "Rewind the footage. See when he left."

Armani clicks a few buttons, and we see the Ford rolling back into the garage. What's most alarming, however, isn't the fact that he left not ten minutes after Val's limo did, but that he had a duffle bag with him.

"What the fuck is going on?" Armani growls, rewinding the footage and playing it again.

I'm about to answer when an email notification pops up on our screen. The sender is unknown, and the subject says, "Live Feed." I usually would discourage Armani from clicking on something as sketchy as this, but with Val gone, I don't try to stop him.

I suck in a breath as a dark room flickers to life on the screen. A man's back is blocking the view, and screams rip through the speakers. I look at my brother, recognizing the voice.

"It's her! Who the fuck is this?"

Her screams turn to sobs as the man lowers himself in front of her and we can finally see her face. She's terrified, her eyes red and cheeks blotchy. She screams again, and the man laughs, then a ripping noise sounds.

His hand cups her cheek. "Don't cry, my love, this is how it's supposed to be."

She jerks her chin away. "Fuck you, Marco," Val grits out, and a chill grips my insides.

Marco.

Marco moves to her side, revealing her whole body for the first time.

"I'm going to kill him!" Armani seethes.

Val is tied to a chair, and not just tied with a simple pair of handcuffs. Rope is twisted around her forearms, gluing them to the armrests. Her legs are wrapped from her ankles to her knees, securing her to the chair's front legs.

She's barely clothed, the remnants of her dress hanging behind her, leaving her in a matching set of bra and panties.

I watch with fury as Marco pulls the dress out from behind her then steps behind her back. "Let them watch us, my love. Let them see how in love we are." Marco slips his hands down her body, and red coats my vision as he dives his hands inside her bra.

Val screams again, thrashing her head, but it's no use. She can't fucking move. But then she says something that has my blood fucking boiling. As Marco removes one hand and drags it down her body, the movement pulls at her bra and exposes one of her nipples, but he doesn't stop there, dipping a hand inside her panties. "No, please," she begs, looking imploringly at someone to the side of the camera. "Sal, please... Help me."

A rage I didn't know I was capable of surges through me. My own fucking brother is in on this?

"I'm going to kill him!" I shout, slamming my fist through the nearest wall.

"Not if I kill him first," Armani growls.

"I'll tear him limb from fucking limb," I start, but then my brother's voice blares through the speakers.

"Not yet, Marco. Wait to defile the little baby girl until the rest of your men arrive. I've heard she likes an audience."

"Fuck you!" she spits, and Marco's hand plunges farther. "Get off of me, you sick fuck!" Val turns her head and latches her teeth onto Marco's cheek, drawing blood. I silently celebrate her little victory, but it falls short when Marco rips himself away and marches in front of her again, blocking our view. The smack that ricochets into my ears feels like a punch to my gut.

Val's hair flies to the side as Marco strikes her face. "You little bitch!" he shouts, landing a backhand on her cheek. My rage is uncontrollable, and my entire body is alight with murderous intent, yet I have nowhere to direct it.

We're fucking powerless.

Helpless.

Marco prowls around her, frantically tapping his phone. Blood seeps from her lips and drips down her chin to her chest, staining her white bra pink.

"Dad, where the fuck are you guys?" Marco growls into his phone. "I can't wait much longer. I need to do this." Val cries softly, her shoulders shaking and head lowered in defeat. "Yeah, I can wait another half hour for all of you to get here, but fucking hurry."

"Thirty minutes until who gets there?" I wonder out loud.

Sal steps forward, sinking to the ground in front of her. "All you do is cry, little baby girl. Cry. Cry. Fucking cry. Your sobs are pathetic and noisy, but I promise you more are to come. Marco's plans for you will have you shrieking so loudly they'll hear you in the deepest *craters* of the moon." Sal emphasizes the word "craters" and my mind spins as a bell rings three times. "Hear that bell, little baby girl? That's the sound announcing your second round of misery. Cry for us. Your tears only make me hate you even more."

Sal stands and backs away, and realization dawns on me. Sal gave us clues—intentionally or not, I can't be sure. I glance at Armani. "I know where she is."

As Marco settles the knife between Val's breasts and slices through her bra, her breasts bouncing free, I punch my fist through the computer screen, unable to see another second. I run from the office, Armani right behind me, and I don't stop until I get to the garage. I choose our fastest car and strap in, tearing out of our driveway.

Marco said we had thirty minutes, and I'll be damned if it takes me more than twenty-five to get there.

We're coming for you, pistol, and when we get there, we're going to slaughter every single person who caused you pain. Even if the one who did it is my own flesh and blood.

CHAPTER FORTY-FOUR

Valentina

THE TEARS WON'T STOP. My eyes feel swollen and puffy as I stare at the ground. I'm too hurt, too lost to look at Sal and see hatred in his eyes again. I won't put myself through that. What kills me is that I finally allowed him in. He finally showed me a bit of who he is, a man who's sweet and caring.

What happened to that man who defended me at the pharmacy?

What happened to the man who went back to the store and bought me all my favorite snacks?

Was it all just a ploy to get me here?

Was every move intentional, done for me to let my guard down so he could pull the rug out from under me at this exact moment?

I almost refuse to believe it, but the evidence is standing right in front of me, his face of stone back in place as he watches Marco strip me of my bra.

I hate that I'm naked like this. It's terrifying and fills me with shame, and I know this isn't the worst of what's to come tonight.

Salvatore's vile words bring more tears than Marco's actions.

"I trusted you!" I shout at Sal as Marco starts exploring my body again. "Was that all a lie? How can you let him touch me like this and do nothing?"

Sal won't even look at me as I jerk my body, twisting my shoulders to try and free myself from Marco's repulsive grasp. He just stares at the ground by my feet, and the only movements he makes are his clenching jaw and his hands squeezing into fists.

I scream in frustration, but every action I make depletes me of energy. I'm getting tired of fighting. Besides, my arms and legs are bound so tightly that I know I can't get out of this on my own.

So I endure it, getting lost in a dark corner of my mind, a place where there is no emotion, no feeling, just numbness. I pretend it's my own hands moving along my skin, touching me in my most secret places. I pretend this is all just a dream.

Staring blankly ahead, I count the blinking lights and clear my head of all thoughts, all feelings, attempting to stay strong. Cool air blows down on me, chilling me to the bone. Goosebumps rise on my skin and my nipples turn to ice, searching for even an ounce of warmth.

But there's nothing warm in here. This room is filled with icy hearts and frozen souls.

Marco pulls his knife on me again, tilts my head back, and presses it against my throat. "Kiss, my love." He nods toward the camera. "Show them how little you care for them. Show them how in love we are."

He nicks my skin, and I gasp. Marco takes my open mouth as an invitation to shove his tongue down it. I can't move, can't breathe, choking on his tongue as he drags it along my cheeks like a fucking psycho.

I gag and cough, and Marco tightens his grip on my hair, keeping the knife pressed firmly against my skin as more footsteps sound. I pray it's the police or the twins, hoping someone has found me, that Payton was able to get help for me.

But to my horror, it isn't anyone on my side, at least not anymore.

Marco removes his slimy tongue and drags the blade down my chest, leaving one hand still entangled in my hair. As more and more men filter into the room, Marco taps his knife against my nipple, and I force myself to remain as still as possible.

I don't cower or look away, staring each man in the eye as they walk in and see my naked body. The last man to walk in the room is none other than Alfonzo Capelli.

"You," I seethe. "My father trusted you."

Alfonzo adjusts his pants, yanking on his suit jacket. "A fool's action, really. Knowing the feelings my son had for you, he shared information about the treaty. It was then we started plotting his demise, as well as your brothers', so you and Marco could lead the next generation of the Cosa Nostra." Alfonzo steps right in front of me, and Marco pulls back on my hair, forcing me to look up. "Of course we only need you to say the marriage vows, and then Marco can lock you up in his basement for all I care."

Marco hums his delight at his father's crass words.

"You make me sick," I grit out. "All of you. How can you stand there and do nothing? I know you have daughters and sisters. You can't call yourselves men when you watch them do this to me. You're cowards. Every single one of you."

Alfonzo grins, displaying his nicotine stained teeth. "Marco, let me have the knife." Alfonzo holds out his hand and wiggles his fingers. Marco reluctantly hands over the blade. Alfonzo crouches down, holding the knife in front of my eyes. "We don't plan on only watching tonight." He grins maliciously as he slips the knife under my panties and slices.

"No!" I cry out as he pulls them off me, leaving me completely naked in front of all these leering men.

"Yes!" Alfonzo shouts victoriously, holding my torn panties up for them all to see. "Now they can see what a fucking cunt you really are."

Alfonzo backs up and brandishes the knife. For a moment, a dot of red light blinks across his face, but it's gone so fast I'm not sure it was even there. "Each man gets to make a mark before Marco fucks her cunt raw in front of all of us," he barks, turning toward his men. "Who'd like to make the mark first?"

"Me."

His response is immediate. I shake my head, still in disbelief as Sal plucks the knife from Alfonzo's hand. Marco moves to stand next to his dad, a sleazy, arrogant smile on his face.

"Why?" I whisper, my chest compressing as Sal rests the flat end of the blade against my cheek.

Sal leans in close to my ear, his words so softly spoken I almost can't hear them. "Because the right choice is never easy." He stands tall, wrapping his hand around my hair. "I'm going to enjoy this." He laughs, then shouts, "Now!"

Gunshots ring out, and the knife is lifted from my cheek and hurled across from me. A sickening thud sounds as it embeds in Alfonzo's chest and he falls to his knees. I scream as more shots are fired, my ears ringing from the deafeningly loud sounds.

An avalanche of people rush inside wearing leather and cowboy hats, stinking of sweat and booze, attacking every suit-clad man in sight. Men fall left and right, the scent of blood misting the air as I pull and yank on the ropes, desperate to free myself.

"I've got you, pistol." Fausto's voice booms from the darkness and my savior rushes to me, cutting me loose. "Armani, I'm taking her out of here now!" he shouts, scooping me into his arms.

Pressing me tightly against his chest, Fausto Moretti barrels through the mass of people until he finds the exit. He practically leaps down the stairs, his feet pounding on the old metal walkway until he kicks open a door and sunlight surrounds us.

I'm outside.

I'm safe.

It's not until I open my eyes and see the graffiti scrawled across the outside wall of the abandoned factory when I realize where we are—The Crater.

Fausto falls to his knees, cradling my body, tears leaking from his eyes. "You're safe. You're safe," he coos, rocking us back and forth.

"Fausto? What's going on? I don't understand any of this."

He kisses my head and finds the strength to stand, opening the door to his blue Jeep. "I don't have all the answers yet, but I promise I'll wring them out of Sal if I have to use my own hands to do it. But first, I want to get you back home."

"But Armani and Sal?" I argue.

He presses a finger to my lips. "Even in a time of your own need, you're worried about others. It's one of the many things I love about you, Val. My brothers are two of the strongest fighters I have ever come across. They have everything under control. I promise."

Fausto takes off his shirt and slips it over me then buckles me in.

With one glance back at The Crater, Fausto shifts the truck into drive, the tires squealing as he peels out of the parking lot. He finds my hand and squeezes it gently, rubbing his thumb across the top in a caring way, and he never lets it go the entire way home.

CHAPTER FORTY-FIVE

Valentina

I can't stop trembling.

I can't stop shaking.

Anxiety has ripped me to shreds, and I don't know if I can stop it.

Back at the Moretti mansion, we learn Sal called ahead and ordered the staff to exit the home. I appreciate that move so much, not wanting all of them to see me like this, with swollen eyes, tearstained cheeks, and in nothing but Fausto's shirt.

I rest my head against Fausto's chest as he takes me upstairs, entering my room. I'm relieved to be inside, to say the least. He closes and locks the door behind him and carries me into the bathroom, sitting me on the sink.

"I know you have questions, Val, and you'll get your answers as soon as they get home. I promise we'll get to the bottom of this."

I don't respond because Fausto seems to be as lost as I am.

"What Sal did—"

"Shh," I murmur, not wanting to hear it, not wanting to think about it.

Fausto heads through the glass shower door to the tub and turns it on, filling it to the brim with warm water and bubbles. He steps back out and walks over to me. "Go soak in the tub, it will ease your body. I know how exhausted you must be."

It's only now that I realize fatigue is written all over him. His eyes are dark and sunken, and blood splatters are all over his face and hands. Fausto is a mess.

When I don't move, he heads out of my bathroom and turns back to face me. "I'll be back to check on you in an hour, okay?"

Words lodge in my throat, so I can only nod, my eyes fixed on the floor. Fausto's footsteps grow distant, and then I hear my bedroom door open and shut. When I'm sure I'm alone, I hop down from the counter and allow my borrowed t-shirt to fall to the ground.

Grabbing two towels from the cabinet, I bring them inside the shower with me and set them on the ground next to the tub before climbing in.

Fausto was right, this is exactly what I need. I dip my entire body under, even my head, before I come up and take a deep breath, resting the back of my head against the rim.

Today has been traumatic in so many ways that I'm unsure if I'll recover. My life flashed before my eyes today, and I felt terror the likes of which I've never known. I was stripped and groped, and my body was used like a sex toy for a sick man.

I've never been this mortified, never felt that kind of shame like I did when all those men poured in from the darkness and gazed at me, chained and naked, while Marco slid his knife all over my skin.

I raise my hand to my neck, feeling the cut there, and immediately start to cry. I don't just cry. I bawl. I scream and yell and wail loudly, letting my emotions run loose as they echo off the bathroom walls.

But I need this. I need to feel. I need to grieve for what was done to me. It's hard to process, and my memories of it are a blur. I wonder if it really did happen or if it was just a dream. Then I see the crumpled shirt on the ground and the feelings overwhelm me again.

I cry until my voice grows hoarse. I cry until no more tears fall from my eyes. Then I just shake, trembling in the water until it grows cold around me.

Pulling the plug, I step out and quickly dry myself, wrapping my hair in a towel. Stepping inside my closet, I slip on a tank top, a t-shirt, and a large hoodie, then a pair of cotton panties and long, baggy pajama pants, the ones that belonged to my brother.

Exhaustion pulls at my eyelids, and my feet drag as I stumble over to my bed and fall into the mess of perfectly placed pillows and elegantly folded blankets. My eyes close and I give in to the fatigue, falling asleep with the plushie bunny Armani gave me tucked in my arms.

I WAKE up to soft snoring sometime later. Fear skates down my spine and my eyes fly open, wondering where I am, but then I see Fausto passed out next to me, wearing gray sweats and a t-shirt. Movement on my other side has me turning to see Armani pressed firmly against me, wearing boxer shorts and nothing else.

Tucked between them, I feel safe, and I start to relax. I must have been tense even during sleep. Darkness has fallen outside, and I sit up on my elbows, my stomach rumbling. Quietly, I crawl from the bed, intent on heading down to the kitchen, when a third body sprawled on my couch catches me off guard.

It's Sal.

He's wearing a clean pair of jeans and a Cubs hoodie. Looking at him, I'd never know he's the Don of the Outfit. Now, sleeping softly, he looks just like any other man.

Well…

Not like any other man. The Morettis have an air about them. It would be impossible not to notice them when they enter a room. They exude power and confidence, their gorgeous faces unmatched against normal society.

And here they are, all in my bedroom, camped out to keep a watchful eye over me, to protect me.

My eyes well again, even because of Sal who was the cause of so much of my pain. He's not off my shit list yet, but I'll hear what he has to say when he has to say it.

Grabbing the door handle, I freeze. My body won't move, and I'm unable to open it as fear grips my insides again. He could be here for all I know, hunting me, unwilling to let me go.

I swallow hard when I feel a body press gently against my back, a hand resting on mine to help me turn the handle.

"I've got you, Val."

I glance over my shoulder, and Sal softly smiles at me, but it doesn't reach his eyes. He still looks weary and exhausted.

I nod and allow him to help me. He holds my hand as we walk through the dark, quiet house to the kitchen. "What are you hungry for?" he asks.

"Food. Anything."

He guides me to the table, and I sit as he moves over to the fridge, pulling it open. "Something hot or cold?"

"Food," I repeat, uncaring what it is at this point.

He closes the fridge and faces me. "One of my favorite nighttime snacks is a big bowl of cereal. Do you like cereal, Val?"

"My God, do I. What kinds do you have?"

Sal smiles and turns to the pantry, opening the glass door. "Cinnamon Toast Crunch, Golden Grahams, Lucky Charms, Coco Puffs, Honey Nut Cheerios…"

The thought of the sweet milk to drink after having a bowl of Honey Nut Cheerios seals the deal. "I'll take the Cheerios please."

Sal plucks the box down and pours us both a bowl, adding the milk before setting it down in front of me. "I pegged you as a Coco Puffs kind of girl," he comments before scooping a spoonful into his mouth.

I swallow my bite. "When I was a kid, it was one of my favorites, but not since I realized how fucked up the roof of my mouth would get after having a bowl."

He points his spoon at me and nods. "Same. Armani is still willing to risk it."

"Not surprised," I mutter between mouthfuls.

After finishing my bowl and putting it in the sink, I fold my hands on the table and look pointedly at Sal, ignoring the black eye on this beautiful stranger. "You have some explaining to do, Sal. The pleasantries are nice and all, but I can't forget what happened today. I need answers."

Sal nods sadly and touches his swollen eye tenderly. "I know you do. You deserve them."

"And what happened to your eye?" I ask as the twins burst through the kitchen door.

"Armani punched him in the face for what he did to you," Fausto announces, and I see Armani's sleepy face right behind him. Fausto rushes right to my side, grabs my face, and kisses me as if his life depends on it. I feel his emotion, his terror, and his desperation at the thought of losing me. I sense it all through just this simple kiss.

Armani practically shoves Fausto out of the way before wrapping his large arms around me and holding me close. "I was so scared, kitten, so fucking scared."

"So was I," I admit, holding him back.

"Who wants coffee?" Fausto inquires.

"Me," we all respond in tandem. A few moments later, Fausto brings a tray to the table like Matilda does, with a carafe, creamer, and sugar. I scoot over and Fausto sits next to me, forcing Armani to grudgingly sit by Sal.

Fausto wraps his arm around me and pulls me close to his side. "Start talking, Sal."

Sal, for the first time ever, looks nervous. His hands are even a little shaky as he sips from his mug before clasping his hands in front of him.

"Let me start off by saying that I don't know if what I did was right or wrong. It felt like the right move at the time, but looking back on it now, I question things. For over a week, I dug for information on Marco, and I confirmed Val's suspicions. He was stalking her. But finding him was like trying to grasp onto a handful of sand. He was being protected."

"Then why didn't you fucking tell us? Maybe we could have helped," Armani grits out.

"Because I'm a selfish fucking asshole who wanted to take care of it myself! I thought I owed it to her." He briefly looks me in the eye but averts his gaze almost instantly, scrubbing the side of his face. "I thought if I could bring him down on my own, she might forgive me for how I've acted since she came here."

"You were reckless," Fausto spits. "You put her life at risk."

"It was the only way," Sal responds. "Marco actually had the fucking balls to call me. Consumed by his delusions, he told me of his entire plan. He said he needed my help to capture Val. I knew neither of you would have gone along with it, you care for her too deeply, so I had to keep you in the dark. It was the only way to get everyone involved at the same place at the same time. I had to risk it, even though I knew you might never forgive me."

Sal swallows and licks his lips. "I had to do it, Val. It was the hardest fucking thing I've ever done, handing you over like that. You can't imagine how hard it was."

"I can't imagine?" I shout angrily. "Were you the one strapped to a chair, stripped of all your pride, while some sleazy men touched your body?"

He shakes his head. "No."

"Oh, then you must know what it's like to have a man you're falling for kidnap you while trying on dresses with your friend?" I recognize my slipup, but it's too late.

Sal's eyes widen, but sadness quickly etches across his features. His lips turn down. "No."

"Then don't sit there and try to tell me what I can't imagine because I can promise you it's not worse than what I had to live through."

Sal slams his fists on the table. "It was the only way, Val! I know how strong you are. I've seen you fight tooth and nail since you've been here. I've seen you stand up for yourself and battle me head-to-head even when I was at my worst, even when I tried to hurt you, when I hated you with every fucking breath in my body."

I throw up my hands in frustration. "But why do you hate me, Sal? I've done nothing to you. You blame me for this… this treaty when I didn't even fucking know about it. You can't even fucking look at me, Sal. Why can't you look me in the eye?"

"Because all I see is your fucking father!" he shouts, veins pulsing in his temples. "When I look at you, I see *him*. My hatred for Carlo Rossi has clouded all the feelings I have for you."

Confusion wraps itself around my mind. "But why, Sal? Why do you hate him so much? I know the Outfit and Cosa Nostra are enemies, but it feels like more than that."

Sal ushers Armani out of the bench and paces the kitchen, massaging his temples again. "Because of something that happened several months ago. Your father took something from me that almost destroyed me. He… He broke me."

At this admission, Armani and Fausto perk up, shifting their bodies toward Sal after sharing one of their twin looks that I wish I could be a part of.

"Tell me, Sal," I beg. "Help me understand."

He shakes his head, a sob escaping his lips as a tear drips down his cheek. "Val," he whispers, "don't make me say it."

"Please!" I scream. "I can't live like this anymore! I can't live with all the secrets! I can't stand how you never look me in the eye, and the few times you have, all I see is hatred staring back at me."

Sal turns to me, his eyes glistening with tears. "He killed my girlfriend, okay? Are you happy now? Your father murdered Gianna right in front of my eyes all because of you."

My heart plummets to my feet, and the twins look at me with shock on their faces. "I—Sal… I don't know what to say."

His tears fall freely now.

"You told us she ran away." Fausto chokes on his words, coming to his brother's side.

Sal pushes him away. "I didn't want you to know because it jaded my opinion of any Rossi. It made me hate Val before I even got to know her. Carlo broke part of my heart, and I didn't want what he did to affect you too. If I kept it from you, then maybe your opinion of her wouldn't be so cynical. Maybe you could learn to love a Rossi and be happy, because I thought I never could."

Sal looks at me with utter sadness. "That's why I never look at you, Val. When I look at you, I see the dying face of the woman I loved. When I look at you, I see her murderer staring back at me."

Emotion clogs my throat. I feel as though I've been shot in the chest with a dozen arrows and impaled by the sharpest spear. Pain like I've never known before dizzies my mind and tears through my heart. I feel shattered, broken, as shame washes over me for the sins of my father.

"I'm so sorry," Armani says, covering his mouth in shock. "Sal, if I would have known, I—"

"You what?" Sal interrupts. "You would have sought vengeance on our future. You would have killed Carlo, and in doing so, pissed on the treaty our father worked so hard to seal. I couldn't allow you to do that. I couldn't let you suffer the burden I had to carry. It was my cross to bear. I was the one who decided to test the limits of the treaty. I'm the one who chose to openly have a girlfriend. I thought I was untouchable, but I was wrong, and my poor choices cost Gianna her fucking life."

Sal turns to me, desperation tugging at his lips. "So I did the only thing I could to survive, I froze my heart. I turned dark and depraved, and bathed in the blood of others. I learned how to be harder and meaner so I didn't fall apart. The family needed me, so I stood firm for them. I never imagined someone could open my heart up again. I never imagined that in spite of how hard I tried to keep you out, that you'd thaw what I thought had drowned in the depths of the coldest ocean. But you have, Valentina. You have."

Sal turns away from us, wiping his face on his sleeves. "A wise man recently told me that sometimes you have to make hard choices. That the right path is not always easy. So I did what had to be done. I sacrificed you in order to catch every last fucking person that tried to overthrow you, who were planning to kill off every remaining heir of

Carlo Rossi. I'd be lying if I said I wasn't tempted," Sal continues. "All I had to do was leave you there. The plan was in motion to take your brothers down. With them dead and gone, the Rossi name would die with them, and I would finally have my vengeance. But then I saw you, I felt you, and your soul called to mine. I knew then if I let this happen then I was no better than Carlo. I'd be worse, and I so desperately want to be a better man than that, to be better for you."

Sal rushes toward me and falls to his knees. "I'll beg for your forgiveness until the day I die, Valentina, but my life is yours if you'll have it, in whatever capacity you'll take me."

"How can you possibly say that?" I choke out. "How can you love me, knowing who my father is?"

"Because you are not your father," Sal replies quickly. "That's something that has taken me a long time to see. You are not the evil man who broke me. You are the woman who saved me. You rebuilt my crumbling wall brick by fucking brick. You are my rock, Valentina, and I will defend you with my life over and over again if that means I get to share the rest of yours with you."

I'm so overwhelmed, so angry and hurt and mad and sad all at once. "And what about Marco? He'll never stop hunting me."

Armani stands up proudly. "He's dead, kitten. They all are."

"All of them?" I ask, and Fausto nods.

"When we saw the video come through and figured out the clues Sal gave us, I called Crystal right away. She had every person in The Crater on standby, ready to come to our aid, and they did, pistol. They helped us save you."

"So it's over then?" I murmur, staring at my cup of coffee.

"Not exactly," Sal says, and I turn to him. "That chapter of your life is over. But this… this is just the beginning."

I think about what he said, replaying his confession in my mind. I understand why he did what he did. I really do. He had to sacrifice me in order to bring down everyone who wanted to destroy the Rossi name. I was the bait, the lure to get them out of hiding.

And it worked.

Every last one of them is dead.

"I forgive you," I whisper softly.

Sal chokes on a sob. "What?"

I turn in my chair and cup his face in my hands. "I forgive you, Salvatore Moretti. I know everything you did was for me even if it was the most fucked up way to show someone you care. I know you did what you thought was right, and in the end, I'm okay, and the people who tried to hurt me—"

"Can never hurt you again," he finishes, and I smile. "You are so much stronger than I ever thought you were. You've proven it over and over again. You'd make me the proudest man in the world if I could call you my wife, and we'd all be honored if you would take the Moretti family name as your own."

Tears fall from my eyes like a dam has just been broken, and I leap into his arms. "Yes. I want that so badly."

Armani joins us, wrapping Sal and me in his arms. "We want it too, kitten."

"Forever?" I ask as Fausto slides in as well.

He kisses my head. "Always. Until the end of time."

CHAPTER FORTY-SIX

Valentina

THE PAST WEEK HAS BEEN... interesting, to say the least. Armani has been overly attentive to my every need like a little overprotective hen. Fausto has battled me about setting up cameras in my room so he can check on me at all times, but I won that fight, insisting no cameras be put into my room. Fausto disagrees, but I think his reasons for pushing so hard are more nefarious than he claims.

Sal... Where do I even begin? He's so unsure of himself it's actually adorable. To see this powerful man crumble, wanting to fulfill my every whim, is such a drastic change that I'm struggling to adjust to it. His black eye is healed with the care of some therapy from their family doctor, but I kind of liked it. I told him it made him look rugged.

That was the first time I'd seen him smile since that night.

Sal is so handsome when he smiles and leaves the stress of his life behind for a moment, just enjoying what's right in front of him.

But something has been bothering me—our lack of intimacy.

Sometimes it's awkward between the two of us, like we both want to do it but neither of us is confident enough to make the first move.

I know Sal thinks I'll reject him after everything that's happened, but I wouldn't. I've accepted the past and have decided to grow from it, not allowing it to weaken me or cause me to be jaded.

I don't think Sal believes I truly forgive him, but I do. I really do. He saved me the only way he knew how, and I'll forever be grateful for it.

Sal has mentioned our marriage more than once, and I know it's necessary to complete the treaty. From what I gather, we might be the only ones left who haven't said our vows.

I know that time is coming soon, but I still don't feel like I'm ready. I'm only eighteen, for fuck's sake, and I am definitely not ready to settle down and start pumping out kids. I want to go to college and live a little first.

The most significant change over the past week is the inclusion of Payton. She's even come to the mansion and spent the night. We hung out in our favorite comfy clothes, ordered pizza, and binge watched every *Harry Potter* movie. It took us almost two days to complete the marathon, but it was the best two days ever.

In fact, she's here now. We've been instructed to get ready for an expensive dinner, and several dresses were brought to my room, tucked inside clear plastic shells to keep them safe.

"Which one do you think would look best on me?" Payton asks, grabbing a sherbet-colored gown.

"You know what I'm going to say." I point at the pink dress.

Payton rolls her eyes. "And you know what I'm going to say—fuck off."

We both laugh as Payton puts the sherbet dress back on the rack and decides on a baby blue piece. It will look gorgeous with her eyes.

I snatch a sparkly black dress, lifting the crinkly cover up and holding it against myself, standing in front of the full-length mirror in my closet. "I think this is the one."

"Oh!" Payton says, fingering the material. "I love it."

We set aside our selected gowns and do our hair and makeup before dressing.

"What do you think they are up to?" I ask her, curious to see her reaction. To my surprise, Payton won't look at me, but her cheeks flush. "You know something, don't you?"

She scoffs. "No?"

"You do!" I accuse, noting how her voice rose, making *no* sound more like a question than an answer.

She turns her back toward me, adjusting the straps on her dress. "I know nothing."

"Fine. Keep your secrets. I'll remember that."

Standing in front of the mirror, I admire the black dress from every angle. It's the kind of dress a movie star would wear on the red carpet.

Short, capped sleeves barely cover my shoulders, and the sweetheart neckline makes my tits look much fuller than they really are. The dress is cinched on my left hip where a slit in the material reaches all the way down to the hem at my ankles, leaving my left leg bare when I walk.

I don't know what the material is made of, it's not sequins or glitter exactly, but when I move, the entire thing sparkles like a cloudless night sky. I add a pair of strappy heels and a small Versace clutch Fausto got for me to complete the outfit.

"What do you think?" I turn to Payton and my jaw drops. She looks like a million bucks! "Girl, you look incredible."

The short, strapless dress hugs her curves. She's paired the dress with nude wedge heels, making her legs look powerful and strong.

"Yeah? So do you!"

She links her arm around mine, and we exit my room, gripping each other tightly for balance as we make our way down the stairs.

Joseph greets us at the bottom, grinning as we walk over to him. "You ladies look magnificent. Please allow me to escort you to your transport for the evening."

Payton and I giggle together as we take Joseph's arms in our hands and allow the sweet, old man to guide us outside. What I wasn't prepared for was the vintage Jaguar waiting for us, the ivory paint shining in the afternoon sun.

A driver dressed in black with white, gloved hands opens the back door when he sees us coming. "Watch your step, ladies."

Payton steps inside first, and I follow close behind her. To say this car is luxurious would be a severe understatement. With tan leather seats and black accents, this car oozes wealth and extravagance.

A bottle of champagne chills in a bucket of ice, and the driver pours us each a flute before strapping into the driver's seat and pulling the car onto the road.

I don't ask where we're going, because I really don't care. I could go to a fast-food restaurant with Payton, and we'd have just as much fun. It doesn't matter what we do together, every second is filled with happiness and laughter.

I turn to look out the back window and see another car following us.

Good.

Sal promised to have men follow us for protection at my request. I feel much better knowing someone is watching my back, even if it's not necessary anymore. As a mafia wife, it will be necessary, so I might as well get used to it now.

We drive through the high-class neighborhood and head into downtown traffic. Payton and I manage to finish the bottle of champagne just as we pull in front of one of the most elite restaurants in downtown Chicago, Chateau de Black.

Black glass, black brick, and a lit awning make up the front. Fabric-covered ropes hold back a line of people who wish to have a table. Payton and I hold hands as our driver opens our door for us, and then we bypass the line.

People glare at us, but we pay them no mind, ignoring their sneers and calls of outrage as a bouncer opens the doors for us. Walls made of sparkling wallpaper and bar tops of exquisite granite greet us. Sparkling chandeliers cast a soft glow from above as a band plays slow-paced, traditional acoustic music.

A seasoned man with salt and pepper hair and an exceptional

mustache greets us from behind a podium. "Ah, you must be Mr. Moretti's esteemed guests. I'm Reginald, and I'd be honored if you two ladies would please follow me to your table."

Reginald guides us through a busy bar area. Men wear tuxedos, and women wear designer gowns, dripping with diamond jewelry. I almost feel out of place here, like I don't belong.

Payton and I struggle to walk in our heels, gripping each other for support, the champagne giving us both a good buzz. Reginald beckons us inside an elevator, but before the doors can close, one of our guards joins us, glaring at Reginald. The man gulps and plasters a fake grin on his face as he presses a button and the elevator travels up.

When the doors open again on the opposite side of the elevator, Payton and I step out onto a balcony overlooking the city, where glass railings give guests an unobstructed view of Chicago.

Several private, candlelit tables are at different elevations, up and down sets of stairs. Each stair is lit with soft, white light, oozing extravagance.

The sounds of softly tapping silverware on dinner plates and the happy clinking of glasses greets us. Reginald ushers me forward, rounding a walkway parallel to the glass railing, before stopping me in front of an empty table set for two. In the center is a vase filled with roses that blesses us with their floral fragrance. Petals and candles are scattered across the table, giving it a romantic ambiance.

"Isn't this gorgeous?" I say to Payton, but when I turn back, she's gone.

"Don't worry about her. She just ran off to the bathroom," Reginald assures me as I tuck my dress under myself and scoot in.

But something isn't sitting right with me.

A few tables down, in the shadows, a figure rises, and I begin to panic. The form-fitting suit does nothing to hide the broad shoulders, tapered waist, and muscular physique as the man approaches, but then Fausto emerges from the darkness holding a single rose in his hand.

"Fausto?" I exclaim, rising from my seat. "What are you doing here?"

He kisses my lips softly. "Surprising you, of course. Did it work?"

"Yes, but…" My words trail off as he helps me back into my seat.

"I have something for you."

I bite my lip as he pulls out a small box wrapped with red ribbon. "Valentina, I brought you here tonight to show you how much I care for you. Before I met you, I didn't know what love was. It was a shadow to me, something you could see but never hold. I thought I was doomed to live my life alone, but then you came along and pulled the rug out from under me."

Tears blur my vision as he grabs my hand in his.

"There are no words I can say to make you understand the capacity of my adoration for you, but I'm here to tell you I love you."

A sob escapes from my lips as he opens the box and displays the ring inside. It's platinum and covered in diamonds, but where you might find a center stone, there is an odd C-shape.

"I love you too," I admit, and I fling myself into his arms. "I love it. Thank you so much."

He squeezes me tight, his own eyes glistening. "Head behind me, where your next guest is ready to greet you." Fausto places the box in my hand and gently presses on my lower back, urging me down the walkway.

My legs tremble as I round a large pillar and find Armani waiting for me. He pushes away from his table, his eyes wide as he takes me in. "Val, you look incredible."

I blush, heading closer to him. "So do you."

Wearing a dark blazer with a white shirt below it, dark jeans, and brown boots, Armani looks gorgeous. Today his hair is pulled back and his beard is neatly trimmed, making him look like a rugged lumberjack who's just learning how to play dress up.

He gestures to a vacant chair at his table. "Please sit."

Armani rushes behind me, pushing the chair under me as I lower myself down. He plops into his seat and scoots it closer. Resting on the table is another small box, this time with a pink ribbon around it.

"Valentina, you know I'm not good with words, but I'm going to try to speak from my heart here." I can see how nervous he is as he lets out a long breath. "Before I met you, I moved through life with blinders on. Even the things I loved most in life had lost their luster. My dedication to the Outfit overshadowed anything else in life. I didn't realize how unhappy I was and how much less I was smiling until I saw you in our dining hall that day."

He scoots closer and takes my hands in his. "You were so sweet and innocent, yet you had a fire burning within you, a fierce desire to live. It's contagious. You've infected me in the best way. You've made me laugh and helped me find my smile again. After only a few short weeks, I can't imagine my life without you, and I'm finally able to admit that I love you."

Armani unfastens the bow and opens the box. A ring identical to Fausto's blinks up at me, the diamonds sparkling even in the meager light. Tears fall freely from my eyes, and I curse myself for not wearing waterproof mascara as he slides the box in front of me.

"I love you too, Armani. I have for a while now."

The smile that stretches across his face makes my heart leap, and he scoops me out of my chair, spinning us around with his lips pressed against mine. After he sets me down, he hands me the two boxes and points down the walkway again. "You have one more stop to make, kitten. I'll see you soon."

With my heart beating loudly in my ears, I head down the perimeter of the balcony and find my final man—Salvatore Moretti. This time, there's no table to sit at. He stands in a spectacular tuxedo, his hair is perfectly styled, and his black shoes shine.

Sal is standing with his hands clasped behind his back, surrounded by huge displays of roses with petals strewn across the floor. Candles flicker on top of pillars of all sizes and float in little glass bowls around him.

"Hey," I say, walking up to him. I tuck my hair behind my ears, my nervousness escalating.

"Valentina," he purrs, his eyes roving over my body. "I'm so glad you came."

I stop a few feet in front of him. "Did you think I wouldn't come?"

He licks his lips. "To tell you the truth, I wasn't sure, but now that you're here, I have something to say."

Then Sal does something completely uncharacteristic of himself—he locks eyes with me. For a moment, he just gazes into my eyes and allows me to see the emotion he tries to hide, the emotion that currently trickles down one cheek.

"My world was so clouded by hatred that I felt like I was drowning in darkness. There was no happiness for me, only pride and duty. My obligation to the Mafia cast a shadow on every other aspect of my life. Men are desperate for my attention, and women are even worse. No one wanted my company because of who I am as a man, instead preening for the Don of the Outfit. It was a hard pill to swallow, the unending plague of blackness that had become my life."

Sal stretches his neck and adjusts his feet, taking a deep breath. "Before I met you, I was sure this was as good as it was going to get. Even though I knew you were coming, I didn't have an ounce of strength left in me to care. I judged you for something you had no control over, hated you for something you didn't do, and my anger almost swallowed me whole."

He reaches a hand across the distance between us and clutches one of mine. "To say you are the light that saved me doesn't seem powerful enough for what you've done. You resuscitated me when I struggled to breathe. You rescued me when life held me prisoner. You, Valentina, shared your soul so generously, your heart so pure and open, that I instantly fell for you."

I gasp as Sal falls to one knee, his handsome face gazing up at me. "You illuminated my world and made life worth living, and because of you, I've become a better man. I promise to love you and treasure you every day for the rest of my life."

Sal brings his arm forward from behind his back. Clutched between his thumb and pointer finger is a ring. The solitaire diamond sparkles as if it has its own light. I clap my hand over my mouth as I realize what he's about to do, more tears leaking from my eyes.

Sal holds my left hand in his. "Valentina Rossi, I love you more than life itself. Would you do me the honor of making me the happiest man in the world and marry me?"

"Yes!" I screech as uncontrollable sobs overtake me. He stands and presses me against his chest, rubbing my back. We're quickly engulfed by the twins. Armani cries softly, though he tries to hide it, while Sal and Fausto sniff back their own tears.

"You are still ours too, pistol," Fausto proclaims. "We will share you, honor you, and love you together."

"As a family," Armani adds, and I cry again, my shoulders shaking.

After wiping my tears away, the twins grab their boxes and pluck out their rings. The three men join their rings together, linking them into one large engagement ring. "Three rings for the three of you," I rasp out on a shaky breath.

Sal nods. "Give me your hand." I hold out my left hand, and Sal slides the joined rings onto my ring finger, the set fitting perfectly. I wiggle my fingers, feeling the weight of it, sure, more than ever, that I'm the happiest woman in the world.

"I love you all so much," I tell them as my three men engulf me once more in a tender embrace. This was never how I pictured my life, but now that it's mine, I can't imagine it any other way.

CHAPTER FORTY-SEVEN

Valentina

It's a surreal feeling, slipping on a wedding dress. I don't want to say this is a day I dreamed of, because that wouldn't really be true. My dreams were of freedom, of a time when I'd remove myself from my father's tight grasp and finally get to live.

I didn't know how different my path would be and how it would change me in the process.

Payton shifts behind me, lacing up the corset back and adjusting my veil, her pretty pink bridesmaid dress flowing around her. I finally got my way, choosing pink as my wedding color. Payton had no choice but to wear it.

And she looks amazing.

Dani and Kristina chat back and forth, fixing each other's makeup and making sure their teeth are free of rogue lipstick.

As I stare at myself, sadness threatens to engulf me. It's hard to imagine getting married without a mother to help me dress and without a dad to walk me down the aisle.

The wedding coordinator bustles into our dressing room. "It's time," she announces, tapping her watch.

Payton helps me stand, and I step up onto the pedestal in front of a triple mirror. My dress is magazine worthy. The bodice is tight, drizzled in sparkling crystals, with a sweetheart neckline. Two diamond encrusted straps stretch up from the front of the bodice to my neck, wrapping around my throat like a collar.

The skirt is puffy and flares out from my waist, glittering with crystals and pearls.

The top of my hair is pulled back, and every piece is curled to perfection. A crown of crystals rests on top of my head, and a long veil cascades down my back, but I think my shoes are my favorite thing—silver flats covered in glitter.

"You look like a princess," Dani gushes, fixing my long train.

I smile, because that's exactly how I feel as I turn to look at myself.

"They are calling for you!" Payton practically screams from the doorway. Dani helps me down, and we rush outside, ushered into place by the wedding planner.

St. Luke's church is packed to the brim as I hide in the shadows. Family and friends, most of whom I've never met, pack the pews of the small church. Kristina walks down the aisle first as the music shifts, and then Dani follows shortly behind her, clutching a stunning bouquet of pink and white roses dotted amongst stargazer lilies.

My men don't know it, but I chose the lilies as a nod to their sister who couldn't be here today. I know how much they miss her, and having this simple flower in our bouquets makes me feel like she's here with us. I can't wait to meet her someday and learn all the dirt she can tell me about them.

My thoughts drift to my brothers as Payton takes her cue as my maid of honor, heading down the aisle. I know none of them could be here, but I can't pretend it doesn't hurt my heart to not have a single one of them with me today.

As the music changes again, I step up behind the double wooden doors, greeting Joseph. He looks so handsome in his tuxedo, with a lily set inside his pocket.

I asked him to walk me down the aisle. He's been nothing but sweet and kind since I met him. The old man choked with emotion and hugged me so fiercely that I couldn't stop my own tears from falling.

"Are you ready, my dear?" he asks as I link my hand through his arm.

I let out a deep sigh. "Are you ever really ready for something like this?"

He laughs and pats my hand. "I guess not, but the time has come and your groom—or should I say *grooms*, await you."

The doors swing open, and a collective gasp rings out from the parishioners and guests. I keep my eyes focused on Fr. Castiglione, unable to look at Sal, Armani, or Fausto, because I know once I do, I'll start to cry.

And I'm going to keep this makeup looking good, dammit.

As Joseph hands me off to Sal, however, I have to lift my gaze. "Wow," he whispers, holding my hand in his. There are no words to explain how gorgeous he looks in his white tuxedo with black accents. Sal looks like a Versace model with his chiseled face and his masculine physique, which is evident through the tailored tux. My eyes shift next to him, to my twins who are wearing the same exact suit as Sal but in reverse colors. "I love you," they both mouth as Sal and I turn to face Fr. Castiglione.

He begins his initial blessing, and I try to hold it together and stay present in the moment, but the ceremony flies by in a blur, and before I know it, I'm kissing Sal and being announced as his wife.

As we turn to face the crowd as husband and wife, I see my brother Lucian perched against the back wall. He clasps his hands together and nods briefly.

That's when I lose it.

Someone came for me.

Someone showed up.

I sniff back the tears as Sal kisses me once more then ushers me down the aisle. Outside, I search for Lucian, but he's gone. The thought of him leaving doesn't make me as sad, though, as it would have at one time. He came, and to me, that's everything.

The rest of the day flies by. Pictures are taken, champagne is consumed, and soon we're dancing the night away in the most epic wedding reception of all time.

The DJ pumps out music, the bass blaring as we jump around and sing and laugh. We decided to forgo the traditional dances expected of us, because it just wouldn't feel right to have my first dance with Sal when the twins mean just as much as he does.

We eat and drink, and I party until sweat covers every inch of my skin. It's not until the DJ ends his final song that my men and I bid our goodbyes to the final guests and head up to our suite.

When the door closes and locks behind me, I turn to see the heated gazes of three very buzzed, very horny men.

I gulp.

What have I gotten myself into?

Fausto shrugs out of his tuxedo jacket. "I'm sorry, pistol, but you only have one man to satisfy your needs tonight."

I look at him in confusion.

Armani grabs Sal by the shoulders and pushes him toward me. "You two have been waiting for this night. Take it. But don't be surprised when Fausto and I watch from the sidelines."

With that very erotic thought, I turn my back on them. "Someone needs to unlace me."

I don't know whose deft fingers unbind me, but as the dress falls to the ground, I don't look back, even when the groans of three men heat my core. Instead, I head right into the bathroom to get ready for this.

Closing and locking the door, I take a careful shower, washing my body and pussy like five times, making sure I'm clean and perfect while keeping my hair the way it was.

After drying off, I open my bag and pull out the sexy ivory lingerie I was almost too embarrassed to purchase from an online store. I slip on the stockings, which stretch over my knee, and hike the crotchless panties up over my hips. I attach the garters and slide my feet into ivory heels.

I fasten the bra behind my back, adjusting the cups. Made of a sheer material with a little knit heart to hide my nipples, the top is unbelievably sexy. I clip my veil back on, add some fresh lipstick, and grab the bathroom door handle.

I almost chicken out. I mean, what was I thinking wearing crotchless panties? I'm not that brave or confident. But then I think of the way those men looked at me clothed, and it gives me all the confidence I need to step out in front of them.

"Fuck," Sal groans, rising from the bed. He's wrapped only in a towel, his body still damp with water.

Fausto and Armani are still somewhat dressed in their tuxedos. They hold drinks in their hands and watch me hungrily.

Instead of cowering from their heated gazes, I let it fuel me. This is my fucking wedding night, right? Is there a night when a woman feels more powerful and wanted than this?

I lift my hair, cock one hip to the side, and spread my legs, making sure they see the lack of fabric between them.

"Get over here now," Sal growls, dropping his towel and striding toward me. I try to walk seductively, crossing my feet as I move.

Sal takes my chin in his hand and crushes his mouth to mine in a possessive kiss. He dominates me mind, body, and soul, owning me in this moment as passion overwhelms us both.

We're both breathing heavily when we pull away, and then he guides me toward the bed surrounded with a white canopy, the twins sitting on a couch directly across from it.

"I've been waiting a long time to do this," Sal murmurs, pulling me onto his lap. But I'm not sitting, no, I'm face down with my ass up and arms and legs dangling in the air.

"Sal, what are you—"

Smack!

Sal spanks my ass so hard that I screech from the burn he quickly rubs away. "It's time for your discipline, baby girl."

The transition from his once demeaning insult of little baby girl to baby girl takes me by surprise, and I moan as he strikes me again, his hand landing on my other cheek.

"You have no idea what you do to me every day. Having to watch you slink around the house in your little dresses and workout clothes, your perfect body lithe and ready for me while I struggle to resist."

He lands two more spanks and I cry out, my core heating at the delicious pain.

"Do you know how many times I had to jerk off to thoughts of you? How many times I couldn't think straight because I wanted you so fucking badly?"

"Ahh!" I scream as he lands another slap on my ass, a harder one, making me wiggle on his lap.

"But I know you like it when I discipline you, don't you, baby girl?"

Sal snakes his hands up my inner thighs, which I part for him like the needy girl I am. He trails a finger in my wetness and moans. "So filthy, aren't you?"

"Yes!" I cry out as he dips a finger inside me and slowly fucks me with it.

"Yeah?" He drags his finger out and down to my clit, rubbing it softly, too softly. "Do you want me to fuck you with my fingers while Fausto and Armani watch?"

"Oh God!" I screech when his hand leaves me and spanks my ass two more times.

Sal soothes the sting, rubbing the skin with his palm. "Now stand up and show them your red behind, baby girl. Show my brothers how filthy you are."

Sal offers me his hand and I take it, gripping it tightly as I slide off his legs and back onto my own. Each movement tugs at my raw skin, and I hiss as I stand up straight and twist my backside toward the twins.

"Fuck, pistol," Fausto groans. "Red looks good on you."

"How about a little peek at that wet cunt of yours, hmm?" Armani asks, his voice gravelly.

Sal answers for me. "She'd love to show you. Now bend forward, press those tits onto the bed, and leave your ass in the air. That's my girl." Sal rubs my back as I do what he asks, resting my upper body on the bedding with my legs still planted firmly on the ground. "Reach around to your ass and spread yourself open, let them see inside of you."

Now it's my turn to groan as, with shaking hands, I spread myself, my fingers slipping on my wetness.

Smack!

"That's for being too fucking sexy!" Sal growls, and I wiggle my ass, the sting lasting longer this time. "I'm going to fuck you so hard, baby girl, and you're going to scream for me, aren't you?"

"Yes," I moan, my face pressed against the bed.

"Good. Now drop to your hands and knees and crawl over to my brothers."

My heels fall off as I obey his order, feeling more aroused than ever with the twins watching Sal boss me around. Every inch of me feels kissed with fire, and he's barely touched me yet.

I crawl over to them, biting my lip and flicking my eyes between them. When I'm right in front of them, I sink back on my heels, and Sal's freshly washed scent fills my nose as he kneels behind me.

Sal's chest is pressed to the back of my head, and his hardness pokes my ass. "Such a beautiful bride." He drags the back of his fingers over my cheek and down my arms, slipping his fingertips under the thin band of material holding my panties over my hips.

He snaps it against my skin, and I jerk. "So pretty."

Fausto and Armani have stripped themselves of their shirts and pants, their boxer briefs doing nothing to contain their erections.

It's empowering to know my body elicits such a reaction from them.

Sal pulls my hair aside and licks down my neck and shoulder, dragging my bra strap down with his teeth. He extends my arm and plants kisses all the way to my inner wrist.

"So soft," he purrs, doing the same on my other arm, and then he snaps my bra strap and my breasts spring free. Sal cups them in his hands and I moan, my head lolling against his chest as he rolls my nipples in his fingers.

He pinches hard, and I hiss, arching my back into his touch. "Does it feel good, baby girl?" he grits out, releasing his hold and moving his hands lower.

"Yes." I'm panting now as he tugs at my thighs with his strong hands.

Sal goes back to squeezing my breasts and toying with my nipples, and my pussy grows wetter with each action.

"You have to follow the next set of instructions exactly. You are to sit on your ass and lean your back against me. Then I want you to spread your legs open as wide as you can stretch them while keeping your knees bent. Show my brothers that filthy little pussy while I fuck it with my fingers."

"Holy shit," Armani rasps, his hand diving into his pants.

I mewl as he drags his hand down my body, cups my pussy, then spanks it. "Faster. Part your legs for their hungry eyes."

I drop on my ass, hissing as my sore cheeks hit the textured carpeting, and then I lean my back against Sal, spreading my legs apart as far as my hips will allow while bending my knees.

Sal kisses the top of my head, flicking my pebbled nipples. "Tell me, brothers, how wet is that cunt? Is she dripping for us yet?"

I chew on my lip as Fausto drags his finger up my slit, making sure to strike my clit as he does. He holds his finger up, stretching my cream between the pads of his finger and thumb. "Drenched," he confirms.

Sal's erection twitches against my back. "Good thing, baby girl. It seems you're ready to come."

My breathing is choppy as he continues his assault on my aching breasts and pointed tips, wetness dripping from my clenching cunt.

Sal slides his hands to my pussy, gathering my cream on his finger before he slips it slowly over my clit. Then his hands disappear, and I whine. My legs begin to close as he spanks my pussy hard.

"Did I say you could close your legs?" Sal rasps, grabbing a handful of my hair. "Keep them fucking open. Let them watch your cunt pulse for more of my touch."

He lets go of my hair, and I lean back on my hands, holding my legs open. Sal comes back a moment later with a dildo and two identical items that I've never seen before. He hands Fausto the dildo and Armani the other items.

Fausto eyes my pussy with an evil smile while Sal tells me what to do.

"Okay, baby girl. This next part will be intense for you. Fausto here is going to fuck you with that dildo. It even has a remote to change how it feels buried inside you."

Fausto clicks the remote and the dildo spins in a circle.

"And Armani has toys for your plump little nipples. They are electric clamps that suck and vibrate depending on which setting he uses."

"Holy shit," I murmur, my arms shaking and thighs trembling as Sal perches behind me again, gliding his fingertips up and down my sides.

Fausto sits in front of me, dragging the tip of the dildo up and down my slit while it vibrates. He rests it on my clit, and I almost come immediately, but he moves away too fast.

He presses it against my entrance and pushes it inside me. "Your pussy stretches so beautifully, pistol," Fausto compliments, pulling it out and working it back inside.

Armani sits next to me, and I hiss as he attaches little suction cups to my nipples. When he turns them on, I startle as they latch on, actually feeling like a man's lips are wrapped around them. He adds the vibrating component as Fausto changes the setting on the dildo to swirl in circles.

It's almost too much.

"There," Sal says, dragging one finger around my clit, but not quite touching it. "Now we all own a part of your body, controlling you from the inside out."

Armani increases the suction, and my cunt clenches on the dildo.

"Please," I beg, not even knowing what I'm asking for.

Sal hums as he slides his finger over my clit so lightly I almost can't feel it.

Fausto increases the force of his dildo, pulling it out and slamming it back in as Sal teases my engorged clit again. My nipples scream, the suction harder, and the vibration makes me lose my mind.

"Please!" I shout, unable to take it another second, and Sal turns my head and captures my lips. He strokes my clit with expertise, and soon I'm lifting my hips to press against his finger, widening my legs farther to take Fausto's dildo deeper inside me.

My orgasm barrels down on me like a freight train that's lost control. It surges through me, electrifying every fucking nerve until stars twinkle in my vision and my body seizes from the force of it.

For a moment, I'm not in my body. Instead, I'm watching from above, seeing these three men play my body like it's their favorite game. When I'm twitching and moaning, Sal calls them off.

Fausto slips the dildo out, and Armani releases my nipples from the suctions. "Fucking perfect," Sal coos, picking up my limp body and carrying me to the bed. "But I'm not done yet. It's time for me to own what was promised to me so long ago."

I expect him to be aggressive and manhandle me. Instead, Sal sets me down and climbs on top of me. As I catch my breath, he kisses my neck, working his way over my chest and gently lapping at my breasts and erect pink buds. He plants soft kisses down the side of my jaw to my lips, his tongue massaging mine gently. "I love you, Valentina, and I always will."

I blink my eyes open, only realizing now they were closed. He smiles down at me so warmly, I smile back, reaching up to cup his face. He kisses me again, the crown of his cock nudging at my entrance. I wrap my legs around him, encouraging him to sink inside me.

He moans against my mouth, pausing once he's fully seated, and then he sits up to watch where our bodies are joined. He doesn't fuck me like a dog in heat, he... makes love to me.

Gently thrusting his cock, Sal takes me kindly, slowly, and passionately. He leans down and draws my nipple into his mouth, softly sucking with his cock filling me.

He moves to my other side, and another orgasm begins to build, the deep heat growing until I can't contain it a second longer. Sal takes his time fucking me at an agonizingly slow pace, his lips now attached to the tender skin of my neck.

It's torture. I crave more of his touch—harder, stronger, deeper.

I move my hips in time with his, our bodies meeting, and the sound of my wetness fills the room.

"Harder," I whisper, chasing my orgasm.

"You want it harder, baby girl?" Sal croons, keeping his slow and steady pace.

"I want you to fuck me like you mean it, Sal."

He pauses, looking at me. "If that's what my queen wants…"

Then he moves, shifting me onto my knees, facing the twins. He fists my hair and pulls me up, sinking into me from behind.

"You want to be fucked by your husband like a filthy little whore? Is that it?"

"Yes!" I scream out as he grips my throat in his other hand, hammering into me from behind. My breasts bounce with each movement, my moans growing louder.

I watch Armani and Fausto strip their boxers and fist themselves to Sal and I fucking.

And I topple over the edge.

My cries of pleasure are piercing as my orgasm licks my skin, kissing the tips of my fingers and toes. My hands curl into fists, and I'm blinded for a moment as pleasure courses through me, owning me, branding me.

Sal pushes me forward and grips my hips, fucking me like a madman, my freshly spanked ass stinging with every fucking thrust. Then I feel his hot cum spurt inside of me and hear his grunts of pleasure as he finds his release.

Breathing hard, we collapse to our sides, my body thoroughly and completely spent.

The twins climb on too, curling beside us in a big, naked puppy pile of powerful Moretti men.

Well, not just Moretti men anymore.

Because today, once more, a woman claims the name, and I have these mafia men kneeling at my feet, calling me their queen with only a single day under my belt.

Mrs. Moretti is here to stay. I've endured trauma and abuse. I've fought and won. I've survived and lived to tell the tale. My path to happiness was fraught with pain, laced with evil, and cursed with the blood of men long dead.

Yet here we are, living, breathing, and coming together to take over the world when everyone rooted against us. Like a caged eagle breaking free from captivity, we will take over the skies, quick to hunt for our enemies. We've risen from the ashes, we've swam upstream, and we've clawed and fought and battled our way to happiness.

And now that I have it, I'm never letting go.

Happiness doesn't always come easily, sometimes you have to fight for it, but once you obtain it, once you give it your fucking all and attain what you've always deserved, it will change you.

Mold you.

Love transforms you into something greater than you could ever be all on your own. It blooms inside of you, infecting your heart and soul, and everyone around you can sense it. It's not just a feeling, it's *palpable*—a real, powerful living entity existing within you.

If only you're brave enough to seek it out.

THE END

DEAR READER

Thank you so much for picking up my submission in the Mafia Wars series. If my words touched you in a positive way, please consider leaving me an honest review. Reviews are powerful, and I promise I read each and every one, for better or worse.
Your support is everything. Thank you for sticking with me over the years as my work has grown and changed, as I've found my place in this industry. I couldn't have done it without each and every one of you.
Thank you from the bottom of my heart, for every message, for every post recommending my books, for every comment you've ever left.
Your support is my fuel, it's what keeps me going.
There is so much more I'm ready to give, and with you at my back, I know I'll have the courage to continue.
XOXO
Lox

ABOUT THE AUTHOR

Loxley lives in a small town in northeast Ohio. In her down time, she loves to play with daughters and have date nights with her husband. During the summer she loves to spend her days on Lake Erie. Loxley loves to read, watch reality tv, play video games, and anything Harry Potter. You can follow her on social media here:

Facebook group:
https://www.facebook.com/groups/loxleysavage

Facebook Page:
https://www.facebook.com/AuthorLoxleySavage

Amazon:
https://www.amazon.com/author/loxleysavage

Bookbub:
https://www.bookbub.com/authors/loxley-savage

Instagram:
https://instagram.com/loxley_savage?r=nametag

ALSO BY LOXLEY SAVAGE

FEATHERS AND FIRE SERIES

(dark & triggering reverse harem romance)

- Bound for Blood
- Cursed To Crave
- Freed By Flames

SINISTER FAIRY TALES

(dark reverse harem romance)

- Seven Sins of Snow
- Broken Beasts of Beauty

THE FORSAKEN SERIES:

CO-WRITTEN WITH K.A KNIGHT

(dark alien reverse harem romance)

- Capturing Carmen
- Stealing Shiloh
- Harboring Harlow

GANGSTERS AND GUNS:

CO-WRITTEN WITH K.A KNIGHT

(dark contemporary reverse harem romance, standalone)

- Gangsters And Guns

AFTERWORLD ACADEMY:

CO-WRITTEN WITH KATIE MAY

(fantasy academy reverse harem romance)

- Dearly Departed
- Darkness Deceives
- Defying Destiny

WICKED WAVES:
CO-WRITTEN WITH ERIN O'KANE
(fantasy reverse harem romance)

- Twisted Tides
- Tides That Bind

AUDIO BOOKS

- Gangsters and Guns - https://www.audible.com/pd/Gangsters-and-Guns-Audiobook/1039405274
- Seven Sins of Snow - https://www.audible.com/pd/Seven-Sins-of-Snow-Audiobook/1774247305
- Broken Beasts of Beauty - coming Spring, 2022

Printed in Great Britain
by Amazon